The Puzzle Bark Tree

Also by Stephanie Gertler

Jimmy's Girl

The Puzzle Bark Tree

Stephanie Gertler

DUTTON

DUTTON
Published by the Penguin Group
Penguin Putnam Inc., 375 Hudson Street, New York, New York 10014, U.S.A.
Penguin Books Ltd, 80 Strand, London WC2R 0RL, England
Penguin Books Australia Ltd, Ringwood, Victoria, Australia
Penguin Books Canada Ltd, 10 Alcorn Avenue, Toronto, Ontario, Canada M4V 3B2
Penguin Books (N.Z.) Ltd, 182–190 Wairau Road, Auckland 10, New Zealand

Penguin Books Ltd, Registered Offices: Harmondsworth, Middlesex, England

Published by Dutton, a member of Penguin Putnam Inc.

REGISTERED TRADEMARK—MARCA REGISTRADA

ISBN 0-525-94639-X

Printed in the United States of America
Set in Goudy
Designed by Leonard Telesca

PUBLISHER'S NOTE

In loving memory of Sallie Ann Sullivan Park
April 18, 1933–March 20, 1998

ACKNOWLEDGMENTS

My deep appreciation to Chip Crosby, Ph.D., for his psychological insights as well as his literary sense.

For their individual expertise and assistance, I would like to thank Dr. Michael Baden, Ken and Kathy Bee, Bill Carney, Detective Lieutenant Doug Buschel, Don Dietrich, Chris Gearwar, Michael Goldsmith, Dr. Harry Iaochim, Dr. Donna Ingram, Frank Leonburno, and Joan Salwen Zaitz.

My love and thanks to my friends and family: Judi Coffey for her enthusiasm; Nancy Drexler for her relentlessly keen eye; Ellen Udelson who remembers the conception of this book and lets me read to her over the phone; my brother, Jon Gertler, and my parents, Anna and Menard Gertler—as always; and my niece, Raquel Flatow, who understands the sometimes complicated facets of family.

My gratitude to Father John Giuliani for the epiphany, and to Joe and Lori Cavise, Anne-Marie Galler, Miriam Serow, and Carolina Lopez— thanks for the dance.

To the wonderful people at Dutton: Ronni Berger (my lifeline), Juliette Gillespie, Lisa Johnson, Robert Kempe, Kathleen Schmidt, and Susan Schwartz—many thanks.

My neverending gratitude to my agent and dear friend Marcy Posner, who is always there to listen at the end of one phone or another—and always has an answer and a laugh.

My deepest appreciation to Carole Baron, my editor and publisher, whose editorial and literary acumen is only outshined by her warmth, honesty, and friendship.

Thanks and love: to my children, David, Ellie, and Ben Schiffer, just for being the lights of my life; and to my husband, Mark Schiffer, for the endless help with the medical aspects of this book—but mostly for this crazy love of mine.

The Puzzle Bark Tree

Prologue

One night, before Grace went to sleep, she asked her. Sit down on my bed, Grace said. Sit down just this once. I have the same kind of dream all the time, Mom. Melanie and I are on a ship and the ship is tossing in the night. A hole is gaping through the hull and icy water is pouring in and coming up to our knees and then rushing past our waists. Faster and faster. And I scream for someone to help us. You're there but you won't save us and you swim away. I need to ask you, Mom, if Melanie and I were on a ship, and the ship was tossing in the night and there was a hole gaping through the hull and water was pouring in so that it came up to our knees faster and faster, couldn't you save us? Wouldn't you save us both?

Her mother looked at Grace as she lay in her bed, the covers pulled up to her chin. Her mother's eyes became wide. She looked almost startled, blinking in what appeared to be disbelief. Looking into her mother's eyes frightened Grace more than the dream of the ship sinking in the darkness. When her mother finally spoke, her voice was raised and trembling. What a foolish question, her mother said. Stupid question. That is a cruel and selfish question, Grace Hammond. Why would you *think* about such things? How could you *ask* such a thing? her mother moaned. She inhaled a breath so rasping and deep Grace wasn't sure what would happen when she let it go. Her mother clasped her hands, then released them, wrung them and twisted them in a way that frightened Grace and made her wonder if her mother would tear them off her wrists.

Grace wailed that she didn't mean anything by her question.

I was only wondering, Grace apologized, pleading for mercy.

Her mother left her seat at the edge of Grace's bed and flipped off the bathroom light. Please, please, leave it on and leave the door cracked open, Grace begged. But her mother just walked away, as though she were an apparition in the darkness.

There were so many nights, when Grace was a child, that she dreamed of ships and boats rocking to and fro on metal-gray waves. She was probably around six years old the first time she had the dream. It wasn't until she was ten when Grace found the courage to confess the dream to her mother. The dream recurred over and over again after that. A boat, sometimes a ship, rocking violently on steely dun water that splashed over the deck and soaked Grace's clothes so they clung to her like onionskin. And, in all the dreams, Grace and Melanie would call out for help, their cries trapped somewhere deep inside their throats, down to their chests, though their mouths were poised to cry.

Grace's daughter, Kate, asked the same sort of thing when she was a little girl. Her question, however, did not come from a dream. It was simply one of those questions that children ask, like why is the sky blue and is there really a man on the moon and why don't we fall off the edge of the earth as it spins? Kate called Grace back to her bed one night after Grace had tucked her in and read *Anne of Green Gables* for the umpteenth time.

If you and Daddy and I were on a desert island and you could only save one, whom would you rescue? Kate asked, her eyes imploring.

And Grace answered, ignoring her own sense of something arcane as Kate posed her question. "I would save us all," Grace said matter-of-factly. "I would save us all."

"But you can only save one," Kate said. "That's the rule."

"I would break the rule." Grace smiled, lifting her chin triumphantly. She enveloped her daughter so tightly that Kate laughed and said she was squeezing her too hard.

They fell asleep together that night and, in the morning, just like so many mornings, Grace wondered why it never occurred to her own mother to simply gather Grace up in her arms and say she would save them both.

Chapter One

It was Jemma who called Melanie to say she couldn't awaken her parents that Sunday morning. Jemma, who had lived with the Hammond family for the first twenty years of her employ and, for the last twenty, loyally took the train up from the Bronx every morning and then a cab to their house in Purchase, New York. She did this every morning save an occasional Saturday and Sunday when there was a church function or one of her friends or neighbors needed her assistance but, what with the snowstorm, she decided to check when the Hammonds hadn't answered their phone. Besides, Jemma thought, it was about time she pulled up the artificial tree from the basement and started decorating. The girls were coming for Christmas this year and that was only the day after tomorrow. The girls, Jemma thought. Grace and Melanie were women now with children of their own, but to her they would always be the girls.

Jemma knew the moment she stepped out of the cab that the Hammonds' house was too quiet. Two newspapers, wrapped in plastic, were jammed into the newspaper box. The blinds in the upstairs bedroom window were still drawn. The lamp did not glow from the living room on that pale gray day. At first, Jemma hoped it was the soporific hush that snowfall causes on a lazy Sunday morning and that the Hammonds were uncharacteristically sleeping. She turned her key in the door and flipped on the light in the vestibule. She called out their names and poked her head into the living room and saw it was, indeed, darkened and untouched.

Usually, Jemma found them sitting side by side in the living room, wearing dark, plaid flannel robes in winter and white-piped pastel cotton robes in summer. They would say good morning and make small talk about the weather. Remind her of a task that needed to be done that Jemma knew to do anyway after forty years. Jemma would roll up the blinds and open a window if the weather was temperate. She would place Mrs. Hammond's copper kettle on for tea and lay out her place setting at the dining table with a crystal bowl of sugar cubes, a china teacup, matching plate of wheat toast, and a small jar of marmalade with a tiny gold spoon. Lately, she put the newspaper's television guide next to Mrs. Hammond's place setting and circled the movies and quiz shows in red. She would right Mr. Hammond's TV tray in front of the television: a bowl of Wheatena, a glass of tomato juice, a cup of Sanka with saccharine that he shook from a small silver envelope. He ate in silence, watching the Dow-Jones trail monotonously at the bottom of the screen. There was no conversation at breakfast. Ultimately, Mrs. Hammond would take her place next to her husband on the sofa. They would watch the game shows and wait for lunch. Sometimes they played gin rummy or Scrabble. But Mr. Hammond had trouble with games lately. He had difficulty distinguishing the suits when he played gin rummy with his wife. He became confused with clubs and spades, hearts and diamonds. The shapes and the colors baffled him. Scrabble was even more daunting. There were too many words he couldn't remember. He stared at the jumbled letter tiles in the rack before him, pushing them about with his finger and shaking his head from side to side, stuck on the words.

When the girls were children, Jemma often carried Mrs. Hammond's breakfast to her room. "Your mama has a weak constitution," Jemma would explain as Grace and Melanie sat at the kitchen table eating their breakfast while their father hid behind the *Herald Tribune* drinking his Sanka. "She needs her sugar in the morning. Now you girls eat and I'll be right back to get you on that bus."

It was easy for Grace and Melanie to believe Jemma. How could you not believe someone who wore shirtwaist dresses with gingham checks? Whose lips were polished with an amber gloss that looked like it might taste like apricot? Sometimes Jemma even painted her nails as well, a deep burgundy and, if the girls happened to be around when Jemma was doing what she called her beauty routine, she'd paint their nails as well. Jemma would sit the girls down at the kitchen table, their fingers dangling in bowls of soapy water. She'd push back their cuticles with an orange stick and file the tips into ovals. This is just like the sa-lon, Jemma would say with the emphasis on *salon's* first syllable. And the girls would laugh and say that they felt fancy.

Once in a while their father would lower the paper that covered his face at breakfast and say something to his daughters. Something like, "How are you girls this morning?" or "Make sure you kiss your mother good-bye." He tried, at the very least, for the pretense of intimacy, of family. Awkwardly, but he tried. Though he was visibly uncomfortable in his own skin, unable to extend even the smallest offering of warmth as though it might scald him or, perhaps, scald those around him.

Jemma walked hesitantly up the stairs that early Sunday morning. She walked slowly, not with the surprisingly brisk pace with which her sixty-four-year-old legs usually carried her. She opened the Ham-monds' bedroom door tentatively with a still-gloved hand and knew from the moment she saw them, side by side, motionless and emotion-less, that they were gone. She let go a cry and ran back down the stairs. The heel of her boot snagged on a piece of loose carpet, causing her to trip, and she righted herself with the aid of the banister. Her hands trembled so rapidly she could barely dial Melanie's number (it never occurred to her to call the police) and still, not believing what she saw, Jemma told Melanie she was unable to awaken her parents.

Melanie and her husband drove the twenty minutes from where they lived, leaving their three-year-old twin boys in the care of a neighbor who, as Melanie always said, was like a grandmother to them. When Melanie and Mike arrived at the house that Sunday morning after Jemma called, they parked their car behind the old black Buick in the driveway. It was apparent that the car had not been used in days. The roof was covered with a crusty layer of snow; the windows were iced over. Jemma was standing just inside the open front door. The pewter chandelier in the entryway shone dimly. Several of the candle bulbs had burned out, making the old gold-colored grass cloth on the walls appear even dingier. Jemma's purple-and-red paisley scarf was tied under her chin, her dull red parka buttoned up to her neck. She clutched her pocketbook as though, at any moment, she was prepared to leave. Powdered snow had blown into the entrance hall and dusted the tops of her boots. As Melanie and Mike approached her, Jemma stepped outside onto the stoop.

"Jemma, you must be freezing, standing here with the door open like this," Melanie said, hugging her gently as if she might break.

"I don't want to go back inside. Maybe we shouldn't go inside," Jemma said, her eyes darting one way and then the other. "Maybe we should just let them sleep."

"It's okay, Jemma," Mike said, glancing nervously at his wife. "We're here now."

Melanie ushered Jemma back into the house and closed the heavy front door behind them. She started to call out hello and stopped, choking on the first syllable before the word could be completed. Despite Jemma's insistence that her parents were merely sleeping, Melanie knew there would be no answer. She knew when Jemma called that there would be no awakening. Melanie placed her coat over the banister, glanced at her father's old brown fedora hanging on the hook beside the mirror. She saw her mother's trench coat hanging next to her father's hat, her threadbare beige cashmere scarf tucked into the sleeve, the fringe dangling through the cuff. She turned the corner and stopped before the arched living room door. Jemma followed by Melanie's side, gripping Melanie's elbow tightly while Mike trailed a few steps behind them.

"Are they in their bedroom?" Melanie turned suddenly to Jemma, asking what she already knew.

"They are. I can't wake them," she repeated. Jemma's face appeared frozen. She appeared to mouth the words almost grotesquely, in slow motion, when she spoke.

Melanie looked at Jemma intently. She saw the coarse curls of gray that sprouted around her temples, the dark circles beneath her eyes that were prematurely rheumy with age. Melanie took Jemma's hands in hers and saw the darkened age spots and reddened thickening around her knuckles as Jemma's hands slowly closed upon her own in what she perceived as both a gesture of desperation and confidence. For a moment, Melanie pictured Jemma's fine-boned face as a young woman, her creamy mocha skin, her once jet-black hair sleeked into a bun at the nape of her neck. Her delicate fingers that nimbly threaded needles, sewed on buttons, hemmed skirts, braided hair.

"It's going to be okay, Jemma," Melanie said in a way that begged for Jemma's assurance, but Jemma only blinked back tears.

"Mel, maybe you and Jemma should wait in the car and let me . . . ," Mike said, but Melanie clearly didn't hear him and he stopped speaking halfway through his sentence.

Melanie started up the stairs, stopped halfway, and came back down. She picked up the phone on the table by the stairwell.

"Melanie, who are you calling?" asked Jemma.

"The police," Melanie said.

"But, why?" Jemma almost pleaded. "Why should you—?"

Melanie interrupted her as the police answered. "We have a problem at Thirty-two Harvest Lane," she said. "Can you send a car?"

"What seems to be the problem?" the voice asked on the other end.

"I think my parents might be dead," said Melanie.

Jemma gasped, covering her mouth with her hand. "Melanie!" she cried. "Melanie! All I said was I couldn't wake them!"

"Jesus, Mel," Mike said. "Jesus. It's all right, Jemma." His arm was slung around Jemma's shoulder now, enveloping her.

"Their, um, housekeeper found them this morning," Melanie continued, raising her hand, wrist bent back, fingers spread tensely, to silence her husband and Jemma as she spoke. "She says she couldn't wake them up." And then, "No, I haven't seen them yet. Yes, the house is intact. No, my husband is with us. There is no evidence of a break-in. Yes, we'll wait outside."

"Jemma, you sit down. They told me not to go upstairs. But I'm going up. Mike, you stay here with Jemma," Melanie said.

"You're not going up there alone," Mike said. He placed his hand firmly on Jemma's shoulder now, stopping her as she took a step away from him to follow Melanie. He knew better than to tell his wife he would go in her stead. "Maybe you want to wait here, Jemma," he said, his hand pressing deeply, gripping too hard. "I'm going with you, Mel."

But Jemma followed Mike and Melanie up the stairs to the bedroom. Melanie sank to her knees as she approached the side of the bed. She saw her father lying on his stomach, his face turned to the side upon his pillow. A lock of yellow-white hair had fallen across one eye. Her mother, silver hair combed, lipstick applied carefully on parted lips, her tired plaid flannel robe closed demurely, the bow tied perfectly, was lying beside him. Her arm rested, palm down, on the small of her husband's back. There was a nearly full bottle of Bell's 20 on their nightstand next to an empty, capless, amber pill bottle and two empty glasses. True, if someone hadn't known better, they would have thought they were sleeping. But the room held the distinct stench of Scotch and the imagined odor of expiration. Mike caught his wife as she listed. She turned her face toward his. Her mouth gone dry. Her eyes wide.

"Mother never wore lipstick," she said to Mike, her lips barely moving as she spoke, her breath coming in short gasps. "Mike, call Grace. Call Grace."

Mike picked up the receiver on the nightstand and dialed Grace's number but Melanie took the receiver from his hand, knocking the heavy black base down in her haste. Mike caught it and held it while she spoke, his other arm holding Jemma to him as she sobbed, short uncontrollable bursts.

It was Adam who answered the phone, his voice still thick with sleep. Even in his sleep, he answered formally: Dr. Barnett. The syllables presented with well-rehearsed clarity.

"I need to speak to Grace," Melanie said breathlessly, and then repeated it a second time before Adam could answer.

Adam Barnett turned his head to the place where his wife slept. The quilt was folded back forming a careful triangle on her side of the bed. The pillow was depressed in the center, rumpled where her head had lain. Grace had gone running despite the winter weather.

"She's not here," he said, clearly unhappy that he had been awakened. "I'll tell her that you called." He glanced at the clock. Eight-thirty. It took him a moment to orient himself to the notion of Sunday morning. He'd never asked Melanie why she was calling so early or noticed that she was out of breath. He hung up the phone clumsily in the darkened room, rolled over on his back, placed his arm crooked over his forehead, and stared at the ceiling. He remembered the days when he and his wife had made love on an early Sunday morning. When they sat together in the living room and read the Sunday paper. But, lately, he awakened alone. Grace was out running.

By the time Grace finished her last turn around the path in Central Park, snow flurries had begun again. Her cap was sprinkled with snow and the bottoms of her running shoes were slick. She skidded a little on the apartment building's marble floors when she entered through the brass-trimmed glass doors. She stepped into the elevator and pressed the top floor. She watched as the lighted numbers ticked off one by one, skipping thirteen, above her head. The doors opened into the vestibule outside her apartment. She hung her hat on the wrought-iron rack outside the apartment's door. Placed her sneakers on the straw mat lined with Kate's boots and Adam's galoshes. Straightened the umbrellas in the ceramic umbrella stand. She was happy this morning. She prided herself on getting up and out early despite the little sleep she'd had. The night before, she and Kate had stayed up late wrapping Christmas presents, drinking cocoa, watching movies of Kate when she was a toddler. There was one movie in particular where Kate had taken Grace's box of costume jewelry that Grace used in dance recitals and adorned herself with every strand of beads imaginable and a magenta feather boa. They rewound the video three times.

"Oh, did you ever have the makings for show biz when you were little," laughed Grace. "Your father used to panic. Not intellectual enough."

"Look at the makeup on me," Kate squealed. "I was, like, a little chorus girl. God, look at me vamping."

"You loved to tap," Grace remembered. "You called the shoes your 'shiny clicky shoes.'"

"I probably shouldn't have stopped," Kate said. "Maybe I'll take some dance classes when I get to Boston College in the fall."

Normally, Kate would have been out with friends on a Saturday night but it had been cold and windy the night before. Grace had made a fire in the living room hearth and Kate said it was just too cozy not to stay home. Grace knew that most of Kate's friends were already away on Christmas vacations and that was the real reason that Kate spent the evening with her. Normally they would have been away as well, but this year was Christmas at her parents' house, an event that Melanie and Grace perpetuated even though each time the day was over, they swore they would never do it again. Melanie and Grace brought Christmas dinner; one of them drove Jemma up from the Bronx. Jemma trimmed the tree. But the day was always stilted and sad, the Hammonds barely moving from their seats while Melanie and Grace tried desperately to make the mood festive. When Kate was small, she seemed to irritate her grandparents. They were like strangers, ill at ease, watching someone else's child who was in the way. When Melanie's twins joined the group three years ago, they were overwhelmed. There was too much commotion. Babies who were seen as well as heard (unlike their own daughters whose care was relegated to Jemma for as long as either Grace or Melanie could remember) unnerved them.

Every other year when it was time for Christmas at her grandparents, Kate would protest and Adam would argue that they should simply go to Aspen, celebrate Christmas there and stop trying to make what his grandmother called a silk purse out of a sow's ear. But Grace didn't want to let Melanie down. Melanie, who kept hoping that things would change. As though one day there might be an epiphany and her parents would relent, allow at least one day a year to be joyous. Grace was better prepared this year for the charade and as soon as it was over, they would leave for Colorado. They had built a house in Aspen ten years ago, nestled at the foot of the mountain. When Adam was younger, he was a racer; now he skied mostly cross-country. But Kate skied downhill with the strength and speed he had when he was her age. And Grace, Grace who never skied until she met Adam, loved the speed, the sense of warmth through her body as the cold air bit her face. She often thought the sensation wasn't dissimilar to passion. As for Aspen, she despised its glitz and glamor, the jet set and their parties, preferring to sit by the fire and read a book while Adam was out and about in what he called his paradise.

He heard Grace rummaging outside the apartment and, still aggravated by the call that had awakened him, met her at the door, tying his black silk robe around his waist as he approached her.

"Your sister called," he said, opening the door, dispensing with hello.

"Melanie?" Grace asked.

He breathed in deeply. "Only sister that we know of, Grace," he said, letting the words out in a yawn. "Doesn't she know that those of us without young children try to sleep late on Sundays? Of course, except for those of us who need to run early in the morning. How can you run when it's snowing outside? Why do you always get up so damn early? I hardly slept at all. My goddamn beeper went off a dozen times. I was up half the night."

Grace ignored his questions. His complaints. She'd always been an early riser. She was never one to sleep away the day. Besides, there had been no snow along the loop. It had only just begun to flurry. Snow melts almost immediately in Manhattan, anyway. Adam viscerally hated the fact that Grace ran, perhaps because deep down inside he knew, if she could, that she might keep running if it weren't for Kate.

"Something must be wrong for Melanie to call so early," Grace said, walking past her husband for the phone.

"Jesus, Grace. Why do you always think that something is wrong?" he asked.

"I can feel it in my bones," she said.

"Your bones," he muttered. "Your damn bones."

Grace dialed Melanie's number. It was Mrs. Hadley, Melanie's neighbor, who answered.

"Oh, Grace, dear," said Mrs. Hadley softly. "Melanie and Mike went over to your parents' house."

"What happened?" Grace asked, feeling the color drain from her face.

"I'm not sure, honey," she said. "Why don't you call them? I'm certain they've arrived by now."

Grace's hand shook as she punched her parents' phone number. Adam watched her silently.

"Grace?" Melanie said, answering on half a ring.

"What happened?" Grace asked in a monotone.

Melanie was unable to speak. "Grace" was all she could say.

"What happened?" Grace asked again. She tried to keep her voice from rising. "Was it the car? I told them they shouldn't be driving anymore, especially in this weather. Damn it, Melanie! Talk to me."

"No, not the car. They're here," Melanie said, finding her voice. "They're in bed. The police are coming over."

"What then? Were they robbed?" Grace asked. She felt her knees go weak. The shake in her hands was uncontrollable. "What happened?" Grace's voice rose octaves. "Melanie, speak! You're scaring me to death."

"Grace, they're dead," said Melanie. "Jemma found them this morning. About an hour ago."

"What do you mean they're *dead?* How can they be dead?"

"I don't know," Melanie said, her voice cracking. Grace could hear her swallow.

"How's Jemma?" Grace asked. "Where is she?"

"She's okay. She's here. Right next to me. So is Mike."

"I'll be there as soon as I can, " Grace said, biting down hard on her lip.

"Okay." Melanie began to sob. "But hurry, okay? Please hurry."

"Melanie, where are they?"

"I told you. They're in bed."

"You've seen them?"

"Oh, God, Grace. Yes."

"And?"

"They're gone, Grace. I told you. They're just gone."

Adam had walked over to the window. He pulled the cord to open the draperies.

"How?" he asked when Grace hung up the phone.

"She doesn't know," Grace said, sitting still in the chair by the phone. Her hands covered her mouth. She touched her lip with her index finger. She had bitten so hard she wondered if it was bleeding.

"People don't just die, " Adam said.

"Maybe some people do," Grace said quietly.

Kate stumbled into the room. Her bright red nightshirt hung just above her knees. Her long, sandy-blond hair was tangled from sleep and hung in her eyes.

"What's going on, you guys?" she asked, stretching her arms over her head. "Who called? What's all the commotion?" She was in mid-stretch when her father said her mother's parents were dead. She stopped her stretch in midair, dropped her arms to her side.

"*Both* of them?" she said, a look of horror coming over her face. "How did it happen? Was it the car? An accident? Who told you?"

Grace tried to stand but the room began spinning. Her ears suddenly felt full. Splotches of black appeared before her eyes. She felt a creeping, heavy nausea come over her.

"Oh, I don't feel well," Grace managed to murmur, sitting down again. "I don't feel well at all."

Adam looked at his wife. Her face was drawn and stiff, the rose in her cheeks had turned to gray. He placed his fingers lightly on her pulse without a word, clearly trained in what to do. Count the beats with the seconds. Concentrate. Listen. Grace wrenched her hand away.

"You have a good strong pulse. You're fine," he said. "I have some calls to make. I'll be in my library."

"I am not fine," she said, thinking that was not the way to feel the rhythm of her heart.

Kate brought a glass of cold water and held it to her mother's lips. Grace's hands shook over her daughter's steady grasp as she sipped. Grace dipped her fingers into the glass, extracted a piece of ice, and brushed it against her forehead.

"I'm better now," Grace said, raising her eyes to her daughter. "I'm sorry. I am so sorry."

"Why are you sorry?" Kate asked.

"Oh, I don't know. You know, Christmas. Everything. All this. I don't know." Grace knew she wasn't saying what she really felt, really meant. It was all so complicated. "I'm just sorry for everything."

"It's okay, Mom. It's okay. It's not your fault."

Grace stood again, her knees still buckling. "I think I'm a wreck." Grace smiled wanly at her daughter.

"I should shower and dress, Mom," Kate said. "I'll hurry. I'll be ready to leave when you are. But I don't want to leave you here."

"I'm going to go talk to your father," Grace said. "Go ahead. I'm fine."

Grace stood at the open library door. Adam was sitting behind his desk, his fingers clasped, his chin resting on his hands as he looked out the window. He turned when he heard Grace's footsteps. "I don't even know what to say to you," he said.

Grace looked at him, thinking that he never did. He rarely knew what to do, how to react. But then, who would under the circumstances? "I told you it would happen this way. You never believed me. I told you, one day they would die together."

"I know. I know," he said. "You felt it in your bones." He shook his head from side to side. Looked at his wife, the melted ice still dripping down her face. "It's so unfair, Grace."

Grace sat down in the leather chair opposite her husband's desk. She looked around the room with its oversize mahogany bookcases. The leather-bound books. Photographs of herself with Kate, photographs of the three of them in Aspen. Adam swiveled his desk chair around to look out the window again. Clouds obscured the view of Central Park, but Grace knew he was staring out the window to avoid her eyes. She remembered when they had looked at the apartment shortly after they were married. How they had stopped by the picture window in what would become his library and gazed out at the city. How they stood with their arms wrapped around each other's waists, walked through the apartment, their footsteps echoing in harmony on the bare hardwood floors.

"This place was supposed to be our Eden, wasn't it?" Grace said, breaking the silence. "That view. We loved the view."

"Don't start," he said, turning his chair back around to look at his wife.

"I have to go to my parents' house," Grace said.

"I know," he said.

"Are you coming with me?" Grace asked.

"My beeper went off a dozen times last night," he said again. "I have to go in today. Lots of sick people. What would I do there anyway?"

Grace said nothing. Lots of sick people, she thought. My parents may be dead, but I'm not.

"No," he sighed. "I should go with you. The roads are going to be lousy. It's supposed to snow again."

"It's already snowing," Grace said quietly. "But that's not why you should come with me, Adam. As for the beeper and the patients, someone could cover you today. It's not a good enough excuse this time."

Adam lifted his head. The color had crept back into Grace's cheeks. He watched as one of her long slender fingers pushed a stray auburn hair from her face. Her shirt had slipped down, revealing her firm molded shoulder, the strap of her running bra. He tried not to see the tears that pooled in her hazel eyes.

"I wonder what they would say if they knew how you grieved for them," he said.

Grace walked around to the chair where he sat and stood in front of him. She studied his face: the aquiline nose, sandy blond hair, the color of Kate's, that was streaked with silver. Opaque gray eyes that once penetrated her and now appeared so vacant, almost helpless. Yes, she was grieving, she thought. But for whom?

Kate was back a few moments later dressed in her blue jeans, a hooded sweatshirt, unlaced work boots, a baseball cap covering her damp hair.

"I'm ready, Mom," Kate said.

Grace walked to the door and called for the elevator. She looked at her husband, tipped her head to the side, a motioning gesture asking him to come. A last chance to make sure he wanted to stay behind.

"I have to go now," Grace said. "They're going to bring the car around."

Grace held the elevator door while Kate kissed her father on the cheek.

For most of Grace's forty-four years, she had felt like Sisyphus. Pushing the boulder up the highest mountain only to have it roll back down. Up and down for so many years, never admitting the task was useless. Part of her felt that the task of being the firstborn was finally over. A greater part of her had a feeling that it had only just begun.

Chapter Two

The throbbing in Grace's temples was palpable. A staccato drumming that became more pronounced as she approached the exit for Harvest Lane. She stretched open her mouth, trying to relieve the tightness in her jaw and the clench of her teeth. Her palms perspired, slipping on the steering wheel as she made the right turn off the exit ramp. Left at the stop sign. Right at the schoolhouse. The first left on Harvest Lane. Sixth house on the left. Number thirty-two on the mailbox. Landmarks that Grace still needed to find her way home.

A blue-and-white patrol car sat in the driveway of her parents' house behind her brother-in-law's old orange BMW. Yellow banners with black lettering, CRIME SCENE DO NOT CROSS, stretched from branch to branch of leafless brittle bushes crusted with iced-over snow. Strange tinsel this time of year, Grace thought. Neighbors huddled behind blue police sawhorses, bundled in down jackets and wool scarves, some still in pajamas, straining their necks, holding mugs of steaming coffee as though they awaited a parade.

No one behind the sawhorses spoke as Grace and Kate got out of the car. They watched them walk up the stone path. Their eyes, in unison, followed Grace's hand as it ripped away a yellow banner, ignoring the command not to cross. They moved their eyes away from hers as Grace scanned the strange faces behind the barriers. Strangers. There wasn't one who could step forward and take her arm. Not one who could call out her name or comfort her. Not even someone who might say they know, once knew, her parents.

It had been years since Grace knew the residents on Harvest Lane. There were Mr. and Mrs. Connelly, whose son Brian had been the first boy Grace had ever kissed. Mr. and Mrs. Rinaldi, whose daughter Angela still sent Grace a birthday card every year. The Millers, the Howards, the Schroeders. They all had kids who played with Grace and let Melanie tag along. Grace remembered every nook and cranny of their basements, attics, kitchens; the kinds of cookies they kept in their cookie jars, the creak of every stair in their homes. But the kids never played at Grace's house. Grace and Melanie knew better than to ask them. It was too much noise, their mother would say. Something might get broken. But Grace always thought it was because things broke too easily in a house of cards.

Grace's childhood friends had grown up and married like Melanie and herself; their parents had retired and moved away. The new families lived in identical houses with cedar siding and brand-new windows. Sapling trees grew on the acres where the old homes had been razed. Wooden swing sets and sandboxes were covered with snow. Her parents had become the eccentric old couple on the street, a reputation not far removed from the one they held as the reclusive young couple forty years before who had not joined neighborhood organizations or gone to garage sales or watched the fireworks on the Fourth of July. The ones who simply stayed to themselves. And then there was the "old" house. The stucco-and-brown-wood Tudor that stood out like a gargoyle among the new models just like the Hammonds themselves who stayed behind instead of following the sun. Grace's heart sank as she looked at the house. The house was in disrepair. Shingles, fallen from the roof, lay on top of the snow. The windowpanes were cracked. The paint on the bricked chimney was peeling. Even in spring, the house looked abandoned. The lilac tree no longer bloomed, the magnolia's branches were half-dead. Rusty gutters overflowed with debris. But then, the house had always looked a bit abandoned, Grace thought, even when she was a child. Its landscaping was reliant on tired perennials left over from the previous owners. It seemed that every year there were fewer blooms. They'd never had a swing set like the neighbors or a sandbox or a basketball hoop. The pachysandra was bare in spots and crabgrass was a sharp contrast to the velvet-smooth green lawns of their neighbors. With each passing year, it seemed that the ivy creeping its way up the stone house became more tangled.

"I bet it was the old man," a young woman whispered to a newcomer who had a child in a stroller, bundled in a snowsuit.

"No, the old lady was pretty frail. She rarely saw the light of day," said another neighbor, tightening his collar around his neck. "The old man's been wandering lately. Saw him the other day strolling around the backyard in his bathrobe."

"Real oddballs," the young woman said. "They never even had candy for the kids at Halloween."

"I heard they were always a little crazy," the man said. "Real kooks."

A white van stenciled with blue lettering, MEDICAL EXAMINER, was parked in front of the house next to several black unmarked cars whose only indication of something official were the half dozen spiraled, thick antennas stuck to their rear windows. Blue-and-white squad cars were parked up and down the street with red dome lights turning and glistening, casting scarlet blazes on the snow. Everything seemed surreal and muted, cushioned by the snowfall. The silence was broken only by the crackle of the two-way radio on the hip of the police officer who stood by the front door. Unintelligible conversation broke through the radio in spurts of static that the officer pressed on and off.

Grace could see Jemma standing by the window in the living room. The hood of her old red parka with the fake fur trim pulled over her head. The paisley scarf Grace had given her several Christmases before (she'd worn it each winter since) was twisting in her hands. She saw Jemma take the scarf and dab her eyes and Grace felt her heart wrench to know that Jemma was crying. She wondered how cold it was inside the house that Jemma was still bundled so. It was always so cold in the house. Grace drew her breath through her nose, held it for a moment, and stopped in front of the police officer who guarded the front door.

"Officer, I'm their daughter," Grace said, her breath letting out like smoke. "Their other daughter. My sister is inside. This is my daughter, Kate."

"I'm sorry, ma'am," he said. "I'm afraid I can't let you in." He blocked them, placing his arm out, though he never touched them, as Grace started through the door. "You'll have to wait here until I can get someone to clear you through."

"My parents live here," Grace said. "I need to go inside."

"Give me a moment, ma'am," the officer said.

The police officer was unhooking the walkie-talkie from his belt when the door opened. A plainclothes detective stepped out. He was wearing jeans and a green turtleneck.

"What's going on, Jack?" the man said to the uniformed officer.

"She says she's the daughter, sir," the officer said, rehooking the walkie-talkie. "Says the girl is the granddaughter."

"I'm Grace Barnett and this is my daughter, Kate," Grace said.

"I'm Detective Douglas Bush. I need to see some identification, ma'am," the detective said gently.

Grace's hands trembled as she reached into the caverns of her purse for her wallet. She handed him her driver's license. Credit cards, loose change, a stick of gum, a small hairbrush fell to the ground. Kate reached down to retrieve everything, placing it back into her mother's bag.

"Let them in, Jack," the detective said to the officer as he looked at the driver's license and then back to Grace. "It's okay." Then, turning to Grace, he held the door open. "Please come in."

Melanie had been sitting on the couch between Jemma and Mike when Grace came in the door. She threw her arms around her sister's shoulders, hugging her tightly. Jemma was standing to the side of them until Grace managed to stretch out her hand, pulling Jemma into the embrace. The three stood there, huddled, heads down, as though in prayer, wrapped around each other. There was barely a sound except for Jemma's muffled sobs. Muted words of comfort murmured as though they were in church. As though the funeral had already begun, Grace thought, or perhaps was over.

"You okay, kiddo?" Mike asked Kate softly, pulling her next to him. He kissed the side of her head. "Your hair's kind of wet."

"I just washed it," Kate said. "We left the house so quickly. Are you okay, Uncle Mike? Aunt Mel?"

"Oh, I guess none of us are doing so great right now," Mike said. "This is rough. Really rough."

"What happened, Uncle Mike?" Kate asked. "It's so sad."

"We don't know yet, honey. Not exactly. Just stick by me, okay?" Mike said.

"Please sit down, Mrs. Barnett," said Detective Bush, breaking up the women's embrace. "I'm very sorry but we have to ask you some questions."

"I'm their other daughter," Grace repeated as she gazed up the stairs. She felt empty. Flat. As though she were floating above the room. Her voice came from somewhere else. She tried to make a fist but she couldn't feel her hands.

"Yes, I know, ma'am," the detective said patiently. "First of all, I'm sorry for your loss, Mrs. Barnett."

"Can I see my parents?" Grace asked. "What happened? How did this happen?"

"They won't let us upstairs," said Melanie.

"What do you mean? Why not?" Grace asked, turning to the detective.

"Please, ladies. We're doing what we have to do," Detective Bush said. "Until we know exactly what happened here, we have to treat this as a crime scene. I cannot permit you to go upstairs. We're collecting evidence."

"Evidence? For God's sake, they died," Melanie said. "They killed themselves. This was no crime!"

"It was that, wasn't it, Mel?" Grace said, turning to her sister. "I knew it, I swear. I felt it."

"In my heart, I knew it was," Melanie said. "From the moment I heard Jemma's voice, I knew. I think even Jemma knew."

"Did you know, Jemma?" they asked, not surprised by their chorus.

Jemma didn't answer. She looked from Grace to Melanie, her lips pressed together but not quite firmly enough to stop quivering. Jemma didn't have to answer. They all knew. Grace and Melanie knew even as children. Grace and Melanie could feel it coming when they would tap on their mother's bedroom door and there would be no answer. They would come home from school and jiggle the doorknob to their parents' room and rap furiously.

She's in there, they would whisper to each other. You know she's in there. Do you hear anything? Put your ear to the door.

Jemma would come up the stairs and find them with their ears pressed to the door, breath held, fingertips tapping softly, hearts pounding. They searched Jemma's face and thought that if her skin could blanch, it would. They watched as moist, silver beads of perspiration formed on top of Jemma's lip, as her breath came in small rapid spurts. Then Jemma would paste a false smile on her face as she moved the girls aside and stood between them, knocking firmly, confidently, on the door, glancing from Grace to Melanie, her face still frozen in a smile.

These old houses, Jemma would say. Plaster walls so thick you can never hear a thing. Your mother must have the radio on.

But the girls knew there was no radio playing. There was never music in the house. They never played music or danced in the living room the way the Rinaldis did when they practiced for Angela's sweet sixteen. Do it again, Grace had said to Mr. Rinaldi, clapping her hands as he dipped his wife, twirled her, swooped her in for a kiss. Marie Rinaldi pushed her husband away playfully. "You think you're a regular Casanova, don't you, Vince? You're a lunatic. And in front of the children!" But Mrs. Rinaldi was laughing. Grace wished she could've watched them dance all night.

"Mrs. Hammond!" Jemma would call through the door. "Mrs. Hammond! The girls are home and would like to say hello to you." And then, to the girls, Jemma would explain that their mother was napping. She would say something like their mother hadn't slept well the night before. Or she would say that their mother had one of her headaches. Her spells, Jemma called them. The spells when their mother would take to her bed and Jemma would bring their mother a cloth soaked in white vinegar and lay it across her forehead.

"I gave her the vinegar while you were at school," Jemma would say. "The vinegar sucked out the ache, I bet. She must have finally fallen asleep. You girls run along and play and I'll call you when she's up."

But the girls knew that as soon as they went to their room and changed from their school clothes that Jemma would go down to the kitchen and reach deep into the tin canister hidden behind the Camp-bell's Soups stacked in the pantry and bring out the skeleton key their father had put there. They knew because a few times they watched, hiding in the cedar closet, across from their parents' bedroom. Jemma would tiptoe back up the stairs and carefully place the key in the door, snap the door open, knocking while she opened it halfway. The same way she knocked that morning, so gingerly, afraid of what she might find. They would hear Jemma breathe a sigh of relief as she found their mother sitting on the green brocade divan in her bedroom, staring at nothing in particular, a small leather-bound book closed in her lap. It appeared to always be the same book, a bookmark in the same spot it had been in weeks before. Their mother's hands were clasped, one atop the other, so tightly, you could see the whites of her knuckles straining over the flesh.

"Everything all right, Mrs. Hammond?" Jemma would ask, fiddling with the venetian blind, straightening the lace runner on her dresser, biding her time in the room. "Can I bring you some tea? Is the headache better now?"

And their mother would clear her throat, which hadn't spoken for hours, and say that she felt better, though still suffering the slightest trace of pain. She would say that she needed to rest and would Jemma please give the girls their supper and see to it that they did their home-work. But Jemma always did that. There was no reason to ask or to say it. Jemma always took care of everything.

Jemma would close their mother's door quietly and slip the key into the pocket of her dress and go back down to the kitchen. The girls would wait, then skip downstairs and ask what was for dinner and Jemma would open the oven or lift the lid on the pot and tell them to guess with their eyes closed as they sniffed. Then Jemma would say they should go outside and take a walk or play next door if the weather was nice. "You'll see your mother later when she's rested," Jemma would say. "Oh, she was in such a deep sleep it was a pity that I woke her. But she says to send you both a kiss."

The day came when they stopped hiding in the linen closet. When they stopped tapping on their mother's door. When they knew there were no kisses sent to them. And then the day came that they knew that it wasn't just that something wasn't right—something was terribly wrong. They discovered that other families went to church on Sundays and ate their meals together. That mothers took their daughters shopping and fathers held them while they learned to ride their bicycles. They realized that even when they saw their mother, she did not see them. She didn't want to see them. And their father closed his eyes as if he were blind. Or perhaps he was simply afraid to look. They asked Jemma why it seemed their house was so different from the others and Jemma said it was different strokes for different folks. Your parents are reserved is all, she said. And perhaps because they didn't want Jemma to feel that she wasn't enough to anchor their lives and make them a home, they simply let it go. Perhaps because they knew it wasn't that Jemma was lying so much as she herself was uncertain of the truth.

"This is rather unusual," the detective said quietly, aware that he was breaking Grace's thoughts. He turned to Melanie. "Mrs. Peterson, why didn't you say this to me before? Why didn't you say that you thought your parents' deaths were suicides?"

"I needed to wait for my sister," Melanie said, her eyes down.

"Anything else?" he asked.

"My mother was wearing lipstick. She never wore lipstick," Melanie said.

"Did your parents tell you they were planning this?" the detective asked, looking back and forth from Grace to Melanie. Like Jemma, Grace thought, looking from one of us to the other for an answer outside her bedroom door.

"I don't know what to make of the lipstick," Grace said. "Our parents didn't indicate that anything was planned. It's an awfully long story, detective. Nothing was ever quite right here." Suddenly Grace was agitated. "Why isn't there an ambulance?"

"The ambulance has come and gone, Mrs. Barnett. It was apparent there was no need for them to stay. I have to ask you some questions, Mrs. Barnett. You can sit here," the detective said, motioning to a dining room chair. "Mrs. Peterson, Mrs. Polk, I'm going to ask you to sit down and please be quiet while I speak to your sister." And then to Grace with his back turned slightly to Melanie, "I've already spoken to your sister and to Jemma Polk. You do know Mrs. Polk, correct?"

"Jemma. Of course. Nearly all my life," Grace said. She had never heard Jemma referred to as Mrs. Polk. "Jemma's very distraught, you know."

"Yes, ma'am, we know she is," he said. "She's doing a little better now, though."

"She was the one who found my parents," Grace said.

"Yes, she told us," the detective said. "We're taking good care of her."

"Jemma has been with my family for over forty years," Grace said. "She *is* family, really."

"Did your mother or father ever talk about suicide?" the detective asked.

"Not as such," Grace said. "They never used the term."

"Please be more specific, Mrs. Barnett. Again, I apologize. I know this is difficult," the detective said. He was gentle. More gentle than he had to be.

"They never used the word *suicide*. Not in so many words. But my mother always said, 'When one would go, the other would follow,'" Grace said.

"Recently?"

"Always."

"Did you think she always meant it?" he asked with the emphasis on the frequency.

"I don't know. Maybe. I'm not sure. I never thought about it. Maybe I should have," Grace sighed, trying to take a breath that wasn't coming. She was squeezing her fingers open and closed.

"Why do you suppose your mother said that?" the detective asked, writing on a small lined pad.

"I don't know. It was just something she said. We never asked her," Grace said. "She was always in her own world, our mother. It wasn't the kind of thing we really wanted to know. They were so much each other's world, my parents. Too much each other's world. Especially lately."

"When was the last time you spoke to your parents?" the detective asked Grace.

"Friday evening," she said. "What's today? Sunday? Yes, Friday evening."

"And what was the nature of the call?"

"I called to see if they were well. I call them once or twice a week. We were planning to have Christmas here day after tomorrow. We had Thanksgiving here last month. Melanie and I brought the food and the kids. This was our year for the holidays. You know, we alternate with our family and our husbands' families."

"How was your parents' state of mind?"

"You mean on Thanksgiving?" Grace asked.

"Well, yes, then, and in general," the detective said.

"It's hard to say. They were as they always were," Grace said.

"And what is that?" the detective asked.

"I don't know."

"Well, how would you describe your parents' demeanor?"

"They were, well, restrained. Nearly reclusive. Not close to anyone but to each other," Grace said. "They kept to themselves. Didn't go out much. Certainly not anymore. Jemma really cared for them. They were only in their seventies but somehow they were old. Actually,"

Grace sighed, "they've always seemed old. My father seemed a little out of it, lately. We saw glimpses of it at Thanksgiving."

"How so?"

"He became confused easily. On Thanksgiving, he began to cry when Mike asked him to watch the parade on TV with him and the boys. He just broke down and sobbed. Jemma told us Dad couldn't remember things like if he'd already had his breakfast. He misplaced his glasses all the time. And, last week, Jemma said he threw a deck of cards across the living room: He was frustrated because he'd forgotten how to play solitaire," Grace said. "And Jemma found him wandering down the street a few weeks ago in the pouring rain. He was in his bathrobe, barefoot. She said he was talking to himself. "

"Had you taken him to see anyone?"

"What do you mean?" Grace asked.

The detective was answered cautiously. "Well, you know, a psychiatrist. A social worker."

"No. Melanie and I had discussed it with one another. But we weren't going to bring it up until after the New Year," Grace sighed, and looked away. "I suppose we shouldn't have waited. He'd always been my mother's rock and he was slipping away."

"What did your mother have to say about his mental state?" the detective asked.

"We didn't discuss it with our mother."

"Why not?"

"Because we discussed it with Jemma," Grace said. She was getting impatient. Becoming annoyed. "We never discussed things with our mother. Only with Jemma."

"Were either of your parents physically ill?"

"As opposed to *mentally* ill, detective?" Grace said, blistering visibly.

"I was not implying anything, Mrs. Barnett. I was merely being specific."

"No."

"Did they have any financial difficulties that you were aware of?"

"No."

"Was there anyone or anything that was disturbing them recently?"

"Not that I'm aware of."

"Were they on medication for anything?"

"My father took pills for his blood pressure. I think my mother took baby aspirin every day."

"Did either of them take sleeping pills?"

"I don't believe so."

"Did your parents drink?"

Grace laughed. "Oh, no. Teetotalers."

"There are bottles of wine and Scotch in the basement," the detective said.

"Gifts. From ages ago. Same with the Scotch. When my father practiced law, clients always sent gifts at Christmas and when he finished a case. He hasn't practiced in a few years, though. He'll go into the office sometimes and just putter around. He likes that," Grace said, painfully aware that she spoke of her father in the present tense.

"There's an open bottle of Scotch in their bedroom," the detective said.

"That's not like them," Grace said. "I don't know."

"There was an empty bottle of sleeping pills as well," the detective said.

"I don't know," Grace said.

"Were you close to your parents?"

"No. Yes. I mean, I don't know. No, we were not close. I don't think anyone was close to them." Grace sighed deeply. "I was devoted."

"Are there any siblings besides Melanie Peterson?" the detective asked.

"No. Just the two of us."

"Any other relatives?"

"Well, our children and husbands, of course. We didn't know our grandparents. They died before we were born. Our parents were only children. No aunts. No uncles. No cousins. No one," Grace said. She looked hopefully at the detective. "Was there a note?"

"I can't say at this point, Mrs. Barnett."

Of course they didn't leave a note, Grace thought. There were never any explanations. Any reasons.

"Where is your husband, Mrs. Barnett?"

Grace realized that her lips were dry and stuck together. She could feel herself pale.

"My husband is in the city. At our apartment," Grace said.

"Why didn't he accompany you?" the detective asked.

"He has to work," Grace said.

"He has to work on Sunday?" the detective asked.

"He's a surgeon. A cardiac surgeon. He's on call this weekend. Please, let me go upstairs. I don't feel so well right now," Grace said, standing now, moving away from the detective and heading toward the stairs.

"I'm sorry. I can't let you go up there," the detective said, his hand placed gently but firmly on her arm, stopping her. "It wouldn't be a good idea, Mrs. Barnett."

"Can't you leave her alone now?" asked Melanie, walking over to Grace, who was sitting again. "She was nearly an hour away when this happened. Can't you see she's upset? You've asked me all these questions. I gave you the same answers."

"It won't be much longer," the detective said. "I know this is hard on all of you."

"When can I see them?" Grace repeated. There is no reason why I can't just go upstairs, she thought, standing up again.

She was tapping on their bedroom door. "Come in," her father said. The hint of his Maine accent boomed so clearly. Her mother smiled, opening the door wide. "Oh, Grace, it's you! To think, Grace, that they all thought we were dead. Why don't they know this is just the way we are? Quiet and keeping to ourselves. What foolishness. What foolishness." And then Grace was standing to her waist in icy water. She heard herself cry. Someone please help us, she cried. But her parents sat still in their rooms. Please help us. Why can't you give me your hand? A voice came through the fog.

"Mrs. Barnett? Mrs. Barnett? Are you with us? Can someone get some ice in a towel? Hey, John, we have ammonia salts in the glove box of my car," Detective Bush called to the officer posted by the kitchen door. "You're okay, Mrs. Barnett. You'll be okay. You went out on us when you stood up. You're going to be okay now."

Grace blinked her eyes open. She felt sick to her stomach. The dream had come again when she had blacked out. She hadn't had the dream for months now. The dream she had in one form or another since she was a little girl. The boat. The icy water. The cries for help ignored. She looked up at the staircase leading to her parents' bedroom. It, too, was roped off with yellow tape. Had it been that way when Grace walked in the door? She couldn't remember now.

"I need some air," Grace said to the detective. "Please, just let me go to the window and get some air." She walked, slowly, using the wall to guide her as though she were blindfolded.

"Just let me open the window," Grace said. She was turning the rusty metal crank on the leaded casement when she heard voices coming from the street. The medical examiner's van was being opened from the rear. There were two gurneys sitting on the pavement, each holding a long red rubber bag. Snow was blowing from the trees, falling on the red bags like confetti. Two men lifted the gurneys into the back of the van, closed the heavy double doors solidly. Grace heard a moan and realized it was coming from deep inside her.

"You weren't supposed to see that," said Detective Bush. "I'm so sorry, Mrs. Barnett."

"How did they get them out there?" Grace asked, sitting down again. Melanie had come over and was standing behind Grace, her hand on Grace's back.

"We removed them through the kitchen," the detective said. "Down the back stairs. I don't think we need to ask any more questions, Mrs. Barnett. I just need a number where I can reach you."

"Where are they taking them?" Grace asked.

"To the county medical center," Detective Bush said.

"Why? They're going to do autopsies, aren't they?" Grace asked.

"It's procedure, ma'am," the detective said, nodding his head. "I'll need a phone number where you can be reached."

"Don't you need someone to identify the . . . my parents?" Grace asked.

"Mr. Peterson did that," Detective Bush said. "I know you want to see your folks, Mrs. Barnett. You'll see them at the funeral home."

The funeral home. That was it. It was final. Grace hung her head and began to cry. The numbness was leaving her. Jemma came over and took Grace in her arms.

"They're with the good Lord, now, baby doll," she said, sitting Grace down on the sofa.

There was nothing Grace could say. She searched Jemma's eyes.

" 'Cause those two was always together and He knew that, Grace," Jemma said, answering the question Grace hadn't asked. "It never could be any other way. You know that, Grace. You always knew that, didn't you, baby? Those two were like peas in a pod. And, lately, with your daddy so sad and confused, I think they just wanted it to all be over."

"Wanted *what* to be over, though?" Grace asked.

"I'm not really sure," Jemma said. "I never was real sure."

"I was planning to comfort *you*," Grace said to Jemma, managing a smile.

"You do, baby. Just by being here with me," Jemma said. "My baby girl, that's what you are. You and Melanie, my babies."

Grace leaned into Jemma the way she did when she was a child. "Jemma, if I start to cry again, I'll never stop," Grace said. "Why do you suppose mother put on lipstick?"

"People do strange things, Grace, when they know they're about to die," Jemma said solemnly.

Jemma and Grace walked outside, a few steps ahead of the others. The five of them stood in the middle of the path that led to the house. The van carrying the Hammonds was gone now. A faint smell of gasoline still lingered in the air. Only two police cars were left in the driveway, their red dome lights still turning. The sawhorses had been removed. The neighbors had gone back inside. The street was empty.

"We'll squeeze you and Kate into my car," Mike said, turning to Grace. "We'll come back later for yours."

Grace protested. She was reluctant to leave the car on the street.

"I'll be okay," Grace said. "I'll follow you."

"Out of the question. I won't let you drive. No one's going to bother with Adam's Mercedes," Mike said, reading her mind. "Come on, Grace. I don't want to have to wrestle you for the keys."

Grace stopped and looked back at her parents' house. The police officer was still standing outside the door. How odd, she thought, the house is guarded. A strand of yellow banner had fallen from the weight of the snow. Grace bent down, picked it up, and crumpled it in her hand.

"Mom? You okay?" Kate's voice broke her thoughts.

Grace began to say that she was fine. She was going to try to square her shoulders and manage a smile. But then she thought of her mother behind the locked door. Her father hidden behind the morning paper. Jemma's skeleton key and the cloth soaked in vinegar. The lilac tree that barely bloomed in spring. The dreams she suffered alone.

"I am not okay, but I will be," Grace said. "I will be."

Chapter Three

Grace sat between Kate and Jemma in the backseat of Mike's car, her head leaning on Jemma's shoulder. Kate slumped down in her seat, her head turned to look out the car window, her fingers laced through her mother's. Melanie tilted her neck back and closed her eyes, her hand resting on her husband's thigh. Mike's free hand covered hers. He drove staring straight ahead.

Mrs. Hadley opened the door, holding Matthew in one arm while Jeremy, his mouth covered with chocolate sauce, clung to the top of her thigh. When the twins saw Melanie, they scrambled down Mrs. Hadley's tall, buxom body like she was a firehouse pole.

Melanie knelt down and held her children on either side of her. "You guys smell like chocolate and garlic," she laughed weakly. "Some combination."

"Spaghetti for lunch and hot fudge over ice cream for dessert," Mrs. Hadley laughed, tightening her apron strings. "They each chose a favorite. I figured they might as well have a treat. At first they were upset that you two left, but they bounced back fast." She was fussing now with a button on her blouse that had come undone, scraping some chocolate sauce off with a fingernail. "I must look a mess. Those two are full of beans, I tell you. Kate, why don't you tend to your cousins? Your aunt and uncle look like they could use a few moments to collect themselves. Lord knows, I do. Everything go all right over there?" Mrs. Hadley turned to Melanie.

There was no good way to say it. "They're dead, Mrs. H.," Melanie said. "They died."

"Jesus, Mary, and Joseph," Mrs. Hadley said, placing her hand to her chest, the button still undone. "What happened?"

Melanie took a bottle of wine from the refrigerator and reached for glasses from the rack overhead. She was taking the glasses down one by one, her hands unsteady as she set each glass on the counter, when one tipped over and broke.

"Look what I did," Melanie said, the detached stem of the glass in her hand.

"Let me," Mike said, picking up the shards. "I'll do it. Go sit down."

Grace stood to the side with Jemma although she was afraid to look at her. She could feel Jemma's eyes on her, following her own as she watched Mike take the glasses from his wife's hands, saw her sister's hip brush against her husband's, listened to the words that passed between them. Jemma looped her arm through Grace's and tugged her to the living room.

"He'll show up soon," Jemma whispered to Grace as they walked through the doorway. "You'll see. He'll be here."

Grace turned her face toward Jemma, embarrassed that she was so transparent.

"He won't," said Grace. "But it's okay. He's working, anyway. I don't need him to be here."

"Yes, you do, Grace," Jemma said. "He's your husband."

Grace shook her head. "It's not like that with us, Jemma," Grace said, lifting her chin toward Mike and Melanie. "Not anymore."

Mrs. Hadley was babbling now, walking in from the kitchen with Melanie and Mike, carrying a glass of wine. She came over and took hold of Jemma's hand. She began pumping it up and down, asking her when was the last time they saw one another. Surely it wasn't as long ago as the twins' christening. No, it must have been their second birthday party. Mrs. Hadley held Jemma's hand in both of her own long after she was finished shaking it. "You poor dear. You poor thing.

What a shock you must have had. I should have known something was wrong when I saw Grace and Kate with you. What could I have been thinking?" Mrs. Hadley said, making *tsk*ing sounds with her tongue as she spoke.

"I keep thinking I should have seen it all coming. She'd always been the fragile one," Jemma mused. "But lately, you'd think that man was going to break in two. It was as though he just didn't know who he was anymore."

Mrs. Hadley said that no one could ever expect something like this to happen and Jemma shouldn't blame herself. How the only thing that anyone could do now would be to pray for their souls.

Melanie drank her glass of wine too quickly and began to sob, saying that the wine had gone right to her head but maybe it was just what she needed to let herself go. She told Mrs. Hadley about the police and the yellow tape and the sawhorse barriers. About the bottle of pills and the Scotch. How her mother and father looked as they lay on the bed. She couldn't see their chests rising and falling ever so slightly the way people's do when they're breathing. She'd nearly collapsed even though she knew, before she'd even seen them, when she'd arrived at the house and it was dark and still, that they were gone. Grace was sipping her wine, looking from one to the other. She watched while everyone talked and cried and reached for one another's hands. The voices converged all at once on her ears, their words mixing together nonsensically, like a cacophony of discords one hears in a dream, in a nightmare. She was unable to discern who was saying what. When had she felt this way before? So detached, removed. Standing to the side, avoiding the commotion. Feeling as though no one knew she was there. As though she were invisible.

"I don't really know what happened," Grace said in a loud voice. And then she realized, embarrassed, that no one had asked her anything as they all turned to look at her. She changed the sentence, pretending she had said something else and they had all misheard. "What happens now?" Grace asked. "Now what do we do?"

"We do need to do something, don't we, Mike?" Melanie asked, dabbing her eyes and nose. "What is it that we're supposed to be doing?"

"We wait. Christmas is Tuesday. We probably won't know too much until after that. Look, I hate to bring this up but we need to call the funeral home," Mike said. "Do they have plots?"

"Oh, God, I never thought of that," Melanie said. "Mother's parents are buried in Pennsylvania somewhere. Dad's are in Maine."

"I'm calling over to Flanigan's Funeral Home," Mike said. "Joe Flanigan's a good guy. He works on the volunteer fire department with me some weekends. He'll walk us through this."

Mike took the phone book off the shelf and left the message. "Hey, Joe. Mike Peterson. We've had a, well, deaths in the family. Give us a call, would you? 555-7829."

It wasn't a half hour before Joe Flanigan called back. It was Mike who explained to Joe what he referred to as the "nature" of the deaths. Grace heard him say that they took their own lives. Suicides, Mike whispered as though whispering might diminish the impact. The way people say someone has cancer or that her husband left her for another woman.

"I'll talk to him," Grace said suddenly, reaching for the phone.

"You sure you want to do this now, Grace?" Mike asked, covering the phone with his hand. "You know, I'll be happy to take care of it."

"I need to do this, Mike," she said.

Joe began by telling Grace that he was sorry for her loss. How the days ahead would be difficult but he was there to help her through in any way at all. How hard this must be on her and her sister. You have to choose caskets, Joe said. Is there a resting place where you would like your parents to be? There are several in the area, he said. Perhaps Celestial Gates. It's only about a half hour away. We'll arrange for cars, for the processional. Limousines for family and friends. Flowers at the funeral home. Donations, perhaps, to a charity or fund in lieu of flowers. What church did they go to? Who would preside? Is there someone special who might give a eulogy? Would a Thursday interment be viable?

Viable? Grace thought, what an odd choice of words. An interment to be viable.

They were about to hang up the phone when Joe said, "Oh, one more thing. You have to choose something for them to wear. Perhaps your mother had a favorite dress. A favorite color."

Grace pictured her mother sitting in her robe and her father's tired blue and gray suits that he wore to work each day when she was a child. She pictured the old brown fedora that her father hung so quietly on the rack by the door at the end of the day. She didn't know her mother's favorite color. Her mother's eyes were hazel, like her own. Once she told her mother that Jemma thought she had her mother's eyes.

You have your own eyes, her mother had said. Not mine.

"Joe?" Grace said. "I'm going to turn all this over to you. The plots. The caskets. The cars. They had no church but Melanie's minister can preside."

"But you'll have to bring me their clothes," Joe said. "And choose the caskets. That I can't do for you."

"Jemma, did my mother have a favorite dress?" Grace asked when she hung up the phone.

"We'll find something nice, Grace," Jemma said softly. "Don't you worry. There are a bunch of pretty dresses hanging in her closet."

For a moment, Grace felt like a child again.

Go play outside, Grace, while your mother rests. Dinner will be ready soon. We'll play a game after dinner, Grace. Something quiet so we don't disturb your parents while they talk, Jemma would say. We'll have a good time. Don't you worry.

"I never really saw her wear dresses, Jemma," Grace said. "When did she buy them?"

"They're old, honey, but they'll do. Your parents traveled when you were small. Your dad would tell me he was taking her someplace where the air was fresh. They went to Arizona once and one time to Switzerland. She wore the dresses then. You just don't remember," Jemma said.

Melanie went over to Grace. She'd seen that look on her sister's face too many times before. The one where her sister looked as though she were drifting far away

"You know, it never even occurred to me that you've been in those damp running clothes this whole time," Melanie said. "Come on up-stairs and I'll give you something dry."

Melanie waited while Grace showered. She had laid out a pair of navy sweatpants and a white T-shirt on the bed. A pair of navy fleece socks. Grace came from the bathroom, drying her hair with a towel. She stopped and smiled when she saw the clothing.

"Thanks, Mel. I can't believe how good that felt," said Grace. "My clothes practically peeled off me." She sat down on the bed. "We're supposed to leave for Aspen on Friday, you know. Mel, I can't go. I just don't want to go."

"I was waiting for that," Melanie said. "So, don't go. You don't have to. Adam's not going to like it, though."

"It's not Adam that I'm worried about. It's Kate." Grace was shak-ing water out of her ear, rubbing her hair furiously with a towel as she sat down on the edge of Melanie's bed. "I don't want her to think I'm forsaking her if I don't go to Aspen. It's her last Christmas vacation be-fore she goes off to college. It's just that I need to be around here after Thursday. After the funeral. We'll have to go through their house, you know. There's going to be so much to do. We'll sell the house, right, Mel? That's what we'll do, right? That's what people do, right?"

Melanie didn't say anything. She just looked at her sister.

"We'll get rid of that house, right? I know this sounds selfish, but I want to start the New Year with a clean slate. I want this all behind me. Am I awful to want to get this over with?"

"Of course you're not awful. We all want this behind us. My God, Grace, it's gone on for so long, really," Melanie said. "Maybe Kate can bring a friend to Aspen. Hey, if I were seventeen, I would definitely want to bring a friend on vacation."

"Why do I feel like I'm abandoning her?"

"This is hardly abandonment. Sending your daughter to Aspen with her father doesn't constitute abandonment. Kate's a bright girl. And she loves you. She'll understand. Maybe not at first, but she will," Melanie said. "Grace? How could they have done this? How could they have ended it all this way? No note. No nothing. No explanation. And right before Christmas so that every Christmas we'll mark the season like this. I will never forget what it felt like to walk into that house and know. I just knew. Right then and there."

"After the funeral, we'll go through the house, okay? Maybe something will be there that they'd have wanted us to find, to see. I have this funny feeling, Mel. Like I'm on the outside looking in. I feel like, this sounds so crazy, I feel like I've been through this before."

The bedroom door pushed open as someone knocked. Five deliberate knocks, a hesitation, and two in rapid succession.

"Your secret knock, Jemma." Grace smiled. "I always knew when it was you."

"Irene Hadley and I cooked up everything in your house, Melanie," Jemma said. She was wearing the apron that Mrs. Hadley had worn earlier. She held a pot holder in one hand. "We made a feast. Come downstairs and eat something, girls." Jemma was walking out the door when she turned around and called to Grace. "I wasn't eavesdropping, but I don't know if you're going to find what you're looking for. You can't find things that were never there."

Jemma started back down the stairs after Melanie and Grace said they would be right along as soon as Grace put on some dry clothes. Grace kissed Jemma on the cheek. But when Jemma left the room, Grace put her face into her hands and began to cry.

"Damn them both, Melanie," Grace sobbed. "Damn them for doing this. Damn them for being the way they were. Damn them for not even saying good-bye."

Jemma heard Grace crying as she walked down the stairs. She stopped for a moment as though she might walk back to comfort her. But then she just drew in a deep breath and said aloud to herself, "It's about time, Grace. It's about time. Let it out, baby. Don't damn them. Pray for their souls."

Chapter Four

When Grace and Kate left on Sunday night, Jemma was wearing one of Melanie's flannel nightgowns, her face was lightly greased with cold cream, her hair pulled back in a kerchief. The kerchief was actually one of Mike's bandannas that he wore when he worked the cameras for outdoor shoots in the heat of the summer.

"It looks a darn sight better on you than it does on me," Mike told Jemma.

"We have everything you need here," Melanie said to her. "I'll even run your clothes through the wash so they're clean in the morning."

It had taken little urging to convince Jemma to spend the night. Melanie needed her: It was that simple.

The twins were sitting cross-legged in front of the television watching cartoons, cozy in their pajamas, drinking warm milk and honey from their sippy cups. Kate was leaning on a pillow beside them, looking much like a small child herself. Grace reluctantly took her jacket from the hall closet.

"You and Kate can spend the night as well, you know. I have extra nightgowns. Even extra toothbrushes. Plenty of cold cream left." Melanie smiled.

Grace said she should get home to Adam. Melanie's eyes looked angry. She started to say something, but Grace placed her finger to her lips. "Kate might hear you," Grace said.

"She's getting older," Melanie said.

"I know," said Grace, hugging her sister to her. "We'll talk, Mel. When all this is over, we'll talk."

"He should have been with you today," Melanie said bluntly.

"He couldn't," Grace said. "In so many ways, he couldn't. To tell you the truth, I don't think I would have wanted him to be."

When Mike drove Grace and Kate back to their car, it seemed un-naturally calm on Harvest Lane. Television screens and Christmas trees flickered in the darkened rooms of houses up and down the street. A woman walked a small dog back and forth along the curb. A group of people stood outside one of the holiday-trimmed homes that blinked colored lights on and off in the darkness. They were saying their good nights, wishing one another Merry Christmas. The police barricades and restrictive tape had been removed, although a few torn strands of yellow banners had blown into the bushes, sprinkled like odd yellow petals. There was something almost Gothic about the house on that winter night. The police had left the light on over the front door, a dim golden glow under a dirty glass shade. But, other than that, the house appeared painfully empty. Then again, Grace thought sadly, it was always empty.

Kate slept in the car on the way back to Manhattan, her feet resting on the dashboard, her jaw propped against the car window. I'm just going to rest a little, Kate had said apologetically as her lids started to droop. I won't go to sleep, I promise. But she had dozed off as Grace knew she would. It was just as well, Grace thought. They were both drained. Conversation would have been a futile attempt at explanation, a litany of possibilities that didn't exist as they tried to answer why and find a reason.

It seemed like a lifetime ago that Grace had walked through the apartment door that morning after her run. Once again, Adam was waiting. He opened the door and kissed Kate on the top of her head. "You okay, little girl?" he asked.

"I'm tired, Daddy," Kate said, lifting her face to kiss his cheek. Her eyes were puffy from sleep. There was a red mark on her forehead where she'd leaned against the car window. "I'm going to bed."

"Melanie told me how they died, Grace," Adam said after he heard Kate close the door to her room.

"When did you speak to Melanie?" Grace asked.

"She called here just a minute ago. She wanted to know if you made it home all right," Adam said. "She told me what happened. This must be very hard on you. I'm very sorry, Grace."

Grace looked at Adam blankly. Joe Flanigan and Detective Bush had used the same sort of language. We know this is hard on you, Mrs. Barnett. We're sorry for your loss. A stranger's sympathy. Perfunctory consolation. Adam hadn't even reached for her, hadn't tried to touch her.

"Hard on me? Yes, Adam, it's hard on me," Grace said in a clipped tone. "You should have been there with me today."

"I'm sorry, Grace," Adam said. "I said before that I was sorry."

"Why didn't you call?" Grace said, her chin jutting out like a defiant child's. "I had my cell phone."

"We already knew they were dead when you left this morning," Adam said. "Your sister was there. And Jemma. There was nothing I could do."

"I'm not a patient or a patient's wife, Adam," Grace said. "I didn't need you to take a pulse."

Grace remembered the first time Adam listened to her heart. He nimbly held two fingers to her neck and kissed her, saying he wanted to feel how her heart raced at his touch. It was a sweet joke back then. But that was twenty years ago. They'd met at The School for Special Children where Grace taught dance. Adam was president of the school board, a position he acquired after operating on one of the students, a Down syndrome child. A cardiac surgeon, Adam had repaired the child's ventricular septal defect, a hole in the wall of the heart that separates the heart into left and right sides. A hole in the heart that Adam easily and successfully mended.

"I'm Dr. Barnett," Adam said, stopping into Grace's morning dance class. "I operated on Toby Abbott. How's he doing?"

"He's wonderful. Look at him," Grace said, sweeping her arm toward the boy.

The child was standing in a group of children, practicing the steps Grace had taught moments before. Adam had still not stepped inside the room.

"Come say hello. He's so happy when he dances. You know, it's so easy to see why they're called God's children," Grace said, beckoning to the boy. "He is the sweetest child. Come here, Toby. There's someone here to visit you. Come see Dr. Barnett. Do you remember him?"

Toby nodded shyly, made his way toward Grace, stopped, and hid in the folds of Grace's soft chiffon skirt.

"I think he's afraid you've come to take him back to the hospital," Grace said.

"I'm not taking you back to the hospital, Toby," Adam said awkwardly. "I just came to watch you dance."

But the child burrowed his face deeper and deeper into Grace's skirt. He started to whimper, murmuring that he was afraid.

"No more needles," Toby whimpered. "I don't like the needles."

"No, Toby, no needles," Adam said, shifting his weight uncomfortably.

But Toby continued to protest. "Go 'way," he said, clinging to Grace. "Make him go 'way, Miss Hammond."

"Maybe you should go now," Grace said. "He's becoming too distressed." She turned her back and clapped her hands. She took Toby's hand and walked over to the stereo, started the music again, kept Toby by her side, and formed a circle with the other children.

"I'll go, but only if you'll have dinner with me tonight," Adam called to Grace as he left the room.

Adam had not really come to watch Toby Abbott. He had come to watch Grace. He had been late at a board meeting a few nights before and Grace had been dancing alone in the studio, practicing, working at the barre, stretching her body in ways Adam found unimaginable. He wanted to meet her.

"So, will you?" Adam asked from the doorway when the class ended.

"You again!" Grace smiled, turning to face him. "Will I what?"

"Have dinner with me tonight? I thought we had a deal," Adam said.

That night, they went out and then the night after that and the one after that. She enchanted him. The way she looked at him so directly with her penetrating hazel eyes. How easily she spoke to him; how attentively she listened. And yet she was also guileless. He loved the way she piled her long auburn hair on top of her head with her fingers flying as she fastened it into a large clip. The way she stood, her feet forming a slight vee. He wrapped his slender fingers in the strands of Italian glass beads she looped around her neck that fell near her navel. He became accustomed to the jingle of her long earrings when she walked or shook her head. He loved the way her flawless white skin looked by candlelight. How her smooth body appeared almost incandescent as she lay beside him. She was alternately his siren, his child, his lover, and, much to his surprise, she was his friend.

Grace did not fall in love with Adam right away. At first she thought this man, who was fifteen years older than she, was too conservative. She was unimpressed with his prominence, his wealth, his position on the board. She was only twenty-five. She had mostly dated young musicians and artists. There was one she'd actually fallen in love with. An artist named Lin who had a ponytail and a penchant for painting her image in duplicates shadowed with dark, mournful hues. He took her to jazz clubs where you could barely see through the thick haze of cigarette smoke. Dinners were hamburgers and French fries and pitchers of beer served on bare wooden tables. Lin had proclaimed to love her and then moved on, saying something esoteric about freedom and likening himself to an armadillo. He gave her a book of Camus, one of her portraits (he'd signed it with a flourish) and was gone.

Adam Barnett was different. He wore suits and ties. His hair was styled and cropped. His shoes shined. He dined at restaurants where the check came to more than Grace paid in rent for her studio on the

Upper West Side of Manhattan. She loved his confidence and his bravado. She loved how he spoke in a deep soft voice that seemed to hypnotize those around him into listening. Love didn't come suddenly the way it had with Lin. She grew to love Adam, not only for the way he was but for the way he loved her as well. He seemed to love her unconditionally, something she had longed for since she was a child.

Less than a year from the day they met, Adam proposed to Grace at the department of surgery's Christmas party. He stood before a crowd of nearly one hundred people and clinked a spoon against his champagne glass. Grace thought she was watching what would be one of Adam's famous toasts. The kind he often made at dinner parties to flatter the hostess. Ones that were mildly self-aggrandizing but, she always felt, well meaning. Sometimes she was almost embarrassed for him, worried that he might be misconstrued as obsequious.

"I want you all to be a part of this occasion," he said. "You people are my colleagues as well as my family. You have all met Grace. With you as my witnesses and with your blessings, I ask Grace to marry me." He pulled something from his pocket. He held a ring between his index finger and his thumb. He reached to Grace with an outstretched arm, his hand extended, holding the ring. "Will you marry me, Grace? Will you?" Adam asked, holding the pear-shaped diamond.

Grace moved toward him. She never said a word. She placed her lips to his ear and nodded her response. He slipped the ring on her finger, though she never looked down at her hand. He kissed her in front of the crowd. A long, soulful kiss that was broken when the room broke out in a thunderous applause. Later, when all the chairs were stacked on the tables, after everyone had gone home, they sat at a table for two. A melted candle, its wick flickering in a small bowl of blue water, struggled to glow. Adam had filled two glasses with champagne before the bar was dismantled. "What if I had said I wouldn't, Adam?" Grace asked him, running her finger along the rim of the glass. "How would you have felt in front of all those people?"

But Adam said there was no doubt in his mind. "But why would you have said you wouldn't marry me?" he asked. "You love me, don't you, Grace?"

And she did love him. Despite his aplomb and self-assurance, she was protective of him. It bothered her that the nurses called Adam "God" behind his back as he glided down the sterile hospital corridors in his green scrubs, his cowboys boots clopping his trademark brashness on the linoleum floor as he strode into the OR. The young physicians gathered around him, the pedagogue, as he performed his miracles. On the occasion that a junior physician prepped a patient poorly or did something to fall beneath Adam's expectations, Adam would turn to the young doctor. "Let me ask you a question," he would say in a booming voice. "Is this man sleeping with your wife, Doctor? No? You say no? Then why are you trying to kill him?"

In short, Adam Barnett despised failure and loathed imperfection. Fine qualities for a cardiac surgeon who often stood for hours squeezing a flat-lined heart in the palm of his hand until it began to beat again with the cadence of life.

Twenty years ago, Grace suspected that emotion was something that baffled Adam. Now, she was certain. The notion of the heart beyond that of a blood-pumping muscle was far too intangible for him to comprehend, too abstract for him to risk tackling. He required procedures, formulas, instruments, and machines. He mandated certainty and reasons in order to live his life. He saw the heartlessness of his in-laws but reduced it to a generic form of misanthropy. Adam dismissed his in-laws as they dismissed him. There was no room in his life for anyone who made him feel invisible or powerless. He insisted that his wife move past her childhood. Urged her to stop searching for something that had never existed and never would. He despised them for disrupting what he felt would be the ideal life, the ideal marriage. If not for his wife's apparent angst over the loss of her parents, both while they were living and now that they were dead, Adam felt their marriage had the potential to be idyllic. But his wife's heart was the one thing he couldn't repair. It was not within his domain or capabilities as a healer. And, so, he often left his wife's heart fallow. To acknowledge the impotence he felt when it came to mending Grace's heart was too great an admission of imperfection. It had been simple to repair Toby Abbott's heart twenty years before. The hole in his wife's heart was too deep a canyon.

Unlike Adam, Grace searched the corners of the heart that Adam's instruments couldn't reach. She often hit an impasse, as though she'd hit a rock or a boulder that she was incapable of moving. The impasses tormented her. She always had the feeling that something lay deep within and could not be retrieved.

Grace questioned so many memories lately. She wondered if she had misled her husband into thinking she would make the perfect doctor's wife. Had she made it clear, fairly, right from the start, that she would resist being groomed like the other doctors' wives? Over the years, she had often felt like an albatross as she stood by Adam's side at a dinner party. The other wives wore designer clothing and thick gold necklaces that told of their husbands' success both in and out of the operating room. Grace continued to wear long costume beads and jangling earrings. Her dresses seemed more for dancing than for medical parties. She insisted that for the price of a Chanel she could outfit herself for the year. In the beginning, she was a novelty for Adam. His Eliza Doolittle, she teased. But, lately, she sadly realized that her edgy bohemian ways were wearing thin with her husband. He no longer seemed to be enchanted, as it were, with the fairy-tale notion of the kingfish surgeon and his maverick wife who still taught dance at The School for Special Children while so many other wives spent time on hospital committees. Perhaps when Adam married Grace he thought he could watch her grow up. That she *would* grow up. But Grace simply continued to be Grace.

The Sunday night that Grace and Kate returned from Purchase, Grace made her bed in the guest room. She stacked a pile of magazines on the bed beside her. Nothing that required concentration. Articles about homeopathic remedies for tension headache, low carbohydrate diets, the wonders of ginseng and green teas. Which movie star was getting divorced, having a baby, having an affair. The next thing Grace knew, it was nearly noon. She had fallen asleep with the lamp burning. The television was still on from the night before. Pages of open magazines were stuck to her arms. She was wondering briefly if the day before had been a dream when the phone rang. It was Detective Bush.

"I hope I didn't wake you," he said. "I have the preliminary autopsy report. I thought you'd like to know. Your parents' deaths were suicides. I know this comes as no surprise to you, but still, this is conclusive."

"How?" Grace asked, sitting up on the bed.

"The report is quite detailed," he said. "I don't know if you want to hear it just now."

"I'm ready," she said, gathering the blanket around her. "Please go on."

Detective Bush read the report. The orange hue of her parents' stomachs indicated they had ingested a lethal dose of Seconal. The empty amber bottle at their bedside was a new prescription. The police had called and checked it out with the pharmacist. They had delivered the prescription the Friday before. All thirty pills had most likely been ingested, the report said. The little bit of Scotch from the bottle of Bell's 20 was immaterial. It was the Seconal that killed them.

"But really, if it's any comfort, all they did was go to sleep," Bush said softly.

Sleep, instead of death, Grace thought. A *home* for a funeral. Arrangements. Interment. Procession. Resting place. *Suicide* was the only word that defied any attempt at euphemism. There was no substitute for suicide. The taking of one's own life. It was, Grace felt, simply profane. As blasphemous as the description of her parents' stomach contents. Something no one should ever have to hear or know.

"There was a note as well," Bush said. "It was in your father's handwriting. It was under your mother's . . . under your mother."

"What does it say?" Grace asked hopefully.

"I can bring the note to your sister's house," Bush said. "But it really says nothing. Nothing at all. The words are crossed out."

That night was Christmas Eve. A slow, warm rain washed over Manhattan, leaving piles of soot-covered snow at the edges of the sidewalks. Grace went with Kate and Adam to a neighborhood restaurant for dinner. Pasquale's. The owner, Pasquale himself, was surprised to see them.

"I thought for sure you'd be away this time of year," Pasquale said. He looked at Grace, remarking that she seemed under the weather. "Maybe some nice soup tonight? We have a great minestrone." Grace smiled and said the soup sounded like just what she needed.

"After the soup, a grappa. That will fix you up in no time," Pasquale said.

"You should be a doctor." Grace smiled, wishing the cure could be that easy.

The three took a banquette in the corner. Dinner was subdued. Adam was paged three times and finally remarked that there was nothing he needed more than the ten days in Aspen.

"The funeral is Thursday, Grace," Adam said. "There's no reason why we can't leave as scheduled on Friday morning. We can pack Thursday night."

"I guess I just want to take things one day at a time," Grace said.

"I'll be glad when this week is over," Adam said.

Grace took the bottle of wine from the silver pedestal at the side of the table and poured herself another glass.

"You're really supposed to let the waiter do that," Adam reprimanded her.

"Under the circumstances, I'm sure he'd understand," Grace said. "As should you. The detective called this morning. The deaths were suicides."

"But you knew that, Grace," Adam said.

"Yes and no," Grace said. "Part of me hoped I was wrong. It's obscene to end a life that way."

"It's not uncommon with the elderly," Adam said.

"But the elderly, in this case, were my parents," Grace said. "This is not a textbook."

"Stop!" Kate said, her teeth clenched, her eyes looking at no one. "Can't we just have a peaceful dinner?"

The three walked home in silence. The rain was a steady drizzle now. The city was dank; the night air, cold and penetrating.

Grace poured a brandy when they got home from the restaurant, not without Adam asking her if she didn't think she'd already had enough to drink.

"I would like to feel numb," Grace said.

"You can't *feel* if you're numb," Adam said.

"I meant it in the spiritual way, not the medical way," Grace said, and walked away.

She watched the endings of several old black-and-white movies on television, sitting on the sofa, her legs curled behind her, sipping the brandy. It was the usual Christmas fare: *It's a Wonderful Life*, which she switched off for *Miracle on Thirty-fourth Street*, finally settling on an animated version of *The Snowman*. She cried at every film. Adam had put on pajamas and was sitting in the leather armchair in his library, reading newspapers he said he'd missed what with the events of the last forty-eight hours. He did come out to say good night, telling her it would be wise if she got some sleep, remarking that he'd had another long day and he needed to sleep, as well.

Grace dozed off several times on the sofa. It wasn't so much that she couldn't sleep as that she was afraid to dream. Her eyes were heavy and her body ached with fatigue, yet every time she felt herself succumb to sleep, she forced herself awake.

It was just past four in the morning when Grace plugged in the strands of white lights on the Christmas tree and put Nat King Cole's Christmas CD on the stereo. She put aside the gifts marked with her parents' names. Their new robes and slippers. A beeping remote control gadget that could attach to her father's key ring (Jemma's suggestion, since her father was getting forgetful and always misplacing his keys). An assortment of jams and honeys and teas that came in a red-and-green wicker basket. A tin of butter cookies dipped in chocolate. Two monogrammed white bath sheets. Grace placed the gifts behind the tree, thinking that when Rosa came to clean, she would give them to her unopened. Rosa could donate them to her church. If only she had thought of it yesterday. Grace piled the rest of the gifts into Kate's old duffel bag. She was careful not to mash the bows that she and Kate had tied so painstakingly on Saturday night. It had been such a joyous night, and now it seemed so far away.

She watched Christmas Eve become Christmas morning. Watched the sky change from midnight blue to a pale silver. Heard the sounds of the city awakening, though all too quietly, but then again, it was Christmas Day. Noted the absence of familiar sounds: garbage trucks chuntering below, street cleaners scraping along the pavement, doormen blowing whistles for taxis, sirens. The quiet of the dawn unnerved her. She felt anxious and displaced. It didn't feel like Christmas. It didn't feel like anything she'd felt before. And yet it did. Something felt altogether too familiar. There was a sense she had of distance, of something that was missing. She felt a profound sense of blame for her parents' death, her marriage, her inability to put her finger on what was wrong and what had gone wrong. It was a feeling that her thoughts somehow were an effigy. Her probing seemed an imprecation. She wished she could stop thinking.

Kate and Adam got up early on Christmas morning. Adam had little interest in making the trek to Melanie and Mike's house, but he poured his coffee, shaved and dressed, and called for his car without so much as a word. Grace and Melanie had agreed that Jeremy and Matthew could not be expected to understand if there was no Christmas. They were babies. They had little concept of death. For them, death was something that applied to a bug squashed beneath their shoes or a plant wilted from too much water or lack of sunlight. Melanie had tried to explain. They understood: They would not see their grandparents again, but they could not fathom the finality or the abrupt ending. More significant, the twins barely knew their grand-parents. They didn't know them in the way that young children associ-ate. The way a grandmother's kitchen might smell of almond cookies or the way a grandfather pulls a quarter from your ear every time you see him. Neither Melanie's children nor Kate could get close enough to sense their grandparents, to know them.

"Is it because they were old?" Matthew asked, a few nights before, sitting up in his bed. "Is that why they died?"

"Yes, they were old," Melanie said, tucking the covers around him.

"Is it like they went to sleep forever?" Jeremy asked.

"A little, I suppose," Melanie answered, uncertain of what to say.

"You're old. Will you die if you sleep?" Jeremy asked, a look of panic on his face.

"No, you have to be very, very, very old," Melanie said. She had been trying to tell her sons some semblance of the truth, not realizing how the truth would translate.

"Not just old like you, right, Mommy?" Matthew said.

"Right." Melanie smiled. "Way older than me."

Mike could barely stand to see the pain on his wife's face. He strove to deflect the questions from Jeremy and Matthew who asked (despite their mother's futile attempts to appear cheerful and offer patient ex-planations), "What's wrong with Mommy? Why does she look so sad?" Mike tried to explain the nuances of emotions, the cleansing necessity of sadness and grief, the slow promise of healing.

On Christmas Eve, Mike had taken Jemma with him to the house where she chose a dress for Jane Hammond and a suit for Alexander Hammond. The dress was pale yellow with a square neckline, cinched at the waist with a belt of the same fabric. The day before that, Mike had chosen the caskets, sparing his wife and Grace the wrenching chore. "I picked the blond oak," he had said to Melanie, his own eyes misting over. "That dark mahogany was so dismal." It was all becoming too much even for Mike.

Christmas lunch was a feast. Melanie had baked a ham and a sweet potato pie, Grace brought a salad and a dish of sausage and peppers from Pasquale's, and Jemma, who had stayed at Melanie's since that dreadful Sunday morning, had baked an apple pie and a batch of brownies. When Melanie and Grace were clearing the dishes, Melanie showed Grace the note Detective Bush had dropped off the evening before. The word *dear* was scripted clearly in her father's handwriting. There were some words with nearly illegible letters crossed out. The letter A, written several times, each time with a line through it as the writing trailed off. It said nothing. Grace only glanced at it. "I'd like to keep it, though," Grace said, folding it in quarters, taking her purse from the kitchen counter and slipping the note into her wallet.

The twins were scooting around the living room on new plastic motorcycles when Grace told Adam and Kate that she did not want to go to Aspen.

"There's something I need to talk about," Grace said. "I don't think I should go to Aspen this year. I need to stay here and, well, tend to things."

Adam's head was nodding almost imperceptibly up and down as Grace spoke. As if he were convincing her to go on, encouraging her to continue her announcement, thinking most likely that a separation would be best right now. Kate listened to her mother, her eyes blinking rapidly.

"This is not possible," Kate said aloud. "How can you not come with us? What will you do by yourself?"

Grace explained that she needed to sort through her parents' home. She needed to be with Melanie and Jemma.

"Jemma's been at that house nearly every day for forty years," Grace said. "I need to be here right now." She put her arm around Kate. "You should ask Alison to go. You two would have such a great time."

For a moment, Grace thought that Kate understood; she looked thoughtful. Perhaps the notion of taking Alison was an instant panacea. But then Kate turned to Grace and cried, "You're no better than your mother! You're pushing me away." Kate ran to the powder room and slammed the door.

"She'll get over it, Grace," Adam said as Grace rose from the sofa. "Leave her alone for a while."

But Grace followed Kate. She spoke to her daughter through the closed powder room door.

"Come on out now, Kate," Grace said. "Let's go upstairs and talk."

"Go away!" Kate screamed. "Just leave me alone."

But Grace was persistent. "Just hear me out," she said. "Then I'll leave you alone."

"I hate all this!"

"So do I. I hate it, too," Grace said, haunted by the vision of her mother's closed bedroom door. "Unlock the door, Kate. Please."

Kate flung open the door and walked past her mother, stomped up the stairs to Melanie and Mike's bedroom. She sat on the foot of the bed, her face turned toward the wall, arms crossed over her chest.

"You couldn't have said anything worse, you know," Grace said quietly, sitting next to her daughter. "You hit me way below the belt. I am not pushing you away. I would never push you away."

Kate was crying. She leaned over the bed and grabbed a handful of tissues from the box on the nightstand. She moved as far from her mother as the bed permitted.

"You're ruining everything if you stay here," Kate said. "We were all supposed to go together. I don't want to ask Alison. I haven't even told her that my grandparents died. It's embarrassing. The whole thing is too weird."

"I can't be that far away right now," Grace said, trying to keep the pain out of her voice.

"Then I'll stay, too," Kate said.

"You can't make Daddy go alone," Grace said.

"Why does he have to go?" Kate said.

"He's looking forward to Aspen. He needs a vacation. A rest. He loves it there. Kate, it's not that I want to leave you. It's that I need to stay here. You understand the difference."

"You're being really selfish," Kate said.

"Come here," Grace said. "Come here next to me. I would never leave you, Kate. You know that. I know this whole thing is weird. It's dreadful. Come here, Kate. Please. Come on."

Kate looked up at her mother and saw her mother's arms were stretched out to her, her head cocked to one side. It was the way her mother held herself when Kate came running out of school as a small child. The way Grace looked on camp visiting days when she was the first one at the gate. She slid over on the bed, placed her head in the crook of Grace's arm, allowed Grace to stroke her hair, kiss her damp face.

"You're all salty," Grace said. "You always got so salty when you cried." She lifted Kate's face under her chin. "Look at me, Kate. I know that you're angry and I do understand. I know that my parents often made you angry. And now, they chose a bad time to die and an unspeakable way to die. And maybe you think I'm being selfish, but I think deep down maybe you can understand. I need to stay here and sort things out. To be here for Mel and Jemma. We need to make some sense out of all this. I suppose we need a reason."

"I hate your parents for this," Kate said, crying again. "I'm way more angry than sad. I feel like they screwed everything up. They always screwed everything up."

"I know, Kate. I wish I could say you were wrong, " Grace said.

"They weren't normal," Kate said. "You're going to say not to speak ill of the dead, but they weren't like grandparents. I see Alison's grandma who's always taking her to Broadway shows and even stuck up for her when Alison put those purple streaks in her hair. And her grandfather always slips her money and tells her these great stories about the war. My grandparents acted like I didn't even exist. And then they go and swallow a bottle of sleeping pills. And I don't even know a frigging thing about their families or how they grew up or anything. And now *you're* screwing up our vacation."

"But I can't be in Aspen right now," Grace said patiently. "I'd feel so removed if I were there right now. I need to be here just to think all this through. It has nothing to do with how much I love you, Kate. You are the most important thing in the world to me."

Kate took a deep breath. "I didn't mean what I said about you pushing me away," Kate said, her head down.

"I hope not."

"I didn't," Kate said, raising her head. "Mom, that party we were going to go to on New Year's Eve—those friends of Dad's, the Whittakers? Do you think they'd let me bring Alison?"

"I'm certain. Alison can go as my proxy." Grace smiled. "Come on. Let's go into Mel's bathroom and you can wash off your face."

"I do understand. I do," Kate said as she splashed her face with cool water. "I'm just so upset. Be careful, Mom, okay?

"Careful? Why? Of what?"

"I don't know. I just worry about you being all alone. Especially now. The whole thing is just so creepy. It wasn't like they died of heart attacks or something normal. I mean, God, they committed suicide, Mom. And what should I tell Alison when she asks why you're not with us? What should I tell her about how my grandparents died?"

"She's your best friend," Grace said. "Tell her the truth. Jemma always told me when I was a little girl, the truth will set you free."

"Sometimes the truth can hurt, too," Kate said, looking at her mother's reflection in the mirror.

"Yes, but at least with the truth, you know where you stand," Grace said. "At least with the truth, you *know*."

Chapter Five

The few visitors who came to the house left early in the day after the funeral. Some of the neighbors had dropped by more as curiosity-seekers than mourners. The Hammonds' doctor and his wife and some parishioners from Melanie and Mike's church had come to pay respects. Friends of Grace and Melanie stopped by to embrace them, offering condolences, setting down cellophane-wrapped platters of cookies and foil-wrapped bowls of pasta. The minister who presided at the funeral read mostly from the Scriptures. He was clearly hard-pressed to eulogize two people whom he didn't know. There was no one there, at the funeral or afterwards, who had the distinction of being a close family friend, save George Thompson, Mr. Hammond's former partner, and his wife, Marge, who were politely among the last visitors to leave. There were no relatives except for Grace and Melanie's husbands and children. Except, of course, for Jemma.

By late afternoon, the last of the visitors had gone. Jemma's cousin picked her up and took her home. Grace had convinced Adam to leave her the car and hire a limo to take him and Kate back to the city. Finally, Grace and Melanie were alone. They sifted through the traces of their childhood home. It was not the shadow cast so much by death that disturbed the sisters, but rather how similar its umbrage was to the one that had cloaked them all their lives. At first, the sisters walked through the rooms like trespassers. Feeling the way one does when one calls out a hollow hello in an empty house, not quite expecting anyone to answer, yet hoping and fearing all at once that they might. But Grace and Melanie heard only the familiar resonance of silence.

Sheer white curtains that could have moved with the slightest breath hung immotile before half-open windows. The empty glass on their mother's nightstand had a faded vestige of violet lipstick on the rim. Their father's tortoise-framed eyeglasses sat on top of the folded-back magazine on the floor by his side of the bed. Their parents' matching, brown-suede, fleece-lined slippers were tossed haphazardly in the bathroom. It appeared as though they left so abruptly. Perhaps because they had.

Melanie and Grace took soft rags sprayed with lemon oil and wiped the silver fingerprinting dust from the surfaces. And then, still holding the rags, they sat on their parents' bed and remarked that it might have been the first time in their lives that they ever did that, unlike their own children who played and rolled and tousled on their beds and found comfort there in the middles of so many nights. Though as the sisters sat on what was no longer forbidden territory, they remained straight-backed, afraid to lie down. They ran their palms over the pale green spread folded at the foot and straightened the tassels on the satin throw pillows.

It is uncommon to be comfortable with long silences, yet since Grace and Melanie were very little girls, they had an uncanny way of communicating even tacitly. There were endless evenings when their parents would sit and read in the parlor while Melanie and Grace played Parcheesi or painted by numbers at the kitchen table. Not speaking. Knowing better than to make a peep. But Grace and Melanie knew well what the other might say.

They inhaled the stale essence of their mother's My Sin on her satin pillowcase and the effete fragrance from dried-up yellowed bottles of their father's Old Spice. They folded the dried cloth still pungently redolent of the acrid white vinegar that Jemma lay on their mother's forehead. Olfactory remnants that stirred a sense of the past yet had never been inhaled so deeply. They studied the silver-framed black-and-white photographs of their parents that lined their mother's chintz-skirted dressing table. They picked them up and stared at them as if they might give a clue who their parents were. As though the photographs might reveal something in an expression, a hand placed upon the back of a chair, the tilt of a chin, the hint of a smile.

Obviously missing were pictures of grandchildren and pictures of Grace and Melanie. It was as though their parents had frozen time before their daughters arrived as intruders. Grace and Melanie had often felt that way: like interlopers who happened upon a marriage that was ill prepared to extend itself beyond two people.

Melanie and Grace walked down the cellar steps, pulling the threadlike strings that dangled from dusky bare lightbulbs as they made their way, stealthily, as if the ground was unfamiliar. The basement had never been finished the way basements often were when a home had children. There was no dartboard or game table. No half-moon leatherette wet bar with chrome swivel stools and a television set like the ones they saw at the homes of their childhood friends. The space was raw: rough wooden beams, a cold stone floor, and patched cinder-block walls. Merely a place for storage save a corner on the metal furnace where Grace and Melanie had furtively etched their initials in 1968 when Grace, at twelve, was eight-year-old Melanie's Svengali.

"This way, one day, someone will know that we were here," Grace had said, using a sharpened paper clip as her pen while Melanie stood watch.

They rummaged through the basement's cabinetry. Rusted metal shelves and dusty drawers in cast-off bureaus. Grace found the gilded box, garishly adorned with rhinestones, that she had given her mother one Mother's Day when she was a child. Grace knew, even at the time her mother opened the gift, that she didn't care for it. Her mother didn't even attempt a smile and merely murmured an "Oh, my," turning it over and over in her hands, as if she were looking for something else. Unlike Grace, who immediately pinned the garish butterfly brooch on her sweater (fake gold, too shiny, with pink-and-blue enamel wings) that Kate bought at a school rummage sale for Grace's thirty-fifth birthday. And every time Grace and Adam went anywhere in the evening for years, the brooch was fastened on the upper left bodice of whatever Grace was wearing. Until Kate, a few years later, laughingly told her mother she no longer had to wear it.

"Oh, Mom, it's so gaudy," Kate had said one day when she was older. "You don't have to wear that."

"But I love it," Grace insisted. "I want to."

"Please, don't," Kate had laughed. "I'll get you something else."

But Grace pinned the brooch to a broad green velvet ribbon and hung it from the mirror of her dresser. Grace's mother never displayed the rhinestone-crusted box. It vanished the moment it was opened. Jemma had said that her mother had put it away for safekeeping when Grace noticed it was nowhere to be seen. But there was the box, discarded, in a drawer filled with carpet tacks, tangled among spools of string, its blue silk lining peeling from the corners. Despite the waning years, Grace felt as though someone had punched her in the stomach.

The cellar held the apparent absence of memories. There were no cardboard boxes marked with bold black letters noting milestones the way that Grace cherished Kate's memories: first grade; second grade; right up through this, her senior year; summer camp; sweet sixteen; her first prom. Seventeen years of memories beginning with the pink plastic baby bracelet Kate wore in the hospital nursery when she was merely Baby Girl Barnett to just last month when Kate's acceptance came from Boston College. Instead, the Hammonds' basement held old brown leather luggage with worn tags and torn paper baggage stubs from trips abroad and out West where Melanie and Grace had not gone along. There were soot-covered bottles of wine with damp, faded labels, a few bottles of Scotch (still partially gift-wrapped), antiquated tools, frayed two-pronged electrical cords, and wickless kerosene lamps. Plastic milk crates of *National Geographic* and prewar encyclopedias, their pages too brittle to turn. Gray steel files marked TAXES and some tattered paper accordion folders imprinted with their father's name, ALEXANDER HAMMOND, ATTORNEY-AT-LAW, on the sides. The artificial Christmas tree and the carton of tissue-wrapped ornaments that Grace and Melanie bought years ago, shortly after Kate was born. Perhaps the baby would change things, they said to one another. Create a feeling of continuity and celebration, of family.

Melanie and Grace retreated back up the cellar steps through the house, their stocking feet padding on the worn beige carpet in the living room. Melanie remembered an evening a long time ago when she boldly turned the volume high on the Zenith radio, changing the station from the news to strains of Perry Como. "Catch a Falling Star" filled the house briefly until their mother snapped off the dial and told the girls that their father would be coming home soon and noise just wouldn't do.

"I asked Mother that night if you could really catch a falling star," Melanie said.

"And she said that was ridiculous and went back to her room?" Grace asked in a question that was really a statement.

"You remember?" Melanie asked.

"No, I don't remember," Grace said. "I guessed."

"But she started to cry," Melanie said. "It was almost scary."

Melanie and Grace sat thoughtfully that Friday night at their parents' house struggling with vain attempts to jog warm memories, making futile efforts to reconstruct and even reinvent times that might have said a family once lived in the house. They searched for something that might have conjured up memories of affection and love, hoping there would be an epiphany that said it had been there but had, tragically, gone unrecognized. But there was nothing saved. Nothing savored.

They carried the accordion files and hefted the steel boxes of tax records from the basement and stacked them around themselves like a fortress. They steeped a pot of tea in their mother's kettle. They were pouring tea when Melanie recalled the summer when the cicadas came like locusts. She hadn't given up yet. She was still determined to seize a memory.

"Remember? We thought they were crickets when we were kids,"

Melanie said. "Mother and Dad didn't bother telling us they were cicadas. And we picked one up and put it in a matchbox and named it
Jiminy. It was Jemma who told us when she found the poor thing suffo-
cated in the morning."

"It makes no difference now, Melanie," Grace said with such bitter-
ness that she even startled herself.

"Don't be like that, Grace," Melanie said.

"We've been here for hours trying to remember something that
made us smile. There was nothing, Mel. It was just the two of us. Well,
Jemma, of course. If not for Jemma, I can't even imagine how life
would have been."

When Melanie and Grace were children, until Melanie graduated
college and got her own apartment, Jemma lived with them. She slept
on a narrow twin bed with a wrought-iron headboard in a room off the
kitchen. The room, connected to a bathroom with a claw-legged tub,
had a small casement window, inlaid with frosted stars, so Jemma
couldn't even see the magnolia tree in the backyard. Under the bathtub, Jemma kept a shoe box filled with adhesive tape, cotton swabs,
Band-Aids, Mercurochrome, a mercury thermometer, St. Joseph Aspirin for Children, calamine lotion, and Pepto-Bismol. "My 'just in
case' box," Jemma called it.

Red-and-white jars of hair pomade sketched with the silhouette of
a woman who the girls thought looked Egyptian, an atomizer bottle of
Lilly of the Valley perfume, a tarnished silver brush and mirror, rose-
water glycerine lotion, a small can of rose snuff, and about a dozen
miniature floral bouquets made of linen-crusted china lined Jemma's
dresser. A red leather Bible filled with bookmarks lay on her pillow. A
black-and-white television sat catty-corner on a folding table. And a
gold-framed picture of the handsome young black man in uniform who
had been Jemma's husband ("my darlin' Cyrus," Jemma always called
him) until he was killed in the Korean War was centered on the table
beside her bed under an ecru-fringed lamp. A tiny white-frilled black-
and-white photograph of a young Jemma and Cyrus sitting on the
hood of an old convertible, with Jemma smiling and wearing a corsage

and Cyrus in a shirt, tie, and suspenders, was stuck in the corner of Cyrus's military picture.

Jemma's room was never off-limits to the girls. Even when their parents caved in and bought a color television for the living room, Grace and Melanie preferred to watch Jemma's black and white while she cooked their dinner. The smell of her pot roast and potatoes mixing with Lilly of the Valley when they gave the atomizer a quick squeeze made them heady. "I know you're squeezing my perfume, girls," Jemma would call to them, laughing. "Not too much or you'll smell like tarts." The girls knew they were Jemma's family. But more, they knew that she was theirs.

And so, that night, as Grace and Melanie poured another cup of jasmine tea, they felt their bodies begin to relax in this home where they had always carried themselves so cautiously and meticulously. And in the stillness that they knew so intimately, they wondered if what they had always perceived as benign neglect and dismissed as eccentricity was not something more. It was Grace who voiced what they were both thinking. It was Grace who said aloud that it was a miracle that neither of them had been infected. That neither of them had gone crazy.

"We haven't found a thing, have we?" asked Melanie as they were leaving the house.

"Maybe Jemma was right. Maybe there's nothing to look for," Grace sighed, shutting the door behind them.

Chapter Six

Grace drove Melanie home. She waited until her sister had gone in the door, as she flicked on the hallway light. Grace was about to back the car down the driveway when she saw Melanie and Mike through the living room window. Mike, tall and burly, waited in the vestibule for her sister. He walked toward his wife and reached out to her. Melanie's coat slipped off her shoulders as she melted into her husband's arms. Like Peter Pan slipping on his shadow, Grace thought.

Grace called home to say she was on her way.

"Alison is spending the night," Adam said. "Makes it easier to leave in the morning. I can't wait to get on that plane. I've never been so exhausted in my life." He didn't ask her how it felt to be in the house after everyone had gone or what she and Melanie had done for all those hours. If she had had something to eat, to drink, if she had cried or laughed. How it was to sit with her sister in the house where they grew up and remember.

"Have you seen my ski boots?" he asked.

"You left them in Aspen," Grace said. "They're in the cedar closet."

It was nearly midnight when Grace walked in the door. The apartment was quiet. Although the girls were sleeping, the television in Kate's bedroom was on, tuned to yet another Christmas movie. Grace clicked off the television along with the lamp by Kate's bedside, picked up sweatshirts and sweaters that didn't make it into Kate's suitcase and were tossed on the floor.

"You okay, Mom?" Kate asked, lifting her head from the pillow.

"Go back to sleep," Grace said, leaning over to kiss Kate's forehead. "We have to get up early."

Grace washed her face and slipped into her nightgown, slid into bed next to Adam, placed her arm across his stomach as he lay on his back. When was the last time I reached for him? she thought. She was desperate for touch, a sense of belonging.

"You're back already?" he asked, shifting his weight, but he turned over on his side.

Grace dreamed of her parents that night. They were young in the dream. Her mother's hair was thick and reddish brown like her own, loosely knotted in a chignon. She was wearing the yellow dress she had been buried in, its full skirt billowing out, a pair of high-heeled strappy sandals, a bright lipstick. Her father was wearing his fedora—rakishly though, sort of tipped on his head. His dark eyes were bright and gleaming, a smile playing on his lips. But suddenly the dream turned and her mother was sitting on the familiar green brocade divan in her bedroom. The yellow dress was now a tattered robe. Her mother's hands were folded in her lap and she was staring out the window, watching her father. He was wearing waders, splashing about in steely gray water that was strewn with yellow ribbons. Police cars lined the shore. Her father's fedora was bopping up and down on the waves as if it were the last remnant of someone who had drifted away.

It wasn't quite dawn when the dream awakened Grace. She hung her legs over the bed, touched her feet silently to the floor, straightened her body and pulled herself up, tiptoed to the kitchen. Her nightgown was stuck to her skin, her hair felt damp at the nape of her neck. She was perspiring, as cold and clammy as she felt in her dream when the water threatened to swallow her.

The kitchen sink was piled with dishes. Kate and Alison must have made a feast last night, Grace thought. Grace scrubbed the remnants of melted cheese from plates, wiped crumbs from the counter, steeped a pot of chamomile tea. It was too quiet in the house. Too dark, too still. It was precisely that expression again: She felt something in her bones. Adam said it was something an old woman would say. She felt like an old woman, she thought. One who was weary and helpless and alone. In a few hours, Kate and Adam would be on their way to Aspen. She wondered if she hadn't made a mistake insisting that she stay behind. She wondered if the next ten days without them would be fraught with dreams of lakes and her parents. She poured a mug of tea and sat at the table. Why, since her parents died, was she compelled to watch the past?

She remembered the summer Jemma decided it was time for Grace and Melanie to learn to swim. She'd always told them stories about her childhood on the Outer Banks of North Carolina. How she spent almost every hot summer weekend at the shores. How her feet got tough from walking over hot rocks that led down to the ocean. How it felt to have the waves carry her out and then toss her back, the coarse sand scraping against her belly. She told them how the ocean seemed to swell come August with just the threat of a hurricane and how the swells lasted through October. Grace had looked at Jemma wide-eyed, longing to tell about her dreams. But she was afraid to tell. Almost embarrassed. Telling would make the dreams feel more real and they felt so real to begin with. It was the one thing Grace feared Jemma might not be able to conquer for her.

It baffled Jemma that Grace never liked the water. Even as a little girl, four years old when Jemma first came to work for them, Grace would kick and scream in the tub when Jemma tried to bathe her. Jemma had tried everything: bubbles, rubber ducks, soaps shaped like roses and frogs. She finally gave up and, wearing a bathing suit, got into the shower and held Grace next to her while she washed Grace's hair and lathered her up, telling Grace to count backwards from eighty and then the whole thing would be over.

At first, when Jemma told Grace she was taking them to the town pool for swim lessons, Grace refused. Jemma was not in the least bit surprised. But Jemma promised her that she would be right there beside her the whole time. Getting Grace into the pool was torturous. Jemma stood backwards on the steps, the flounce of her lime-green flowered bathing suit floating on the pool's surface like a hoop skirt. She held her arms out to Grace, her fingers beckoning, coaxing her into the water.

"Come swim to me, baby," she said. "Come on. Kick. It's only inches until you get to me. I'll catch you. I won't let you go."

Despite the strength of the swim instructor, a woman with muscular arms who wore a white bathing cap fastened tightly on the side of her head, Jemma had to be right by Grace's side. Grace insisted that Jemma's hands be right around her: one skimming her back, suspended above her; the other floating in the water below her belly.

Grace flip-flopped around in the water, sputtering and spitting. "Tap me so I know you're still there, Jemma," Grace said, her voice raised and panicky as she came up for air. "Say something."

"I'm right here, baby," Jemma would say. "I'm not going anywhere."

Grace learned enough to keep afloat and dog paddle. She didn't take long strokes across the pool like her sister.

"Melanie's a fish," the swim instructor said proudly, looking at Grace with disdain as she struggled to dog-paddle, her neck stretched upward, her breath coming in croaking gasps. She hugged the rim of the pool, stopping every few seconds to look around her.

"I want to like it, Jemma," Grace said, treading water furiously even though she was clinging to the side of the pool. "All the kids are having such a good time." She paused. "Does anything scare you?"

And Jemma said there was no one alive who wasn't scared of one thing or another. "But you have to look fear square in the eyes so it sees you looking," she said. "Stare it down. Then it won't get under your skin."

Jemma had hoped the sand and the soft gentle July waves of the sea would calm Grace. She thought Grace might enjoy collecting seashells and building sand castles. One Saturday, she packed a picnic basket with chicken sandwiches on fresh rye bread and thick slices of salted tomatoes. She filled two thermos bottles with freshly squeezed lemonade. She wrapped home-made chocolate chip cookies and crisp salted pretzels in foil.

Grace had tried to be excited. She and Melanie sat in the backseat of the car sucking on Charms lollipops, the wind blowing the hair around their faces, their thighs sticking to the upholstery. They wore bathing suits under their new pink terry jackets. Jemma had gone to the five-and-dime the day before and bought them the jackets along with sand pails, shovels, an umbrella, and a beach ball.

"It's a perfect day for the ocean," Jemma said, adjusting the car's rearview mirror, looking at Grace in the backseat. "You'll see when we get there how there's suddenly a breeze. It feels like the temperature drops by ten degrees."

Jemma set down a blanket and twirled the umbrella into the sand. Grace was sitting with Melanie, watching Jemma dig the umbrella deeper and deeper when she became sick to her stomach.

"I don't feel so good," Grace said. "I feel like I'm going to throw up."

"Maybe it was that twisty beach road that got to you," Jemma said. "The fresh air will do you good. Just breathe in deep. Roads like that make your tummy feel like it's doing somersaults." She gave Grace a handful of pretzels. "Here, these will settle your stomach. Eat them nice and slow."

Jemma took the girls' hands as they walked along the sea. They collected shells in the pails and made sure they only picked up the ones with holes in the tops.

"We'll pass some thread through the holes and make necklaces when we get home," Jemma said. "We can paint them with your watercolors."

They poked crabs with sticks and watched them burrow through the sand. They built drip castles with buckets of water that Jemma hauled back from the surf. When Jemma blew up the beach ball, her cheeks puffed out like a blowfish, and Grace laughed. The three of them batted the ball back and forth with their fists, the girls giggling as they dove for the ball, falling on the sand.

It was Grace who missed the catch and caused the ball to drift into the ocean and Melanie who ran to get it. It landed a perfect distance for Melanie to dive into a small breaker that was cresting toward the shore. She stood up, laughing, the water just past her knees. Another wave came behind the first, this one just a bit higher, foamier, knocking her down, promising a swift ride to the muddy edge of the shore. She wasn't up to her waist in the surf when she grabbed the ball, punching it playfully back to Grace. But Grace had paled visibly when Melanie ran into the water. Screamed when her sister briefly disappeared under the breaker. Louder when Melanie disappeared momentarily under the next. Her cry was so loud, so bloodcurdling, it pierced the susurrant timbre of the beach. Even the lifeguard stood on his perch, blowing his whistle instinctively, not really knowing why. Everyone on the beach stopped what they were doing and turned to look.

"It's okay, Grace," Jemma said, her hands on Grace's shoulders. "I'm right here. She's not even past her knees."

"I want to go home," Grace cried. "Please. Let's go now."

Melanie was beside Grace by then, tugging on her arm as though to wake her. But Grace didn't feel her. She was staring at the ocean, crying over and over for Jemma to take them home. Jemma kneeled in the sand and held Grace to her. She brushed the sand off Grace's skinny legs and stroked away wisps of hair that stuck to Grace's sunburned face, but she couldn't get Grace to calm. Grace cried until the hiccoughs came, causing her to choke and cry even harder.

"You're being dumb, Grace," Melanie said. "You're just a scaredy-cat."

"Now, that's enough out of you, Melanie," Jemma admonished. "We don't need name-calling."

Jemma carried Grace over to their umbrella, Grace's legs wrapped around Jemma like a spider's. She sat the girls under the beach umbrella, unwrapped the chicken sandwiches, and poured Grace a cup of lemonade, but Grace just stared at the food and said she wasn't hungry. She tried to make Grace laugh by holding her nose while she drank, telling her that was a sure-fire way to cure the hiccoughs, but Grace couldn't even manage a smile. Jemma told them a story about when she was a little girl and she and her friends drew sundials on the muddy sand when the tide went out and how the tide came back and washed the sundials away, but Grace wasn't listening. Finally, Jemma said it was time to go. Grace, who sat now with a towel covering her legs, her beach jacket pulled around her, looked green despite her sunburn.

On the drive home, Jemma put Grace next to her on the front seat. Jemma sang "This Old Man" with Melanie, who wasn't happy about sitting alone in the back, let alone leaving the beach. Grace didn't sing. She leaned into Jemma with her eyes closed, taking in the faded scent of her Lilly of the

Valley and the rose snuff that Jemma had broken off and tucked inside her gums.

"I don't like water, Jemma," Grace said seriously in almost a monotone, her eyes shut so tight that she saw sparkles from the sunlight that beat through the windshield. "Don't bring me here again."

"I know that, baby," Jemma said. "We won't go back to the water. Not for a long time. But why don't you like the water, baby? You won't even give it a chance."

"I am afraid that it will make me disappear," Grace said. "Just like it made Melanie disappear."

"But she didn't disappear, Grace," Jemma said. "She's right here."

Grace shut her eyes and leaned on Jemma's shoulder. She didn't say a word. Not until Jemma tucked her into bed that night and said I love you and she held Jemma as if she never would let her go.

Grace rode the elevator downstairs with her husband and daughter the morning they left for Aspen. She watched as the doorman loaded their bags into the trunk of the limousine, stood beside Adam as he patted his breast pocket for the airline tickets. She was wearing her running clothes, a wool baseball cap pulled down over her eyes. The sleeves of her fleece were too long and nearly covered her hands. She watched as their limousine rounded the corner and headed uptown toward the Triborough Bridge for the airport. She stood for several minutes after the car was gone from view, her hands tucked inside the too-big sleeves. How would she fare without her daughter and her husband for the next ten days? she wondered. For a few moments she thought perhaps she could run upstairs and pack. Grab a cab. Surprise them at the airport. But she knew it was too late. And in what seemed like a burst of movement that propelled her forward, she ran toward Columbus Circle and sprinted into the park.

By late Friday afternoon, Grace had gone through every drawer and cabinet in the apartment. She sorted socks and folded sweaters into neat piles. Polished shoes and sterling silver. Threw out old magazines, expired medications, and chipped coffee mugs. Alphabetized compact discs and videotapes and dusted every book in Adam's library. She took a dance class at a studio on Broadway. It wasn't until she was faced with the prospect of eating dinner alone, even at Pasquale's, that she called Melanie.

"Can I spend the weekend?" she asked. "I'm not up for a table for one."

"I thought you'd never ask," Melanie said. "I already made up the guest bedroom. I even bought an extra steak."

"See you in an hour or so," Grace said. "I'm on my way."

Mr. Hammond's partner, George Thompson, called Melanie's house on Sunday morning. He had been mired in paperwork for the last several days, he said. As Alex's partner, this was quite a shock. There was much to get together, he explained. Legalities and specifics to unravel and decipher regarding Alex and Jane's estate. And then to Melanie, who had answered the phone, he caught himself. "Forgive me, my dear. Here I am, going on and on about business when this is such a deeply personal loss for you. Precisely why I'm calling. I thought it would be helpful to you and Grace if you saw your parents' wills before the New Year. Perhaps this will ease any pragmatic concerns you may have regarding their estate."

"You mean, we can have a reading of the will?" Melanie asked.

"We don't do that anymore," he explained. "There's really no such thing as a reading of the will. That's a bunch of Hollywood hype. Usually, I'd just serve each of you with a copy. But seeing that you have been through so much, I thought we could meet at the Purchase house in the morning. Say around ten? You might want to invite Mrs. Polk. There are some things that concern her as well."

Jemma took the train up on Monday morning. Melanie waited in the car while Grace stood on the platform. The train chugged slowly into the station. Jemma was the only person to get off at the stop. She was wearing a new red parka, a white cashmere scarf and hat that Grace had bought her for Christmas.

"You smell like old times," Grace said, embracing her. "You still wear Lilly of the Valley. You shouldn't use that snuff though, you know. It's so bad for you."

"It's my one vice," Jemma said. "I'm too old to give it up, baby girl. You spoiled me with this cashmere scarf. Come the warm weather, I'll be loath to take it off."

Jemma talked a great deal on the drive to Harvest Lane. It was a knee-jerk reaction to pick up the phone that morning, she said. To call them. Ask if they needed anything. If the heat was working right, if they'd taken in their newspaper.

"All weekend long, for that matter, my hand kept reaching for the phone. I kept feeling as if I wasn't where I was supposed to be and had forgotten to get on the train. You do the same thing nearly every day for forty years and then stop doing it and all of sudden you don't know where you are anymore," Jemma said, her voice trailing off as Melanie's car pulled into the driveway.

Jemma opened the door to the house. The key was on a baby blue rabbit's-foot chain. "I'll always keep this key," Jemma said. "Even after this house is sold and the locks are changed."

Jemma hung her coat and scarf next to the other coats and hats. She stroked her hand over Mr. Hammond's fedora, straightened Mrs. Hammond's trench coat, turned down a fold on the cuff.

"Everything's so gritty," Jemma said, wiping a thin layer of silver dust off the coat rack with her fingertips. "The house could use a good cleaning."

"Melanie and I dusted the upstairs on Thursday night," Grace said. "It was covered with fingerprinting dust up there. Some of it floated down here, I guess."

"We're going to take care of all this together," Jemma said softly, patting Grace's hand.

"I know," Grace whispered, her words slightly catching in her throat. She was caught off guard, overcome with emotion. "We'll all get everything squared away. I'm just not quite ready yet to tackle it yet. But I want to get it done. Get it all behind us."

"I know, baby," Jemma said. "We'll get there."

Jemma went into the kitchen and set the kettle on to boil. She took out four cups and saucers and set them on a tray with spoons, four frayed calico cloth napkins, and a bowl filled with different flavored tea bags. She was pouring a container of sour milk down the drain when Grace walked into the kitchen.

"Thompson's here," Grace said.

Thompson was a formal man. Unlike Alexander Hammond, whose suits were often rumpled and looked as though he might have slept in them, Thompson was immaculate. He wore a gray pinstripe suit and a shirt with French cuffs, starched stiffly and pinched together with gaudy cuff links of filigreed gold. Thompson was the front office man when Alexander still worked at the firm. He was the one who met with the clients while Alexander tended more to details on paper. Thompson was never called George or Mr. Thompson. He was just plain Thompson. Even his wife, Marge, called him Thompson, something Grace once wondered about when she was a teenager and pictured the two in acts of intimacy where Marge was perhaps screaming passionately "Thompson!" The image still made her smile.

Thompson took a seat at the head of the dining table, hefting his heavy black briefcase on the wood just as Jemma set a quilted place mat underneath to cushion the blow. He positioned his half glasses on the tip of his nose and raised his eyebrows, looked at the women sitting around him at the table.

"I have here your parents' last wills and testaments," Thompson said, clearing his throat. "They were recorded just three weeks ago, updated for what, of course, became the final time. In fact, your parents had what are called reciprocal wills, wills that can be interpreted as one since the documents are mirror images of one another. Often the deceased leave notes or letters within the will to accompany the document. Just so you know, right off the bat, there was nothing of that nature left within for any of you. It's pretty straightforward. I know this is hard for all of you. Before I begin, again, Grace and Melanie, if there is anything at all that I can do, please let me know."

"For Jemma, too," Grace said.

Thompson nodded to Jemma. "Forgive me. You, too, Mrs. Polk. I am aware of your devotion and loyalty to Mr. and Mrs. Hammond," he said stiffly as he dunked an herbal tea bag in a mug of boiled water.

"They were my family," Jemma said.

But Thompson just went on. He wasn't one for sentiment. "You'll all get your copies. In the meantime, I will paraphrase a bit. You don't need to be bogged down with legal mumbo jumbo. I assume we're all comfortable?"

"We're ready now," Grace said.

"They've left things quite clean, as it were," said Thompson, lifting his teacup with a pretentious pinky-up as he continued. "All succession, estate, or inheritance taxes which might be levied against the estate will be paid out of the residuary estate. There should be no surprises for any of you.

"For Jeremy and Matthew Peterson and Katherine Barnett: The net proceeds sale from the Purchase house is to be divided equally among the three grandchildren. Proceeds from the aforementioned sale will be held in trust for the benefit of each child with John Glass, your parents' accountant for the last ten years, as trustee and myself as alternate trustee. Mr. Glass is also the executor of the will.

"The furnishings of the house as well as vases, dishes, household appliances, books, records, and all personal effects are to be sold at auction. Additionally, net proceeds from said auction should be divided equally among the grandchildren and held in trust as set up in Article Nine.

"Your mother's jewelry, consisting of a diamond engagement ring (total one carat in a platinum setting valued at seven thousand dollars), one sixteen-inch strand of pearls with an amethyst clasp (valued at two thousand dollars), a gold seashell necklace with matching earrings (valued at three thousand five hundred dollars), and a diamond-and-sapphire bracelet (valued at twenty-five hundred dollars), has been left to Melanie."

"And to Grace, I assume?" Melanie asked, interrupting him. "I assume that Grace shares in the jewelry as well?"

"No. Your mother left the jewelry to you alone, Melanie," Thompson said. "Just to you. It is rather irregular, I know, seeing that there are two daughters. For you, Mrs. Polk, in appreciation of what is termed a lifetime of devotion and service, the Hammonds left a flat sum of twenty-five thousand dollars."

"And to Grace?" Melanie asked again angrily. "What about Grace?"

"Melanie, it's okay," Grace said. "They provided for Kate. That's all that matters."

"Now, now, now. They actually saved the best for last. The residuary estate does not include the following, Grace. They most certainly have not forgotten you, my dear. It says right here that Grace Hammond Barnett is the beneficiary of their house at Sabbath Landing," Thompson said, smiling broadly.

"A house?" Grace asked. "What house? What is Sabbath Landing?"

"I never heard them mention a house," Jemma said. "What on earth—?"

"Well, I must say I am rather surprised. I don't quite understand. You are not familiar with this house?" Thompson said, interrupting Jemma.

He pulled the deed out of the folder in his briefcase. "Says right here that in 1950, your parents purchased a twenty-five-hundred-square-foot dwelling in Sabbath Landing, New York. Let me paraphrase: Said dwelling rests on four acres with southeast view of Pilot Mount, northwest view of Hester's Peak."

"They own another house?" Grace asked. "Are you sure it's not a mistake?"

"Oh, no. There's no mistake. They most certainly do own another house," said Thompson. "And in a magnificent area. There's a grand old hotel in Sabbath Landing. The Alpine. Marge and I have spent many fine weekends there. Of course, come the end of September, it gets pretty darn cold. Must be frigid there now. Doesn't really warm up after that until June."

"Have you been to the house?" Grace asked, a shiver running up her spine so vividly she shuddered.

"Well, no," said Thompson. "I admit, it's a bit odd that your father never mentioned it, since he knew that Marge and I often went up there. But then again, your father, may he rest in peace, was not, well, loquacious, shall we say. Oh, it's a gorgeous spot. Way back in the 1930s and 1940s, people snatched up property for a song up there. Before the DEC came in and started to say you couldn't do this and you couldn't do that. Your parents' house was built in 1868. Sounds like it's quite special. Built of cypress. They say that cypress never rots, you know."

"Why me? Why would they have wanted me to have that house?" Grace asked.

"That I can't answer," said Thompson. "I'm a bit dumbstruck, to tell you the truth. I would have thought you girls knew the place."

"Well, we don't. We've never been there nor have we been aware that they owned it," Grace said. She was becoming irritated. "*Where* exactly is this house? How do you get there?"

"Oh, it's easy," Thompson said. "About a five-hour drive from here right up the Thruway. But you don't want to go there now. As I said, it's too damn cold there now. You couldn't even get out to the house."

"Well, there must be roads," Grace said. "I mean, people live there, don't they? They probably all have four-wheel drives."

"People live there, all right, but not where this house is," Thompson said, pulling an aerial photograph from a worn brown envelope. "It's a beauty, isn't it?" He held the photo in front of Grace. "There it is. A real log cabin on Canterbury Island. About a mile and a half off the coast. Right smack dab in the middle of Diamond Lake."

Chapter Seven

Thompson finished his tea. He dabbed his mouth too delicately with the corner of a calico napkin and handed the deed and the photograph in the worn brown envelope to Grace. Grace never rose from the sofa when she took the envelope in her hands. She lifted her head to Thompson and thanked him, trying to look him directly in the eyes, hoping she might see a hint of something that he wasn't telling her but knew. Something he might have been keeping from her or waiting for her to ask. There was nothing. He nodded his head. Smiled at her. Wished her well.

Jemma picked up the tray of cups and saucers and carried them to the kitchen while Melanie ushered Thompson out the door. He sputtered more amenities, the banal recitation Grace had tired of hearing over the last week. Sorry for your loss. My deepest sympathies. Marge sends her condolences. Once again, let me reiterate: if there is anything you need. Grace heard the low drone of Thompson's voice, the empty yet appropriate words, trailing on and on until she heard Melanie shut the door behind him.

"What do you think this is about?" Grace asked, waving the aerial photograph at Melanie as she walked into the living room.

Jemma was wiping her hands on a dish towel. She sat down next to Grace, peering over her shoulder at the picture.

"I have no idea," Melanie said. "You would think that as bizarre as this last week has been, things couldn't get stranger. And now this.

Jemma, do you know? Did they ever go to that house? Had you ever heard them mention Diamond Lake?"

Jemma shook her head. "What I find so odd is that if they had a house in the middle of a lake, why didn't we ever go there? I bet it's beautiful there in the summer. I couldn't even get your folks to take you girls swimming when you were kids. Remember? I was the one who took you for those swim lessons. For the life of me, I can't understand why they'd have a house by a lake and not even tell us."

"What are you going to do with it?" Melanie asked, turning to her sister.

But Grace didn't answer. She had opened the envelope. She was studying the aerial view. The house was all but hidden in a layer of trees. The deed said it was twenty-five hundred square feet, but it was hard to make out the size or the shape from the photograph. There appeared to be dirt paths leading around the island, what looked like a patio of sorts high above the lake on one side, dots that looked like a table and six chairs. Lower, at water level, there was a dock with what looked like a boat tied to a rafter. The island was not flat in the way one might imagine an island. It was hilly, rising sixty feet above the lake's surface according to the deed's speculations. The house stood center, a good hike up hill from the lake below. But the age of the yellow-tinged photograph, the distance from where it was taken, obscured the details.

"It doesn't look like the kind of place that Mother and Dad would have gone," Grace said. "It seems so remote. But then again, maybe that was so much like them. Maybe it was a place they went to by themselves. Or maybe it was just an investment." She slipped the photo back into the envelope. "I don't understand. I don't understand any of this at all. Most of all, I don't understand why they left it to me. Why leave an island to someone who has a fear of water?"

Jemma said that her cousin Stella was having a small gathering that night for the New Year. It was getting late, she said. She should probably get back to the Bronx.

"You're going to stay the week with Melanie, aren't you, Grace?"

Jemma asked hopefully, looping the cashmere scarf around her neck. "You shouldn't be by yourself tonight. No one should be alone on New Year's Eve."

Grace nodded. She told Jemma not to worry. Assured her that she wouldn't be by herself. But after Grace and Melanie dropped Jemma off at the train station, Grace told Melanie she wanted to get back to her apartment.

"I won't be much fun tonight, I'm afraid," Grace said. "There's something about that photograph. About that house. I just need to think. I feel like I'm racking my brain for something and I'm just coming up empty."

Melanie said that Mrs. Hadley and some of the neighbors would be by that evening. That Mike had bought champagne and lobster tails for the occasion.

"It'll be so quiet and low-key," Melanie implored her. "Please stay." But she knew by the look on her sister's face that Grace's mind was made up. "I can't convince you, can I?"

"Maybe I'll come up tomorrow for New Year's Day," Grace said. "I'm not in much of a party mood, I guess. I feel so—I don't know—so agitated right now. If I get lonely, I'll drive up, though. Honest."

It was nearly five-thirty by the time Grace got back to Manhattan. Night seemed to have fallen early. The smell of snow saturated the air with a cool, damp stillness. The streets of the city were already thick with revelers bundled up against a brisk wind that whistled through the concrete. She passed a group of young men in coats and tails, sequined top hats, already mildly inebriated, walking with women wearing ball gowns and half masks studded with rhinestones. Arm linked in arm. Laughing. Grace went to a Chinese restaurant and brought in food. Stopped at the liquor store and bought a chilled split of champagne and a bottle of Pinot Noir. She bought a bouquet of white roses at a corner flower mart that doubled as a deli.

"Happy New Year, Mrs. Barnett," the doorman said as he opened the door for Grace, her arms laden with packages, her overnight bag slung over her shoulder. "May I take those for you?"

"I can manage," she said. "Thanks, though. And Happy New Year, Jerry. Hope it's a good one."

The elevator door opened on Grace's penthouse floor. She set the bags down on the kitchen counter and put the roses in a pitcher that was sitting by the sink. She opened the wine and, still with her coat on, poured a glass before stepping onto the terrace. It looked so barren out there in the winter. The furniture was covered with thick green plastic. The planters where she grew what she called her rooftop tomatoes and cucumbers, the buckets that held pink yarrow and red begonias in the spring, were filled with sticks and leaves. She looked out over the city. Heard the comical horns of noisemakers juxtaposed to urgent sirens that came in short bleats as police cars cruised the city streets. It would be a busy night in Manhattan, she thought. Strange to be without Kate and Adam. She couldn't remember a New Year's that she had been alone. She remembered many when she was lonely.

Once, when she was six years old, her parents took her to a restaurant somewhere in the country that had a wishing well. It was New Year's Eve. She had thrown a penny into the well, leaning over, watching the copper until it disappeared. She closed her eyes tightly and wished for a night like the one they were having, where the four of them were all together, although she wished there could be laughter and more conversation. Grace remembered that night after dinner once they were home. How her father lit a fire in the hearth and opened a bottle of champagne for himself and her mother. Melanie was sleeping on a quilt by the window while Grace worked on a mosaic kit that Jemma had bought her. She was wearing a dark green velvet dress with a lace pinafore she'd gotten for Christmas, another gift marked TO GRACE FROM SANTA.

Grace watched her mother's lifeless eyes stare into the fire as it flickered and popped. Her father poured Grace a ginger ale in a champagne flute. As the church bell tolled ten chimes that night, she watched her father lean into her mother's cheek and wish her Happy New Year, murmuring something into her mother's ear. Two hours to go, he said, but we won't make it until midnight, will we? he said aloud. And then her father kissed Grace on the top of her head. For auld lang syne, he said, and she lifted her head from the mosaic tiles and asked what that meant. *It was a simple kiss without an embrace. Not the kind that Mike or even Adam gives their children. It means the good old times,* her father said. And Grace remembered that her father had tears in his eyes.

Her mother still did not kiss her that night. She looked at Grace vacantly as she rose from the chair by the fireplace and said she hoped the New Year would be good to her. Then, she went upstairs to bed. Her father carried Melanie upstairs, slumped over his shoulder like a rag doll, Grace walking behind him, carrying her patent leather Mary Janes dangling by their buckles.

She startled out of her thoughts when the phone rang. It was Adam calling from Aspen.

"We're on our way to the Whittakers'," Adam said. "I'm wearing my tux and Kate and Alison have on blue jeans with these glittery shirts. You think that's okay? I mean, we're so disparately dressed. Not to mention glitter with denim."

Grace laughed for what felt like the first time in days. Adam was so formal. "I'm sure it's just fine," she said reassuring him. "Why are you leaving so early? It's only what? About five-thirty there?"

Adam said that John Whittaker had gotten a new billiard table and they were going to start the party early with a one-on-one before the crowd came. She was tempted to tell Adam about Thompson and the will but then decided it wasn't the best time. Besides, Adam hadn't asked what she'd done that day. He didn't seem to be concerned about how she was faring by herself.

"Why aren't you with Aunt Mel and Uncle Mike?" Kate asked, picking up another extension.

"Hey, you. How are you? I'm just going to rest tonight," Grace said. "You know, I was with them all weekend. A little hectic there, what with the boys and all. I'm enjoying the peace and quiet. I have a good book. Why aren't you wearing that black dress we agonized to buy for tonight?"

"Because all the kids are wearing jeans. We might even go ice-skating over at the lodge. There's a deejay. Are you sure you're okay,

Mom? It doesn't seem right to be alone on New Year's Eve," Kate said. "I wish you were with Aunt Mel."

"I'll go up to Mel's tomorrow. I'm fine, Kate," Grace said. "Really, I am very content. I even bought champagne. Have a wonderful time tonight."

"Won't we talk to you at midnight?" Kate asked.

"By midnight for you, I will be sound asleep," Grace said. "I'll talk to you in the morning. Happy New Year, sweetheart."

Grace did not place the receiver back on the cradle. She pressed the buttons down with her finger and listened for the dial tone. Punched four-one-one.

"Sabbath Landing, New York," she said. "The Alpine Hotel." She dialed the number. Heard the tinkling of piano music in the background when the desk clerk answered.

"I know this is very last minute," she said. "But do you have any rooms available?"

It didn't take but a moment for the clerk to say they had a suite but no rooms.

"Suite has a lake view," he said. "It's a little pricey at the moment, given the holiday. Two-fifty for tonight, but tomorrow it drops to one-twenty-five."

Grace said she would take it.

"How many nights and for how many people?" the clerk asked.

"At least two nights," Grace said. "One person."

Grace read him the digits from her credit card. "You'll hold the room for me, won't you? I'll be there quite late," she said. "And I need driving directions from New York City."

She thought there was a hesitation in his voice when she said she was coming alone, but he gave her directions. It was as Thompson had said, a straight shot up the Thruway, some quirky turns before you get to Fort Hope, and then more after that.

"There's a train, as well, ma'am," he said. "Next one up is at three o'clock tomorrow out of Penn Station. Pulls into Fort Hope. About a forty-minute drive to here."

"Thanks," Grace said. "I need to get there tonight." Before I lose my nerve, she thought to herself.

Grace took the suitcase she was planning to take to Aspen. She packed blue jeans and running clothes. A blue wool dress with a scoop neck and a black dress with a cowl. Why am I taking dresses? she thought. A pile of fleece shirts. A worn plaid shirt that had belonged to Adam. More turtlenecks and T-shirts. She put in her hiking boots, a pair of heels, flannel pajamas, a stack of magazines, her Walkman, and the deed with the photograph. She was disorganized. Unfocused. She forced down the lid of the suitcase, hefted it off the bed. She put the untouched Chinese food in the refrigerator with a note to Rosa, grabbed the scrawled directions she'd left by the phone, the car key from the kitchen table, and shut the lights in the apartment.

Traffic heading south to the city was fierce at nine o'clock on New Year's Eve. Cars lined up for tolls, bumper to bumper. But northbound, there were few cars. It wasn't until Grace turned off the exit for Fort Hope that she realized how far she had driven, how rapidly the hours had passed. She hadn't turned on the radio or played the compact discs she had brought for the ride. She just drove.

It was a right turn off the exit. The road was narrow now. Dark and curving. Poorly lit save for bright yellow arrows with reflectors indicating where the road turned sharply, dipping as it wound around what appeared to be a mountain. Signs for cars to downshift, deer crossing, school bus stops, a hospital.

Grace drove through Fort Hope, a larger town than the ones she had just passed through. Towns that could easily be missed, she thought, if she blinked. Fort Hope was clearly the tourist mecca, although it was boarded up for winter. Grace was certain that in summer it probably smelled like taffy and fudge and fried clams. There was a place called Fairytale Town on one corner. A giant pirate, probably thirty feet tall, guarded the entrance. One eye closed, the other covered in a patch, his head tied in a sculptured red bandanna, one hand on his hip, the other gesturing toward a large white fence that opened onto a now-drained moat. A yellow-haired princess, another gargantuan sculpture, stood in the center of the amusement park, ticket windows in the wide folds of her molded pink skirt. There were several slides leading to three painted blue pits, a miniature golf course, a glass booth with red velvet curtains holding a robotic fortune-teller, head wrapped in a turban, ears hung with gold earrings. Everything was still and lifeless.

Fort Hope also had a wax museum and haunted house. Restaurants every few yards advertised clam rolls and lobster rolls and cold Labatt beer with welcome signs to OUR CANADIAN NEIGHBORS. In between there were stores advertising T-shirts and Indian moccasins, taffy, fudge, homemade ice cream, and offerings for temporary tattoos. But the shop windows were bare and gated. Motel pools were covered with tarpaulins; padlocks dangled from the gates around them. Marquees with block letters spelled CLOSED above crudely lettered signs advertising free phone and cable TV. SEE YOU IN THE SPRING, some said. HAPPY HOLIDAYS.

Grace glanced at the directions and made a sharp right turn at the fork in the road where Fort Hope's three-mile stretch came to an end. There was a sign to Sabbath Landing. Thirty miles, it said. Thirty-eight miles to Minerva's Shelf. The road, now called Diamond Drive, narrowed even more as Grace headed toward Sabbath Landing. If possible, it was even more winding. There were bungalow colonies every few hundred feet on either side. Stores that sold bait and night-crawlers, fresh milk and small groceries. Marinas with signs for water skiing, wake boarding, and parasailing were shut down. More restaurants. A stable. Houses that doubled as shops sold wicker porch furniture, fresh corn and tomatoes. But everything was dormant in winter.

She looked at the odometer and saw she had driven a good thirty miles. It was then she saw the clearing on her right. SCENIC VIEW. A stretch of something silvery glimmered in the darkness under the embryonic January moon that seemed to light the sky through the thin layer of clouds. It was the same moon that shone over Manhattan, struggling to light the skyscrapers through the urban smog. She noticed the temperature on the car's thermometer had dropped. It was eighteen degrees now as she approached Sabbath Landing. When she'd left the city, it was a palatable thirty-one.

Sabbath Landing was tonier than the other towns. Tonier than Fort Hope. No motels on this strip. Just shops that sold quilts, antiques, and even books. There was an ice cream parlor, a Realtor, and several large restaurants—airy and elegant, unlike the ones she'd driven by in Fort Hope. One restaurant, The Birch Tavern, looked as though it had a light on. There were strands of shimmery crepe paper lying in the street outside, metallic deflated balloons hanging over the door. A sign at the end of the strip read ALPINE HOTEL with an arrow pointing right. She drove over a small bridge and suddenly there were globe lights and wreaths and life. WELCOME TO THE ALPINE HOTEL, a small billboard read. WE ARE OPEN.

Grace pulled up to the entrance at the top of the long paved driveway. She walked into the lobby, heard the piano music she had heard over the phone just five hours before. Except for a few people sitting on sofas, the festivities were over. Men languished, smoking cigars, their feet up on coffee tables, bow ties and cummerbunds undone. Women slouched beside them in wrinkled gowns, high heels kicked off on the floor beside them, loose tendrils of hair falling around their faces. They all had the sleepy satisfied looks of those who have had too much to drink, too many dances. They were sitting too close, laughing softly, kissing, their champagne glasses on the side tables. The pianist, a man with a shock of black hair and a thick mustache, tinkled a tune from *Phantom of the Opera* on the keyboard. A woman sat next to him on the piano bench, her head resting on his shoulder. Grace rang the small bell on the desk. A weary clerk came out from the back.

"I'm Grace Barnett," she said. "I made a reservation earlier this evening. I'm sorry to get here so late."

"Perfectly all right, madam," the young clerk said, clearly forcing himself awake. "Welcome to The Alpine and Happy New Year. Your suite overlooks the lake and Hester's Peak."

She signed the register, refused help with her one bag, and took the elevator to the sixth floor. The suite was musty and damp. She flipped on the switch that lit two small lamps in the corner of the living area. A basket of flowers and a box of chocolates sat on the coffee table. She walked into the bedroom and bathroom and did the same: turned on the light, looked around. Walked back to the living room and pushed up the window. The cold night air mingled with a sweet scent of pine. The shadow of the mountain was a silhouette in the distance. She saw what appeared to be a footpath trimmed with stone benches and halo-gen globe lights. And there, at the end of the path, was Diamond Lake. True to its name, it glistened, frozen, in the moonlight at the foot of the mountain. And as fearsome as it was to gaze out at the lake, as audibly as her heart pounded, although she shivered in the cold night air, Grace was suddenly struck by a tremendous sense of peace.

Chapter Eight

There was a small basket of supplies in the bathroom. Grace showered and lathered her body with a minted gel. Washed her hair with pine-scented shampoo. Creamed her arms and legs with a lavender lotion. I'm a bouquet, she thought to herself. And then she thought how weary she was. From the drive, the week, the vicissitudes of emotions she had endured since that Sunday morning when Melanie called from their house. She put on the terry-cloth robe that hung on the back of the bathroom door, wrapped her hair in a towel, and lay down on the bed. She was leafing through a tourist magazine about the area when she fell asleep.

The dream came. Grace was calling to her mother to save them as the water swirled around them, swallowing them in an icy vortex. The muscles in her throat clutched and tightened as her cries attempted to escape. And as she struggled to awaken, she felt as though she were strangling, sputtering, barely able to breathe.

She sat up against the pillows. Rigid. Her legs and arms painfully stiff. Her skin was moist and cool. She looked about the strange room. The orientation of the bed was not the same as hers at home. The window was on the wrong side. Finally, her eyes found her suitcase sitting on the strapped luggage stand, lid open. The now-familiar worn brown envelope holding the deed lay on top of her bright red fleece, and she remembered. She pulled her knees up to her chest, hugged them to her, rocked herself gently back and forth as she did when she was a child. Shake it out, she thought. It was only a dream. She glanced at the clock on the nightstand. Five-thirty. She'd only slept a little over two hours. She thought of the Chinese food she'd left in the refrigerator at home. She hadn't eaten since yesterday afternoon at Melanie's house. She was starving.

Grace got up and took the towel off her head, her long auburn hair falling in ringlets from the dampness. She loosened it with her fingertips. Her hairbrush caught in the tangles. She splashed cool water on her face. Brushed her teeth. Ran a lipstick over her mouth. She leaned forward and looked at herself in the too brightly lit mirror. Caught a glimpse of herself in the gold-toned magnifier anchored on the wall.

"You look every one of your forty-four years right now," she said aloud, relieved at the sound of her voice.

She put on blue jeans and a navy turtleneck. Hiking boots over tweed socks. Grabbed the blue down parka that she had thrown over the couch when she'd walked in the door. She stopped to look out the window again. It was overcast. The ice on the lake looked opalescent. The sky, like mother of pearl above the shadowy silhouette of Hester's Peak. A group of people, seemingly a family, in bright orange jackets were pulling a small tent a few feet out on the lake, shuffling along as though they were skating. There were children, gliding back and forth as though they danced on glass.

The desk clerk said it was too early for The Alpine's restaurant to be open for breakfast, but there was a diner, about two miles down the road, in Sabbath Landing. "Just as you head out of town toward Fort Hope. It's open year-round," he said. "Mostly fishermen in there this time of day."

At first Grace wondered why all eyes turned to her through the windows of the diner as she parked her car right in front. It didn't take but a moment for her to realize that a silver Mercedes was an oddity in town. The street was lined with old Chevy pickups, their beds cluttered with dirty Styrofoam coolers and buckets with rusted handles; an old army-green Jeep, rusted station wagons with wood-paneled rocker panels. Wind chimes tinkled as she opened the door to the diner, making such a ruckus she thought she should reach up to stop their jingling and clanging. The smell of bacon and sausage and strong coffee made Grace feel even hungrier. Her stomach was growling. A waitress, in her late fifties, hair dyed black with a maroon henna tint, overweight, in a pair of tight black pants, a white blouse with flounce collar, a yellow corsage pinned to her bosom, greeted Grace with a slightly stained menu encased in plastic.

"Morning! Happy New Year! Counter or table, miss?" she asked.

"Happy New Year. Could I have a booth?" Grace said. "Over there, okay?" Grace pointed to one at the back of the room even though all of them were empty.

"Any place at all. Not exactly our busy season," the waitress laughed. "You wouldn't recognize this place come Memorial Day. They stand knee deep outside just waiting to get a seat for the boysenberry pancakes. I like it in the winter, though. Quiet, you know? Coffee?"

The waitress, her name tag said HELEN, was already pouring coffee into Grace's cup before Grace could answer.

"Can I have the number four?" Grace asked, setting the menu down on the table. "I'll have the eggs over medium, and can I have the sausage *and* the bacon? The hash browns. And an English muffin instead of toast. And jam. But not grape, please."

"Now that's what I like," Helen said. "A gal with a healthy appetite. Now, how do you stay so skinny? All I have to do is look at food. Be right back."

Grace didn't quite know what to do with herself while she waited for breakfast. She doubted that the diner had been silent before she walked in. A long row of men on swivel stools with pale blue vinyl seats lined the counter. They wore dark wool knit caps, rough plaid shirts, and dark jeans. Their jackets, faded once-dark colors, well worn and salt stained, were heaped on a rack in the corner. The counter was set with a covered cake plate that held Danish pastries and doughnuts. There were bottles of ketchup, Tabasco sauce, and mustard in bent metal racks. A leaky assortment of syrups in glass-and-chrome pitchers. Large plates set before the men were heaped with eggs and pancakes. The old jukebox on the table had square red buttons embossed with well-worn letters and numbers. She turned the wheel on top, flipped the selections forward and back, reading the cardboard pages. Lots of Sinatra. Patsy Cline. Johnny Mathis. She grabbed an old real estate guidebook (the newsprint kind that supermarkets give away) sitting on a table behind her and turned the pages. Delis and bungalow colonies for sale. Bold print advertising plots and parcels of land with lakefront footage. "Life begins here," said an ad for a trailer space described also as "a little piece of heaven." Voices at the counter began to chatter again, beginning with whispers and rising to a more robust crescendo. She was becoming comfortable now. Less of an anomaly. Part of the landscape.

We got the freeze-over already, the voices said. Early this year. Last time it came this early was around 1980. Looks like good blue ice. Least four inches thick, I bet you. Should be a good season.

Helen set down Grace's breakfast. "We call this one the Lumberjack," she said, grinning. "If you'd gotten the one with the pancakes, then we call it the Paul Bunyan."

"Well, I'm no lumberjack, but I'm as hungry as one. It looks great," Grace said. "Could I get some more coffee? And, also, can you tell me how I would go about getting out to those islands in the lake?"

Helen laughed. "The islands? Oh, my dear, the fellas were just saying how the freeze-over came early this year. Usually we don't get ice in until February, but not this year. Nope, we got the ice in now, and it's frozen solid. And those islands are a good two miles in for the closest. Your best bet is to wait till the thaw, dearie. The ice goes out around middle of April. You a photographer or something?"

Their conversation piqued the interest of the men at the counter. Grace noted they had stopped speaking again. They all turned around on their stools, their eyes unabashedly focused on her. She was about to put a bite of hash browns in her mouth when one of the men spoke.

"Folks don't usually go out to the islands after the first of November," he said. "Most of the islanders batten down the hatches come October. Make sure the place is secure for winter. Rule of thumb around here is we're still pretty cautious so soon after the freeze-over. There are still currents out there. Especially around those islands."

"I saw people out on the lake this morning, though," Grace said. "They had little tents with them and they were walking around on the ice."

The men laughed aloud, in unison, but the man just smiled. "Tourists acting like ice fishermen. They stay right near the shore where they think the ice is firm. Funny thing is—or not so funny—the shoreline is probably the least safe spot. They think they can get themselves to land if need be, but it's pretty risky. Those tents, by the way, are called shanties. Keeps the ice fishermen out of the wind. I should introduce myself; I'm Lucas Keegan. Luke," the man said, walking toward Grace, extending his hand.

Grace smiled. "I see. Grace Barnett. Nice to meet you." She shook his hand. It was rough, the nails cut short, grease embedded in the cracks. Not like surgeon's hands, she thought, picturing Adam's elegant slender fingers, his buffed manicured nails. "I can't imagine there's no way out to the islands. I mean, what if there was an emergency or something?"

"Well, that's true. Now, we have ways of getting there if there's a problem. A fire or something. Maybe an electrical problem. You're mighty determined, aren't you?" Luke said. "Better get yourself a hat and some gloves first. I noticed you when you came in. Dressed kind of flimsy for January in Sabbath Landing. Where you from?"

"New York City, and I *am* determined." Grace smiled. He had noticed her, she thought. He has beautiful eyes.

"I didn't hear what you told Helen," Luke said. "Are you a photographer? Lots of people from those outdoor-type magazines come up to these parts."

"No," Grace said hesitantly. "I'm just up for some relaxation. Fresh air, you know? Not too many places seem open this time of year."

Luke laughed, "No, it's pretty quiet, all right. Of course, some bait shops are open year-round for a bucket of shiners or grubs. Speaking of which, I've got to run. I guide around here. I'm either out on the lake or guiding the woods by seven in the morning depending on what month it is. Right now, I'm doing the ice-fishing. Party of five fellows from the city are waiting for me and the grubs. Starting a little later this morning, what with last night being New Year's Eve. If I can be of any help, let me know. Just ask for me. Or for Helen. She always knows where to find me."

"Maybe I'll do that," Grace said. She couldn't stop looking at Luke's eyes. They were blue. Nearly turquoise. He had a shock of gray hair that stuck out the back of his knit cap. Broad shoulders. Long, muscular, lean legs in black jeans. A worn black leather jacket.

"Where're you staying?"

"The Alpine."

"By yourself?"

Grace lowered her eyes. She hesitated, her mouth opened slightly, not knowing what to say.

"My apologies," Luke said. "I shouldn't be so nosy. I talk too damn much."

"No, not at all," Grace said. "My husband and daughter are away on a ski trip. Out West."

"Well, The Alpine is a fine place," Luke said. "My son worked at their waterfront for a half dozen summers. My wife waitressed there for a few summers, too. Nice to meet you again, Grace. Enjoy your stay. Don't forget that hat."

The wind chimes jingled when Luke walked out the door. Grace paid the check. Three dollars for breakfast. She left a two-dollar tip.

"Hey! Thanks!" Helen called to Grace as she walked out the door. "Come back and see us again."

When Grace got back to The Alpine, a cleaning crew was straightening the lobby where the festivities had been the night before. A woman in a gray dress was dusting. A man in a white jacket was running a noisy Hoover over the Oriental rugs. The desk clerk was standing behind the desk—shuffling papers, trying to look busy—when Grace approached him.

"I was just wondering," she said. "Is there any place to go around here at night? You know, besides the restaurant in the hotel? The town seems like it's mostly shut down."

The Birch Tavern was the spot where the locals went for dinner, he said. Pizza, burgers, pasta, he said. Nothing special. On the weekends, sometimes, there's a band. They've got a small dance floor. "I don't know that you'd want to be there by yourself, though," he said gently. "The hotel restaurant might be preferable."

Grace went upstairs and turned on the television in the living room. There was a selection of movies on pay-per-view, most of which she'd already seen. She pulled out the deed and the photograph, studying them carefully. Hoping something might jump out at her. Something that might explain why the house on the island was left to her.

She waited until nine o'clock and called Jemma. The answering machine picked up and Grace realized Jemma had spent the night at her cousin's. She wished her Happy New Year. I hope all your dreams come true, she said, but felt guilty when she fibbed: I'm at the apartment, she said. But I'm heading up to Mel's, and I'll call you later. Jemma would worry if she knew where I was, she rationalized. She's been through enough lately.

Grace dozed off on the sofa, the deed resting on her stomach, one hand holding the aerial photograph. She turned when she awakened, grabbed the photograph as it began to slip off. She felt a sense of relief: She'd had no bad dreams.

Adam answered the phone when Grace called Aspen. She was grateful that he hadn't been sleeping, although his voice sounded thick, his speech slightly slurred. He had too much to drink last night, she thought. Kate was showering, he said. They were about to head out. Had a great time at the Whittakers'. The kids went ice-skating at the lodge. He beat John Whittaker at pool. Elaine Whittaker had a face-lift and looked ten years younger. Barely recognized her at first, he said. It was an obvious afterthought when he asked Grace how she was. It was merely a formality when he wished her Happy New Year, a long pause before he asked what she had done for New Year's Eve.

Grace prefaced what she said next. Choosing her words carefully, eliminating emotion from her voice. "Well, I had a rather unusual evening," she said. "Now promise you won't say a word until I'm finished. Then we can talk." She told him about the meeting with Thompson. The provisions of the will. Canterbury Island. Sabbath Landing and the weekends that Thompson spent at The Alpine and how her father never said a word about owning a home off the shore. How she had planned to spend New Year's Eve at the apartment. That she didn't feel like being up at Melanie's. How she got Chinese takeout and bought herself roses and even a split of champagne. How dismal the terrace looked when she stood outside.

"Get to the point, Grace," Adam said, his voice laced with impatience.

"I want you to understand though," Grace said. "I was thinking, maybe I should just go up to Melanie's and not be alone when the idea came to me. It was like a force out of nowhere, Adam. I just had to come here."

"Are you telling me that you're in Sabbath Crossing?" Adam asked sternly.

"Landing," Grace said. "Sabbath Landing. And, yes, I am. I drove here last night. I didn't get here until nearly two in the morning, but it was an easy trip. The roads were clear and dry. I was certainly sober. And it's a beautiful spot. The mountains. Diamond Lake. It's the strangest thing, Adam. You know, I have this fear of water and yet I look out at that lake and I am so drawn to it somehow. I can't explain. Not even to myself."

"Sure, because the goddamn lake is probably frozen. You're practically at the Canadian border, for Christ's sake. Call me crazy, but I don't think a woman should be driving alone to some frozen redneck town in the middle of the night. And on New Year's Eve? What the hell were you thinking, Grace? You think you're going to find something there? They left you some run-down beach house is all this is about. Threw you another bone. Christ almighty, Grace, when are you going to let this crap go? You think you're going to find your answers in some two-bit resort town?"

"That's not it," Grace said quietly. "You're wrong. I wish I could make you understand. From the moment Thompson told me about this place, I had to come here. And it's not a redneck town. It's not like that at all, Adam. It's beautiful. I mean, it's kind of boarded up for the winter, but still, it is so peaceful. I have to know why they had a house here and never told us. I can't imagine why they left it to me."

"This is insane being there by yourself. Driving there in the middle of the night. I think you should go home, Grace. I'll prescribe you a sedative."

"That's ridiculous. I'm fine. I don't need a sedative. I know exactly what I'm doing. I feel exhilarated being here." Her heart was pounding now. She drew in a breath. "And I'm not going back home right now, either. I want to give it a few days here. If it makes you feel better, I'll call Melanie and see if she'll come up. There's a train that runs from Penn Station to Fort Hope. That's a town about forty minutes from here. I'll ask her, okay?"

"I know about Fort Hope. It's a real honky-tonk town. I'm beginning not to care what you do, Grace," Adam said bitterly.

"Well, that's truly a shame, isn't it?" Grace said, getting angry now. "Make sure you tell Kate that I called. Give her my love and tell her I'll call later. And, Adam, don't tell her where I am."

"What difference does it make if it is as you say, if it's such a beautiful spot?" Adam asked sarcastically.

"Please respect my wishes, Adam," Grace said softly. "Please."

"You're wasting your time and my money," Adam said angrily. "You're not going to find one goddamn thing. I've come across a lot of people in my line of work. All types. Your parents took the cake. They were misanthropes, plain and simple. Selfish and self-involved. Jesus, Grace, don't you see? You need to stop looking for answers. There are none. None that you want to hear."

"I guess I'll either prove you right or wrong, won't I? Take care, Adam." And she hung up the phone.

Grace's hands shook slightly when she dialed Melanie's number. "I didn't wake you, did I?" she asked.

"Are you kidding? The kids have been up since six. I just tried you," Melanie said. "Where were you? Out running? Happy New Year."

"Happy New Year, Mel. Guess where I am?" Grace took a deep breath and told her. "Why don't you come up here?" Grace asked when she finished. "It's about five hours by train. There's a three o'clock out of Penn."

"Oh, my God, Grace. Do you think I could? Hang on, okay? Hang on just one second," Melanie said. "I need to talk to Mike."

Grace heard them talking. Heard Mike's voice rise for a moment as he tried to take it all in. She heard the urgency in Melanie's muffled tone as her hand covered the mouthpiece, making scratching staticky sounds. She heard Melanie tell Mike about The Alpine. Even Thompson and his wife go there, Mike, it's fine. I'll be fine.

"He says if Mrs. Hadley is willing to stay during the day, I should go," Melanie said breathlessly. "He actually thinks it'll do me good to breathe the mountain air. Can you believe it? I'll call for train schedules in case I miss the three o'clock. And I'll call Mrs. Hadley. Talk to you later. Keep your fingers crossed. Hey, is it cold up there?"

Grace laughed. "Oh, yes. It's cold. Bring a hat." She thought of the man at the diner.

That night, Grace met Melanie's train in Fort Hope. It had just started to snow as they drove the winding road back to The Alpine.

"I was afraid you'd think I was crazy to come here," Grace said.

Melanie nodded her head and smiled. "Then I'm as crazy as you are. I was a little surprised. But not that surprised."

"Look at the lake." Grace pointed as they rounded the turn into Sabbath Landing. "Look at the moon. The lake is frozen solid, you know. The ice is in."

"Listen to you with the local jargon," Melanie said with a laugh. "No wonder they call it Diamond Lake. It practically glistens. You know, you drive this road like you've been driving it your whole life."

Grace smiled. "I know. It's amazing. I feel like I know every turn."

Chapter Nine

"I need to get gas," Grace said, just before they were supposed to turn into The Alpine. "There's a Sunoco up ahead."

The Sunoco was barely a gas station by current standards. Two short rounded pumps stood side by side. An old red Coke machine stood next to a newer machine filled with candy and chips. A sign offering free firewood was scrawled in black on a crude piece of plywood. The station itself was a white brick house, an American flag waving over the small front porch, yellow curtains in the upstairs windows. A pile of old tires sat on the porch partially hidden by a rail of broken spindles.

"Do you think it's still open?" Grace asked, pulling up to the pump, glancing at the clock on the dashboard. "It's nearly nine-thirty."

"It doesn't look like it's ever open. This place looks practically turn of the century," Melanie said. "I bet it was a blacksmith shop once."

"Well, there's a light on inside and smoke coming out of the chimney. Someone's here, I guess. I'm going to honk," Grace said.

A man in a gray woolen balaclava came out from the house. He wore a heavy brown corduroy jacket with a matted fleece lining, soiled beige leather gloves. He stood at the driver's window, his hands flapping his arms to warm himself.

"Fill it, please," Grace said, barely cracking the window. "Supreme. I'm glad you're open."

"Just about to close," the man said, puffs of warm breath visible in the cold night air. "But sometimes, even if the sign says closed, I come out to give folks their gas. The wife and I live inside. She gets mad when I come out and all folks want is directions. These pumps are the only game in town. You gotta drive to Fort Hope otherwise or up to Minerva's Shelf." He looked up at the sky and sniffed the air. "Snow's going to blow in hard by morning. It'll leave enough behind so that we have to shovel."

Grace turned off the engine, comforted now by the man's conversation, the notion that he had a wife. His balaclava had frightened her at first, as did the darkness of the station, the silence and the solitude of the town on a snowy night.

"I've lived in Manhattan for too long," she laughed, turning to Melanie. "Boy, you can really smell that gasoline. The last time I smelled that, I was a kid."

Grace was lost in thought when the man knocked on the car window.

"Grace? Grace?" Melanie said, poking her in the rib cage. "He wants to get paid. You're on another planet."

"Your pumps aren't fixed yet, are they?" Grace asked as she handed him her credit card through the window.

"Nope. We got to tend to that in the spring or they'll shut us down. We ain't environmentally updated yet. Still got that stink. Managed to get by this long, though."

"It makes you kind of queasy, doesn't it?" Grace asked.

"You get used to it, I guess. Don't bother me anymore. Have a nice night, ladies. Keep warm."

Snow was falling faster now as they pulled up The Alpine's drive. The wind was blowing in cold sharp snaps, causing the branches on the pine trees to bend. Grace gave the car to the valet, shielding her face from the cold while she waited for him to bring her the ticket.

"Want to sit here and warm up?" Grace asked, pointing to two rose-colored chairs by the hearth in the lobby.

"That fire feels so good," Melanie said, placing her jacket over the arm of the chair, peeling off her gloves. "I can't wait to see everything in daylight. I could smell the pine just walking in the door."

"Wait until you see it. It's breathtaking. Listen, we can order tea here before we head upstairs," Grace said. "Maybe even get a bite to eat. Unless you're tired."

"Oh, no. This is perfect. I'm hungry. Mrs. Hadley packed me a picnic for the train but I ate it before the train left the station. Egg salad. I figured I'd better eat it quickly before it started to smell rotten," Melanie laughed. "I slept the rest of the way after that."

A waiter came over with a small menu in a leather case. They ordered Irish coffees instead of tea. Hamburgers and French fries.

"I haven't had a hamburger in ages," Grace said. "Adam says they'll clog my arteries."

"How is Adam? And Kate? I never even asked you: Did you tell them you're here?"

"Good. They're fine. Adam knows. I told him this morning. Kate was in the shower, but I'll call her later. And you were right, Mel. I spoke to Kate on New Year's Eve and she sounded like she's having a wonderful time."

"And what did Adam say?"

"Well, let's just say he was less than pleased that I'm here," Grace sighed. "I think I'm becoming an emotional burden on him."

"A burden? Oh, for God's sake, Grace. Some burden. Mike still can't get over the fact that Adam let you drive up to Purchase that morning. He can't believe he let you go alone."

"He had to work. He was on call."

"Oh, bullshit. Family emergencies take precedence over patients. It wasn't like he was performing surgery on a Sunday. Even I know that."

"Adam's very practical. He said they were dead anyway so there was nothing he could do," Grace said.

"Oh, really? And what about you? Doesn't he care about the nonanesthetized living?"

"He is who he is, Mel. Adam doesn't do well with complications unless they're surgical."

"I'm sorry. Maybe I shouldn't talk like this to you, but he makes me angry. I don't like to see you hurt."

"I'm not hurt. I'm not saying his attitude doesn't bother me," Grace said. "It does. He doesn't know how to comfort me. He doesn't know what to do. But sometimes I think perhaps I'm just inconsolable."

"Do you still love him?"

"He's the father of my child."

"I'm not talking about history or sentiment. I'm asking you, do you still love him? I mean, really love him?"

"Sometimes I think I do and other times, I just don't know anymore. Do I love him? Honestly? Not the way I want to love someone. It's been like that for a long time. Not that I think you go along being idiotically happy forever. And then I wonder if it's me. Maybe I wouldn't be happy with anyone at this point. Our marriage was never like it is with you and Mike."

"Don't think we don't have our moments. It's not so perfect. But Mike is there for me. God knows, he was there for me that Sunday."

"But that's my point. Adam would have been there in body only. Even after the funeral, he was more interested in getting to Aspen. He's not comfortable with emotion. At least not with my emotion."

"How does he deal with patients? How does he tell families when there's a bad result?"

"He tells people ahead of time that results are never guaranteed. And he's a surgeon, don't forget. He doesn't have long-term relationships with his patients."

"Doesn't he realize you're not a patient?"

"Maybe it's the only way he can function," Grace said. Her mind was wandering again. "I bought myself white roses and champagne and wine the night after Thompson read the will. I stood out on the terrace with a glass of wine, all prepared to have a night at home alone and feel strong and independent and I felt so sad. And now, look where I am."

"Well, I think it's wonderful that we're here," said Melanie. "And I think it's perfectly reasonable to want to see the house."

"Adam would prefer if things were simpler, I guess. I think the notion of a mystery house makes him feel threatened somehow. It makes him feel helpless. He's a healer, you know?"

"Maybe the physician needs to heal himself," Melanie said.

Grace laughed, "You're beginning to sound like Jemma."

"I am, aren't I?" Melanie smiled. "Look. Let's drop it for now. Let's just relax. It's so peaceful here. This lobby is so beautiful. Look at the beamed ceilings."

Grace was silent. She stared into the fireplace. Watched the yellow flames dance. Listened to the fire crackle and pop, sending small sparks through the screen. She heard her sister speaking, but she was thinking of the man in the balaclava at the gas pumps in town. The putrid smell of the gasoline.

"Melanie? I had this thought when we were at the Sunoco station. I remembered once being somewhere in the heat of the summer. We were with Mom and Dad and stopped to fill up the car. I remember saying that I felt sick to my stomach. I guess it was from the stench of the gas fumes. And Mom gave me a mint. You know those big thick pink-and-white ones like you get in a restaurant? The kind wrapped in cellophane that taste like a candy cane? And a Wash'n Dri. She gave me a Wash'n Dri and then she put her hand on my forehead and told me to hold the Wash'n Dri next to my nose and suck on the mint so I wouldn't feel so sick. Where do you think we were going, Mel? Dairy Queen maybe? Why do I remember a Dairy Queen?"

Melanie laughed. "Talk about a non sequitur."

"I know. I know," Grace said. "But I'm remembering something."

"I don't ever remember going with them anywhere warm. And in the car? When did we ever drive anywhere with them? And I never remember going to a Dairy Queen." But then Melanie stopped laughing. "The really sad thing is, I never remember Mom being tender like that."

But Grace thought she remembered a cherry bonnet poured over a soft vanilla cone. Standing outside, leaning on a fence with her parents and Melanie. Melanie eating spoonfuls of a hot fudge sundae covered with rainbow jimmies. Fudge dripping down her blouse.

"Ice cream is the best cure for an upset tummy, isn't it, Grace?" her mother said, placing a cool hand on the back of Grace's neck, pushing her hair from her face.

"You think ice cream cures everything, Jane." Her father smiled.

"Now, that is simply not true, Alex," her mother protested with a mock pout. "Just some things, that's all. Oh, my goodness, look at that child's shirt! Covered in fudge! I'll have to soak that in Clorox. Grace, your lips are red as roses from that cherry bonnet. They look like petals."

"No, Mel. We did go to a Dairy Queen. Maybe you were just too young to remember. Dad said that Mother loved ice cream. My lips were all red from a cherry bonnet. You were having hot fudge."

"Fudge? I hate fudge. Too rich. I've never been big on chocolate. Maybe it was butterscotch. Are you sure it wasn't butterscotch?"

"I have such a funny feeling since I smelled that gasoline."

"I think this Irish coffee got to you. Or the fumes," Melanie said. "I think you're dreaming."

"Speaking of dreams," Grace said, turning from the fire to her sister. She held her breath for a moment. "Speaking of dreams, there's something I want to tell you."

"Go ahead. You can tell me anything."

"No, I'd rather tell you when we're upstairs. I'll get the check."

"It's nothing bad, is it, Grace? I've had enough bad news lately to last me a—"

"No, it's not bad," Grace said. "It's just troubling me. Let's get the check and go upstairs. Then I'll tell you."

Chapter Ten

"Look at the view," Melanie said, standing at the window in the suite. "Look at the shadow of the mountain."

"That's Hester's Peak," Grace said as though she were boasting.

"It's almost mystical, isn't it?" Melanie said. "So, tell me."

"Let's get settled," Grace said. "Go ahead. You get into pajamas first."

"I'm dying of curiosity, you know," Mel said.

Melanie was wearing a flannel nightgown and a pair of white socks when she flopped down on the couch in the living room. "Boy, it's cold in here. Maybe we ought to turn the heat up. This is like when we were girls and we'd have pajama parties with each other. I feel like we should be swapping diaries or playing Truth or Dare. Okay: Truth, Grace."

"Well, there's something I never told you and I'm thinking that maybe I should. The only one I ever told was Mother."

"You're kidding, right? You told Mother? Not Jemma?"

"I think it was my first and last reaching out to her. You see, since I was really little, I had this dream. You were in the dream, too. It's not exactly the same dream each time but it's the same kind of dream. You and I are drowning or about to drown. We're in cold water and it's dark outside. Not nighttime, I don't think, but I'm not sure. It's more just sort of colorless. Sometimes we're on a boat and the boat is sinking. Sometimes the water is just choppy and sometimes it's just like this icy vortex and we're getting sucked in. There's always water. Cold water.

And in the dream, Mother is there. I ask Mother to save us and she says she can't save us both so she just walks away and Dad goes with her. And I watch them. I watch them walk away. By the time I'm waking up I can feel myself trying to scream for help but it's like I'm choking. Like the words are stuck in my throat. You know, in a nightmare when you try to speak and you just can't find your voice? Anyway, I told Mother the dream and asked what she would do if that really happened. I asked if she would save us both."

"And?"

"And she became distraught. Not really angry, but she got this wild look about her. I'll never forget. She said it was a selfish dream. That there was something wrong with me to talk about such things. Even dream or think about such things. I felt so evil, Mel. So wicked and embarrassed after I told her. But, when Kate was about that age, maybe a little older, she asked me questions like that. I don't know that they were dreams exactly, but I remember one time she asked if the three of us, Adam and Kate and I, were all on a desert island and I was the savior but could only save one, who would I save."

"And, of course, you said you would save everyone."

"Of course. No matter what, I said I would save us all. That I didn't care about what I was supposed to do or could do or anything. It was hands down. Save everyone. Mother never said anything like that. It would have been so easy."

"How old were you when you told Mother?"

"Six. Give or take."

"Why didn't you ever tell Jemma?"

"I was embarrassed. Once Mother reacted the way she did, I was certain there was something wrong with me. I was too ashamed to tell anyone after that. I never even wrote the dream in my diary."

"Poor little kid," Melanie said, shaking her head. "But, Grace, I think a lot of people, particularly children, have the same kinds of dreams over and over. I once read that blind people dream that they can see. For me, well, I always dream that I can drive a manual shift and Mike laughs at me because I've tried and for the life of me I can't coordinate my hands and feet enough to shift and clutch. But why is this bothering you so much now? Kids dream crazy things. Even Matt and Jeremy, even at three, they've had some doozies."

"But that's just it. I still have the dream. And it still terrifies me. You'd think I would have outgrown this by now. I had the dream last night. And the night after Mother and Dad died. I still wake up in a cold sweat. I shake when that dream comes. And before that, well, it was months ago that I had the dream. . . . It's just that it always feels so real."

"I just thought of something. When you'd wake up when we were kids, howling in the middle of the night, that wasn't foot cramps, was it?" Melanie asked. "You always said you got foot cramps because of the dancing."

Grace smiled. "No, it wasn't foot cramps."

"Why did you say that it was? Why didn't you at least tell me?"

"I was the big sister. I didn't want to worry you. Now we're more even."

"Well, it doesn't worry me, but I think maybe you should talk to someone about it. You know, a professional."

"Now you sound like Adam."

"Thanks a lot. Have you ever told Adam?"

"Never. He would commit me. When I told him I was here, he said I probably needed medication. Antidepressants. I'm too emotional for him. Too probing. He'd tell me to ignore it. To get over it or get help."

"Well, I think you ought to talk to someone when you get back home. Maybe the dream is pretty straightforward, Grace. Maybe you've always felt like you were drowning since you were a child. I don't want to sound like an analyst but, you know, gasping for air, gasping for affection. Maybe the dream is a parable."

Grace ran her hands through her hair and pushed it back from her face. She drew in a deep breath, letting it out slowly. "Thank you, Sigmund." She nodded with a weak smile. "I often wondered why they bothered to even have children. We were probably both unplanned."

"I was always certain that I was," Melanie said, smoothing a finger-nail with an emery board.

"You never told me that."

"Oh, yeah. Once I asked Mother why she bothered to have a sec-ond child. I was around fourteen and I was angry at her for something. Maybe just because of the way she was. Anyway, I asked her and she said that she was sorry. And I didn't know if she meant sorry for having me or sorry that I felt that way."

"How come you never told me that?" Grace asked.

"You had just gone off to college. But you know what? It was no more awful than the things that weren't said. I don't even care any-more. I got over it a long time ago."

"I'm not as emotionally healthy as you are, I guess," Grace sighed. "I envy you."

"Oh, no," Melanie said. "You're very strong. I just have an advan-tage. You see, I always had you. You had four years without me. You made all the difference in the world for me. I never knew what it was like to be their only child. I never had to suffer alone."

The years, even the days, before Melanie was born were a blur to Grace. She could not remember her mother's round pregnant belly, but she wondered if she ever pressed her head against it and felt the baby kick the way Kate did when she was four and Alison's mother was pregnant. She could not remember when the changing table wasn't set up in the corner of her room, stacks of cloth diapers folded on its wicker shelves, before Melanie arrived. She didn't recall the time before Melanie was born and the bedroom was her own. When the bedroom did not have the sweet pungent smell of antiseptic from the metal diaper pail or the second twin bed that stood oppo-site her own before Melanie's crib was placed there, or when the cane-seated rocker where Jemma fed Melanie her bottle didn't have a place by the win-dow. It was as though Grace's life began the day that Melanie came home, a tiny bundle with dark hair peeking out from under a pink blanket, eyes shut tight, her lips pursed and heart-shaped, sucking at the air.

Grace's mother left for the hospital sometime in the middle of the night about a week before Melanie came home. At breakfast, in the morning,

Grace didn't ask where her mother was. It hadn't even occurred to her that she was gone. Jemma made cocoa and cinnamon toast that morning. While she watched Grace spoon extra sugar into the cinnamon mix, she explained that her parents had left the night before to get the new baby. Grace was nonplussed, more intent on sweetening her toast.

"That's enough sugar, now, Grace," Jemma said patiently, taking the spoon from her hand. "The baby will be home in a few days. Your parents went to get her last night. You have a little sister."

Grace's face lit up. Jemma had spoken of the baby coming before but suddenly she was real. "A girl?" Grace asked, her eyes wide and hopeful. "Will she play with me?" And Jemma laughed and said that one day she would but she had to get a little bigger first.

Grace hadn't gone to visit her mother in the hospital. She never stood at the window of the nursery with her father and saw the new baby through the glass. Angela Rinaldi was the one who brought the omission to Grace's attention one morning. They were drawing a hopscotch in Angela's driveway with a fat piece of blue chalk when Angela (who was a very grown-up five and a half) asked Grace if she had seen her baby sister yet. Angela said that when her brother Joey was born, her father took her up to where the mommies are and the nurses held Joey behind a window.

"Daddy took pictures with a magic camera that spits out the paper and there you are. He took one of me with Joey behind the glass. Why don't you get your daddy to take you to see the baby and buy a magic camera? The nurses gave me candy, too," Angela boasted.

"My mommy will be home soon," Grace said, tossing her penny and hopping all the way to the ninesies, never stepping on a line. It was the first time Grace had an inkling that her family didn't do things quite the way that other people did.

Jemma took Grace for a walk the day Melanie came home. Usually, Grace would ride her tricycle while Jemma skipped beside her, a wire hanger bent as a hook so Jemma could pull her along. Jemma said to leave the trike at home that day. They were going for a chitchat and constitutional instead. Grace had laughed. A what? What's that?

"It's an airing out of your mind and your body. Gets your blood flowing and your mind sharp," Jemma said.

"Oh, Angela," Grace bragged to Angela who was skipping a rainbow woven rope when she and Jemma stepped outside. "Jemma and I are going for a constipational." And Jemma laughed so hard, Grace thought she might burst.

It was a warm day in early May. The first day that Jemma didn't insist that Grace wear her cardigan, or at least bring it along "just in case." Grace was wearing a plaid skirt that kept hitting her in the back of the knee and every few seconds she stopped to scratch.

"It keeps tickling me," Grace laughed. "It hits me right in that crease. You know, the knee pit."

Jemma shook her head and smiled, said she would make a hem that night unless Grace preferred to grow another inch or two really fast.

"At this rate it's going to be dark by the time we get anywhere and back, Grace. Let me show you a trick." Jemma pulled Grace to her. She rolled the skirt from the waist band, poufing her blouse out to cover the bump. "There you go," Jemma laughed. "Now it won't get you in the knee pit."

"You're the smartest person I ever met, Jemma," Grace said. "You always know just what to do."

Grace hopped up on a low stone wall, Jemma holding her hand while Grace pretended to be on a tightrope, arms held straight out to the side exaggerating her balancing act.

"Today's the big day, Grace," Jemma said. "Your baby sister's coming home."

"Can I hold her?" Grace asked, taking a small jump on the wall, stopping the tightrope walk. Her mouth opened wide and stayed that way for so long that Jemma said to close it or she'd catch flies. "Can I give her milk from the bottle and burp her? And help change her diaper?"

And Jemma smiled and said that Grace would do all those things. "She's going to share your room," Jemma said. "We're going to hang some pink eyelet curtains and get you a new pink spread for your bed. Your daddy's putting a crib where the extra bed was. We'll take the extra bed up from the *basement when Melanie's big enough. What do you think, baby? Do you like her name? You're going to be Melanie's big sister in a new pink room."*

"But Jemma, how come my daddy didn't take me to the hospital like Angela's daddy did with her? Angela got to see Joey through the window and got her picture taken."

Jemma set her mouth for a moment and thought. "Because your mommy and daddy want you to see the baby for the first time at home. That's much more exciting than through a big old glass where you can't touch."

Grace jumped from the wall and threw her arms around Jemma. "This is the best day of my life," she said. "You and I will take the best care of her."

"Your mama, too, baby. She'll take care of her and you both," Jemma said.

Grace looked at Jemma as though she was about to say something and then said she wanted to tightrope-walk again. "Let's turn around so we can go home," Grace said. "I want to see the crib and make sure everything is perfect for Melanie."

Melanie interrupted Grace's thoughts. "You're thinking so hard, Grace," Melanie said softly. "Where are you right now?"

"I can remember the day you were born so clearly. But I can't remember a thing before that. Sometimes I wonder if that dream is really a dream. Maybe it's a memory, Mel," Grace said. "To tell you the truth, it scares me to death."

Chapter Eleven

The man at the gas station was right. In the morning, Grace and Melanie awakened to the sounds of shovels scraping the pavement. Men in scarves and knitted caps piled the snow in even mounds on either side of the path, tossing handfuls of salt and sand. Diamond Lake was coated with white powder. Branches on the pine trees were heavy, straining, under thick layers of snow. In the distance, Hester's Peak looked like it had been dribbled with frosting. Children's voices, their laughter, carried on the wind as they built a snowman on The Alpine's lawn. Their words, indecipherable but clearly gleeful as they reached the windows of the suite. Except for the children's voices, the morning was quiet.

"It's the first snowfall since they died," Melanie said as she and Grace stood at the window overlooking the lake. "I miss them, you know. I'm not sure what I miss exactly, but I miss them."

"I've always missed them," Grace said.

"Maybe that's what it is. But this time they're really gone," Melanie said.

"We should call Jemma," Grace said, wiping a single tear that hadn't yet fallen. "I left a message yesterday morning. I promised to call again today."

"She called before I left yesterday afternoon. I forgot to tell you. She asked when I expected you. You didn't tell her where you were, did you? You said you were coming to me, didn't you? I got so nervous that I was lying. I just said you'd be here 'later on' and dashed off the phone. I said that Jeremy and Matt were arguing and I had to run, but I was really racing to the train."

"I was pretty abrupt, too. It's hard for me to lie to her. But I was afraid she'd worry if she knew I was here by myself."

"She knows us so well, Grace. I swear, she was trying to trick me into saying something. She knew something was up." Melanie laughed. "The woman is a witch. A good witch."

Jemma let the phone ring three times before picking it up.

"Hi, it's Grace. Where were you? Took you a while to answer."

"The question is where are you?" Jemma demanded. "You know, I have eyes in the back of my head, Grace Hammond."

"Barnett," Grace giggled.

"Don't you be so smart," Jemma said.

"I'm in Sabbath Landing. With Melanie. She got here last night. But you knew all this, didn't you?"

Jemma finally laughed. "Well, I didn't know about Melanie until I called Mike an hour ago and he said you two were out getting your hair done. He's a worse liar than the two of you put together. As for you, Grace, I knew you weren't at the apartment yesterday. I had a feeling in my bones you went up to that place."

"How?" Grace asked, smiling when Jemma talked about her bones. So that's where I get that expression from, she thought.

" 'Cause when you lie to me, Grace, your voice gets higher."

"Not true!" Grace was almost squealing.

"Oh, yes. And there you go again. It was so high on my answering machine you could have shattered glass. Are you two all right? You're going to that island, aren't you? When on earth did you get there?"

"New Year's Eve. Well, actually, I arrived after midnight so the eve was officially over. Mel took the train up yesterday."

"You drove there by yourself on New Year's Eve? You've got some kind of nerve. Where do you come off driving all by yourself so late at night—a woman alone on the road."

"I have a cell phone," Grace laughed.

"Never mind that. Are you going to that island?"

"I don't know about the island. The lake is a sheet of ice. But seek and you shall find, right, Jemma?"

"Not always. Sometimes you can seek and get lost, too."

"Jemma, I have a question. Did we ever go to Dairy Queen with Mother and Dad? Did Mother like ice cream?"

"What's this all about now? Now don't you go changing the subject."

Grace told her about the man at the gas station. The stench of the gas fumes. The memory of the candy-cane mint and the cool tow-elette. The fudge dripping down Melanie's shirt. The cherry bonnet like lipstick.

"Your mother always said that anything cold gave her a headache. And she despised fudge. I brought her a batch once from the beach at the Outer Banks and she tossed it in the trash and wept. Later she said she was sorry. She hoped she hadn't hurt my feelings. But I was already used to your mama and all her ups and downs. I figured she was proba-bly just having one of her spells was all. I think you're confusing your memories, Grace. I think you're grieving more than you realize. Grief can play tricks on the mind, baby. What are you going on about ice cream for?"

"Wait, Jemma. Why would she get so upset over fudge?"

"It wasn't the fudge, Grace. Your mama was what we used to call high-strung in the old days. Small things sometimes just set her off. Like there was this song. 'Catch a Falling Star.' You know the one? By Perry Como? Put it in your pocket? Save it for a rainy day? Well, any-way, one time I was humming it and your mama said never never never sing that song again. I felt terrible. She took to her divan that day and was in her room for hours. She wouldn't even let me fix her the cloth and vinegar. I'd just started working for you all, too. I'd only been there for about three months. I figured that song must have brought to mind something that just made her so sad. Like with me and Cyrus. There are still some songs I can't listen to. Songs that Cyrus and I would dance to. They still make my eyes smart."

"She was lucky to have you. Someone else might have up and left. They might not have been so understanding."

"Maybe so. But, you see, I was smitten with someone. I had to stay close by."

"You never told me that!" Grace said. "With whom?"

"With you, baby girl. You stole my heart the minute I laid eyes on you. I'll never forget. You were wearing a pink-and-white checked dress. Blue cardigan. Red socks. A headband with yellow silk flowers. What a little ragamuffin you were. But you said you'd gotten all dressed up for me 'cause I was company. That was the day I had my interview. You just tugged on every one of my heartstrings."

"Oh, Jemma. I wish I could remember that day. Listen, I'll call you tomorrow. Please don't worry. We're fine."

"Tell Melanie I said that you two should take care of each other."

"We will. I love you, you know. I don't know sometimes what I'd do without you. What I would have done without you."

"I know, baby. And I love you, too."

Melanie was pulling a turtleneck sweater over her head when Grace hung up the phone.

"She knew we were here, didn't she?" Melanie said as her head popped through. "I told you she knew."

"Well, she sure guessed," Grace said.

"*Casablanca*'s on TV this afternoon. How about we order room service and curl up? I'm so glad we're here even though I miss the boys. This is just what I needed, Grace. Tonight we can go to that Birch Tavern, okay? Right now, I could use a good brisk walk."

"You can walk, Mel," Grace said. "I can use a good fast run."

Chapter Twelve

White lights were draped over the doorway and woven through the bare trees outside The Birch Tavern. The Birch, as the locals called it, was a two-story log cabin that stood on the lakefront side of Diamond Drive. A tinny speaker that looked like a small megaphone, perched below one of the upstairs windows, played a scratchy version of "Silver Bells" into the street. Inside, dark wooden tables and red bentwood chairs were grouped by the large picture window overlooking the lake, each one decorated with a single red silk rose in a bud vase, salt and pepper shakers, and a caddy made from a Budweiser six-pack carton filled with mustard, ketchup, paper napkins, and plastic cutlery. The bar, a long polished mahogany stretch inlaid with black and white mosaic tiles, seemed elegantly incongruous. To the side of the bar was a large beveled window framed in stained glass overlooking Diamond Drive.

Grace and Melanie took two stools at one end of the bar. It was early. Not much past seven o'clock. There was only one other customer, sitting on the opposite end. A man with long white hair, an unkempt white beard, a short glass of an amber liquid in front of him. He looked like he was falling asleep. His head nodded down, his chin almost resting on his chest until he would jump with a start and right himself again.

"Not to worry. He's harmless," the bartender said, wiping the counter in front of Grace and Melanie with a loose damp rag. "That's Trout. Real name's Bart Lambert. One of the town fixtures. He was born here. Christmas Day, 1930. Earned his name catching more trout on Diamond Lake than anyone around. Comes in every day around five for his Jack Daniel's and leaves around eight after he's tossed back around four of them. He lives just across the street, so we don't worry too much about him getting home. Edith, his wife, died last year. He's lonely, is all. Used to be the fire chief, believe it or not."

Trout nodded to the women, suddenly awake. Raised his glass in a toast.

"Were we that obvious?" Grace asked the bartender.

"Not really. But he's a scary-looking guy, old Trout. I figured I'd just put your mind at ease. What I can get you two?"

"Can we get food?" Melanie asked.

"Pizza is pretty much it for tonight. New Year's Eve tapped us out and the snow last night fouled up deliveries. Usually, we've got burgers, too. But we got some pepperoni for a topping. We can toss a salad."

"Perfect. And two glasses of red wine," Grace said.

"We'll have a crowd coming in later," the bartender said. "It gets pretty filled up in here. By the way, I'm Bill."

"My sister, Melanie, and I'm Grace. Nice to meet you."

"Where you gals from?"

"I live in New York and Melanie lives in a suburb of the city called Katonah," Grace said.

"A city girl, eh?" Bill said.

"Geographically only. I like it here," Grace said. "I'm beginning to feel very much at home."

"Pretty quiet, though, compared to the big city."

Grace smiled. "Quiet can be just what a body needs sometimes. It's just what we're looking for."

"I have twin boys," Melanie said. "Three years old. I can use quiet."

"Well, I bet you can," Bill said. "And I bet you can use that wine, too. Coming right up."

By eight o'clock The Birch began to fill up. Helen, the waitress from the diner, came in with a portly man in a red cable-knit sweater.

They sat at the end of the bar next to Trout. Helen's hand patted Trout's forearm as she took the stool next to his. Grace caught her eye and Helen waved, whispering something into her companion's ear as she did.

"Who's that?" Melanie asked.

"Helen. The waitress from the diner," Grace said, waving back.

"Aren't you quite the townie," Melanie teased.

Bill came over and poured two more glasses. "On the house," he said. "Stick around. We'll crank up the jukebox and things'll get hopping. We're the only place open nights in winter. Us and the gas station."

"We filled up there last night. That place looks like an antique."

"It is an antique. Used to be a blacksmith shop. Did you meet Sam in that crazy headgear he wears?" Bill laughed. "He doesn't take that damn thing off until June, I swear. Says he's got some inner ear problem and can't take the wind whistling through. I told him I think he's got a hole in the head from those fumes."

"He's getting the pumps fixed in the spring," Grace said.

"Now, there you go. You're a regular Sabbath Lander. Sam's wife, Jeannie, is convinced those fumes have gone to Sam's head. She hasn't opened a window on that house in twenty years 'cause of that stink," Bill said, glancing at the door. "Well, look who's here. If it isn't Lucas Keegan. Recovered from New Year's, I see. Care to finish that Black Velvet?"

"You won't let me live that down, will you, Bill? Hello, Grace," Luke said, ignoring Bill now. "Good to see you again."

If Melanie could have fallen off her bar stool at that point, she would have. She tugged on Grace's sweater so hard that Grace nearly tipped over herself. Grace threw her head back and laughed.

"Luke! Hello again. I want you to meet my sister, Melanie. Melanie, Luke and I met in the diner the other morning. He gave me a lesson in ice-fishing."

"Did you get to those islands, yet? I dare say you didn't, what with that snow last night. And that snow was just a tease. Come the end of

February we're knee deep up here and digging out until April. Have you been here before, Melanie? Beautiful country, isn't it?"

"Never. It really is wonderful. We were going to drive up the mountain today, but we don't have four-wheel drive. But we walked by the lake. It's kind of nice to be out and see people," Melanie said. "It's so peaceful here. Not too crowded."

Luke laughed. "Well, right now it's quiet, all right. But come the tourist season, after Memorial Day, you can barely walk on the street. It's packed. This place is like two different towns depending on the season. We look at winter as our rest period. Gives us a chance to recuperate and bear up for summer."

The jukebox started playing. "Summer Wind." Helen and her man got up to dance.

"They've been married since they're sixteen," Luke said, tilting his chin in their direction. "Forty years. No kids. They live up between here and Minerva's Shelf. Look at them. They take ballroom down in Fort Hope. Wait till George dips her. She's like a will-o'-the-wisp when she dances with him. They come here just about every night."

"Grace is a dancer," Melanie said.

"No kidding?" Luke said, turning to Grace. "Where do you dance?"

"I teach at a school for children with disabilities," Grace said. "I was never really good enough to perform. But I do love it. What does your wife do? Will she be here later, too?"

"My wife passed on eight years ago Thanksgiving time," Luke said.

"I'm so sorry," Grace said, embarrassed. "I thought you said she worked summers at The Alpine."

"I probably did. I have this nasty habit of speaking about her in the present tense," Luke said. "No, she worked there years ago. Our son, Chris—he's twenty-two now—he worked there at the waterfront after Meg died. Cancer. He's off in New York City now. Got himself a scholarship to Columbia University. I just hope he comes back here. Wanted a taste of the big city, you know? I've lived here all my life. Most folks who leave here end up coming back. Once you get this place under your skin, it's hard to let go, so I'm hoping. How about you, Melanie? Any kids? You said you have a daughter, right, Grace?"

Melanie told Luke about the boys, took their picture from her wallet. Double trouble, Luke said. Grace showed Luke a picture of Kate dressed in her prom gown, amazed that he remembered she'd mentioned her at the diner that morning.

"She's a beauty," he said. "What's her name?"

"Kate," Grace said. "She looks like her father."

"Kate. Katherine, right? Well, I don't know what her father looks like," Luke said. "To me, she looks like you. So, listen, what's your fascination with our islands?"

Grace turned to Melanie. "Why don't you explain? You're better at these things than I am."

"Our parents died recently," Melanie said diplomatically, leaving out the details. "They left Grace the house they owned on one of the islands. But we've never seen it. Actually, we never even knew about it until last week when the lawyer told us."

"Hold on, now. Your folks had a house up here and you've never seen it? They buy it recently or what? For retirement?"

"Oh, no. They bought back in 1950. I think maybe they rented it out or something. It's a little odd, we know," Melanie said.

"Well, not really. I mean, some folks bought property up here for investment. Real estate here keeps getting more and more valuable. And people don't always talk about their investments, not even to family. If you don't mind my asking, how come they just left it to you, Grace? Just shut me up if I'm getting too personal."

"No, no. Not at all. That's probably one of the questions of the century. But, in all fairness, they left other things to Melanie and to the rest of our family. I guess they had their reasons. I'll know more when I see it," Grace said.

"Maybe it has a dance floor." Luke grinned.

"Maybe," Grace said, smiling. "Does this town have an ice cream parlor?"

"Kind of cold out for ice cream, don't you think?"

Grace laughed. "Yes. I was just curious."

"There's a Baskin-Robbins down the street that opens in the spring. Pretty fancy. Even has one of those coffee bars in it. When I was a kid, there was a Dairy Queen, but when Baskin-Robbins came in, they went out of business. Couldn't compete with all those fancy flavors. I still miss that Dairy Queen. Best shake in town."

Grace held her breath. "Where was the Dairy Queen?" she asked.

"Next to the Sunoco up by The Alpine. You okay? You look a little pale."

"I'm fine. Too much wine maybe."

"Hey, Billy! The lady is suffering from that cheap wine you guys buy. How about getting her a seltzer with a squeeze of lemon and sugar? Works like a charm every time, Grace. So, tell me now, which island is yours?"

"Canterbury Island."

Luke had turned around to pull a pack of cigarettes from the pocket of his shirt when his hand froze in midair. He looked Grace in the eyes, his lips parted slightly.

"You don't say? Well, that's a fine one," he said, continuing the movement with his hand. "One of the higher altitudes. Know that one well. Fished those shores many times. Quite close to The Alpine, really. Maybe about five and a half miles north. Listen, tomorrow I have a group that's booked me for a day of ice-fishing, but what do you say we all meet here tomorrow night, say around eight, and make plans to head out to Canterbury day after tomorrow? I'll pull you ladies out with my snowmobile. Hook the old toboggan on the back and set you two right on it. It would be my pleasure."

"Is that safe?" Grace asked. "I thought you said the lake was treacherous."

"Well, I'm an expert," Luke said confidently. "And I think this situation qualifies as an emergency, don't you?"

"Well, I don't know," Grace said. "We'll see. I don't want to go if it's dangerous. To tell you the truth, I'm afraid of the water."

"It's not water. It's frozen solid."

"I guess I'm better off doing this before the thaw, then, aren't I? Well, we were thinking about going to the library tomorrow and reading up on the town. You know, get to know something about this legacy of mine."

"Well, I think if an expert wants to haul us out, then I'm game," Melanie said. "We will definitely be here tomorrow. Same time. Same place."

"I have to give it some thought, " Grace said. "I'm not as impetuous as my sister."

"Oh, no. She's not impetuous. She just drove here in the middle of the night. Alone. On New Year's Eve."

"Well, whatever you two decide. I'm willing and able," Luke said. "Nice to see you again, Grace. Good to meet you, Melanie."

Melanie turned to Grace as they got into the car.

"Did you see the way he looked at you?" Melanie teased. "I'm jealous. He was practically looking through you. Gorgeous eyes."

"Oh, for goodness' sake, Mel. I'm married," Grace said.

"You're married, Grace, but you're not dead," Melanie said.

"Don't you think that's weird about the Dairy Queen being next to the gas station?"

"No," Melanie said drawing the word into several syllables. "I think most small towns had Dairy Queens at one point. Especially beach towns. I bet if you'd asked about an old hot dog stand you would have found out there was one of those, too. You're reading too much into your dreams."

"But that wasn't a dream. It was definitely a memory."

"You're forty-four years old. Childhood memories get contaminated with age, you know. There are a million towns in this country that had Dairy Queens. I bet that Purchase even had one when we were kids. And I bet it had a fume-ridden gas station, too. What are you saying, Grace? That we've been here before? That's ridiculous. We would know if we'd been here before. Jemma would know, for sure. She would have said something."

Grace sighed. "Maybe you're right. Sometimes I think I am going crazy. Dreaming about lakes and Dairy Queens. Running off on a toboggan with a stranger."

"I kind of like the toboggan part," Melanie said.

Luke watched Grace's car pull out onto Diamond Drive through the picture window. He turned to Bill, pushed his glass forward. "One more for the road, Bill," he said.

"Nice buggy they're driving, eh? Say, Luke. Did I hear them say Canterbury Island? That place has been shut down forever. Trout was the caretaker there for years, right? His kid watches it now, doesn't he?"

"Yup. That's the one," Luke said.

"What's it, for sale or something? What'd they say their names were again? Melanie and who?" Bill asked. "I think the redhead had eyes for you, Keegan."

"Melanie and Grace," Luke said.

Grace Hammond, he thought to himself.

Chapter Thirteen

When Kate called the next morning at ten o'clock, Grace and Melanie were still sleeping. Grace picked up the phone, knocking it against the corner of the table so it clattered. Her voice creaked out hello.

"Mom? I can't believe I woke you!" Kate said. "I just wanted to talk to you before we went out on the slopes. Dad gave me the number. Where *are* you?"

"Hi, sweetheart. Sorry. I tried you a couple of times, but once you were in the shower and I guess the other times you were skiing. How is it out there? Are you having fun?"

"It's great, Mom. Pure powder. Alison and I are having a blast. Mom, where *are* you? Daddy said you would explain."

How typical of Adam, Grace thought. I said, "Let me tell her," but of course I never said not to give her the number. Just a little touch of Barnett drama.

"I'm in a town called Sabbath Landing. Upstate New York in the Adirondacks. I'm with Aunt Mel. We're staying at a place called The Alpine. It's a beautiful old hotel, Kate. We have a view of mountains and the lake. Diamond Lake. It's a little cold but gorgeous."

"But why are you there?"

"Well, right after you and Dad left, Thompson met with Mel and Jemma and me about my parents' wills," Grace said, filling Kate in on the details. "And me, well, they left me a house up here. So, Aunt Mel and I came up to check it out."

"A house? That's wild, Mom. Is it nice?"

"Well, the lake is frozen so it remains to be seen whether or not we get out there."

"I don't understand. What difference does it make if the lake is frozen?"

"The house is in the middle of the lake. Diamond Lake. It's on its own island. Canterbury Island."

"Canterbury Island? That's so cool. It sounds so romantic. How come you never told me about it?"

"Well, I never knew until Thompson told me."

"This is too weird. An island. But you can't get out there if the lake is frozen. I suppose you could always ice-skate, right, Mom?"

"We'd have to take a snowmobile, I'm told."

"A snowmobile? Mom! Those things are wild. You can't drive a snowmobile."

"No, no. But there are people up here who will take you out on them and maybe we'll do that. Probably not, though, so don't worry," Grace said, thinking that lately she was fibbing all too much. "But at least we're getting a feel for the town. And a rest."

"I don't get it," Kate said. "Sounds like they left you a Trojan horse."

"It does, doesn't it?" Grace said thoughtfully. "I never looked at it quite that way."

"Mom? Maybe you should just wait for the spring to see this house. I'll go with you."

"Now, that's a good idea," Grace said.

"No, I mean it, Mom. Why can't we go up in the spring? The three of us?"

"Okay, sweetheart. That sounds good. Now, look, take care. I love you."

"I love you, too. *You* take care. Kiss Aunt Mel. I miss you."

"I miss you, too."

Grace and Melanie ate breakfast in the diner, biding their time before the library opened. The fishermen were already out on the lake.

The diner was empty except for a few people who straggled in and out, sitting at the counter for a cup of coffee, reading the local *Gazette*. The front-page headline told of a fire that tore through a Minerva's Shelf boathouse on New Year's Eve, destroying a vintage Cruiser. Helen was off that morning. Her replacement said she was helping to clean up the mess from the fire. Each time the wind chimes on the door jingled, Grace looked up. And each time it wasn't Luke who entered, Grace was disappointed.

"He's probably out on the lake," Melanie said quietly.

"Who?"

"Oh, come on, Grace. It's me you're talking to," Melanie said. "You keep checking out the door."

"I know. I'm being so ridiculous, though. It's just that, well, he was so nice to talk to," Grace said. "Do you still want to go to the library? Everything else is closed unless we want to browse the bait shop."

"Ugh. Let's go." Melanie gulped down the rest of her coffee. "Let's do a little research about your new hometown."

"Very funny," said Grace. "Maybe we can walk there. It'll do us good to move."

A small antique shop strung with white icicle lights was open on the corner. A wagon wheel leaned against the side of the shop; a Patty Play Pal doll stood in the doorway, bundled in a snow jacket, holding a pair of antique child's skis. A Victorian dollhouse sat in the window.

"Wow, something's actually open. I'm cold and I love these musty old shops. Let's look around," Melanie said, pressing her face against the window.

They spent an hour inside the shop. The proprietor sat behind the glass-enclosed counter. He was smoking a pipe filled with Borkum Riff; the bag of tobacco lay on the counter beside a large leather-trimmed ashtray. He nodded when Grace and Melanie came in but went back to reading a book, clearly used to people just browsing. There was a tray filled with costume jewelry, purple and blue beads in twisted strands, malachite earrings, chunky bracelets encrusted with different color stones.

"I love this junk," Grace laughed. "Adam will probably short-circuit if I bring more of this home."

Melanie sat on a small milking bench sifting through a crate of antique cameras. "I have to get one of these for Mike," she said, holding up an old Leica. "He collects these old things. Look at the shutter on this one."

Grace was holding a strand of shiny crystal beads in front of her sweater. "These are great, aren't they? They look like flapper beads."

By the time they got to the library, it had been open for nearly an hour. A small white clapboard house standing at the edge of Diamond Drive, the library was nearly a mile from the diner. A few steps up led to a small front porch. Two green wicker rockers sat on either side of a pot of silk geraniums. A tall metal canister filled with damp sand stood by the door, a modern red-and-white decal for no smoking pasted on its side. A cigarette lay on top of the sand, still smoldering. A sign on the door said The Free Library was open daily from noon until six except on Sundays when the library was closed. A bronze plaque on the side of the building said the town's library was started by Hester and Isaac Wright in 1857, dedicated to the values instilled by books, reading, and writing.

"Look at this place," Grace said, reading the plaque over the door. "Maybe Hester Wright is the one in Hester's Peak. This place is so full of history."

"It better be full of heat," Melanie said tugging on Grace's arm. "Let's go inside. I'm freezing. So disgusting that someone would leave that stinky cigarette in the ashtray."

The librarian was standing on a step stool, placing books back on shelves in the children's room when Grace and Melanie came in the door.

"Be right with you," she whispered. "Oops, so used to whispering and no one's even in here."

Grace and Melanie waited while the woman placed the last book back on the shelf. She stepped down from the step stool, dusted her hands off on the red apron tied over her brown corduroy skirt. Put the half glasses that were dangling around her neck back onto her nose.

"Now, how can I help you?" she asked in a louder voice.

"We're visiting the town and wanted to look at some of the local history books," Melanie said. "Maybe some old news clippings, things like that."

The librarian pointed them to a small corner with the sign REFER-ENCE hanging over a bookcase. "We have books that date back to 1850," she said proudly. "You can't take them out, though. But you can sit here and read them. And, of course, we have a drawer of microfilm that *The Gazette* put in order for us. Dates back to the 1920s. Enjoy yourselves, ladies. I'm Margaret Buckley. Call me if you need any help."

There were six straight-back chairs, three on either side, at a worn mahogany table in the center of the room. Grace chose a book of newspaper clippings dating from 1850 through 1930. The clippings were not originals but copies pasted in chronological order. On the cover of the book was a picture of a small redbrick house, a white picket fence around it, a horse and carriage waiting outside.

"Look at this," Grace whispered. "It's the gas station we went to. Back when it was a blacksmith's, I bet."

"The gas station is white, though," Melanie said.

"Painted, silly."

There were old photographs of the trolley that ran through the town, clippings of births and marriages and deaths. News stories about rowboat accidents, drownings, horses running wild, local politicians (one of the town officials, a close friend of Lincoln's, discussed the as-sassination in an interview), and town scandals (a young woman of sixteen, the third wife of a wealthy older town resident was found dead in the barn by her own hand—it was the third time the man had been widowed). A small article discussing the many islands on Diamond Lake stated that legend had it that there were 365 islands except on the leap year when another mysteriously appeared for a day and then sank back again into the lake.

"Let's get to the 1950s," Grace whispered. "What about the microfilm?"

The drawers for the microfilm were labeled accordingly, by month and year. January 1931 through June 1931, July 1931 through December 1931, and so forth.

"The deed says that Mother and Dad bought the island in April 1950. That would be here," Grace said, trailing her finger along the drawers. "Here we go. January 1950 through June 1950."

Melanie wound the spool under the bulky machine, threaded the film in and around with expertise.

"How do you know how to do that?" Grace asked.

"I taught high school, remember?" Melanie smiled. "My other life. I wasn't always opening cans of SpaghettiOs. I've sunk from *Beowulf* to *Barney*." She turned the dial until the film scrolled to the month of April. "Grace! Look at this. In the real estate section: Lamb's Island sold to Mr. and Mrs. Alexander Hammond on April eighteenth, 1950, for the sum of fifteen thousand dollars by Edwin Lamb. Taxes to be assessed."

"Lamb's Island?"

"They must have changed the name after they bought it," Melanie said. "You know, like those people near us who bought that farm called Stonybrook. The Stone family had owned it for years, but when the Green family bought it they changed the name to Greenacres Farm. I'm sure that was it."

"So why not Hammond Island?"

"Who knows?" Melanie said. "Maybe just for the sake of privacy. You know them. Let's keep looking."

Grace stacked up the small white boxes of microfilm on the table beside Melanie. "I'm going to get more," she said.

"Pull July 1956 when you were born and see if there's anything. I mean, they were homeowners here. People always list that kind of stuff," Melanie said in a loud whisper.

Melanie popped the reel into the machine and scrolled. "Look, Grace. Here you are. A daughter, Grace Ann Hammond, was born to

Alexander and Jane Hammond at—what? Saint Mary's Hospital in Sabbath Landing, New York, on July twenty-eighth, 1956? What? Grace, you were born in Sabbath Landing?"

"What? Oh, my God." Grace had been standing over Melanie's shoulder, peering down at the screen. She sat in the chair next to her sister. "Oh, my God."

"Did you ever see your birth certificate?"

"No, Mother and Dad said they lost it. I almost ordered a copy after I married Adam because I wanted to change my name legally to Hammond and not use Barnett, but Adam was so opposed that I never bothered. I've always used my passport for identification. Dad got me one when I was around ten. I remember going with him to the post office and to this place where I had my picture taken. He signed for me. Any time I ever needed to show proof of anything, I just used my passport and my driver's license. Dad had to have a birth certificate to get me my passport, though. Mel, this is so creepy."

"Maybe they were summering up here when Mother went into labor. That would make sense."

"Yes, but why not tell me? I feel so strange. I feel like I don't know myself all of a sudden. They told me I was born in Manhattan at Physicians' Fifth Avenue Hospital where you were born. I always just assumed we lived in Manhattan and moved to the suburbs just like everyone else. Why would they lie to me?"

"Go get some more film, Grace. Bring me some more," Melanie said.

"Why would they lie about where I was born?" Grace asked again, setting down another stack of film she held in her shaking hands. "Here. I went through until 1960. There's a gap from July 1959 through December 1959 and January 1960 through June 1960. The boxes are missing. You can see in the drawer where the film boxes would have been. Someone must have taken them out. Answer me. Why would they lie about where I was born?"

"Why? Who knows?" Melanie said, a rubber band held between her teeth that she had taken off one of the tapes. "Maybe they were afraid

you'd want to go to your birthplace and they didn't feel like making the trip. Who the hell knows? I tell you though, this whole thing
is beginning to make me angry. Too many lies. Too much goddamn
secrecy."

"You know what this means, don't you, Melanie? I've probably been
to that house before. Maybe I was just an infant but still . . . I must have
been there. Maybe I even went home to that house when I was born. I
don't understand, though. Why would they keep that from me?"

Melanie just looked at her sister. "I don't know. I wish I could come
up with a better answer. But I just don't know. And I don't understand.
Anything."

Margaret was walking past them when Grace stopped her. "Margaret? You know a whole year of microfilm is missing from the drawer,"
Grace said. "Has someone checked them out?"

"Well, that is just so irresponsible," Margaret said. "Let me have a
look." She opened the drawer and searched where Grace had already
looked. "I'll be darned. No one checked them out. You can't check
these out. These are not supposed to be removed from the library. Oh,
well—things always turn up around here. What exactly are you looking for, anyway?"

"Information about Canterbury Island," Grace said.

"I wish I could help you, " Margaret said. "I'm not familiar with all
those islands. Not too many books about the private ones. Is Canterbury private or state-owned? I'll look for that microfilm. There were
only a few folks in today besides you two, and one of them was looking
through microfilm. Maybe he just put the boxes back in the wrong
drawer."

"Maybe we should search around," Melanie said. "We don't mind."

"Well, I'd prefer to have a look myself," Margaret said. "I'm sure I'll
come across a lot of misfiled things. It'll give me an opportunity to
clean the place up a bit, too. Why don't you come back tomorrow? I'm
sure I'll turn them up by then."

Chapter Fourteen

It felt like more than a mile's walk back to the car from the library. The glimmer of sunlight that peeked through the library windows a few hours before was hidden now behind thick layers of clouds that had rolled in over Hester's Peak, casting a caliginous pallor over the lake. A brisk wind stung their faces as Grace and Melanie walked up Diamond Drive. The antique shop had flipped the welcoming sign on its door to CLOSED. SEE YOU AGAIN, it said. Patty Play Pal and the wagon wheel were safely inside. The shop was dark.

The Mercedes was boxed in next to a double-parked Blazer with a snowplow on the front, the engine running, a man sitting inside drinking a cup of steaming coffee from a blue-and-gold paper cup. The window of his car was slightly open. He nodded as Grace put the key in her car door.

"I'll move," he said. "I'm just warming up with some coffee. Going to be a storm tonight. Nor'easter blowing in from Canada. Been keeping track on the radio. Could be a long night for the plow."

"Take your time. I hope it's not too bad tonight," Grace said.

"More snow the better in my business. Course, if you're lucky, it'll turn a bit and head more inland. If I'm lucky, we'll see at least eight to ten by morning. Not too bad, really. Have a nice evening, ladies."

The windows of the Mercedes were coated with a thin layer of ice. Grace ran the defroster and the wipers. She and Melanie watched the wipers scrape back and forth over the windshield. They didn't speak.

Grace put on the radio. They listened to the weather report the man had just told her.

"Weather's a big topic up here, I bet. That and bait and guns and hunting season. Luke said he guides the woods in winter," Grace said, realizing she liked the sound of his name. "Do you suppose he hunts? Is that what he means by 'guiding' the woods?"

Melanie laughed, "I would place bets that he's not leading Boy Scouts. I'm sure he hunts."

"It bothers me that he'd go out and shoot something," Grace said. "It seems so barbaric."

"Well, I suppose if you eat what you shoot, it's somehow justified," Melanie said. "You know, every time you eat a hamburger . . . "

"I know, don't remind me," Grace said, waving her hand. "I should call Adam when I get back to the room."

"What reminded you of Adam? Shooting? Or the fact that you're thinking about Luke Keegan?"

Grace gave her sister a mock dirty look. "Hamburger. Hamburger reminds me of Adam. Hamburger clogging my arteries."

Just as she expected, the answering machine picked up when Grace placed the call to Aspen. "I suppose you two are still out on the slopes," Grace said. "I just wanted to let you know that Mel and I are fine. Resting. Relaxing. Enjoying each other's company. We'll be out to dinner tonight. My cell phone doesn't always work here because of the mountains. I'll call you later. Love you both."

"Grace, my cell phone works here just fine," Melanie said as Grace hung up the phone.

"I know. So does mine," Grace confessed. "I just didn't want Adam calling when we're at The Birch tonight. And I didn't want him to get a no answer."

It took Grace nearly an hour to dress for the evening.

"I'm so sick of everything I own," Grace said, amused, tossing another shirt onto what was now a pile of clothing on the chair. "You'd think I was going on a date or something."

"Well?"

"Don't be ridiculous," Grace said.

"So, what's all the fuss about, then? We're only going to a bar."

"You're a pesty roommate," Grace teased. "You're worse than that Laurie my freshman year."

She ended up wearing blue jeans and a black turtleneck, a pair of black boots with a heel.

"You won't be able to walk in the snow with those boots," Melanie said. "You'll slip."

"We'll park right in front. I can't dance in the rubber-soled hiking boots," Grace said with a smile.

"Dance? Oh, I see. Were you going to dance with me?" Melanie teased.

"Maybe," Grace called as she walked into the bathroom. She was applying mascara to her lashes, her eyes wide open, head back, her mouth forming a slight O when Melanie came in.

"It's nice to see you looking so happy," Melanie said, sitting on the vanity chair beside her. "You're . . . what's the expression? Filled with anticipation."

Grace stopped applying the mascara. The wand was poised upward in her hand. "I like him, Mel. Something about him makes me feel very safe. Which, of course, is ridiculous since I really don't know a thing about him. I feel this—now this will really sound adolescent—this connection."

Melanie stood up from the vanity chair and stretched. "Go for it. But I need a reality check. I've got to go call Mr. Mom." Melanie looked at her watch. "Bath time should be over. Mrs. Hadley's probably home by now."

Grace heard Melanie laughing on the phone with Mike. "Well, you should know the difference between the space pajamas and the airplane pajamas. That's right, you have to read the book twice. Once for each of them. Welcome to my world, honey. You'll lose brain cells by the minute. Now, if you don't mind, Grace and I are going to paint the town red. I love you, Mike."

"I don't think I've laughed with Adam in years," Grace said when Melanie hung up the phone. "I want to laugh with someone again. I want to talk and laugh and make love and take long walks. Do you think I'm asking too much?"

"Grace," Melanie said, shaking her head. "You are hardly asking for anything at all. Come on. It's after eight. The Birch should be hopping."

Trout was sitting in his usual seat at the bar when Melanie and Grace walked in. He nodded to them, then turned his head up to the television mounted on the wall. A younger couple was sitting on the far end, deep in discussion, facing one another, hands held on the man's knee. Grace was disappointed. She was certain Luke would have been there. But Melanie, a few steps ahead of Grace, stopped suddenly.

"Hi! Well, you seem deep in thought," Melanie said, tapping Luke lightly on his shoulder. He was at the bar, his head bent down as he swirled the ice in his drink.

Luke turned, almost jumped. His face broke into a smile. He was dressed differently this time. His hair was clean and combed, slicked back off his forehead, curled just over his collar. His skin had a ruddy glow to it. He'd been ice-fishing that day. The wind and few hours of sun showed around his eyes and cheekbones. He wore the usual black denim jeans but this time with a black button-down shirt, open at the neck, revealing a small silver owl on a thin chain. He stood up from his seat and smiled. "So good to see you both again," he said. "I was hoping you'd be here." But when he spoke, he was unmistakably looking at Grace.

Grace inhaled a small breath through her nose, tilted her chin slightly upward. "It's good to see you, too, Luke," she said.

"Hey, Bill," Luke called. "Two red wines, please." He turned to Grace and Melanie. "Red wine, right?"

"Perfect, thanks. I hear we're getting a big storm later tonight,"

Grace said. "I guess that pretty much eliminates any chance of getting to the island tomorrow."

"Pretty much," Luke said. "But there's always a chance the storm won't hit. And there's always the next day. How long are you staying?"

"My husband and Kate will be back in the city on Sunday evening. I have to be home by Sunday afternoon," Grace said.

"Well, let's see. Today's Thursday. That gives us a little time. How about you, Melanie?"

"I said I'd be back by tomorrow evening," Melanie said. "Mike's been an awfully good sport. I couldn't possibly stay the weekend."

"Oh, Mel. You have to stay," Grace said. "You *have* to. We might not get out to the island until Saturday."

"So, I guess this means you've decided to brave the ice." Luke smiled. "Well, barring a second storm, I promise I'll get you two out there by Saturday. Did you ever get to the library? Did you meet Margaret? Her husband, Gus, he owns the nursery behind the library, says she's got the house catalogued. Says she files his socks by color."

Grace laughed. "She's very organized. Although we were going through *The Gazette*'s microfilm and a year was missing from the drawer. She wasn't too happy about that. Maybe tomorrow we'll go back and see if she found it. She said it was probably just misfiled."

A song came on the jukebox. "Unchained Melody."

"Grace, want to teach me to dance?" Luke asked.

"Oh, no, I really shouldn't," Grace said.

"Why not? You afraid I'll step on your toes?" Luke said. "Look, I can take my boots off." He started to unlace one of his work boots.

"Go ahead, Grace," Melanie said.

"No, no, no. Leave your boots on," Grace urged, placing her hand on Luke's shoulder. "I've had my toes stepped on before. Not with boots like those, of course."

"Okay, but you lead."

Melanie watched her sister walk onto the dance floor with Luke Keegan. She smiled as Grace tossed her head back and laughed at something Luke whispered in her ear before he ceremoniously placed his hand on her waist and bowed. She watched her sister's body relax and lean in closer as they danced. They stood still in position a few moments after the song ended. Luke placed his hand on the small of Grace's back for a brief moment and led her back to the bar.

"Well, he was a faker," Grace said. "He's a wonderful dancer. A natural."

"I haven't danced since Meg died," Luke said. "She'd always beg me to dance and I'd balk."

"Luke, did Grace tell you that we found out she was born in Sabbath Landing? We looked it up on the microfilm, and she was born at Saint Mary's Hospital. Can you believe that? She's a native," Melanie said, purposely changing the subject.

"You don't say?" Luke said. "Well, I guess at some point your folks sure spent some time here. When's your birthday, Grace?"

"July. So we figure maybe they were summering here when I came along. You'd think they would have stayed put in Manhattan and not taken a chance that Mother could go into labor on an island, though. Especially with your first. I think I barely moved from the phone the last month of my pregnancy," Grace said. "I must have been to that house before. I don't remember, though. But I must have been there."

"This place draws you to it. I suppose they figured they'd just take their chances," Luke said. "Labor or no labor. First child or not."

"Except they always told me I was born in Manhattan. It's a little creepy. How far is Saint Mary's from here, anyway?"

"Just before you come up Diamond Drive from Fort Hope, there's a left turn inland. About five miles up the hill is Saint Mary's. I've spent far too much time there. With Meg. Of course, Chris was born there, as well, so that was a good time. What else did you find out?"

"Well, that the island used to be called Lamb's Island. They bought it from an Edwin Lamb," Grace said.

"Edwin Lamb owned several motels down in Fort Hope, as well," Luke said. "He passed on about two years ago. His wife sold the Fort Hope properties and moved down to Hollywood Beach. She'd been saying for years how she wanted to move to Florida. Said the winters here were getting too cold for her."

"Well, I can't wait to see the house," Grace said. "I think I feel more trusting of your snowmobiling expertise since I've seen what a good dancer you are."

"Well, then you'll have to dance with me one more time just to make sure," Luke said, winking at Melanie.

"I have to powder the proverbial nose," Melanie laughed.

"Am I being too forward?" Luke said as Melanie walked away. "I know you're married, Grace. I hope I'm not making you uncomfortable. I'm just enjoying your company."

"No, it's fine," Grace said. "I feel very comfortable. I feel like I've known you longer than a few days."

"Well, I'm pleased to hear that. Sometimes you just meet someone and you feel like you've known them a lifetime," Luke said, looking at her intently. "Listen, I need to ask you something and, again, if I'm getting too personal, just tell me to shut up. Sometimes I talk too much. But why isn't your family here with you?"

"We had plans to go to Aspen. In Colorado. We own a home there. My husband loves it. It's his heaven on earth. But this year, after Mother and Dad died, I really didn't feel like going. I'm not crazy about Aspen, anyway. It's very, well, social. A little too glitzy for me. Besides, this year I just needed to stay back home with Mel and Jemma. Of course, I'm here and Jemma is by herself."

"Jemma?"

"Jemma is, was—I don't know how to put it—our parents' housekeeper. But she was the one who really brought us up. Our mother wasn't well. She was weak her whole life and Dad was working. The usual. He was a lawyer. Anyway, when I found out that my parents left me the house, I decided to come here instead."

"When did your parents die? Amazing isn't it how older people so often die within months of each other?" Luke said.

"They died on Sunday, December twenty-third. At least that's the date we posted," Grace said.

"I don't understand," Luke said.

"They died on the same day. Last month. They committed suicide," Grace said, swallowing audibly. "Jemma found them. She'd come in to check on them."

Luke felt his heart pounding in his chest. He turned his head from Grace and took a long sip of his Black Velvet. "I don't know what to say, Grace. What an awful thing for you. And Melanie. How did they do it? Why?"

"Pills. It was peaceful. Thank God. That's my only consolation. Painless. The doctor told me it was as if they simply went to sleep. But the thing that bothers me is that in order to do something like that, to take your own life, you have to be in such pain. Such deep spiritual pain. And I can't understand why none of us saw it. The last few months, my father was suffering from what we think was the beginning of Alzheimer's or some sort of senility. My mother depended on him so greatly. I think maybe that's why they did what they did. Maybe she couldn't go on without him and she saw him slipping away and they both just decided to end it before everything got worse. Now look who's talking too much, " Grace said.

Luke took in a breath. He was looking into Grace's eyes. "You poor baby," he said, wondering how her husband could leave her behind at a time like this.

"No, I was quite insistent that Adam and Kate go," Grace said defensively. "Really, I just wanted, needed, to be by myself."

Melanie came back from the ladies' room and sat down next to Grace, placed her arm over her shoulder. "You look awfully down at the mouth," she said. "What's going on?"

"She told me about your parents," Luke said. "How they died. I'm so sorry. I ask too many questions and I guess I opened up the dam. I should learn to keep my mouth shut."

"People are bound to find out sooner or later," Melanie said. "It's something we're going to have to deal with. We'll either have to tell the truth or lie. I guess depending on whom we're talking to, we'll decide."

Helen and George were on the dance floor now. The young couple who had been talking so intently were dancing, as well. Luke turned to Melanie. "Okay, you're my next victim." He smiled, pulling Melanie onto the dance floor. "I'm feeling like a regular Gene Kelly tonight."

It was nearly midnight when Grace said they should get going.

"One last dance," Luke said to Grace.

Melanie watched again as Luke held Grace to him. This time he held her hand low by his hip while his other encircled her waist. She's not dancing like a dancer this time, Melanie thought.

Luke still had his hand on the small of Grace's back as they walked over to Melanie. "I tell you what," Luke said. "If the storm blows in, I'll let you two sleep in. But if it stays north, I'll call your place at six and we'll head out to the island. What's the room number?"

"Suite 318," Melanie said without a hesitation.

Luke walked them outside. The air was still and cold. He opened the passenger door for Melanie and closed it once she was settled inside the car. He walked Grace around to the driver's side, placed his hand on her arm as she reached for the door handle.

"Thanks for the dances," he said, kissing her cheek. "You're waking up my heart again. Good night, Grace. Sweet dreams."

Grace turned to Melanie as she drove away from The Birch. "Why do you suppose he's going out of his way for us?" she asked. "Maybe it's not such a great idea to go out to an island with him. I mean, we hardly know him."

"Oh, now the paranoia sets in," Melanie groaned. "Everyone in town knows him, but he's going to take us to an island and hold us captive along with the other unfortunates who fell into his lair. Grace, for God's sake. He likes you. Don't you get it? He's taken with you."

"I'm married."

"Look, I give off a married vibe. You don't, okay?"

"I don't feel the married vibe."

"Well, apparently neither does Luke Keegan. You only go around once, Grace. What did he say to you outside the car?"

"He said I was waking up his heart again. But I'm very confused. Part of me feels all excited and part of me feels guilty and underhanded and deceitful."

"I'd go with the excited for now."

"Since when did you get to be such an hedonist?"

"I'm living vicariously," Melanie laughed.

"Oh, great. Glad I can be your fantasy. Pray that it doesn't snow, Mel. I would love to see that island in the morning. I like him so much. What is happening to me?"

Melanie laughed. "I don't know, but I know it's good. This is definitely good."

"I'm a little afraid to go to that house," Grace said, pulling the car up to The Alpine.

"I'll be with you, Grace," Melanie said. "Together we're invincible."

"It's in the middle of the lake, though."

"Remember what Luke said, Grace. It's solid ice now."

Chapter Fifteen

It wasn't six o'clock when the phone rang the next morning.

"Good morning," Luke said brightly. "I didn't wake you, did I?"

"Guilty," Grace laughed weakly. "It's okay. The alarm is set to go off in about ten minutes. You sound wide awake, though."

"I've been up for hours. Listening to weather reports. Storm's on delay. Stuck around Ottawa. Say I pick you two up in an hour?"

"We're going?"

"We're going. Got the snowmobile gassed up and a couple of blankets on the toboggan. We can grab some coffee at the diner before we head out. You okay with this, Grace?"

She hesitated a moment before answering, "I think so. The lake is frozen? No thaw?"

"Solid blue ice. Couldn't ask for more."

"Okay," Grace said. "We'll be in the lobby at seven."

"Dress really warm, okay? Remember. Layers. Lots of layers. It's cold out on the lake with the wind blowing. Remember that hat."

Melanie had gotten up. She was standing at the window, parting the curtains. She turned around as Grace hung up the phone. "No storm yet, huh?" she said. "I guess we're going."

"I'm nervous," Grace said.

"Don't be. The lake is frozen. I'm sure he runs those snowmobiles all the time."

"That's not what's making me nervous. I have this funny feeling. I can't explain it."

Melanie stretched her arms over her head and yawned. "Go take a shower," she said. "It's going to be fine. You're letting your imagination run wild. I'm going to call Mike. I'm sure the boys are up."

Luke pulled up to the lobby in a black Chevy pickup truck promptly at seven. He stepped out when he saw them, opened the door for them.

"Watch your step." He grinned. "It's a lot higher up than that Mercedes."

"It's warm in here," Grace said, sitting next to Luke, loosening the scarf from her neck.

"Warmed her up for a half hour this morning. She was frozen solid. One of these days I'll clean all the crap out of my garage so I can put the truck in at night. Listen, how do you feel about coffee at my place? The snowmobile's right at the slip behind my house and my place is closer to the island. It'll save us some time."

"Sounds fine," Melanie said. "How's your coffee?"

"Oh, easily confused with Starbucks," Luke said, deadpan.

Grace was quiet on the drive to Luke's house. Melanie and Luke chatted past her. Grace's back was almost stiff as she leaned back, letting her sister take up the conversation. Melanie told Luke how tired Mike had sounded when she called earlier that morning. How the boys were already clamoring, jumping on top of Mike as he lay in his bed. How the best words she'd ever heard were, "I don't know how you do this all day long, Mel."

"You okay, Grace?" Luke asked at one point. "Still sleeping? We're almost there. I live just a ways up this mountain. My place is about halfway between Sabbath Landing and Minerva's Shelf. I'm really more of a post office box than a town."

Luke turned right down a muddy dirt road. "This leads to my place. I'm right on the water."

The house was a graying clapboard Cape. Two stories with a front porch. Window boxes were falling apart, filled with snow and split from the weight of the ice. A rowboat, covered with a tarpaulin, sat on cinder blocks in the side yard. A wicker swing, suffering from a bad case of chipped paint, hung from the porch ceiling, down on one side where a hook had pulled out.

"It looked a darn sight better when Meg was alive," Luke said apologetically. "I really let it go. It lacks a woman's touch, doesn't it? Meg used to plant those window boxes with pansies every spring."

Luke led them around to the back of the house. The snowmobile sat on a small deck at the frozen lakefront. He pointed to a mass of land about two or three miles in the distance.

"That's Canterbury Island right there," he said. "It's one of the larger islands. It won't take us but fifteen minutes to get out there. My boat's docked here in season, but it's down at Clark's Marina now." Luke placed his hand on a group of small bushes near the deck. "These here are called rose of Sharon. In the spring, they've got pink and white blooms. Kind of look like hibiscus. You should see it here in the summer. You wouldn't recognize the place."

Inside, the house looked like it belonged to a man who lived alone. A copy of *The Gazette* sat on the floor by a worn plaid reclining chair in the living room. Empty vases and planters were lined up on a sideboard. An open box of cereal and empty milk container sat on a cluttered dining table. A navy blue sofa, its cushions sunken, was speckled with lint. A stack of logs sat in the corner next to a wood-burning stove. A photograph of a woman and a shirtless boy standing on the deck of a boat sat on what once had been used as a plant stand. The woman was smiling, a bright red kerchief tied to hold her long dark hair in place. Her eyes, like the boy's, were dark. She stood behind him, her hands on his shoulders as he held up a fish.

"Meg and Chris. That was taken about a year before she got sick," Luke said, coming up behind Grace, who was holding the photo in her hands. "Chris was only about ten at the time. I should really put out a new picture of him."

"She's very pretty," Grace said, putting the picture down.

"Yes, she was," Luke said softly.

"This view is unbelievable," Grace said, walking to the sliding doors overlooking the deck and the lake. "You must want to just stare out the window all day long. For me, well, it's awfully close to the lake, though. I told you, didn't I? I'm afraid of the water."

"Yes, you told me," Luke said gently.

"I have been for as long as I can remember. When Jemma came to work for us, I was around four and she told me that I wouldn't even get into the bathtub. She used to shower me with her swimsuit on."

"Did something happen?" he asked hesitantly. "Did you have a bad experience?"

"No, I've never been much of a swimmer, that's for sure. I took swim lessons and hated them. Nothing's ever happened. I guess it's just one of those things."

Melanie wandered into the kitchen. "If you tell me where things are, I'll make the coffee," she called out.

"Don't trust me?" Luke asked. "Coffee's right there on the counter. Coffeepot's on the stove."

"On the stove?" Grace asked. "You mean it's the kind you *boil*?"

"What can I say? I'm an old-fashioned guy," he said.

"I guess you are," Melanie said. "Well, I'm out. It's all yours. I'm good as long as I can pop in a filter and flip a switch."

The three sat in the living room and drank the hot thick coffee from mugs. Luke turned on the weather scanner and listened to the report. "If we're going to go, let's go now. Weather's going to roll in again by noon. We should get out there so we can get back before the wind picks up speed. Looks like that nor'easter's going to land here after all."

They walked down to the lakefront. Luke checked the ties on the toboggan, making sure it was fastened tightly to the snowmobile. He took Melanie's hand and helped her step into the toboggan, handed her a brown wool blanket to wrap around herself. As he reached for Grace, she pulled her hand away. "I can't," she said, breathless. "I can't go out on that lake."

"It's frozen solid, Grace," Luke said. "It's not even a lake right now. There's not the slightest trace of water. I promise. You'll be fine. You can close your eyes and before you know it, we'll be on the island."

"I can't," Grace repeated. "I can't. I can't do it."

"Then how about you come sit up front with me on the snow-mobile? It seats two. Sit right behind me like on a motorcycle and hold on tight."

"I don't know," Grace said.

"Grace, you've been waiting to do this," Melanie urged. "Listen to him. Listen to me. We're going to be fine. Sit up there with Luke. Go ahead. You'll regret it if we don't go. Come on, Grace."

Luke sat on the snowmobile and took Grace's hand as she slung her leg over and sat behind him.

"Pull that hat down lower on your head. Now, put your arms around me and hold on tight. Ready, Melanie?" he called over his shoulder, turning the key in the ignition. "We're off."

The wind was whipping around them as the snowmobile bounced and scraped along the snow-covered ice. "Over there to the right is Buddha's Island," Luke called through the wind. "See that smoke coming off the mountain on Hester's Peak? There's a group of cabins up there and a couple of small ski trails."

But Grace wasn't listening. Her head was turned sideways, pressed against Luke's upper back, nestled in the soft leather of his jacket, her arms gripped tightly around his waist.

"Okay," Luke called. "This is it. We're going to pull up on the shore. We're going to bump a little. Hang on. Now that wasn't so bad, was it?"

Grace loosened her arms from around Luke's waist. Her head was perspiring. She pulled off her hat and shook out her hair. Melanie climbed from the toboggan.

"Wow, look at this place," Melanie said. "Where's the house, though?"

"The house is way up the hill. You can't see it from sea level. Look through those trees," Luke pointed.

"Luke, there's smoke coming from the chimney," Grace said. "I don't understand. Is someone here?"

"I'm going to explain everything to you, Grace," Luke said. "Everything."

"What do you mean?" she asked.

"Just trust me," he said. "Just promise that you'll trust me."

"I've been here before, haven't I?" Grace asked suddenly.

"Yes."

"When?"

"A long time ago."

"How long have you known this?" Grace asked, almost angry. Her eyes welled up with tears.

"Only since you told me the house was on Canterbury Island."

"Did you know my parents?"

"I'm going to tell you everything. Everything. I promise. You have to trust me. Please," Luke said. "Give me your hand."

Chapter Sixteen

The deed was accurate. The island rose a majestic sixty feet above sea level and measured eleven acres. The path leading up to the house, a narrow strip of soil carved through the rocky terrain and dense forest, was treacherous. A glacial moraine, Canterbury Island was wooded and overgrown with weary drooping pines and tired hemlocks, stately oaks, beech trees nearly thirty feet in diameter, and now-dormant blueberry bushes. Luke walked ahead of Grace, holding her hand behind him, Melanie bringing up the end of the single file. Occasionally, Luke would stop to toss a log out of their way, warn them of uneven spots in the earth or burrow holes in the ground where they could turn an ankle or misstep. Two squirrels scurried from behind a wood pile crusted with mold and friable earth, covered with thin lacy cobwebs. Farther down the path, a one-armed statue of a discus thrower stood on what was once a paddle tennis court, now overgrown with weeds and covered with a fresh layer of snow. A low white picket fence, broken in more places than it was intact, tangled with weeds and sticks, enclosed what used to be a garden.

The house sat dead center on Canterbury Island's highest point, a single-story structure built from wide cypress logs and topped off with a stone chimney. The house was square and boxy, an oversize log cabin. A balcony overlooking the lake, constructed from a lighter, newer wood, was obviously an addition placed at a later date than the original dwelling. A large branch from a pine had snapped, and hung precariously, resting bent and crooked over the balcony's railing. As they approached the house, the smell of the burning wood reminded Grace of late autumn. She remembered when someone, somewhere, had burned leaves after raking them into soft mounds. A sense of long ago came over her. She was comforted by the familiar scent. But then, without warning, a shiver ran up her spine. She stopped as they came to the bottom step that led up to the house, tugging Luke's hand to a stand still.

"Just tell me," she said. "When was the last time I was here?"

"You were a baby," Luke said.

"How old?"

"Three."

"Was it summer?"

"It was late fall. November. The first week of November. 1959."

"How can you remember so exactly? Why?"

Despite the cold, streaks of perspiration glistened on Luke's forehead. His mouth was dry, cracking at the sides. He ran a gloved hand over his face. "The steps up to the door are a little shaky. Be careful."

"How do you remember the month? The year?" Grace asked. She was staring up at the house, watching the smoke curl from the chimney.

"I'm going to tell you," Luke said. "Let's just get inside."

A man, in his late thirties, dressed neatly in jeans and a plaid shirt, opened the door.

"Kevin, this is Grace," Luke said, pulling Grace slightly forward. "And this is her sister, Melanie." Luke turned to the women. "This is Kevin Lambert. You remember Trout from The Birch? Well, Kevin here is Trout's son. Trout used to be the caretaker for the house. Kevin took over about seven years ago. Too much for Trout, especially when Edith became ill."

"It's good to see you both," Kevin said. "Come on in. I made a fire in the stove."

"How often are you here?" Grace asked, looking at Kevin.

"Not too often," Kevin said. "Maybe once a month in season. Just to air the place out. I haven't been here since the fall. This was a special trip for my friend Luke here. He wanted a jump start on the place for today. Warmed it up for you and your sister."

"Thanks," Grace said absentmindedly. "I take it no one lives here."

"No, no one lives here," Kevin said. He cast a quizzical look at Luke, who turned his face away.

"What's going on?" Melanie asked, catching Kevin's glance.

"I'm going to explain everything," Luke said. "Let's go sit down."

The front door led into a great room with exposed beamed ceilings, outlined with picture windows. There were no curtains or shades. Nothing covering the large beveled glass windows the way the windows were covered at the Purchase house with heavy venetian blinds. A large black cast-iron stove stood on a brick platform at one end. A basket of short logs in a brass pot with a delft handle sat next to the stove. A dark polished wood floor was partially covered with a deep-red braided rug in the center and two hooked rugs with a butterfly design on either side. A long oak bookcase filled with books stood against the far wall.

"This certainly doesn't look like my parents' house," Grace said. "Has anyone else ever lived here?"

"No one since your folks bought it," Luke said. "It's just the way it's always been."

"It's so warm. The colors, I mean. The reds and blues," Grace said. "The house we grew up in, in Purchase, it was so—well, so pale."

"This is a home," Melanie said quietly. "It really looks like home."

A dark wood cabinet, metal-screened on either side, held an old stereo. The words RCA Victor were scripted on one corner of the cabinet next to a small brass plaque of a dog and a megaphone. On the cabinet's lid was a stack of bare 78 recordings, coated with dust, scratches visibly gouged into the vinyl. Lena Horne. Johnny Mathis. Billie Holiday. Tony Bennett. Perry Como.

"Mel! 'Catch a Falling Star,' " Grace said, picking up the album that lay on top of the pile.

"Oh, my God," Melanie said. "Let me see." She turned the record over in her hands. "Maybe Jemma was right. Maybe she wouldn't play it because it brought back a memory."

A half dozen watercolors of sailboats signed JH and dated 1957 and two large gilded oval mirrors hung on the walls. Two mismatched over-stuffed armchairs (one a worn burgundy velvet; the other, beige with a red-and-purple crewel pattern) sat in front of the bookcase. The velvet one had a matching ottoman. A pillow embroidered with a bouquet of violets leaned against the back of the patterned chair. A sofa, ticked in a red-and-white stripe, formed a slight U shape. It, too, was scattered with brightly embroidered pillows, a plaid blanket folded over one arm. A square wicker table at one end held a lamp and a small clock. A round, darker-colored wicker coffee table with a glass top stood in front of the sofa. A pile of *Life* magazines and a few *New Yorkers*, old issues dating back to the 1950s, were stacked beside a ceramic burnt-orange bowl. The bowl was filled with pinecones so old they appeared almost white, their scales peeling away; some spilled over, littering the table. A glazed black lacquer ashtray was pushed to the side, a brass cigar cutter in its center. A cranberry glass candy dish on a pedestal was filled with Mary Janes, their wrappers unfurled, the candies exposed and brittle from age.

Grace looked up at the tarnished brass chandelier hanging from a center rafter. She brought her head down slowly, looked from right to left, as though she were waiting for something. There were doors, half-open on either side of the room.

"Where do the doors lead?" she asked.

"To the bedrooms. There are three bedrooms," Luke said, studying her face. Her face had lost its color. He watched as she licked her lips, barely moistening them. "There's another door around the bend in the hall. That's the bathroom. This was one of the first islands to have plumbing. It's high up enough. If it were lower down, then the waste would leech into the lake. Still old knob-and-tube electric. We're running electric off the generator right now."

Grace murmured, "I see," and walked slowly into the kitchen. It was a small square room with a rectangular table at the center covered in a blue-and-white checkered oilcloth. The walls were wood paneled except for the area behind the stove that was tiled. Wood-framed cabinets with glass windows revealed bright yellow stoneware dishes. The stove, a white six-burner propane, had a copper teakettle on a back burner, two bright yellow pot holders hooked over the oven door. Two coffee cups and saucers sat upside down in a dish drainer to the side of the sink. A tall baker's rack stood against the kitchen wall, its grated steel shelves lined with green glass. On the first shelf was a sign, heart shaped and hand painted with a border of daisies: HOME SWEET HOME. And on top of the glass shelves, below the sign, were photographs. Grace recognized her parents. Her mother in a dressy suit with a peplum, a corsage pinned to her jacket, her face slightly turned to her father beside her, smiling broadly, a boutonniere in his lapel. A plaque on the frame: JANE AND ALEXANDER, APRIL 1948. Her mother's hair was long, to her shoulders, flipped gently at the ends. Her father's trademark fedora was tipped rakishly on his head as it had been in one of Grace's dreams.

"Mel, look," Grace called to the great room, lifting the photograph carefully from the rack. "I bet they were on their honeymoon."

"They're so young," Melanie whispered, taking the photograph from Grace's hands.

"It reminds me of the one Jemma kept in her room. You know, the one of her with Cyrus," Grace said.

There were other photographs: A group of women sitting at a round table, dressed in gowns with soft folds at the bodice. Men standing behind them wearing tuxedos, their hair parted off-center and slicked back. A handwritten number in a metal holder sat at the center of the table, next to an arrangement of flowers with a taper candle. A picture of their mother in a sleeveless sundress cinched at the waist with what seemed to be a matching belt. It was hard to tell in black and white. She was standing behind a pram, one hand resting on the carriage, the other holding the hand of a child standing beside her. The child was smiling. Unruly hair fell in soft curls around the child's face. The child wore loose overalls and a T-shirt.

"That must be you in the pram," Grace said to Melanie. "God, I looked like such a tomboy here. I wonder where this one was taken."

Melanie held the photo and looked closer. "That's not you, Grace," she said, pointing to the child. "That's a boy."

"Are you sure? A boy?"

"Look at his shoes."

Grace picked up another faded photograph of a child. A girl wearing a dress that looked more like a pinafore. Her arms were skinny and bare. Her hair tied in a high ponytail with a big bow.

"Me?" she asked, holding the picture out to Luke and Melanie.

"You," Luke said softly.

"And this? Who's this?" she asked, picking up another photograph. Again, the other child. This time the child clearly looked like a boy. He wore a striped polo shirt and baggy shorts. His feet were bare. He was smiling, standing next to a rowboat, a tooth clearly missing on the side. He held up a fish still on the line. The girl in the pinafore was there, leaning away, shrinking back from the fish. "Who's the boy?"

Luke ran his finger around the edge of the silver frame.

"That was Alex," Luke said, his voice choking as he spoke. "Alexander Hammond Jr. Your brother."

"My brother?" Grace turned her head to look at Luke. "I don't have a brother."

Melanie's hand covered her mouth and moved to her cheek as she spoke. "I don't understand," she said. "I don't understand."

"I thought you told them, Luke," Kevin said angrily. "You said you'd tell them before you brought them here."

Luke wiped a tear that had fallen to his cheek. "I didn't know where to begin," he said so quietly his voice was barely a whisper. "She didn't know about the house. I knew then that she didn't know about Alex."

"What do you mean this *was* Alex?" Grace asked. Her mouth was set, her eyebrows knit together, unable to take her eyes off the photograph. "Where is he? What happened to him?"

"There was an accident."

"What kind of accident?"

"I'm going to tell you everything."

"Is he . . . Is he dead?" Grace asked.

"Yes."

"How?"

"He drowned."

"Oh, no," Melanie said. "Oh, God."

"It was here, wasn't it?" Grace asked. "On this island?"

"Yes," Luke said, tears streaming down his face now.

"My dream," Grace said turning to Melanie. "My dream."

"I know." Melanie nodded. "I know."

"What dream?" Luke asked.

"I have this dream. All the time. That I'm with Melanie and we're drowning and our parents can't save us. It's not a dream is it, Luke? Was I here when he drowned?" Her eyes had a wild look to them; her hand covered her mouth. "Answer me, Luke. Answer me."

"Yes. You were here," Luke said.

"Oh, God," she gasped. "Did you know him? Did you know my brother?"

"Oh, Grace," Luke said, taking a bandanna out of his back pocket and blotting his eyes.

"Please tell me. Luke?"

"Alex and I were nine when he drowned. You were three. The kid sister." Luke tried to smile. "I still miss him, Grace. I still think of him every day. See, he was my best friend."

Chapter Seventeen

Grace sat beside Melanie on the sofa, her hands folded on the picture of Alex and herself. Melanie held an embroidered pillow against her chest.

"Tell us what happened," Grace said, looking at Luke.

"You don't remember a thing, do you?" Kevin asked. He was standing by the wood-burning stove, about to stoke the fire.

"Nothing," Grace said. "Did you know Alex, too?"

"No. I never knew Alex. I wasn't born yet when it happened. I've only heard the story. My dad was here. He came out on the rescue boat."

"Trout? Trout came out here?" Grace asked.

"Grace, I'm going to tell you what happened. Just listen. I'm going to tell you everything," Luke said. He took the ottoman from the chair and pushed it in front of Grace. He placed his hands over hers holding on the picture and began.

Your parents bought this house in 1950 when Alex was just a newborn. They had a small house on the mainland. Up in Minerva's Shelf. There used to be a small college up there called Wright University, named after the same folks who started the library down here. Anyway, your dad taught courses at Wright in American history. He was a lawyer, but all he really did were some real estate deals in town and mostly for free. He loved to teach. And your mother taught there, too. English. It was actually this one course on Chaucer which is why your parents named this place Canterbury Island. You know, from that book? The Canterbury Tales? And she painted, too.

Dabbled, she called it. See these watercolors? She did all of these paintings. See where they're signed JH? Jane Hammond. She used to sit sometimes right by the lake and sketch while your father smoked a cigar. My dad used to love to tell me stories about your folks after they left. I guess it made him feel like they were still around or something. He told me that your mom would stop to wave the smoke out of her face and tell your father she might as well be standing behind a city bus the way he was puffing away. He was good-humored, your dad was. He'd just laugh and she'd get even madder. But she was never really mad. It was like a game they played. The only time I ever saw her get really annoyed was when your dad gave Alex and me each a puff and she told him not to get us started on that filthy habit. And your dad, well, he pulled the cigar right from my mouth and said we had to listen to her. He said how she was right.

Your mother loved reading, too. My mom used to say that Jane ate books instead of reading them. No, devoured was what she said. Jane devoured them. And your mother read to you before you could even speak. And to Alex and me. Some nights when I'd sleep over, she read aloud to us. Robin-son Crusoe, of course. No better island book than that one. We'd be lying in our beds and she'd sit on the floor beside us with that plaid blanket that's over the sofa across her legs and read until she'd see our eyes get heavy. She'd always say "More adventures tomorrow, boys." It was like her signa-ture. We waited for her to say that and then she'd kiss us both good night.

Anyway, just after Alex was born, up at Saint Mary's, Ed Lamb put this place up for sale. Ed was opening the motels in Fort Hope and he and his wife were spending less and less time here on the island. In those days, you could get these islands for a song and Ed made your parents a deal that really sang. See, your dad helped Ed with the closings on all his motels and Ed really wanted your folks to have this island. Your folks weren't paying for housing on campus, but money was tight, anyway. But this house, well, the price was so right they couldn't afford to turn Ed down. And your mother, she loved it here. Ed Lamb said when your folks visited them out here, your mom'd always say this was the most peaceful place on earth.

Little by little, over the next few years, your dad built on. My dad and your dad were buddies. My dad was in construction, a foreman on the crews renovating Ed's motels and even up at Wright where he worked on building the student union. Even though your dad was educated and mine wasn't, they became friends. Fished together. Smoked cigars together. Your dad loved to build. Loved to work with his hands. On the weekends, when my dad wasn't working on the construction crews, he'd come out here and help out. The two of them built that balcony on the side of the house. They built the picnic deck on the other side of the island and bricked in the barbecue pit. Built the paddle tennis court, too. We'd come here nearly every weekend. Our moms would be baking cookies and gabbing away. But sometimes they'd just sit and read. Right where we are now. Your mother with a book and mine with a magazine. Redbook. My mom loved Redbook. But one weekend every month or so, when my dad worked the Power Squadron, my folks stayed on the mainland. In the 1950s, the Power Squadron was the closest thing we had around here to a lake patrol or a Coast Guard type of thing. The squadron was two guys, volunteers, a Chris-Craft Cruiser with a first aid kit, a litter that looked like a hammock on sticks, and a radio. When it was my dad's turn for duty, he took it real seriously.

Alex and I knew each other from day one. When we were around five, we went to the same kindergarten. The island is considered part of Sabbath Landing and because your folks owned the island, Alex got to go to the school. He could have gone to the one in Minerva's Shelf since your folks taught at Wright, but having us in the same school made it easier for your mom. See, on the days your mom taught, my mom took Alex home with us. There's only one school in Sabbath Landing. Goes kindergarten through twelfth grade and, back in those days, there was only one kindergarten classroom. And there were only ten of us in the classroom. Anyway, Alex and I became buddies. Really good buddies, not just kids who were always together because their parents were friends. I'm an only child and Alex was the brother I never had. Weekends through, say, November, my dad would bring me out here and Alex and I would help your dad and mine, hammering nails and carrying wood. Our dads let us sit on the dock and hang some fishing line over and we'd pull up bass and toss them back in the water. I think the part we liked best was digging for the worms. Come September, my mother said it was too cold and damp out here for her, but my dad and I kept coming till the ice came in.

I remember that it was summer when you were born. Summer before Alex and I were heading into first grade. I remember the night because it was so hot and I was having trouble sleeping. I remember my dad brought Alex over in the middle of the night. Your folks had an old World War One Klaxon that Ed and his wife left on the island. It's really loud. A siren. Really piercing. The deal was, if my dad heard the Klaxon, he should jump in our boat and go pick up your folks and Alex because that meant your mom was in labor. Well, the next thing I knew, Alex was in my room with his sleeping bag and my mother was all excited and nervous and my dad drove your folks to Saint Mary's.

They had a big party for you about two months later. The christening, I guess. Your mother wanted to have it here on the island but the party was at our house instead. Their place at Wright was small so my mom said she'd have it. It was too hard in those days to get everyone out to the island house where your folks really wanted it to be, and your dad was worried that the weather could be bad. Your parents. They were something else. Your dad did so much work for free around here it was crazy. He'd end up not charging people on closings just because he got friendly with them. And if anyone had any kind of legal problem, your dad would help them out. And your mother. She would carry you around on her hip and you'd see her painting by the shore, right down there where we walked up that path. You'd sit on her lap while she picked wild blueberries along the path here. When you got older, you'd just be playing at her feet while she read to you and Alex and me and our dads were off fishing or building. And your mom, she always had a radio, a transistor, playing.

"She played music?" Grace asked. "She liked music?"

"Oh, she loved music. She was crazy for Perry Como. Alex must have heard it so much that he was always humming that song. He loved it. You know, the one about the falling star?"

"Oh, Grace. The song. That's why the song . . . ," Melanie said through tears.

"What happened with the song?" Luke asked. "What are you talking about?"

"We'll tell you later," Grace said. She sat with her back straight, her eyes glued to Luke's face, afraid to move. "Just go on. Go on."

So skip ahead and you were about three years old. You loved being by the lake and watching the stick bugs jump over the water. You were the bravest little thing. You never flinched when a dragonfly flew right next to you, mostly because Alex—if he told you not to worry about something, you believed him. You weren't bothered by worms or nightcrawlers, but for some reason, you hated the fish when they hung off the hook. You know, when we'd reel them in and they'd squirm and flop around until we threw them back in the water. And Alex—well, Alex was some kind of big brother. He'd catch a fish and if you were around he'd tell you to close your eyes while he'd pull it up. One time, I was teasing you, dangling the fish at you and you screamed. Well, Alex, he grabbed my shirt and kind of shook me. Don't tease her, he told me. Don't make her cry. He was real protective.

Alex and I were allowed to take the raft or the rowboat and go out on the lake. By the time we were just six, we were strong swimmers. We'd grown up on this lake and grown up on it pretty much together. There was nothing about fishing and boating that we didn't know. And we were good about things. We knew to wear those big orange life preservers even though they were a pain. We could look at the sky and read the clouds and the breeze and tell if weather was rolling in. We knew where every rock and every old pier or dock was buried under the lake and how to avoid them. We knew how to read the buoys. Couple of times we messed up, though. Like one time we saw thunderheads but we hadn't caught anything and we stayed out longer than we should have. Caught holy hell when we came back and the lightning had come. Our parents were standing at the dock and we knew we were in big trouble. After that, we weren't allowed in the boat for a week. But there was one rule we knew we couldn't break. One rule we'd never dare to break. We were never allowed to bring you down to the lake without one of the grown-ups there. That was something that was drummed into us over and over again. We knew if we did that, there would be no second chance.

Well, one day your folks were closing up the house for the season. It was

November 1959. Early in November. Right after Halloween because Alex and I had spent the last few days sort of arguing. He wanted to be a pirate and I wanted to be a cowboy for Halloween but we made a deal that we would be the same thing. Anyway, we shot it out with that thing, you know rock scissors paper shoot, and I won, so we were cowboys. We'd trick-or-treated in my neighborhood on the mainland and everyone recognized us and said hi and Alex said that pirates would have been a better disguise than cowboys. It was the first argument we ever had. Well, that day when your folks were closing down the house, it was the first time Alex and I had been together since Halloween. We fished from the dock that day and at first we hardly even spoke. We just sat side by side but then we started laughing about how this girl named Dottie got so scared by this kid who was dressed like a skeleton on Halloween night that she wet her pants.

Our dads had finished tying down tarpaulins on the deck furniture when my dad said we had to get home. It had sort of drizzled all day and by the time we left, it was really pouring. Trout was manning the Power Squadron alone that day and my dad said he really ought to get back to the mainland. How it wasn't fair to leave Trout alone when he was the one supposed to be working with him even though November was a quiet month. I asked my dad if I could stay the night, but he said the next day was school and we should get back.

Your dad was out on the picnic deck on the other side of the island when we left. He was putting some shellac on the table. Your mom was up at the house fighting with the storm windows. I said good-bye to Alex and my dad and I got into the boat. It was cold that day. The wind was snapping across the lake. I had my jacket zipped right up to my neck. When dad and I got back to the mainland, he called my mother from the Squadron office to say we were back. She asked him to run to Val's—that was the general store—to buy another roll of waxed paper before he came home. My mom, she was always baking stuff. Well, we were at Val's when we heard the Klaxon sound. I remember my dad saying to Val how they must be trying to put the damn thing away for the winter. He laughed at first. Said how Ham (that's what he called your dad) wasn't so handy without him. But then it went off again. And again and again. And my dad asked Val to call my mother and tell her we were heading back out to the island. I remember he said how he hoped your dad hadn't set something on fire over there messing around with his new gas-powered generator. My dad and I went back to the Power Squadron hut. Got Trout. Checked the first aid kit. Dad wanted me to stay in the hut by the radio but I said I wanted to go with him. Val had two pirate eye patches left at the general store and I'd bought them. I wanted to give one to Alex. I was going to tell him that next Halloween, we'd be pirates for sure. I was going to tell him that he was right, pirates would have been better.

When we got there, my dad and Trout and me, your parents were on the dock. Your dad was soaked to the bone. Your mother was sitting on the ground, her head in her hands, shaking back and forth. And she was moaning. The raft was tied to the dock and you were standing by yourself off to the side. And Alex was lying there on the dock. He was lying on his belly but I could see his face turned to the side and he was white as the sky was that day. My dad gave Alex mouth to mouth and put his fingers on the pulse on his neck. And then I remember how he looked at your father and shook his head ever so slightly from side to side and how your dad just crumbled into my father's arms. Me, well, I was just in shock. It was like nothing was real. Trout came over to me and put me in the Cruiser with a blanket around me. And then Trout took blankets and wrapped one around you and sat you down where you'd been standing and wrapped another one around your mother. He told me to use the radio and call into the police down at Fort Hope, but the radio wasn't working right. Maybe it was the winds that day, I don't know. But I couldn't get the damn thing to signal. I kept saying Mayday the way I'd heard once in a movie and I kept trying to make my voice louder, but nothing would come out.

Trout and my dad took you and your mother into the house and Trout stayed until my dad came back later. My dad carried Alex and put him on the litter and then we lifted him onto the Cruiser. Your dad was with us. I didn't stay on deck, though. My dad made me go below and I was throwing up the whole way back in the head. The radio began working when we got closer to shore and the ambulance met us at the dock and took Alex to Saint Mary's. It was like no one could say it yet. My mother came down to the dock to get me and I remember how her face looked. She had on her apron under her coat and she was covered with flour and her face was as white as the flour. I never saw my mother look so scared to death in my life. She took me back home. Your father rode the ambulance to Saint Mary's. And my dad went back to the island with one of the other volunteers. Practically everyone in town was down at the dock by then. They went and got you and your mother and Trout.

Luke stopped to compose himself. He ran his hand through his hair, took the bandanna from his pocket and blew his nose. His jaw was set, his mouth a straight line. He rested his eyes on a vacant corner of the room.

"Luke," Grace asked. "Do you want to stop for now?"

He heaved a deep sigh, turned his face to hers. "No, I need to finish."

Over the years, we tried to put together the pieces of that day. It wasn't until I was older, twelve maybe, that my dad told me what he thought happened. He figured that somehow you wandered down to the dock. I guess your mom thought your dad had you and your dad thought your mom had you. You must have walked down to the dock and climbed into the raft when no one was looking. We knew you'd been in the raft because one of your hair ribbons was in it. Though my mother always said that maybe Alex just wanted to treat you to a raft ride. But I said that he would have known better. I said that he would never have broken that rule. That the life preservers were still hanging by the dock. But who knows? I mean, we'd broken rules before, Alex and me. Who knows? We never really knew exactly what happened. Alex must have slipped when he was climbing either into the raft or out of it. The rocks were covered with lichen and the wind was blowing. Alex was wearing sneakers and the soles must have been real slick on the moss. He hit his head and slipped under the water. He knew how to swim but he lost consciousness. The water is shallow there at the edge and you must have climbed out of the raft. Like I said, one of your hair ribbons was in it. You ran up to the house and got your parents but it was too late. You must have fallen a few times running. Your knees were all scraped and bloody. It had to have taken you at least fifteen minutes to get up to the house on those little legs.

It was too late by the time your parents got down to the lake and too late for sure by the time my dad and I got there in the Cruiser. Alex was gone. My dad said that Trout was holding you in his arms when he went back there after the ambulance took Alex away. He asked Trout why your mother was just sitting off by herself and Trout said she didn't want anyone near her. He said that every time he tried to speak to her or comfort her, her body just went rigid and he was afraid she'd have a seizure or something so he just let her be. It was as if your mother disappeared that day. Not her body. Her mind. My dad said she was just staring straight ahead. I remember they said she was catatonic. I didn't know what it meant.

Your folks left here a few weeks later. Your mom never went to Alex's funeral. She was at Saint Mary's for quite a while. Sedated, they said. You and your father stayed at our house and my mom took care of you. Your dad spent the days with your mother. You were quiet. Real quiet at our house. You played and you drew pictures. Lots of boats. You drew lots of boats. And you never mentioned Alex. You refused to go to the lake. You refused even to look at it. Our house was right on the water and when Mom would go out back by the lake to hang the clothes on the line, you stayed with me. As a matter of fact, you wanted me there all the time. Sometimes I just sat there, next to you on the living room floor, while you drew pictures. But you never said a word. One time I asked you if you knew where Alex was and you just looked at me and turned your face away. Certain things, even though I was only nine, I'll never forget. I asked Mom what was wrong with you, why you didn't ask for Alex. She said to give you time. That time was a great healer. She said you were just a baby and the whole thing was just too confusing for you, but you'd come around.

When your mom got out of Saint Mary's, your dad brought her to our house and got you. Your mother was sitting in the front of their station wagon and your dad put you in the back. Your mother never got out of the car. She just sat there, looking straight ahead. My mom went and tapped on the window and your mother never even turned her head. She didn't even look like your mom anymore. Her eyes were glassed over. I remember how I thought that she looked real old all of a sudden. Your father kissed my *parents good-bye. Kissed both of them and hugged me. You just waved and took your dad's hand. And that was it.*

No one ever saw your parents again once they left. No one ever heard from them again. They never went back to the island. Never went back to Wright. They left the house on campus and didn't take anything with them. Not clothes. Not books. Nothing. Your father never even saw my dad again. He sent a letter a few months later and asked if my dad would arrange for someone to watch the house. In the letter, he asked that the house be kept the way it was. And we did. Right down to the candy dish and the cups in the dish drainer. Keep it up like Jane would have wanted it but wash down the dock and throw the raft away, the letter said. Hire someone like a caretaker. And every month, a check came to our house for the caretaker and every year a check came for the taxes. The postmark was always the same: New York City. The check was cut from Manufacturers Hanover Trust.

I always wish that the image of Alex lying on that dock wasn't the one he left me with. And now, since I met you, I have this other image I can't shake. Jesus. I haven't slept in nights. I remember you from that day, Grace. When I realized it was you, it all came back to me. How you looked. Shivering cold and covered with dirt. Bloody knees. Standing off by yourself. Frozen. Eyes as wide as saucers. Your clothes all soaking wet and clinging to your little body like onionskin.

Grace set Alex's picture next to her on the couch. She knelt on the floor beside the ottoman where Luke sat with his head in his hands now. They moved toward each other without a word, wrapped in each other's arms as they wept.

Chapter Eighteen

Grace wasn't sure how long Luke held her in his arms. Her eyes were closed. She did not shake or tremble the way people do when they weep. Again, she felt like Sisyphus, but this time the boulder at the bottom of the hill would stay. It was as though the task was done. Her anguish was oddly replaced with relief, much the way a mother holds her child who is, perhaps, late from school. The agony of wondering is erased by the child's presence on the doorstep, the softness of her flesh, the smell of sweat in her hair, the breathlessness of her speech after she has run home. Luke's shoulders shook up and down. Gently. Rhythmically. The sounds of his tears muffled in the curve of Grace's neck.

Grace heard the wind whistling through the trees and smelled the charred logs burning in the Franklin stove. She imagined laughter and music in the great room. For a moment she saw her mother's face when she was young and wore a flowing skirt. But the vision was quickly replaced by the picture of her mother's face, taut and pinched, as she sat on the divan in her bedroom in Purchase, a small leather-bound book on her lap, her hands clasped tensely on its cover. She tasted Luke's tears on her lips, felt them sting her cheeks and dampen her hair. Finally, she spoke. Pulling away reluctantly, turning to Luke, forgetting there was anyone else in the room.

"I want to remember," she said, her mouth so close to Luke's he felt her words warm his face. "I want to remember so badly and I can't."

"You were so little," he said. "So frightened."

"I'm even frightened now," Grace said.

"We protect ourselves sometimes," Luke said. "Maybe I shouldn't have told you. Maybe I shouldn't have brought you here."

"I would have found out eventually if you hadn't told me now, Luke. It's better to hear this from you. How could I have forgotten him? It's not just Alex I want to remember. I wish I could remember *them*."

"Your parents?"

"My parents. I wish I could remember them before all this happened. The people you knew were so different from the ones I knew," Grace said. Then suddenly, "Luke, you took that microfilm from the library, didn't you? It was you, wasn't it?"

"Yes."

"Why?"

"Why do you think? So you wouldn't be alone when you found out. So you wouldn't see the obituary and the news stories without me. So I could tell you and explain everything. So you'd understand. So you wouldn't leave here without saying good-bye."

"When were you there? At the library?"

"Minutes before you got there. I saw you and Melanie walking up Diamond Drive and I ducked out the back door. I didn't think you'd get there as early as you did."

"We actually got there later than we'd planned. We went antiquing," Grace said, a tranquility coming over her. She took Luke's face in her hands. "I would never have left, Luke. And you, you'd better put everything back. Margaret wasn't happy."

"She knew I took them," he said. He placed his hand over one of hers on his face.

"A conspiracy?"

"A conspiracy," he managed a weak smile. "She still doesn't know *why* I took them, though. I told her I'd explain another time."

Grace stood up from where she knelt next to Luke and walked over to Melanie.

"You okay?" she asked her sister, standing in front of her, placing her hand on top of Melanie's head.

"I'm okay," Melanie said, sniffling. "I keep thinking about my boys. I just want to hold them in my arms and never let them go."

"I know," Grace said. "I know. You will." She turned to Luke. "I want to see the rest of this house."

"Which room first?" Luke asked, standing now, walking over to Grace.

"My room," Grace said. "I want to see my room."

The room was small. It had a narrow Adirondack bed, two railings on either side to keep a small child from tumbling out. The bed came straight out from the wall, covered with a bright pink-and-yellow quilt. A large brown bear, a red ribbon faded with age around its neck, leaned against the pillow. An oval pink-and-yellow braided rug partially covered the wood floor. Next to the bed was a matching nightstand, a lamp with a pink voile shade that looked like a tutu, and an alarm clock with Minnie Mouse ears. There were shelves filled with picture books, bedtime stories, books of poetry, coloring books, and boxes of crayons. A low six-drawer dresser with an eyelet antimacassar running down the center leaned against a wall hung with a hand-painted mirror. Small bottles of perfume, a silvered hairbrush, comb, and mirror, pastel grosgrain ribbons, two Ginny Dolls, and a music box lined the antimacassar. The music box, a ballerina, had porcelain arms stretched over her head. Grace tipped it over gently, wound the key on the bottom, and watched the ballerina twirl.

"Greensleeves," she smiled. "I bought one like this for Kate when she was little. Hers is a horse, though. She had a thing for horses when she was little. Black Beauty."

"That last Halloween, you were dressed as a ballerina," Luke said softly. "I hadn't thought about that until just now."

"I was?"

"Your mother made you wear a winter coat because it was so cold that night. And you were crying. You said no one would know you were a ballerina under the coat. It's funny what comes back to you."

"I want to see Alex's room now, " Grace said.

Alex's room, just across the hall, was a mirror image of Grace's in red plaid. Balsawood airplanes dangled on threads hung from the ceiling. A chessboard and pieces were set up on a table, clearly midgame. A shelf of Hardy Boys books, Jules Verne, and *Robinson Crusoe*. Toy soldiers. Fishing poles leaned against the wall in the corner partially covering a dartboard. A good-size bass mounted on a plank hung over the bed.

"Your dad and Alex played chess together. They made those airplanes, too," Luke said. "I was with Alex the day he caught that bass. Six pounds, but it fought like it was sixty. I kept telling Alex he probably caught a boot and he got so mad at me. Trout was the one who had it mounted for Alex. Said it was his first trophy fish."

"Who are these boys?" Grace asked picking up a photograph on Alex's dresser.

"That's us. First day of first grade. Our mothers were big on taking first day at school pictures. That's me on the right. The one with the crew cut. I wanted to wear a hat, but my mom wouldn't let me. Alex teased me until my hair grew in. He said I looked like I'd been scalped."

"Did you mind that he teased you?"

"Hell, no. That was all part of everything. We were boys, you know. It was always good-natured. It was always who could catch the bigger fish, throw the ball harder, run faster. That kind of thing. If we'd gotten older together, we would have fought over a girl, but then we'd both have let her go."

"I want to see my parents' room now," Grace said, taking the picture of Alex and Luke.

Her parents' room was wreathed with curtainless windows, surrounded by trees. A double bed, the mattress sagging under a lumpy featherbed, sat in a corner covered by a bright embroidered floral quilt. An old pedal sewing machine on a scratched dark wood table stood under one window next to an easel with a half-finished painting. Grace recognized the painting as the paddle tennis court she'd passed walking the path up to the house: Her mother had sketched the discus thrower lightly in pencil. She ran her fingertips lightly over the painting, then bent down to rummage through a cloth-lined wicker basket filled with odd buttons, eye hooks, and snaps.

There was a tall dresser, a man's dresser, its top cluttered with a painted tin bowl holding an assortment of fishhooks, a pile of loose change mixed with collar stays, a folded handkerchief, a black-and-white tube of Chap Stick, a few loose, graying Bufferin tablets. A humidor sat toward the back next to a large box of wooden matches. A dressing table, a tilting oval mirror in its center, and a tufted stool, both trimmed with red-and-white-striped chintz skirts, sat under another window. Grace lifted a bottle of Shalimar and a gold-cased lipstick sitting on the glass top before looking at the silver-framed photographs that took up most of the space: Alex in a pile of leaves, Grace leaning against him, his arms holding her, legs splayed out around her. The four of them around a birthday cake on the kitchen table. Another where her mother's face was scrunched against a baby's cheek. The baby wore a woolen helmet tied beneath the chin. Her mother was smiling in a way that Grace had never seen before. Her hair was long and wavy to her shoulders, blowing back in a breeze coming over the lake behind them.

"Who's the baby?" Grace asked

"You," Luke said.

"Mel, do you see this?" Grace asked, holding the picture out to her. "I have almost the same picture of Kate and me. Without the lake. We took it in Central Park."

"She looks like—" Melanie said, but Grace didn't let her finish the sentence.

"A mother. She looks like a mother." Grace covered her mouth with her hand. Shook her head from side to side. "Mother always wore My Sin, though," Grace said, picking up the Shalimar and then the lipstick. "She wore lipstick the day she died. Where does this door go?" Grace asked jiggling the knob of a door between the two windows.

"The balcony," Luke said turning the latch.

The balcony was lined with planters. Sticks poked out from the old soil where the snow didn't quite cover them.

"What did she have in these?" Grace asked.

"Oh, Grace. I don't remember. Flowers. That's all I know. Some sort of flowers. Your dad would haul them over on the boat from the garden center every May," Luke said. "No one ever sat out here after your mother planted the flowers, though. Too many bees. But still, every spring, your dad carted over the flowers."

"I need to leave here now," Grace said suddenly. "I can't stay here anymore." And with that, she ran from the balcony through her parents' room.

"Grace! Where are you going?" Luke called after her.

"Leave her for a minute, Luke," Melanie said, tugging Luke's arm. "She'll be fine. Just let her get some air. It's a lot for her. She was the one who spent her life dreaming dreams that were really memories. It's not the same for me. It's not even the same for you. I mean, at least you've always known what you remembered."

Melanie and Luke walked into the great room. Kevin was sitting on the sofa now, a cup of coffee in his hand. "She went outside," Kevin said. "She didn't take her coat. She's going to freeze out there."

"You want to go?" Luke asked, turning to Melanie.

"No, I think you should," Melanie said.

"You're sure?"

But before Melanie could answer, Luke put on his jacket and slung Grace's over his arm. He stopped outside the door to the house and looked around. "Grace? Grace?" he called her name, listening to it echo through the trees. He walked around the side of the house and saw her standing, her hands wrapped around opposite arms, her head down, shoulders heaving. "Put your coat on, Grace. Here. Put it on."

She did not protest. She unwrapped her arms and placed one into each sleeve as Luke held the coat behind her.

"I'm sorry," she said as she slipped on her jacket. Tears streamed down her cheeks. "I have a balcony outside my apartment in the city. Every spring, I plant flowers. Yarrow and begonias, usually. And every summer we get so many bees out there that Adam says he doesn't know why I bother. And every winter, the flowerpots look like those on Mother's balcony. They're almost unrecognizable in winter. All of a sudden I began to think that life can repeat itself and you might not even know why. I can't explain." She turned to him and smiled through her tears. "We're a fine pair. I'm crying over what I can't remember and you're crying over what you can't forget."

"Look up at the sky," Luke said. "The storm is getting closer. Feel how still it is out here now. The wind was blowing so hard before."

"The proverbial calm before the storm," Grace said. "I wish they had told me. Told someone. All those years, I wondered why everything was always, well, always just so sad. Why my parents were so *different*. Maybe if they had told someone, we could have helped them."

"They died that day with Alex, Grace."

"No, but they tried to, didn't they?" Grace said. "I can't believe they even had another child."

"I told you. Your mother was already pregnant when it happened," Luke said. "What month was Melanie born?"

"May. May 1960."

"The accident was November 1959. Your mother was about three months pregnant."

"I've sort of ignored Melanie through all this. Do you think she's all right? She wants to go home."

"She's doing okay. I think she's worried more about you. Come here. There's something I want to show you," Luke said. "Careful here. The path pitches downward."

Luke took Grace's hand down a steep section of the path. He walked ahead of her, backwards, his hand holding hers, guiding her. At the end of the path was a small round wooden table and two small chairs under a tall pine tree. Below, Diamond Lake was visible through the clearing.

"This was our place," Luke said. "Alex and my place. Look here. Alex carved our initials in the table. In the summer, we'd take a pitcher of Kool-Aid out here. And Lorna Doone cookies. I remember most of the days being real sunny. The sky and the lake were so blue. Sapphire blue. We'd play cards, Spit and Old Maid, under this tree here. Now, look at this tree. " Luke took a knife from his pocket and unfolded the blade, slipped an edge of the blade under a piece of the bark. "Look at this." He snapped out the one beneath the one he had removed. "Look how the pieces fit into one another. Most trees, the bark grows vertically and comes off in big hunks. This one, it's like the wood is almost petrified or something. It won't crumble like most bark. And look, it grows horizontally. And each piece fits into the other. See?"

Grace took the pieces of bark from Luke's hand. They were a deep red on one side, a mottled gray on the other. The edges were sculpted and rounded, irregular, grooved and carved like pieces of a jigsaw.

"What kind of tree is this?" Grace asked, turning the pieces over and locking them together so they fit perfectly into one another. "Look, they click right in. It's amazing." She looked at Luke and smiled.

"It's an eastern red pine. Nothing very special except it's probably been here for almost three hundred years. But like I said, trees don't usually grow with the bark this way. But the soil here is so shallow and the roots can't reach the water because the island here is so high up. It's like the tree is growing at a deficit to begin with because it can't get the nutrients it needs. I don't know the exact scientific reasons. I asked someone, this guy I know who works at Fort Hope Forestry. I wondered if I was remembering this tree the right way or if it was just like a kid's memory, you know? Anyway, I brought him samples of the bark and he came out with me a few summers ago to take a look. He said the tree had to compensate somehow in order to survive all these years the way it did. It had a rotten environment to grow but it, well, it adapted so that's why the bark grows crazy like this. I mean, this tree even survived the winters out here."

"What kind of tree did you say this was?" she asked, still looking at the pieces in her hand.

"Eastern red pine. But when we were kids, we called it the puzzle bark tree," Luke said. He looked at the sky again. "We should really get going before the storm comes in."

Grace closed her fist over the pieces of bark.

"I'm ready," she said. "Luke, where is Alex buried?"

"In town. In the town cemetery."

"Can you take me there? Do you know where his grave is?"

"I go there every Christmas."

"You do?"

"Never missed one. I always leave something for Alex. My mother said that way I would remember him. Not that I ever would have forgotten him, but still . . . The first year, I left him my old pirate eye patch and once I left him a rainbow-painted lure that I sprinkled with glitter. I never was a pirate after that Halloween. Actually, I never even trick-or-treated again. Even when Chris was little, Meg always took him. I just couldn't bear it. Last month, on Christmas Day, I went to see Alex. I left him some pieces from this puzzle bark tree."

Chapter Nineteen

They took the same path back to the dock that they had walked up hours before, but it only appeared as though they left the island the way they came. Kevin stayed behind to close up. He planned to douse the embers in the Franklin stove and reset a stubborn storm window in the kitchen that he kept meaning to repair all winter. A brittle gasket on the refrigerator door needed to be replaced.

"What about the pilot light on the stove?" Grace asked.

"The propane is turned off," Kevin said curtly.

"Of course it is," Grace said, slightly embarrassed.

Melanie smiled gently. "You're getting possessive of your house."

"Our house," Grace corrected her.

"No, this is your house, Grace. It was never mine or meant to be mine. It never was," Melanie said.

"I don't quite know what to do with it yet," Grace said.

"You'll figure it out," Melanie said. "I can't help but think there is a reason for all this. A reason why they left it to you."

"We really ought to get going," Luke said. "Kevin, don't you stay too long here, either. This could be a big one if it lands."

It started to flurry as they hiked back to the dock. Grace stopped and looked around her.

"This was the spot wasn't it, Luke?" Grace asked as they stood at the slip. Luke nodded. "It's hard to believe. It looks so untouched. So innocent."

Grace sat behind Luke in the snowmobile, her arms holding him around the waist. But she felt different this time. There was a sense of comfort, of familiarity. She leaned the side of her face into his back, sheltering herself from the lake wind. He reached an arm behind him, letting go for just a moment, reaching for her as if to make certain she was there.

Luke covered the snowmobile with a tarpaulin and hauled the toboggan up on the porch. Grace and Melanie waited in the living room. He walked into the house, stomped the mud and snow from his boots outside the front door.

"What's the plan now?" he asked. "Who's going where?"

"I want to get back to the hotel and pack up," Melanie said. "I'd like to catch the three-fifteen back to the city."

"You're not really leaving?" Grace asked. "What about me? You're going to leave me here alone?"

"You're not alone," Melanie said. "Grace, I have to go. I *need* to go."

"What about the storm?" Grace asked.

"The train will beat the storm," Luke said.

"I need to get home," Melanie said turning to Grace. "I need to see those babies of mine."

"If you want to make that train, then we'd better get a move on," Luke said glancing at his watch. "It's nearly two now." He turned to Grace with an urgent look in his eyes. "What about you, Grace? What are you going to do?"

"I'll stay," she said. "I want to stay."

Luke and Grace waited in the sitting room of the suite while Melanie packed. He had insisted on driving them. Insisted that the Mercedes could not maneuver the slick road the way his pickup could. He parked the truck in front of the ticket office, hopped out, and took Melanie's bag from the bed of the truck.

"You two go in," Luke said. "I'll wait here."

"It's okay—," Grace started, wanting to say he could come in as well, but Luke stopped her.

"No. Spend some time with your sister. I'll be right here waiting," he said. He turned to Melanie. "It was good to meet you. I hope I see you again sometime on a better day. You hold those boys real tight now." He smiled.

"I will," Melanie said. "And I hope I see you again, too." Luke extended his hand, but Melanie reached up and kissed his cheek. "Take good care of her," she whispered in his ear.

"You're doing this on purpose, aren't you?" Grace said when the two were standing on the platform.

"What are you talking about? Doing what on purpose?" Melanie asked.

"Leaving."

"It's time for me to go, Grace. I told you I couldn't stay through the weekend."

"No, but you could stay through tomorrow and then we could drive back together."

"There's a storm coming. We may not be able to get back tomorrow."

"Oh, so I'll be snowed in by myself."

"Hardly. Luke will be here," Melanie said. "Besides, you don't want to leave. I do."

"I'm married, Mel."

"I know you're married. And you keep reminding me," she laughed. "Who are you trying to convince?"

"We haven't even had a chance to talk about everything," Grace said. "How can you leave?"

"I know, but all I can think about are Jeremy and Matt. We'll talk. I feel so, so numb almost. Like the outsider here. You? What about you?"

"Me, too. Numb. It all seems so unreal."

A scratchy voice over a loudspeaker announced the train was pulling into the station.

"Call me if you need me, okay?" Melanie said, lifting her suitcase. "I'll leave the cell phone on."

"You are somewhat of a brat, you know," Grace said.

"Yeah, I know," Melanie said hugging her. "I know. And, Grace."

"What?"

"Oh, God, I don't know. Just don't hold anything back. It seems to me we have a family history of holding back."

Grace hugged her sister to her. "I know. No more holding back." She wiped a tear from her cheek.

"You okay?" Melanie whispered.

"I am. I am surprisingly okay."

"He's a nice man, Grace. I can tell," Melanie said.

Grace watched the train pull out of the station. Waited until she could barely see the red taillights in the distance. She walked down the steps to where Luke's truck waited. The windshield wipers were slowly going back and forth. The snow was turning to rain. When he saw her coming down the steps, he got out of the truck and walked around to the passenger door, holding it open for her.

"You didn't have to do that," Grace said.

Luke smiled. "A simple thank-you will do."

Grace laughed, "You're right. Thank you."

"Where to?"

"I don't know," Grace said. "I need to make some calls. I need to call Jemma. And I need to call Adam and Kate. I should probably go back to the hotel."

Luke was staring straight ahead as Grace spoke. He was shifting the truck into drive when he said then that's where he would take her. "The Alpine it is, ma'am," he said with forced cheer. It bothered him that she had to call Adam.

"What about you? What are you going to do?" Grace asked.

"I guess I'll head back to my place. Maybe clean it up a bit. I don't know."

"Well, what are you doing for dinner?" Grace asked.

"I haven't thought about dinner."

"I see." She nodded, looking at him. His face looked weary. But more than that, he looked uncomfortable—or maybe she simply sensed that he was. He licked his lips, swallowed hard.

"Hey," she said. "Where are you?"

"I'm not sure," he said.

"Will you have dinner with me?"

He turned his head to her and smiled. "I would love nothing more than to have dinner with you," he said. "How about I pick you up around six and we head over to The Birch?"

"I'm not up to seeing anyone at The Birch tonight. Not up for the music. Besides, Trout will be there and I'm not quite ready to talk to him yet, though I want to."

"Then how about my place? I make a great steak." He could tell that Grace was hesitant. He was suddenly nervous. Maybe suggesting his place gave her the wrong impression. "Of course, there are other places around. There's a place down in Fort Hope that's open year-round except there's no guarantee the buffet's not left over from last summer."

Grace laughed. "Your place is fine. I'll be ready at six."

They were driving in silence until Luke spoke.

"You *are* going to talk to Trout, though, right?"

"Before I leave. At some point." Grace nodded. "He was the only other one who was there that day. The only other living one, that is. You don't think he'll mind, do you?"

"Oh, no. He knew we were going there this morning. Kevin told him. My guess is that he's waiting for your call."

"Tomorrow then. Maybe tomorrow."

"Don't take this wrong, Grace. I know it's been a rough day. But I'm so glad to be with you. So glad you're here with me," Luke said, his face reddening.

Grace didn't answer him. She placed her hand in the center of the truck's seat. He covered it with his own. He left his hand on top of hers until they pulled up to the awning of The Alpine.

"I'll be back at six," he said.

"What if the weather gets bad? You might not make it then," Grace said, opening the door of the truck as she spoke.

Luke reached over and held her coat sleeve as she was stepping down from the truck.

"If you'd waited, I'd have come around and opened that door for you. And I will absolutely be here at six come rain, sleet, or snow and right now it's beginning to look like this storm is fizzling into just a regular hard rain, anyway."

"See you later," Grace said, but then she leaned into the truck before shutting the door. "And, Luke? I'm glad I'm here, too."

The heat was turned up so high in the suite that the windows were steamed over. Grace rubbed a spot on one of the panes. Hester's Peak was shrouded in a thick haze. The few remaining snowflakes were becoming more transparent. Rain flooded through the downspouts on the hotel's facade. Suddenly, the scenery looked dismal, drenched in precipitation that couldn't seem to make up its mind.

Grace pulled her damp woolen hat from her head, tossed it on the coffee table, fluffed her hair with her fingers. A small coffeepot sat on a side table in the living room. She filled it with water, turned the switch, tore open a cellophane packet with tea bags and a wooden stirrer. She needed to talk to Jemma.

"Hi, it's me," Grace said when Jemma answered the phone. "How are you?"

"Oh, Grace. I swear. I was just thinking about you. I was hoping you'd call. You know, I wrote down the number of that place you're staying on the bottom of a tissue box and then fool that I am, I threw the box away when it was empty. For the life of me, I couldn't remember the name of the place. I was about to call Mike."

"The Alpine."

"The Alpine. I racked my brain. How are you? How's Melanie?"

"I'm fine. Mel left this afternoon. She wanted to get home to the boys."

"Why didn't you go back together?"

"I'm not quite ready to leave here. I went to the house this morning, Jemma. Mel, too. We were both there."

"And?"

"And it's a beautiful spot. Of course, it's covered with snow now and a little run-down, for sure. I mean, no one's lived there for forty years."

"You mean it's just been sitting there?"

"Well, no, they have a man who watches it. It's been kept up, you know, but no one's lived in it. It's the way it was forty years ago."

"I don't understand. Why would your folks have a house and never go there?"

"Oh, it's such a long sad story, Jemma. I wish you were here. Face-to-face with me while I tell you."

"You're worrying me now, Grace."

"I just don't even know how to begin," Grace said, her voice breaking into a sob.

"Grace? Oh, for goodness' sakes, Grace. What's wrong? What happened?"

"I'm sorry," Grace said. "I wasn't planning to cry. There was a child, Jemma. They had another child before me. A boy. I had a brother. And he drowned on the island. He was only nine years old. And after that day when he drowned, they never went back there. But for some reason they wouldn't let go of that house." Grace could hear Jemma breathing heavily. "Jemma, are you okay? Say something."

"I don't know what to say. I can't believe this. Those poor people. My Lord."

"They were grieving all their lives," Grace said, recovering her voice. "But I am so confused, Jemma. I am so angry that they never told any of us. We could have comforted them. They just drowned in their grief. And I feel so guilty."

"Guilty?"

"Well, it's such a long story, but the day Alex drowned, I was there."

"Alex? Oh, God. Alex. Just like your father."

"I don't remember, but I was there. My parents were up by the house and we were down at the lake. But we weren't supposed to be. Well, at least I wasn't. That was the one place I wasn't allowed. No one knows whether Alex was sneaking me out in the raft for a ride or whether I wandered down there. I mean, either way, I feel like it's my fault."

"Who told you this story? Grace, you're rambling on, baby, and I'm trying to take it all in."

"See, I should have waited until I was with you."

"No. It's okay. Who told you all this?"

"The man who took us to the island. Luke."

"Who is he? How did you find him?"

"He was Alex's best friend when they were kids," Grace said. "How I found him is another long story."

"Was he there when it happened?"

"No, he'd gone home already. But he was back later that day with his father after . . . after Alex drowned. I feel like it was all my fault somehow."

"Grace, I don't understand why you keep saying that. I'm getting very confused. Why don't you just begin at the beginning."

"Because it seems that one way or the other, I was the one Alex was trying to save or help or maybe take out on the boat," Grace said, winded after telling the story. "No matter how I look at it, it seems to come back to me."

"How old were you, Grace?"

"Three."

"Exactly. Three! Three! Do you remember when Kate took that safety pin and stuck it in that outlet?"

"I can't believe you remember that. The whole socket blew up. She burned her fingers."

"Right. Now how old was she?"

"Oh, I don't know. Three. Maybe close to four."

"And?"

"And what?"

"Was it her fault?"

"Of course not. She was just a baby."

"Exactly. She was just a baby. Just like you were. So even if you were someplace where you weren't supposed to be and this boy, your brother—my God, your brother—was trying to help you or play with you or whatever, it's not your fault. You can't do this to yourself. Listen to me. For God's sake, Grace, Alex wasn't more than a baby himself. Nine years old."

"I wish I could remember what happened that day, Jemma," Grace said. "I wish I could remember Alex. Maybe it was my fault. Maybe if I hadn't wandered away. Luke said that my father thought my mother was watching me and my mother thought my father was watching me. It was November and they were closing up the house for the winter. But if I hadn't wandered down to the lake . . . "

"But you don't know if you wandered."

"No, but let's assume that I did. Let's assume because it's the likely way it happened."

"Who says? That Luke fellow?"

"Oh, no. Not Luke." Grace felt suddenly protective of him. "Luke says no one knows what really happened."

"So?"

"So, I still can't help but feel, well, responsible somehow."

"Grace, where were you when Kate stuck that pin in the socket?"

"I was cooking dinner."

"And Adam? Where was he?"

"Reading the paper. In his study."

"And?"

"And what?" Grace found herself sounding impatient.

"And didn't each of you think the other one was watching Kate?"

"Well, there wasn't much reason to even watch. I mean, we were all in the apartment."

"So, whose fault was it?"

"I don't know. Whose?"

"No one's, Grace. It was no one's fault."

"But Kate was fine. Alex—"

"How did he drown?"

"He slipped on a rock. He hit his head and drowned because he lost consciousness. The water wasn't even deep."

"Oh, Grace. It's such a horrible thing. There is nothing worse on earth than a child . . . But, baby, you didn't put that rock there. I mean, at three, was Kate responsible? You can't do this to yourself."

Grace began to cry.

"Grace, listen to me. When I lost Cyrus, I thought my world ended. And in some ways, it did end. It made no sense that he was taken from me. We had only been married for six months when he was killed but I had been with him since I was fourteen years old. For months after he died, I didn't want to leave my mother's house. I just sat in my bedroom and stared out the window. It was like I couldn't feel my fingers and toes. I could hear my heart beating in my head so I knew I was alive but I remember feeling that I was gone and I wished I *was* gone. Like your mama. Except people knew what happened to me and one day they just dragged me out of that room. And that was when I started going to church for real. I mean, I had gone to church as a child but I didn't pay it the mind I did after that. All the people around me pulled me out from this dark hole I was in. If it hadn't been for my friends and my family, Lord knows how I would have ended up. But your mother. Your father. They didn't tell anyone their story. No one knew. So, how could anyone help them? Especially you? You were a child."

"I'm so sad, Jemma. But I'm also so angry. Why didn't they tell anyone? Why didn't they let us help them?"

"You can't be angry at them, Grace. Anger is a useless emotion. You have to try to forgive them."

"Forgive them?"

"Yes, forgive them. You yourself said they were grieving their whole lives. Why don't you come home, Grace? Come on, I'll come stay with you at your place until Adam and Kate get back. I'm worried about you being there all alone right now."

"I'm not alone, Jemma. I'm having dinner tonight with an old friend."

"Who? An old friend of yours? Up there?"

"Luke. You know, the man who took us to the island. Lucas Keegan. " Grace hesitated as the words caught in her throat. "I told you he was Alex's best friend."

"Is this all right, Grace? Do you know what you're doing?"

"He's such a nice man, Jemma. Do I know what I'm doing? All I know is that whatever I'm doing feels right for the first time in a very long time."

"Good Lord, Grace. I'm not sure I like this."

"It's fine. This I can promise you."

"I wasn't born yesterday, you know."

"I never said you were. He's very kind, Jemma. You'd like him, I know it." Grace felt like a child trying to convince her.

"You're married."

"I know. I keep telling Melanie," Grace found herself laughing.

"Telling Melanie what?"

"That I'm married. I know that."

"I swear, I'm getting more confused by the minute. Don't you see? You're like an open wound right now. You have to be careful."

"I will. I will be careful. One last question and then I want to call Adam and Kate. Jemma, what was that book Mother held on her lap all the time?"

"Oh, my. I'm not real sure. Some sort of short story book, I think. It looked like English words, but it wasn't."

"*The Canterbury Tales?*"

"That was it! How did you know that?"

"The island. Canterbury Island. Mother was a teacher at a college up here. She taught an English course about that book. I think it was her favorite."

"A teacher. Good Lord. I can't hardly imagine your mother being a teacher. What about your father? Was he a lawyer there?"

"He was, but he taught at the college, too. And he always helped people in the town. And he fished and he loved to build. And Mother read and she painted and she loved music."

"My God. It's like we're talking about two different women."

"She was a different woman before . . . before all this happened. But they stole so many things from Mel and me. For God's sake, Jemma, Mother wouldn't let us play a radio."

"I'm telling you, you won't have any peace until you forgive her, Grace. Your father, too. You need to forgive them."

Grace remained silent on the other end of the phone.

"Have you told Adam and Kate?" Jemma asked.

"No. I'm going to call Adam now, but they're probably still on the slopes. I'm not going to tell them anything until we're face-to-face. Kate will get upset and worry and Adam, well you know Adam, his reactions aren't always best for me."

"If you don't mind my telling you, I wouldn't mention Lucas to them. I don't think it's a good idea."

Grace paused before she spoke. "You surprise me sometimes, Jemma. Why would you say that?"

"Something I just feel things—"

"In your bones?" Grace asked gently.

"These bones are pretty reliable, baby. You're raw right now, Grace. You have to be careful. Don't do anything you might regret. You have to promise me."

"I won't do anything I'll regret. I promise. What would I do without you, Jemma?"

"And don't be so angry. Anger never got anyone anywhere."

"I think it got me here, though, didn't it?"

Chapter Twenty

Grace had decided not to tell Adam and Kate she had visited the island in a phone call. She wanted to be with them when she told them. She pictured Kate's face as she unveiled the secret and wondered if that same look of horror would come over her as it had when she told her how her grandparents had died. She questioned her strength, her capability to soothe her child. How could she comfort her child when she was barely able to comfort herself? As for Adam, maybe if he saw her eyes when she told him the tale, she would engage him enough to elicit a genuine reaction rather than the ones she was usually given where he was almost dismissive, wanting her angst to be over and no longer turn his world upside down. If only Adam could pick up her pieces sometimes. Retrieve all the splintered morsels of her heart.

She wondered if she could successfully mask her voice, control her emotions, when she called them and made small talk. She toyed with the idea of leaving a simple greeting on their answering machine. Something chatty and innocuous. It was still early in Aspen. Most likely, they were still skiing and she could get away with just leaving a message. But she wanted to speak to Kate. Like Melanie, she found herself longing for a tactile sense of her child. For now, she would settle just to hear Kate's voice.

She looked at the clock on the nightstand, turned on the television, turned it off again after flipping through several channels. It was nearly five o'clock. She ran the shower, waited until the steam billowed outside the bathroom door, slipped out of her clothes layer by layer, letting them drop in a pile on the floor. She stood while the water rushed over her body, washing away the sweet scent of pine and the sticky sap that the puzzle bark had left on her fingertips. She imagined the faint smell of ashen air from the Franklin stove, Luke's tears along with her own, twirling down the drain. As she tipped her face and let the stream from the shower run down her neck, she couldn't help but think she might be washing away memories she seemed to be making as well as those she couldn't remember.

The phone was ringing as she turned off the faucet. She grabbed the terry-cloth robe from behind the bathroom door and ran.

"Grace? You're out of breath," Adam said.

"I was in the shower. I ran for the phone. You're back early. How are you?"

"Just fine. Just fine. You're missing quite a time out here. I skied the black diamonds this morning. Haven't done that in years. Kate and Alison were right there beside me. We're all quite exhausted. And you? What are you up to?"

Thoughts ran through Grace's mind before she answered. What am I up to? she thought. He didn't say that he missed her, not that it would have mattered. He never said he missed her. Instead he told her what she was missing. Even when they'd first met, he drew her into his world as though, until then, the world she lived in was mournfully devoid of his. She pictured Adam and Kate in their sleek ski outfits, smoked goggles offsetting tawny windburned suntans against a background of white. She envied them for a moment. The abandon of their days this past week. The tony New Year's Eve party at the Whittakers'. She envisioned her daughter flying down the mountain beside her father. And there she was sifting through a lifetime shrouded by an overgrown island. She felt a profound sense of isolation, a frightening sense of distance, a dread that all the things she could offer Kate might pale beside the opulence of Aspen, of flying down a mountain.

"Grace? You there?" Adam said, his voice aggravated.

"I'm here," she said, clearing her throat. "We're resting mostly.

Reading. Tonight we're having a quiet dinner." She didn't say that Melanie had gone home.

"Sounds too low-key for me. When are you heading back?"

"In the next day or two. I'll be back before you and Kate get home on Sunday," Grace said.

"Did you see your island?" he asked, drawling the word *island*.

"The lake is frozen," Grace said, evading the question, implying she hadn't gone by omission. "Can I talk to Kate?"

"Sure thing. Hold on. By the way, you might want to call Rosa and tell her to turn up the heat in the apartment on Saturday. Also, tell her to get some milk for my coffee on Monday morning."

"I've already *asked* her," Grace said, clearly annoyed. "She knows, Adam."

"Well, just make sure. And, by the way, Grace, I loved your subtle distinction between asking and telling." She heard him call loudly to Kate. At least she wasn't in earshot when he spoke to her the way he did.

"So, I hear you skied the diamonds, " Grace said, trying to sound cheerful, forcing the irritation from her voice. "That's a feat."

"Dad made me do it," Kate laughed. "I was perfectly happy downhill. The only reason I agreed was that he bet me. Twenty bucks. Oh, Daddy is correcting me. *Dollars.* Twenty *dollars.* I've got to speak the King's English around him. Did you go to the island?"

Again, "The lake is frozen. I'll tell you everything on Sunday night. How's Alison?"

"Oh, she's great. We're all going to the Whittakers' again tonight. I tell you, I can take just so much of Elaine Whittaker, though. I mean, she's nice, I guess, but she flirts with every man in the room like you wouldn't believe."

"She does, does she?"

"It's sick."

"Oh, well. It's just Elaine's way. I doubt she means anything by it."

"There're a lot of women like her out here. Face-lifts and fake boobs," Kate said.

"Kate Barnett! Listen to you. I thought Elaine only had a face-lift."

"Well, I think they went a little lower. Alison thinks so, too. Not that Alison knows what Elaine looked like before, but Alison says they look fake. You know, a little too firm. I mean, they don't move. And this other woman, her name is Shelby. She's Elaine's decorator. Says she's English aristocracy, Lady something-or-other. Anyway, she's a definite plastic job and, ugh, what a flirt. It's gross. Oh, now Daddy's shushing me. Where are you going tonight?"

Grace was laughing. "Just to dinner. Boring evening, I'm afraid."

"Can I say hi to Aunt Mel?"

"She's napping, actually."

"Oh, okay. Well, say hi for me. I want to go to Sabbath Landing with you in the spring, Mom. It's pretty cool out here but I miss you."

"Oh, Kate. I miss you, too." Grace felt the lump in her throat. "I'll take you here one day. Does Dad want to talk to me again?"

"He's on the other line."

"Oh? With whom?"

"That Shelby woman. Dad wants to put a gym and a sauna thing in the basement here. I told you, she's a decorator so she's been coming over with carpet swatches and tile samples and all this junk. I'll tell him to call you back."

"No. No, that's not necessary. I'll call again tomorrow. Take care, sweetheart. I love you."

Grace sat on the edge of the bed for a few moments. She went into the bathroom, picked up her clothes from the floor. She dropped the robe from her shoulders, gazed at her breasts in the mirror. Boob jobs, she thought. No one could accuse me of one of those.

She blow-dried her hair quickly, not bothering to straighten the curls. Put on a pair of khaki corduroy pants, a black turtleneck she had washed out the night before, her heavy rubber-soled boots. She glanced at her watch. It was nearly six o'clock. She took her coat from the sofa, flicked off the lights, hung the room service menu on the doorknob for her morning coffee, and left the room. She was halfway down the hall to the elevator when she turned around. She walked back to her room, removed the menu from the doorknob, and slipped it into her purse.

Luke's truck was already waiting when she got downstairs. He jumped out when he saw her coming. Opened the door for her. Held her elbow as she climbed in.

"I'm not sure whether this chivalry is making me feel special or feeble," she laughed.

Luke's face reddened. "Shit. I'm politically incorrect, aren't I?"

"Oh, no." Grace smiled, thinking Luke was the sweetest man she'd ever known. "I'm just not used to it. I didn't mean to make you feel bad."

"Did you make your calls?"

"I did."

"Some weather, isn't it? It's snowing one minute and raining the next. It can't seem to make up its mind. Did you speak to your daughter?" Luke said, turning the truck out of The Alpine's driveway, turning on the windshield wipers.

"I spoke to Kate and to her father," Grace said, aware of the way she defined Adam. "I didn't tell them anything, though. I'd rather tell them in person. It's something that requires more than just a phone conversation, don't you think?"

"Oh, yeah. I do," Luke said. His mind was wandering. When she told Adam, once she was back home, would he take her in his arms? Would she cry and would he wipe away her tears?

Grace interrupted Luke's thoughts. "Did you ever try to call them? Did anyone ever try to call them after they left here?"

"Who? Your parents?"

"Yes."

"Oh, my dad tried. Several times. I guess they were determined not to be found. He tried to call them through the bank where the checks were cut. That was really the only contact we had with them. They didn't even have their mail forwarded. Mom sent Christmas cards to Wright for years. She always hoped they'd finally give a forwarding address, but there was nothing. You know, there wasn't a lot of communication back then. I mean, now you can get anyone's number any-where. Back then—well, it was different. Here we are," Luke said, pulling into his driveway.

Grace waited while he walked around to her side of the truck. She opened the door, but waited until he was in front of her to step down.

She smiled. "I'm getting the hang of this."

"About time." Luke grinned.

There was a clean scent when he opened the door to his house. The newspapers that had been piled by the chair were stacked neatly under the coffee table. One of the empty vases was filled with flow-ers. The small dining table was set for two with candles, place mats, wineglasses.

"Oh, Luke," Grace said. "Everything looks so beautiful."

He laughed, "I've been like the white tornado. I figure if the steaks fail, the atmosphere will help. Steak, baked potatoes, salad, okay? It's the best I do. And red wine. The bottle's open. I had a glass before I left."

"Where did you get the flowers?"

"The A&P in Minerva's Shelf. Apple pie for dessert."

"You baked a pie?" Grace's mouth fell open.

"No, I defrosted it. Mrs. Smith baked it." He smiled at her. "I'm go-ing to fire up the grill, okay?"

Luke slid the door open to the patio facing Diamond Lake. Lit the coals and fanned them with his hand. Grace sat on the sofa, ran her hand over the seat. She noticed the lint had been vacuumed.

"The steaks smell great," she called, reaching for the wine bottle on the coffee table. She poured two glasses.

"It's just the old grease burning off right now," Luke said, walking back through the door. "Boy, are you easy to please." He took the glass of wine from her and sat in a chair opposite the sofa. "Did I ever show you what Chris got me for Christmas?" He pulled a silver chain from under his sweater. "An owl."

She reached her hand to the owl around Luke's neck, holding it gently between her thumb and forefinger. "It's so pretty. What's the significance?"

He took a deep breath and smiled. "Ready for the recital? 'The owl stands for communication between spiritual and physical realities. It stands for wisdom, vision, and insight.' Not bad?"

Grace let it drop gently back to its place, her fingertips grazing the hair on Luke's chest. "I wouldn't take it off, either, in that case," she said. "Chris must be very special."

"He is. Got the best of me and his mother. None of the bad stuff," Luke said. He took a sip of his wine. "You know, this is the first time I've had dinner company in years. I'm not much of a cook. Meg always cooked. When she got sick, we ate mostly frozen stuff. Edith Lambert always helped out. And my mom—she was alive back then—she brought stuff, too. My folks died a few years ago. One after the other. Sometimes it feels like everyone just left at once."

"I know," Grace sighed.

"I'm sorry. I didn't even think about what I was saying. My mom had a heart attack and then my dad had a stroke about a year and a half after that. With yours, Jesus, that must have been such a nightmare."

"It was, even though we almost expected something like that. It was always so clear to us that they would leave us in a way that was, I don't know, not typical, you know? And for sure, they couldn't have lived one without the other, but I don't really want to talk about this. Tell me about Meg."

"We met in high school. Tenth grade. Got married when we were nineteen. Lived in Vermont for awhile. Outside of Burlington. I went to college up there at UVM. Got an environmental degree like Chris. Meg got sick when Chris was eleven. You know, I lost Alex so fast and then I spent years losing her." He turned his face away. "What about you? Your marriage?"

Grace's eyes looked down at her hands.

"Adam is much older than I am. He'll be sixty on his next birthday. Adam is one more thing I have to figure out in my life."

"What does he do?"

"He's a cardiac surgeon."

"I wouldn't have pictured you as a doctor's wife," he said.

Grace laughed, "Well, fortunately, that's not my only definition."

"Tell me about Kate."

"She's the love of my life. And believe me, she's not without her moments. She is your typical teenage girl. High maintenance. Demanding. Can scream at the top of her lungs. But she's a good kid. More perceptive than most. And bright. Really bright."

"Does she want to be a dancer like her mother?"

Grace shook her head. "Oh, God, no. She's a good athlete, but she has two left feet when she dances." She hesitated. "She wants to be a lawyer."

"Like her grandfather," Luke said tenderly. "I better check that grill. You stay here. It's cold outside."

Grace took her coat from the hook, wrapped her scarf around her neck, and followed him outside. She slid open the glass door and stood beside him as he took the steaks from an aluminum pan where they'd been marinating. There was a fine gentle rain.

"Where did that big storm go?" Grace asked, pulling her coat tighter around her.

"It's funny up here in the mountains. Sometimes these storms lock in and sock you real hard and other times they turn and go off the coast. My dad always said they're like women: You never know from one moment to the next."

Grace looked out across the lake. It was covered with a fine mist. Luke watched her.

"I never get tired of the view," Luke said. "It always amazes me."

"It must be clearing because there are a few stars up there," she said, looking up at the sky. "When I was little I wished on them. You know, 'Star light, star bright, first star I see tonight.'"

"Chris and I used to sit out here and he'd name all the constellations. What did you wish for?"

"What do you mean?" she asked, looking away from the sky, turning her face toward his. She pictured him sitting with his boy. Thought about him pointing to Orion, Ursa Major. Jemma had done that with her. Jemma once said, if she could, she would pluck the stars from the sky for her.

"On the stars. What did you wish for?"

"Oh, all kinds of things. I don't remember."

"What would you wish for now?"

She hesitated. "I'd wish I could remember Alex. Luke, I keep meaning to ask you. Did Alex like chocolate?"

Luke laughed, "Alex? Oh, he loved chocolate. I told you how there was a Dairy Queen in town, next to the Sunoco? Well, we'd go there on our bikes and Alex always got the same thing: hot fudge sundae. Why did you ask? Do you remember something?"

"Did our parents ever take us to the Dairy Queen?" She was shivering.

"I'm sure they did, Grace. Honestly, I don't remember. Why are you asking all this?"

"Because when I filled up my car with Melanie at the Sunoco, I had this memory of being at a Dairy Queen with my parents and Melanie, and Melanie getting chocolate all over her shirt. But Melanie doesn't like chocolate. I think I was remembering Alex. I wish I could remember what happened that day on the island."

"It's not something you'd want to remember."

"But I need to know what happened that day. Luke, I keep wondering if it wasn't somehow my fault."

"Oh, Grace." He turned and held her shoulders. "No, I swear to you. It was never your fault. It was no one's fault. It was just an accident. A horrible accident."

"That's what Jemma said. I called her this afternoon. But what do you think happened? I mean, how do you think it happened?"

"I don't know for sure, but it doesn't matter. Whether you went where you shouldn't have gone or he took you where you two weren't supposed to go . . . what's the difference? You were a baby, Grace. In some ways, so was Alex. Christ, he was only nine years old."

"I keep thinking about the dream when Melanie and I are in icy water and I'm calling to my parents to save us and no one can help us.

But it wasn't a dream, Luke. It's never really been a dream," she said. "Don't you see? It's really Alex and me in the dream. Just like it was Alex and me at the Dairy Queen. It's all just buried so deep inside." She stepped away from him, stood closer to the edge of the patio overlooking the lake, looked up at the sky again. Grace said, still facing away, "What would *you* wish for?"

He came behind her and placed his hands on her shoulders. "I would wish there was something in my power to take away all your pain," he said.

Grace did not turn around as his hands pressed into her. She reached her left hand up to cover his left hand. "It's your wish, though," she said softly, stroking the top of his hand. "Wanting all the hurt to go away would be *my* wish."

A warmth came over him at the softness of her touch. He inhaled the scent of her damp hair. Her words, almost whispered, made him long to bring her closer. "But that would be my wish, too," he said, trying not to see the glimmer of her wedding band in the moonlight.

Chapter Twenty-one

Luke carried the salad and baked potatoes from the kitchen. Grace sliced a loaf of bread while Luke lit the candles.

"Let me feed the fire," he said as Grace sat down at the table. "It'll just take a minute."

He tossed a log into the stove, wiped his sooty hands down the sides of his jeans, and rolled up the cuffs of his plaid shirt to his elbows. He sat across from her at the table.

"Here's to you," he said, lifting his wineglass.

"Here's to Alex," Grace said.

"To Alex," Luke said, touching his glass to hers. "You two have the same coloring."

"Did he freckle in the summer?" Grace asked.

He smiled, remembering. "I guess he did because he was full of freckles. Do you?"

"I hide under hats and sunblock," she said. She paused for a moment. "I'd like to visit his grave."

"I'll take you," Luke said.

"And I want to talk to Trout tomorrow, too," Grace said.

"Everything at once?"

"I have to leave on Sunday."

There was an uncomfortable silence. Luke shifted in his chair. Grace took a sip of her wine.

"I hate to think about you leaving," Luke finally said. "I guess I blocked it from my mind."

"I can certainly understand blocking the mind," she said.

"What are you going to do with the island?" he asked, shaking salt on his steak.

"I'm not sure. For now, just have Kevin watch it. I'm going to leave everything as is for now. I need to think about it," she said. "I can't understand why they kept it. I mean, if they weren't going to ever go there again, why didn't they just sell it? Let it go?"

"I think it's called restitution."

"What do you mean?" she asked, her fork raised in midair, looking at him intently.

"At some point, maybe they were planning to take you there and tell you everything. Maybe they just never got around to it or couldn't because it never got less painful. It seems to me that by leaving it to you, it's like restoring it to a rightful owner. It's like their way of explaining. Making peace with it."

"You didn't know them the way I did," Grace said, shaking her head from side to side.

"No, I didn't. I knew them before they were destroyed," he said.

She looked at him from across the table. Her eyes brimmed with tears.

"I don't mean to upset you, Grace. But look, they *were* destroyed. I mean, I can't even fathom how I'd feel if Chris—"

"Stop," she said, raising her hand, fingers spread. "Don't even say it."

"So, imagine how they felt, Grace. They suffered the unthinkable. You need to forgive them."

"That's what Jemma said. But they never forgave *me*."

"You? Oh, no. I think you're wrong about that. You see, I don't think they ever blamed you. I think they just distanced themselves from you. From Melanie. From all their old friends, old places, old bonds. It's easier to go on when you have nothing to lose, isn't it?"

"But that's so wrong."

He was silent for a moment. "Yeah, maybe it was wrong. But I guess it was the only way they were able to handle their grief. You're talking about people who took their own lives in the end, Grace."

"Maybe by merely existing, I poured salt on their wounds. Like I was some sort of living bad memory. A constant reminder."

"I don't think that was it," he said softly. "It's what I said before. They couldn't risk losing anyone again. The sad part is, they felt the only way not to lose anyone was not to love anyone."

This time neither of them minded the silence. There was the familiar sound of silverware, a knife scraping against a plate, the tapping of a glass as it was set down on the table. It was a necessary, comfortable quiet, the kind that descends over two people who can read each other's thoughts with no need for conversation.

"Will you come back in the spring? I tell you, you won't recognize the place in the spring. And the summer. The summers up here are golden," Luke said. His voice broke the silence like the gentle tinkle of wind chimes.

"I'll probably come up with Kate," Grace said. "She wants to see the island. Everything's delicious, Luke."

"Specialty of the house." He smiled. "Unfortunately, there's only one specialty. Do you cook?"

"I do cook. I actually like to cook. Adam prefers to go out, but I like to make dinner a few nights a week."

Adam. The mention of his name made Luke's back stiffen. He felt as though he was no longer alone with her. Grace sensed a change in his demeanor. Maybe it's just my imagination, she thought. But she was certain that his eyes were looking away from her now, searching for a place to rest that might seem casual, less telling. She watched his hand as he picked up his wineglass. It looked almost incongruous against the delicate stem. She had noticed his hands the first day she met him at the diner. His hand was rough as it gripped hers. But his touch had made her take a breath so deep she was afraid to let it go.

"I don't like eating in restaurants," she said tentatively.

"What?"

"I said, I don't like eating in restaurants. I'd rather be at home but sometimes, lately, it's easier just to go out. It makes the one-on-one more manageable."

"How do you mean?"

"It's distracting. Adam and I seem to have less and less to say to one another lately," she said.

Was his reaction to Adam's name obvious? He pictured her sitting at a white-clothed banquette with her husband. He wondered if Adam appreciated the way she looked in candlelight. If he coveted the delicate line of her jaw, the smoothness of her neck, the flecks of gold and the intensity in her eyes.

"You don't have to tell me this, Grace," Luke said, embarrassed at his transparency.

"I know I don't," she said, prodding the salad with her fork. "But I want to. We always go to dinner where people know us. Adam loves the attention. The fawning. You know, 'Good evening, Dr. Barnett.' 'Very good, sir' when they pour his wine. That sort of thing."

"Tell me about your dancing."

"Oh, there's not so much to tell these days. I teach at the school four days a week. Ballet, jazz, tap. Some of the kids are really fantastic. I mean, they have disabilities, but when they dance it's as though they're in another universe, you know? I just started teaching a hip-hop class for the older kids. Now, that class does me in. I'm much too old to be hopping up and down for an hour," she laughed. "But the kids love it and some of them are really good. And then, on weekends mostly, I run in Central Park and I take some classes at the studios on Broadway. Mostly ballet."

"I guess you always liked ballet," Luke said. "I mean, you had that music box and the costume."

"All little girls want to be ballerinas. Even Kate with the two left feet went through her ballet phase. Jemma started me with the ballet classes when I was probably around six. I just never stopped dancing." She smiled. "You know, you're a pretty good dancer."

Luke threw his head back and laughed. "I think it was my partner," he said.

Grace blushed. "I didn't lead, did I? I have a tendency to do that."

"No, you were perfect," he said tenderly. "You know what we need? We need some music." He got up from the table. "What do you like?"

"Everything."

"Dan Fogelberg?"

"I haven't heard him in a hundred years," Grace said.

"Well, it's time then," Luke said. "He's one of my favorites." He held a record album in his hand.

"Oh, God. Kate calls that 'vinyl.' You still have a turntable?"

"I'm a dinosaur. I promised Chris I'd buy a CD player. He bought me tapes and a cassette player for the boat and I can't even get used to that. There's just something about a record, you know? I even love the way it smells. I keep trying to tell you, I'm just an old-fashioned guy. Records. Opening car doors."

She heard the drop of the needle and the slight scratch as the music started with a skip.

"I love this song," she said. "That line, 'It's never easy and it's never clear, who's to navigate and who's to steer.' "

They finished their meal. Luke poured the last drop of wine into Grace's glass.

"I'll open another bottle," he said.

She heard him open the kitchen drawer, the pull of the corkscrew.

"Are you trying to get me drunk?" she teased as he poured.

"You don't really think that, do you?" Luke said. He stopped pouring. He looked almost stricken.

Grace laughed, "Oh, Luke, I was joking. Just teasing you. You really *are* an old-fashioned guy, aren't you?"

He set the bottle on the table, took the glass from her hand. He got down on one knee and held her hands on her lap in both of his. "I am old-fashioned. So before you have any more to drink, and before I do—"

He let go of her hands and took her face between his palms. He kissed her mouth. Gently. So softly she thought it felt like butterflies. But then he covered her lips with his own, slightly parted as though he was waiting to see how she would receive him. He pulled away and looked into her eyes, still holding her face between his hands.

"Okay?" he asked.

She didn't say a word. She leaned into him, placed her hands around his back. She parted her lips over his. She felt his hands move down her side, press against the small of her back, and pull her toward him. He kissed her neck, the line of her jaw, her lips, his body leaning into her.

"Okay," she murmured, her eyes closed as he kissed her neck. She felt as though she might melt.

"You sure?" he whispered.

"I am positive."

He took her hand and pulled her from the chair. Her legs felt so weak she wondered if she might stumble. Her skin felt moist and warm. He pulled her close to him. She would have sworn she could feel his heart beating as he leaned against her. She reached up between the two of them. Unfastened the buttons of his shirt. Slowly. One by one. She pressed her hands against his chest, rubbed them over his stomach, taut and firm. She felt the cool dampness of his skin under her fingertips. His chest rose and fell slowly, a controlled urgency to every breath he took. He took her hand and led her to the sofa, placed a pillow behind her head, covered her with his body.

There wasn't a moment as he made love to her that he stopped kissing her. Not a moment where she didn't feel a part of him and he a part of her. She felt the way she had when she danced with him, as though she had been making love with him for her entire life. Their bodies moved in rhythm, anticipating one another. He filled her, seal-ing every corner of her heart that had been overlooked, picking up all the splintered pieces. There was a gentleness when they finished, a tenderness mingled with a forceful passion. The record had ended long ago. The needle wafted back and forth on the smooth edge of the vinyl. He was lying next to her now, but he hadn't let her go. It was the first time in so many years she hadn't felt alone after making love.

She had forgotten what it was like to feel a part of someone else. Another image, she thought, that she had successfully blocked from her consciousness. She listened to the rain tapping on the roof, tasted the salt from his body on her lips, felt the strength of his arm cradling her. She wondered how she could ever go back home.

"I didn't even notice that the record stopped," Grace said, running her finger down the middle of Luke's chest to his stomach.

"Funny, I still hear music." He smiled at her, turning his face to hers. "Stay with me tonight, Grace."

She nodded. "I will."

Luke got up and walked to the stereo. Took the needle from the turntable and locked it into its perch. He carried a candle into the bedroom, blew out the other, picked up their wineglasses.

"Come with me," he said, pulling her from the sofa, wrapping an afghan around her. Her body was firm and sleek, and yet under him she felt so soft, so pliable and willing. "You're beautiful," he said kissing the side of her forehead, holding the blanket in place against her skin.

They walked to his bedroom. The bed was covered with a patchwork quilt in deep blue and burgundy. There was a tall bureau, a desk with a dark green glass-shaded lamp, a wooden valet. It was a man's room, not a bedroom shared.

"I gave Meg's things to the Goodwill last year," he said, answering her thoughts. "It was time. Even Chris said so. I kept my dresser. Moved the desk from the living room in here so the room didn't look so bare. Bought a new bed. Chris bought me the valet. He said it would add a masculine touch. Funny kid." He turned down a corner of the quilt. "Lie down with me."

She tucked herself under his arm. Her face nestled in the nook below his shoulder. He lifted himself and turned, leaning over her on his elbow.

"What do you see?" he asked, looking into her eyes.

"Your eyes. They're nearly turquoise, you know." She twirled the owl hanging around his neck between her fingers.

"They never want you to leave," he said, stroking her hair. His mind drifted as they lay together in the candlelight.

After Alex was gone, he had spent hours alone in his room. He ate his dinners in silence, poking at his food with his fork, barely touching his food. "You need to eat, son," his father would say. "You need your strength if we're going to fish out on the ice tomorrow." But he didn't want to ice-fish anymore. Not without Alex. Luke could feel his mother's eyes glance at his father over Luke's bowed head, silently asking what they should do. She would lean over, place her hand on his arm to coax him, but he recoiled at his mother's touch, pulling his arm from her as though her touch might burn him.

For months after Alex's funeral, there were long winter nights when Luke would sit at his desk, one corner of the room lit by a dim gooseneck lamp. He would craft lures, painting their tails with chartreuse paint, tying delicate nylon lines around small oval weights. Occupying his thoughts with the complicated business of weaving intricate knots to distract himself. He longed to shake the memory of Alex's laughter, the feeling of their shoulders rubbing together while they fished, that final vision of Alex lying still and ashen on the dock.

He remembered one night not long before the Christmas after Alex died. He and his parents had just trimmed the tree, but he had excused himself. Putting baubles and lights on a tree that year was intolerable. He was sitting in his darkened room. He heard his mother's footsteps come up the stairs, watched as she pushed his door open slowly, saying his name as though it were a question as she entered. She sat on the edge of his bed. "Luke? Luke? Why don't you turn on more light?" she asked quietly. "You can hardly see what you're doing."

Luke shrugged his shoulders, muttered that the light was plenty bright.

"Alex is still with you, you know," she said tentatively, biting the side of her lip to keep it from quivering.

His mother walked over to him and placed her arms around his skinny shoulders as he sat at his desk. He shook her off, almost pushing her. He flailed and cried to leave him alone but she refused to go. The small round weights rolled from the desk onto the floor, bouncing and scattering across the hardwood with pinging sounds. The nylon knots that hung so perfectly

from the lures and the weights were tangled now. The small glass jar of chartreuse paint had tipped and spilled. He cried that she ruined his lures,
screamed that she had no business coming into his room and bothering him.

"Just go away," he sobbed. "Get out of here."

"You're not upset with me, Luke," she said, her mouth a straight line
across, her breath coming in spurts. She swallowed hard. He froze and
glared at her through his tears. And then, like a marionette whose strings had
been let go, he collapsed and wept in her arms. He was angry at Alex for
leaving him. Angry at himself for leaving early that day when his presence
might have saved his friend. He was ashamed that he allowed himself to dis-
solve into the comfort of his mother's arms as she wiped the tears from his
face with her palms.

He remembered his mother's words that night. Remembered how he had
longed to believe the words of rapture she whispered in his ear while she
stroked his hair. "The kingdom of God is in you and all around you. You will
feel Alex again one day. You'll feel his shoulder rubbing against yours. He'll
be there when you tie your lures, when you toss a ball as far as you can,
when you run with your face in the wind. He hasn't left you, Luke. Open
your heart and you'll find him."

When Grace walked into the diner that first morning, he had felt
something the moment she opened the door. The wind chimes au-
gured the presence of something gentle, their clusters tinkling like
crystal prisms. A gust of cold wind had rushed through the opened
door of the diner, but a feeling of warmth, a serenity, engulfed him
when he saw her. Her windblown hair, her willowy body settling into
the booth. He watched as she plucked off her gloves, finger by finger,
laid them on the table beside her, smiled up at Helen. He heard the
anticipation in the pitch of Grace's voice when she asked about the islands. Absorbed her disappointment when Helen cautioned her about
the ice. Wondered what this stranger was touching that he felt so deep
in his soul. At The Birch, when Grace's mouth rounded the words
Canterbury Island, he felt as though someone were calling out to him,
crying that they had found what he had been searching for.

He looked at Grace beside him. Her fire-flecked hazel eyes, sinewy build, porcelain skin, her wavy auburn hair. He covered her body with his and loved her again.

Grace fell asleep in Luke's arms that night. She dreamed a shooting star fell from the sky. She dreamed that Luke caught it. Held it out to her while she wished. In the morning, the sun's rays streaked through the bedroom windows like a searchlight. Luke's arm lay across her stomach.

"Did you have sweet dreams?" he whispered.

She nodded. "I dreamed you held the stars for me while I wished. They fell from the sky and you caught them in your hands."

He lay beside her. His bare shoulder rubbed against hers. He closed his eyes and remembered two small boys fishing side by side in a rowboat when the sun was setting. He felt the wind in his face as he raced Alex up the hill on the island. He watched a ball fly through the sky as far as he could throw it. He took Grace into his arms. He was overwhelmed with peace.

Chapter Twenty-two

Alex's grave was tucked away from the narrow paved road that wove its way through the cemetery. It sat on the edge of an even narrower dirt path. Luke said that in the spring, the path was lined with yellow tulips. For now, the path was barren. Their feet sank into the snow, baring the cedar chips underneath that had turned to mulch and mud.

The headstone was simple: ALEXANDER CHARLES HAMMOND JR. OCTOBER 19, 1950–NOVEMBER 5, 1959. It wasn't long after his ninth birthday, she thought. She remembered Kate's ninth birthday, the one where Kate had said it was the last one before she would become "double digits." BELOVED SON AND BROTHER. Grace placed a single red rose on the snow by his grave, touched her fingers to her lips, and placed a kiss on the word *brother*.

Luke entwined his fingers into hers. His head was bowed.

"It wasn't sunny the day of his funeral," he said. "It was cold and I remember thinking that the sky was so white. There was a gunshot during the service. In the distance. It was nearly Thanksgiving and folks were out shooting turkey. And I remember thinking, how could anyone possibly celebrate Thanksgiving with Alex gone? I mean, what on earth was there to be thankful for? Alex and you and your parents were supposed to come to our place that year for Thanksgiving. Truth is, my dad was going to take Alex and me turkey shooting the day that turned out to be the funeral."

"What happened that year on Thanksgiving?" Grace asked.

He looked up at her. "You know what? I don't even remember. I remember the color of the sky, but I can't remember what we did on Thanksgiving."

Without speaking, they walked the path back to Luke's truck, their steps falling in unison, the vapor of their breath visible in the winter air.

"We need to go to the library," Luke said. "I need to return the microfilm. I left it in the glove box."

Margaret was sitting behind her small mahogany desk when they walked into the library. She lifted her head and smiled.

"Twice in one week, Luke," Margaret whispered. "You're becoming a regular."

He placed the boxes of microfilm on her desk. "Bet you didn't think you'd get these back."

"Are you going to tell me why you needed them now?"

"It's an awfully long story, Maggie," Luke said. "I promise I'll tell you one of these days. In the meantime, do me a favor. Loop them up for me, would you?"

Margaret glanced at Grace. "You were in the other day, weren't you, miss? How can I help you?"

"She's with me," Luke said, and introduced them.

"You're right," Grace said. "I was here with my sister."

Grace pulled a chair next to Luke at the microfilm reel. He scrolled to two articles from *The Gazette*.

TRAGEDY ON CANTERBURY ISLAND

November 6, 1959. Alexander Charles Hammond Jr., the son of Jane and Alexander, was killed instantly about 4 o'clock Sunday afternoon when his head struck a rock and he was drowned in the shallow east basin off Canterbury Island. It is conjectured that the child slipped on a moss-covered rock while climbing either onto the dock from a small raft tied near the shore or into the raft. There was no one in the vicinity except his 3-year-old sister, Grace. The toddler ran up Canterbury Island's steep hill to summon her parents, who arrived at Alex's side when it was too late.

The Power Squadron, summoned by the Hammonds' Klaxon, arrived roughly an hour after the child suffered the injury. Although cause of death is listed as drowning, it is clear from the coroner's report that drowning occurred after the boy had already lost consciousness from the blow to his head.

Funeral services will be held at the Sabbath Landing Town Cemetery on Wednesday at noon. The Reverend Albert Wood will preside. In lieu of flowers, donations should be made to the Alexander Hammond Jr. Scholarship Fund at Wright University in Minerva's Shelf. Interment is private.

MYSTERY SURROUNDS HAMMOND FAMILY

May 5, 1960. Jane and Alexander Hammond literally disappeared two days after their son's funeral. The boy, Alexander Charles Hammond Jr., drowned after losing consciousness when his head hit a rock exactly six months to this date on Canterbury Island. Mrs. Hammond did not attend the funeral. She was under heavy sedation for several days at St. Mary's Hospital. Mr. Hammond, a pallbearer at the funeral, was there with his 3-year-old daughter, Grace, who was in the care of Mrs. Edith Lambert, wife of Bartholomew "Trout" Lambert of Sabbath Landing.

The Hammonds, formerly professors at Wright University in Minerva's Shelf where Mrs. Hammond taught courses in English Literature with a focus on Chaucer, were longtime residents of Sabbath Landing and Minerva's Shelf. Mr. Hammond, a professor of history, was a well-known real estate lawyer in Sabbath Landing. According to sources at Wright, the Hammonds left their small campus cottage intact, leaving behind clothing and personal effects. Sources do concede, however, that the bulk of their personal effects were in the island home. The island home has not been placed for either sale or rental and is being cared for by Mr. Lambert. According to Mr. Lambert, a check comes monthly to cover both the home's upkeep as well as Mr. Lambert's salary. The check, drawn on The Manufacturers Hanover Trust Bank in Manhattan, is signed by an officer of the bank. The bank would not release the whereabouts for Mr. and Mrs. Hammond. Mr. Lambert has been unable to contact them.

Close friends of the Hammonds Mr. and Mrs. William Keegan could not be reached for comment. Their son, 10-year-old Lucas Keegan, was young Alexander's closest friend. The two attended the Sabbath Landing School since kindergarten. Lucas is currently in Mrs. Taft's sixth-grade class.

It is rumored by sources at St. Mary's Hospital that Mrs. Hammond has given birth to a third child since the accident that befell her son and first child. The anonymous hospital spokesperson said that maternity records were mailed to the Hammonds' physician but would not state the location or give the physician's name. Mrs. Hammond's mental state since her release from St. Mary's psychiatric unit last year is unknown. Mrs. Hammond was hospitalized the day of her son's accident for one week. The diagnosis was shock with borderline catatonia. Physicians in St. Mary's psychiatric unit recommended against her release. "We felt it was premature," Chief of Psychiatry Dr. Leon Stone said in an interview yesterday. "We felt her release was a precipitous transition."

The Hammonds and their daughter left Sabbath Landing the day after Mrs. Hammond's release from St. Mary's.

"Psychiatric unit?" Grace whispered.

"She was distraught, Grace. They watched her there. Medicated her."

"Like a suicide watch?" she asked.

"I don't know. I suppose," Luke said, shaking his head. "You know, I never saw either of these articles. My parents must have hidden them from me."

"How did you know they were here, then? What made you take the film?"

"I didn't want to take any chances. I figured there must have been stuff written and when I heard you and Melanie say you were coming to the library, I wanted to work fast. I told you, I didn't want you to hear the story from anyone but me."

"You are unbelievable," she said, slipping her arm through his, leaning her head against his shoulder. "Is there more?"

Luke started to scroll down, but Grace stopped him. "You know what? I don't want to see any more," she said. "Let's just go. It's enough."

It was just after five o'clock when they left the library. The streets in Sabbath Landing were dark. There was a crescent moon pushing through the cloudy sky. The few shops that had been open as they walked up the hill to the library were closed now. Signs fashioned like clocks with cardboard hands were turned over in the window begging COME AGAIN.

"I could use a drink," Luke said. "What do you say we go over to The Birch? Trout'll be in soon, I bet. You still want to talk to him, right?"

Grace nodded. "I do," she said softly. "I'm a little apprehensive, but I do."

"He's not going to bite your head off, you know," Luke said. "He's a real sweet guy. Always was."

"No, I know that. It's just that, I mean, he was there. I mean really there."

"Not when it happened, though."

"No, but right afterwards. I don't want to upset him."

Trout was already sitting in his regular spot at the end of the bar, a short glass of Jack Daniel's in front of him. His head was craned to a hockey game on the television suspended overhead.

"Well, look who's here. You're getting earlier and earlier, Keegan," Bill said from behind the bar.

"You're ruining my reputation," Luke laughed. "You remember Grace? Now, say hello and tell the lady you were kidding about my drinking habits."

"Nice to see you again, Grace. And, yes, I was just razzing my pal here. What can I get you?"

Bill set down a Black Velvet for Luke, a red wine for Grace. Luke clinked his glass against hers. "Want me to take you over to him?"

Luke carried their drinks to the end of the bar.

"Mr. Lambert," Grace said, standing to the side of Trout's bar stool.

"My name is Grace Barnett. I was wondering if I could talk to you about something. Do you know who I am? I met your son, Kevin, at the house on Canterbury Island. I used to be Grace Hammond."

"Do I know who you are? Of course, I know. That first night you came in here, Helen told me you'd been asking questions about those islands. Well, she pointed you out to me, said your name was Grace and I saw that red hair of yours and I had a feeling who you were right away. I thought, by God, that's Janie and Ham's girl."

"You did?" She smiled. "Really?"

"Well, I didn't know for sure, but something told me it was you. Course, since then, my son Kevin's filled me in."

"Is it all right if I ask you some questions, Mr. Lambert?"

"Well, I tell you what. First of all, you got to call me Trout 'cause I don't know who this Mr. Lambert is." He smiled. "And second of all, you got to understand that my wife, Edith—may she rest in peace—and I held you in our arms. That was the last time I saw you and if you don't mind, I'd like to say hello to you again in the way I feel is proper." He reached his arms out and folded her in like a child. Trout's eyes misted over as he embraced her. "I've been waiting forty years for this, little one," he said, letting her go and holding her at half an arm's length so he could look at her. "You know the last time I saw you was at your brother's funeral. Edith was watching you that day. Luke here, he was standing between his mom and dad right in front of Reverend Wood. Ham right next to Will Keegan. Edith and I stood in the last row with you, holding you. You kept going back and forth from one of us to the other. You were crying for your mama. You damn near broke my heart. I swear, I still miss your folks. It's a rare day goes by when I don't think of them. Kevin told me they passed away."

There wasn't more for Trout to tell other than what Luke had already told her. He'd gone out there that November afternoon with Will Keegan and Luke on the Cruiser, none of them expecting what they were about to find. Trout said that Janie, as he called her, became a ghost that day. There were dark shadows under her eyes and her pupils were fixed like someone who'd had a bright light shining in them. Ham, he said, was all but shaking life into the limp body of his boy. And Grace, well, you Grace, he said, you were soaked to the bone. Like a little waif standing off to the side. Shaking, you were. Part from the cold and part from not knowing what was going on, I guess.

Trout said it didn't surprise him when Janie and Ham never came back to Sabbath Landing. Oh, he waited for them. Never stopped waiting for them, really. Every summer, he opened up the island house and as the years went by and he'd hear the roar of motors on the lake (most people back then just had rowboats but somehow he figured Ham for buying an outboard, he said), he'd look around and think maybe this time it would be Ham and Janie coming home. Of course, it never was. He'd open the house for the summer season and shut it down again come the first of November. Check the propane and the generator, make sure there was a pile of short wood for the stove in the fall. The first thing I did after they left was to throw out that raft, Trout said. Took it home and burned it in my yard.

"Edith had smelled the rubber burning and she never came out to ask me what that putrid smell was. She knew," he said. "And when I came back in she said it was about time I got rid of that thing. That maybe we'd all feel better now somehow. I'd also dumped that rock into the lake. The one Alex slipped off that was leaned up against the dock. I used every ounce of strength to push it and I watched it sink right to the bottom where it belonged. Cursed it all the way down."

"Trout, how did it happen, do you think?" Grace asked.

"The accident? Alex slipped on the dock and hit his head. That boy was a fine swimmer. But he lost consciousness and drowned in what wasn't even a foot of water," Trout said.

"I know, but that's not what I'm asking. I mean, why were we both down at the dock? Luke told me I wasn't allowed there. Ever."

"To tell you the truth, we never could figure that out. But you know what, Grace? It didn't matter. It's like I told your father the day I was out there. Your father was going on and on about how he should have scrubbed the moss off those rocks. How he knew they were slippery be- cause he damn near fell earlier that day when he was fixing one of the posts on the dock. He showed me how he even had the chlorine ready to scrub off the moss, but he got busy with something else and figured he'd do it later on before they all left. Ham, I told him, you can't beat yourself up. See, what happened to Alex is the definition of accident. It's the definition of tragedy."

"My father blamed himself?"

"I think we all blamed ourselves. Will Keegan was carrying on that he never should have left so early that day. I cursed that old Cruiser for going at a snail's pace. Kept thinking if only I'd gotten there sooner—"

"Did my mother blame herself, too?" Grace asked softly.

"She didn't say a word. She screamed if I went near her. Screamed as though her flesh was on fire when I tried to touch her. Janie was one of the sweetest gals I'd ever known and from the moment I landed on that island that day, it was as if she had slipped out of her skin and someone else had slipped right in. I can't blame them for never coming back here, your folks," he said. "Kevin tells me the house is yours now."

Grace nodded. "I'm still trying to understand why they left it to me. I have a younger sister. Melanie. We never knew about Alex. No one ever told us anything. The first we heard of any of this was yesterday when Luke told us."

"Your mother was pregnant when the accident happened. Edith said she couldn't believe she didn't lose the baby after such a shock. Your parents never told you what happened?"

Trout cast a glance over Grace's head at Luke. Luke shook his head. "It's true. They never told them."

Trout took a long sip of his drink, held the glass between both hands, and dropped his chin down to his chest.

"When did your folks pass on?"

"Last month."

"Last month? The both of them? Good Lord, what happened?"

"They committed suicide," Grace said, tears streaming down her face now.

Trout slammed his open palm on the bar. He was silent for a few moments. "How long you staying here?"

"I'm leaving in the morning," she said. "But I'll be back in the spring. I have a daughter. Kate. She wants to see the house."

"Well, you make sure you call me when you come back here, you hear? And look, here's my number. Give me a pen, would you, Bill?" he called to the bartender. Trout scribbled the number on a napkin. "Anything I can do, you give me a call. Now you take care, Grace," he said, hugging her. "God, it's good to see you. All grown up."

Luke drove Grace to The Alpine. He waited at the lobby bar while she packed and called Kate and Adam.

"I'm getting an early start tomorrow morning," she told Adam. "I'll be home well before you are."

"So, you never did get to your island, did you?" Adam asked.

It was hard to resist. "Actually, I did," she said almost defiantly.

"And?"

"And I'll tell you all about it tomorrow."

"I guess it will be a short conversation, won't it?" he asked.

"You might be surprised, Adam," she said, seething. "Could you put Kate on, please?"

"Mom? Did you see the house?" Kate asked.

"I did."

"Is it nice?"

"It is more than nice. It's actually very special and I'll tell you everything when I see you. Are you ready to come home?"

"Yeah, I am. Are you? Did you take any pictures?"

"Just one. I can't wait to see you," Grace said, thinking of the photograph of Alex and Luke as boys between the sweaters in her suitcase.

Luke was standing in front of the fireplace when Grace came into the lobby.

"I'm ready," she said.

He picked up her suitcase and carried it out to his truck. They drove in silence to his house. Once again, she sat next to him, leaning her head on his shoulder.

"What if he calls and finds you checked out?" Luke asked.

"Adam? Oh, he won't."

"How can you be so sure?"

"I'm certain. I called them from the room. I told them I was leaving early in the morning."

"How early?"

"By seven. I have to leave by seven. That way I'll be home by noon. Their plane gets in around one."

They walked into Luke's house. Grace turned on the lamp in the living room and sat down on the couch. Luke brought in two glasses of red wine and placed them on the coffee table.

"We could scrounge around for leftovers, but I'm not even hungry, are you?" Luke said, feeling much the way he had felt once, long ago.

"I'll be back, Luke," she said gently, slipping her arm through his.

"I know," he said. "If I were to tell you the truth right now, I would tell you that I'm frightened. I don't want to lose you, Grace. The funny thing is, I don't even know how much I have you. Does that make any sense to you? It's like I can feel you slipping through my fingers."

"If there is anyone who has me now, anyone who holds my heart, it's you," Grace said, outlining his face with her finger. "There's so much for me to figure out. But I promise you this: I will figure everything out."

"What if you figure wrong?" He laughed self-consciously, lighting a cigarette. "I guess I'm thinking that maybe you'll get back home and figure that you don't want some run-down house on some overgrown island that's filled with bad memories. Maybe you'll sell the place and wonder what you were thinking hanging around with some fisherman."

Grace looked at him and shook her head as she spoke. "You don't know me very well. That's just not true, Luke."

"What if all this has been because of, well, just emotion?" he asked. "What if what happened between us is because we just needed this right now?"

"Maybe that's how all this started, Luke. But it's different now," she said softly. "I know how I feel about you. How strongly I feel. I know. Leaving tomorrow is something I can barely think about."

They made love that night and again when they awakened before sunrise. At six-thirty, just as the sun was rising over Hester's Peak, Luke drove Grace to her car at The Alpine.

"When will I hear from you?" he asked, holding her close to him.

"Soon," she said, feeling as though she was afraid to move away from his arms. "I just need to think everything through. Soon, though. I promise."

She was turning onto the interstate when she glanced at the seat next to her. Camouflaged by the gray leather upholstery were two interlocked shapes from the puzzle bark tree.

Chapter Twenty-three

Grace had crossed over the bridge into Manhattan hundreds of times before. She had seen the silhouette of the city skyline against the horizon, witnessed the sun straining through the clouds, felt herself blinded by the mirrored reflections bouncing off the glass skyscrapers. The bridge spanned a river junction where railroad tracks converged in a twisted confluence of steel rails and ties that seemed to be going nowhere. It was a dreary scene. There was a row of low dark buildings with flat roofs, their concrete walls marred with graffiti. Thick black smoke mushroomed into the air over torn billboards behind dormant water towers.

She thought of the way Diamond Lake glistened in the moonlight, how the mountain appeared charcoal-brushed against the mottled sky, the way the pine trees yielded to the weight of snow. She longed for the winding roads of Sabbath Landing, the streets lit by strings of crystal lights, the now familiar faces at The Birch. It had been only a few hours since she left and yet it all felt so far away, not unlike a dream. Mostly, she longed for Luke. She yearned to breathe the citrus of his cologne, the faint scent of tobacco, to feel the strength of his arms as he held her, the gentle way he touched her, the warmth of his mouth when he kissed her.

The city streets accosted her as she drove down Broadway. The quick bleats of sirens, irate drivers leaning on their horns, shrill whistles from doormen hailing cabs for black-garbed couples waiting under awnings. She thought how impossible it would be to hear the tinkle of a wind chime in what suddenly seemed to be urban chaos.

This city she had once found exhilarating suddenly left her overwhelmed. She pulled the car down the steep dark ramp of the parking garage in her building, carried her suitcase into the elevator, watched the numbers blink sequentially as it climbed to the penthouse. She placed her boots on the mat outside the apartment door next to a pair of Adam's tasseled loafers. Inserted her keys in the tumblers and turned the two heavy locks, heard the click and fall of bolts as they unlatched. She stepped inside the apartment door, felt for the switch along the wall, and flicked on the chandelier in the marble-floored foyer. Rosa had placed a vase of daisies on the lowboy in the hall, balanced a note between the stems saying the refrigerator was filled with breakfast food. Welcome home, it said. See you Monday.

It would all begin again in the morning, Grace thought. Adam would sit at the dining table reading his newspaper, drinking his coffee, tearing the edges off an English muffin, silencing his beeper as early morning pages came in from the surgical suite. Kate would drink her juice and fly out the door, her hair still damp, Grace calling after her that she should eat breakfast. Grace would leave for the school. Her leg warmers, ballet slippers, a canvas portfolio of sheet music, a zipper case of compact discs in her knapsack. The children would flock around her in the studio, playing with the folds of her chiffon skirt, telling her about their Christmas vacation, banging the piano keys in discord. She would clap her hands and call them to attention while she popped a CD into the player and they would line up like soldiers. She thought of Luke and his records. The gentle tapping of rain on the roof after he made love to her. She wondered how it was possible to follow a routine so reliable and steadfast when her entire life, the touchstones of her very existence, were no longer the same.

She unpacked her suitcase, placed the pieces of puzzle bark between a soft pile of silk scarves in her bureau drawer, lay the deed on the bed, slid the photograph of Luke and Alex under her bed pillow. She heard the apartment door open. Heard Kate's voice call "Mom," the rustling of her daughter's ski jacket, Kate's eager steps toward her parents' bedroom.

"Look at you, all suntanned!" Grace said, meeting her daughter in the hallway. "You look wonderful!" She kissed her. Helped her off with her jacket. "I missed you. Let me look at you."

"Me, too," Kate said, hugging her mother as they walked back into the bedroom. "I missed you, too, Mom."

Adam came in behind them. How could it be, Grace thought, that he can spend hours traveling and not look the least bit rumpled? He wore heather-green corduroy slacks, a gold tweed jacket, a black turtleneck. His fine silvery hair was neat and combed. His tan so even it looked as though his face was stained café au lait. He bent down and kissed Grace's cheek.

"You smell like smoke," he said, sniffing her sweater.

"I wore this in the bar last night at the hotel," she said, feeling herself flush, picturing Luke as he lit a cigarette. "Lots of smoke in there."

"What should we do about dinner?" Adam asked. "Where's the mail?"

"Rosa put it in your study. In a wicker basket on the couch," Grace said. "I thought we'd get take-out."

"Call the Chinese place, then," he said. "And change that sweater. You reek."

Grace pulled her sweater over her head, holding it to her face for a moment before tossing it into the hamper. She grabbed a fleece top from her drawer, leaned into the mirror over her bureau, and studied her eyes. She didn't look any different, so why did she feel so unlike herself?

It was the usual twenty minutes before the food arrived.

Kate laughed, "Boy, talk about fast food, huh, Mom? Really cooked to order. Are you going to tell us what happened at the island?" Kate was setting out glasses and plates, nibbling on dried noodles.

"Get your father." Grace nodded, pulling the small white cartons of food from a shopping bag. "I'll tell you while we eat."

Grace was filling a pitcher with ice water when Adam came into the kitchen. He pulled out his chair and sat down. Grace thought that Luke might have taken the heavy pitcher from her hands. She watched as Adam reached across the table and loaded his plate with lo mein thinking that Luke would have waited for her, served her first, held out her chair. *I'm just an old-fashioned guy*, she heard him say.

"What are you looking at?" Adam asked, his hand suspended for a moment before placing the serving spoon down.

"Nothing," Grace said. "I'm not looking at anything."

"So, Mom, tell us. We're waiting," Kate said.

"Ah, yes. Grace's mystery island," Adam said.

"I don't know where to begin," Grace said, ignoring her husband's barb. "I guess the best place is always the beginning, right?" She paused briefly. Not knowing whom to face, she looked down. "I had a brother."

"You what?" Adam asked at the same time Kate looked up at her mother as though someone had shattered glass.

"I said, I had a brother. When we were little, we lived on the island with my parents. He was six years older than me. He drowned. His name was Alex."

"Like grandpa," Kate said with a gasp.

Grace nodded. "Like grandpa," Grace echoed. When was the last time Kate had called her father grandpa?

Neither Adam nor Kate spoke while Grace told her story. Adam sat with his fingers steepled, his eyes intent on his wife's face, his own face expressionless, his jaw rapidly and methodically pumping. Kate leaned her chin in her left palm, a napkin crumpled in her right hand wiping slow-flowing tears that trickled down her face.

There were details that Grace omitted. Abstractions she carefully excluded although they were the very the pulp of her story. It was Adam's stone visage that prevented her from explaining the way she felt as she walked through the rooms of the island house. He wouldn't understand what she had felt in her gut. The wrenching significance of pinecones in a bowl, teddy bears, books, crayons, quilts, balsawood airplanes, a chess game unfinished, two mugs left over from an afternoon when life came to a halt. When her world as she knew it ceased to be part of the plan.

Her monologue was pithy, almost terse. She told her story slowly, carefully, without tears. The town was small enough so that once she began making inquiries about the island, word got around, she said. There was a woman named Helen who waitressed at the local diner, a bartender named Bill at a pub in town, a man called Trout who had been there the day that Alex died, and a man named Lucas Keegan. She had purposely blended Luke's name into the landscape of characters, bracing herself to make certain there wasn't a hint of anything in her voice that might say Luke was more than merely a facilitator who helped her retrace a lifetime.

"It turned out that Luke Keegan was my brother's best friend," she said, keeping her eyes from blinking. "He drove Mel and me out to the island on a snowmobile with a toboggan tied on the back."

"I can't believe you went out on the lake," Kate said. "You hate the water."

"I don't hate it. I'm afraid of it. But it was ice," Grace said. "But even though it was frozen, I was still afraid." She didn't say her throat had clutched and felt like it would nearly close but Luke had promised she could trust him. She didn't tell them how Luke talked through the wind as she rode behind him on the snowmobile, her arms wrapped around him, her face burrowed in the strength of his back.

"It wasn't until we got there that Luke told us what happened that day," she said. And as she told her husband and daughter she felt as though she were back in the great room. She felt Luke beside her. The warmth of his face against hers. She could taste his tears, feel the sweat and heat from his body. She prayed that no one saw the images that danced through her mind: the way Luke had wrapped her in the afghan and led her to his bed. How he held her, looked into her eyes as he made love to her by candlelight and when the morning sun streamed through the window.

She told them about the dream where her pleas for help were ignored as she stood in the icy water. How she had come to realize the image of the child whom she'd always thought was Melanie was, in fact, Alex. How she hoped that somewhere, in the recesses of her mind, Alex was not forgotten.

"The island house is high up on a hill," she explained. "I suppose I screamed or called to my parents but I was too far away for them to hear me. I was three. My voice wasn't strong enough to carry the distance." She sighed. "In the dream, I call and they ignore me. In reality, I suppose they simply couldn't hear. There's a difference between hearing and listening, isn't there? But that dream, the more I think about it, wasn't really a dream."

She told them about her mother's love for Chaucer and painting and music. Her father's propensity for a good cigar, how he loved to work with his hands, and practiced law for free. That they both were teachers.

"There were photographs of the four of us all over the house," Grace said. "Mother was pregnant with Melanie when it happened."

It was then that Grace began to really cry. She grabbed another napkin from the table and wiped her eyes. "When my father got sick these last few months, when he started to become forgetful and disoriented, I think Mother felt she was losing him. He was the one who protected her and he was slipping away. I guess that's why they ended it the way they did," she said, recovering her voice. "But, really, when Alex died, that was when they both ceased to exist. That was when their lives ended. Their suicides were merely a formality of what already was."

"Why can't you remember Alex?" Kate asked, blotting her eyes.

"I'm not sure," Grace said, shaking her head. "Maybe it's because I was so little when it happened. Maybe because the way he died was so horrendous that I've just blocked it out. I have a picture of him in my room, though. I'll get it for you. I took it from the house."

She brought back the photograph and held it before Kate. "He's the one on the left," Grace said, standing behind her daughter, her hand resting on her shoulder.

"Alex looks like you, Mom," Kate said softly, running her finger across the glass. "Who's the other boy?"

"That's Luke," she said, her mind drifting again.

"Did he remember you?"

"Who?"

"Luke. Did he remember you?"

"He did," Grace said. "Of course, I was just a baby, but yes, he remembered me."

"What's he like now? What does he do?"

"He's a fisherman. And a hunting guide." *What's he like now? Grace thought. He is smart and strong and gentle.*

"I hope you gave him something for his trouble," Adam said, reaching across the table to take the picture.

"It wasn't like that," Grace said, disturbed with his choice of words. "He was happy to take us out there. After Alex died, I told you, my parents just left. No one ever saw them again. Telling us the story, taking us to the island—well, it was closure for Luke as well. I told you, he was Alex's best friend."

"The guy is almost fifty," Adam said. "I can't imagine that after all this time he hasn't felt a sense of closure. I mean, he was nine years old, for Christ's sake. That's pretty dramatic."

"I don't think so. I think he felt a connection with us. I mean, we're Alex's sisters," Grace said; the notion of being Alex's sister was somewhat startling.

"I think you could use some help with all this, Grace," Adam said, helping himself to more lo mein.

"What kind of help? My heart is broken. It breaks for me, my parents. Even for Melanie. The funny thing is, my heart has often felt broken and I never knew why."

"Well, now you know," Adam said. "Pass the rice, would you, Kate?"

"It's a little more complicated than just *knowing*, don't you think? My parents lost a child. I lost a brother," Grace said, her lips parted and dry.

"What's done is done, Grace," he continued, ignoring her. "I hope this finally quells your constant quest for what you so tritely call clo-sure. You have your answers now, Grace. I trust you're going to get rid of that house."

"Get rid of the house?"

"Who needs it? A place like that is nothing but a liability. The in-surance has to be astronomical. Knowing your parents, they probably didn't even have any coverage. And, don't forget, it probably needs updating. The place is probably a tinderbox. Bringing it up to code alone would be—"

Grace interrupted him, "You know, Adam, until about five minutes ago I hadn't decided what to do with the house. But you've helped me. Now I know."

"Good. At least that's settled."

"I'm going to keep the house, Adam. I think my parents left it to me as restitution," she said, quoting Luke.

"Restitution? For what?"

"As a way of explanation."

"That's a lot of crap."

"I'm keeping it. I may not be able to bring back Alex or them, but I will cherish that house. There can be summers there again. Kate can come with her friends. With her husband one day. Our grandchildren."

"You're terribly confused, Grace."

"No, Adam. I want that house to . . . to stay in my family," she said, her head bowing down as she spoke. "It's mine, Adam." She lifted her head and looked at him. "It's mine."

"You must be insane." Adam stood up, threw his napkin and the photograph on the table, and marched out of the room. Grace heard the library door slam shut.

"I would go, Mom," Kate said quietly. "I would go there with you."

"You'd like it there, Kate," Grace said. "Go ahead, honey. Finish unpacking and get your things organized. It's a school day tomorrow. I can clean up here."

"What about Dad? Shouldn't you say something to him?"

"Just leave it alone right now," Grace said. "Go ahead, Kate. You have plenty to do."

Grace meticulously folded the tops of the small white containers and placed them in the refrigerator, stacked the plates in the dishwasher, tossed the napkins in the trash. When she was finished, she walked down the hallway to the library, the photograph of Alex and Luke in her hand. She knocked on the door.

"May I talk to you?" she asked through the door.

"It's not locked," Adam answered.

Grace walked into the room and sat on the couch. "I'm keeping the island. It's my only legacy."

"You're out of your mind," Adam said, his finger pointing at Grace's face. "You can't even remember that fucking place and you're talking to me about legacies? You need a psychiatrist."

"A psychiatrist? I'm grieving, for God's sake." Grace stood in front of her husband. "Adam, this is my life. If I put this behind me, I put my life behind me. What I just told you has made me who I am. To put this behind me, I would have to pretend to be someone I am not. I need to take all this and let it become a part of me the way it always should have been. You can't reduce my pain, my parents' pain, to a diagnosis." She walked out of the room and Adam heard the slam of the bedroom door.

"I want you to call Dr. Alan Muller in the morning," Adam said, flinging the bedroom open. "My secretary will call you with his number. He's chief of psychiatry at the hospital. If you don't call him, I will. For God's sake, Grace. Recurring dreams. Broken hearts. Suicide as an understandable solution? The notion that you want to keep some rundown island house. I tell you, you've upset your daughter with your ravings. You've finally lost it, Grace."

"No, Adam," Grace said. "I think I finally found it." She walked past him into the bathroom, closed the door, turned the lock.

Adam pounded his fist on the bathroom door. "If you don't call Muller in the morning I'll—"

Grace opened the door. "You'll what? You can call Muller until you're blue in the face," she said. "And you're the reason that Kate is upset. You, with your vitriol and your carrying on. You must bleed ice water, Adam. You are impotent, impotent do you hear me, when it comes to repairing the heart. Especially mine."

She shut the door in his face. Then she turned on the shower full force and drowned him out.

Chapter Twenty-four

Adam slept in the library after the argument. He never attempted to come into the master bedroom. He left his pajamas on the hook of the bathroom door; his slippers remained in the closet. Early in the morning, shortly after five, Adam stumbled into the bedroom, shirtless, wearing rumpled trousers. Grace heard his footsteps and turned onto her side, the way a child feigns sleep. She saw the silhouette of Adam's tall, lanky frame as he stepped from his boxer shorts and tossed them into the wicker hamper. He turned on the night light, and she thought his face looked haggard as he leaned into the closet mirror for a closer look, running his fingers through his fine silver-blond hair, stroking the stubble on his chin. Perhaps what struck Grace the most was that he never glanced her way. She felt invisible. Just yesterday morning she had watched Luke walk from the shower, a towel wrapped tautly around his waist, his dark thick graying hair slicked back from his forehead, beads of water still dripping from his sideburns. He had leaned over the bed where she sat propped against the pillows, waiting for him, and kissed her.

You smell so good, she murmured, nestling her face in Luke's neck. What is that?

It could be you, he whispered, sliding into the bed beside her again.

Grace hadn't slept well. It wasn't so much that she and Adam argued that prevented her from sleeping. It was more that each time she'd closed her eyes, she thought of Luke. She shivered when she thought of his touch, the look in his eyes when he made love to her, the gentle tone he took when he spoke to her. She thought of the afternoon on the island when he told her the story of Alex and how right it felt when they fell into one another's arms. And then the image of Adam's angry face, the cold penetration of his words about the island, interrupted her thoughts.

I hope you gave him something for his trouble. . . . I hope you're going to get rid of that house.

It baffled her how Adam was able to retreat the way he did after they had harsh words. But perhaps, last night, he slept in the library because he *couldn't* sleep, she thought. But that was unlikely. He had the ability to tune out and recover. It was similar to the way he conducted himself after a middle-of-the-night page from the hospital: After a crisis, there was little residue.

Grace listened while Adam ran the shower. She glanced at the clock. Only five-twenty. Why was he leaving so early? Probably to avoid another confrontation at breakfast, she thought. She watched him dress in the dark as she pretended to sleep. Then, like a cat burglar who had taken what there was to take, Adam left the room stealthily. She heard the squeak of the hinges on the hall closet and the wooden hangers knock against each other as he pulled down his coat. She listened as his cowboy boots scraped across the hardwood floors and heard his footsteps halt as his beeper went off. She heard the faint lift of the receiver, the low monotone of his voice as he spoke.

"Look, my first case is at seven," he said. "Don't fuck up my OR schedule this time, Ruth. I'll raise Cain if it happens again." And then Grace heard the receiver slam, the door close firmly on the latch, and the whirring sound of the elevator within the walls.

Grace tiptoed into Kate's room at seven-thirty and awakened her.

"School day," Grace said, pulling up the blinds. "Get up sleepyhead. Party's over."

"Are you and Dad still fighting?" Kate asked sleepily.

"It'll all work itself out," Grace said.

"What's that supposed to mean?" Kate yawned, sitting up in bed.

"It means that we all go through rough times, but we work them through. Get going now, Kate. I can't be late my first day back to work, either. Christmas vacation is over, miss."

"Where's Dad?"

"He left early this morning."

"Why?"

"He's operating. It's Monday. I guess he wanted a jump start," Grace said with forced cheer. "Come on, Kate, get going. See you in the kitchen."

Teachers at Grace's school offered their condolences that morning as she sat drinking tea in the faculty lounge before she taught class. They had seen her parents' obituary in the newspaper, they said. At first, Grace just nodded and smiled as they comforted her with all the perfunctory words she had become too accustomed to hearing. She skillfully avoided their furtive questions as they tried to determine cause of death. Questions poorly disguised as sympathy as they tried to determine how an elderly married couple dies on the same day. We saw the obituaries. How dreadful to lose them both at once, they said, waiting for an answer to the odd circumstance as they emphasized the simultaneity. Exasperated, Grace looked a woman named Loretta right in the eye and said they had committed suicide. Loretta's hand flew to her mouth in a gesture of horror. For a moment Grace felt bad that she had unduly shocked her, but Loretta was too obviously probing under a cloak of compassion. Grace tried to deflect the blow she felt she had inflicted on Loretta, explaining that her father had what they believed was Alzheimer's and that her mother had ailed her entire life. But as she spoke, Grace was painfully aware that she wasn't telling the truth. The truth, however, was too complicated to explain. Or perhaps it was that it was deeply personal and, simply, too sad.

The children came into Grace's studio and took their dance shoes from their cubbies in the back of the room. A second-grader named Amanda, who wore a heavy brace on her right leg and a pair of round steel-rimmed glasses, handed Grace two yellow roses wrapped in a sheath of cellophane.

"My mommy said to give you this and tell you we're sorry," Amanda said, her brown eyes magnified behind thick lenses. "You know, my grandma died right before Christmas, too, Mrs. Barnett."

Grace lightly kissed the top of the girl's head. "I'm so sorry to hear that, Amanda. You tell your mommy I am sorry for her loss, too," Grace said.

"I miss my grandma," the child said, dropping her chin to her chest. "A lot."

"Then think of her really hard," Grace said, lifting Amanda's face under her chin. "And you'll feel her somehow. And when you visit the cemetery, bring something with you to place beside her."

"Like what?" Amanda asked, her magnified eyes even rounder.

"Oh, I don't know. Your favorite flower, maybe. A drawing that you make just for her. Something to remember her forever." And Grace smiled because she thought that Luke would have said the same. It was at that moment that the ache inside made her eyes well up with tears and she wondered how she could continue to miss him the way she had since she left Sabbath Landing. And, for the first time since her parents died, she felt a memory deep inside from a place far away. She missed them.

Grace helped Amanda with her dance shoes and clapped her hands to call the class to order. The children danced to "The Colors of the Wind" that morning. Grace gave them long chiffon scarves in pastel colors and told them to twirl to the music in any way they felt it.

"Wave your arms over your head in the air, slowly as if you're dragging them through muddy water. Now, pretend that the water is clear and blue and move your arms faster," Grace said, her arms above her head, swaying back and forth, as she stood before the class. "As though you're swimming now," she said. "You might even make believe you're floating."

When class was over, Grace went to her usual spot in the cafeteria. She was hungry, having eaten so early. It was nearly ten-thirty. The toast she had at home wasn't enough to hold her until lunch. She was lost in thought when Esther, the school secretary, tapped her shoulder. She startled at the touch. Her mind was in Sabbath Landing.

"You have a phone call," Esther said.

"A phone call?"

"A Lew somebody."

"Lew or Luke?" Grace asked, her heart skipping a beat.

"I'm not sure, Grace," Esther said apologetically. "He spoke kind of fast. But he's on hold."

Grace followed Esther to the office and picked up the old black phone.

"This is Grace," she said, anticipating.

"Lew Erickson," the voice said.

Grace had known Lew and Joyce Erickson nearly as long as she'd known Adam. Lew was a cardiologist, what Adam called a noninvasive guy, at the hospital.

"Lew! Are you making another surprise party for Joyce?" Grace teased. "I don't know if she's gotten over her fortieth yet."

"No, not this time, Grace. Listen, everything's going to be okay, but Adam's had an MI."

Grace gasped. "An MI?"

"A heart attack. Myocardial infarction."

Grace knew what an MI was. "Oh, no. Oh, my God." She was shaking.

"He's stable. He's in the cath lab as we speak. About halfway through an angioplasty. Dave Stevens is the interventionalist. Good man."

"An angioplasty?" Grace asked, stunned. "When did this happen? Where?"

"He collapsed during his morning case. He's okay, Grace. I can send someone to accompany you here. How about if I ask one of my staff to get you? I can even call Joyce."

"I can get there by myself. Just promise that you're leveling with me. That he's okay."

"He's wide awake, Grace. He's one tough son of a gun," Lew said affectionately. "I'll meet you outside the cath lab. Second floor, Cove-leigh Wing."

"I know where it is," she said.

Esther looked at her as she hung up the phone. "What happened?"

Grace nodded, swallowing hard. "My husband had a heart attack," Grace said, her mind flashing back to the red rubber bags and the medical examiner's van parked in the driveway on Harvest Lane. The phone call that had come from Melanie that morning.

"What happened, Melanie?"

"They're gone, Grace. I told you. They're just gone."

"I think someone should take you to the hospital. You shouldn't go alone," Esther said.

"I'm okay." Grace nodded. "The doctor said he's stable. I want to be by myself, Esther. Just please call Janet Clark and see if she can sub for me this afternoon, or maybe the kids can sit in on Joe's general music class."

"Don't you worry, Grace. We'll take care of it. You just go to your husband. That's where you belong."

The security guard didn't stop Grace at the entrance to New York Medical Center. He'd known her for years.

"Hey, Mrs. Barnett. Haven't seen you in ages . . ." His voice trailed off as Grace ran onto the elevator, not acknowledging him. The eleva-tor stopped on the second floor. How many times when she was younger had she waited for Adam by the elevators outside of the surgi-cal suite? How often had he taken her hand and walked her to the doc-tor's lounge while he changed from his green scrubs to flannel slacks and navy blazer? Those were the days when they started to have din-ner at Pasquale's. The days when she was the young wife of the incom-ing chief of cardiac surgery. Now, suddenly, she was a patient's wife. The warm, close hospital air mingled with the pungent odor of anti-septic and disinfectant masking God knows what else made her sick to her stomach. Her mouth was parched and her eyes burned. Her gait slowed to a deliberate pace as she made her way down what seemed an endless stark corridor to the cath lab as though she were in a trance.

Grace opened the swinging doors to the catheterization unit.

"Mrs. Barnett!" The nurse, an older white-haired woman, jumped up from behind the desk.

"Liz," Grace said, her hand covering her mouth. The last time Grace had seen her was at the Department of Surgery Christmas party just before her parents died. "Where is he?"

Liz took Grace's arm. "He's still inside. Let me page Dr. Erickson for you. Come sit right here," Liz said, pointing to an empty chair behind the nurse's station. "Can I get you something? Some water? I want you to sit down. You're very pale."

Lew Erickson came out of the cath lab moments after Liz dialed his pager.

"Please don't let her stand up, Doctor," Liz said. "I don't like her color."

Lew crouched down beside Grace, balancing on one knee. "I always listen to Nurse Lizzie. She's been here longer than I have." He winked. "So, that husband of yours is one pain in the neck. He won't stop asking questions. We've threatened to muzzle him."

"He's talking?"

"Can't get him to pipe down."

"Why did it happen, Lew?"

"I can't tell you why it happened," Lew said, his demeanor becoming more serious. "I can tell you that I've been after Adam to see me for years. Grace, he's a typical cardiac surgeon. Never even had a stress test. Christ, I told him just a couple of weeks ago that he should come in just so we could have a look. I mean, he had no symptoms, but he's almost sixty, for Christ's sake. And he liked his wine and what he called the 'occasional cigar,' didn't he?"

"Was there any warning at all? I want to know everything," Grace said.

Lew sat down beside Grace and told her. Earlier that morning, not past nine, Adam was suturing an artery during his first case of the day.

It was apparent to the OR staff that he was particularly agitated that morning, even for him. Lew had been up in the gallery watching since it was his patient who was having the surgery.

"It was tough case and, to make matters worse, the patient was a VIP. Big shot from administration. The surgical fellow finished up. Thank God, he's one of our best ones. Usually, I don't watch the cases but, as I said, this one was different. It all happened very fast, but I noticed that Adam was losing dexterity. His pace was slowing down like he was distracted or something. He started pulling at his gown and shifting his mask with his gloved hand and it was pretty obvious he was having difficulty breathing. I knew then and there that something was wrong. Really wrong. Adam would never break sterility. And then all of sudden, his eyes just rolled back in his head and he hit the floor. He must have known something was happening to him. I can bet that he was scared out of his mind."

Lew explained that the anesthesiologist, Carl Jeffries, and Nancy Davis, the circulating nurse, came to Adam's assistance after he collapsed. Carl felt for a pulse in Adam's neck—it was, as expected, weak and thready. Nancy ran into the corridor and called for help. Dr. Barnett's collapsed, she called urgently to staffers loitering in the hall. Before anyone could blink, a gurney was wheeled into the OR. Several technicians and Carl lifted Adam onto the stretcher and started an intravenous. They placed a portable monitor beside Adam on the gurney, electrodes attached to his chest, and rushed him to the emergency room. The electrocardiogram taken in the ER showed that Adam was having an acute myocardial infarction. A massive heart attack.

"We called the cath lab as soon as we saw the EKG," Lew said. "His blood pressure was ninety over sixty, but he was conscious again. And it was unbelievable, he kept talking, asking questions. I told you, even in the lab now, he's asking us where the blockage is, how the ventricle looks. There's no worse patient than a doctor, right, Grace?"

"What does the angioplasty do?" Grace asked, ignoring Lew's attempts to cheer her. "I've heard the term a million times, but I don't really know what it is." Her face fell for a moment. "I never had to know before."

"They're passing a catheter, a tube, that goes from an insertion point in Adam's groin up to his aorta. Then they'll inject some dye into the artery and where they see the blockage, they'll open it with a balloon. Then they inflate the balloon on the end and it opens the occluded, the blocked, artery. And they'll put in a stent, looks like the spring on a ballpoint pen, to keep that artery open."

"A tube goes to his heart?"

"Well, to the aorta, really."

"And he's awake through all that?"

"Yup, wide awake. Oh, they gave him local. Novocaine. I'm telling you, Grace, the moment that balloon goes in there, his chest pain will stop, his BP will go back up. He'll be good as new."

"Was it bad? I mean, was the chest pain bad?" Grace asked, her eyes filling with tears. She remembered watching her husband that morning. He hadn't looked well to her. His face looked drawn and weary. How would she have felt if they hadn't gotten to him in time? What if that morning had been the last time she had seen him alive as she pretended to be sleeping? She always told him never to go to bed angry.

"He said the pain felt like a ton of bricks. But, look, he could have been alone or driving his car when this happened. He took a big hit, but we got to him early. His chances are real good."

The door to the cath lab swung open.

"All done, Lew," the doctor said, pulling off his mask. "Looks good."

"Dave, this is Adam's wife, Grace. Grace, Dr. Dave Stevens."

"Quite a guy, your husband. I can't count the times he said that he hoped to hell I knew what I was doing," Dr. Stevens laughed. "Made me swear to bring the films to him in CCU. He's a lucky guy. Lucky he was right here when it happened." Dr. Stevens glanced at the digital display of the beeper on his belt. "I expect him to do fine," he said looking at his wristwatch and then back at Grace. "I've got to run. I've got another case that's been waiting over an hour. If you need any-thing at all, Grace, just give me a call. Lew? Give her my number and pager, will you?"

"Now what?" Grace asked, staring at the lab's door.

"They're going to clean him up and get him to CCU now, Grace," Lew said. "It's going to take them about a half hour. He knows you're here, though."

"Can I see him?"

"Too much radiation floating in there," Lew fibbed, wanting to get Grace away from the unit. Adam still looked grim. He knew she was better off seeing him out of the lab. "Come on, let's grab some coffee and get you a big sugary doughnut to put the color back in you. You'll see him when they've got him all cleaned up and tucked into CCU."

Adam was in Room 7 of the coronary care unit. He lay on the bed, his face turned toward the window when Grace walked into the room. His arms lay lifeless by his side, palms down, an intravenous in either one. Clear tubing ran from a Foley catheter inserted into the tip of Adam's penis to a urine-filled bag hanging at the bedside. Oxygen prongs attached in his nostrils made his eyes appear sunken and hol-low. His hair was matted on his head. Small purple bruises sprouted around the various tubes that were anchored in his arms. Beneath the hospital gown, electrodes ran from his chest to a steadily beeping monitor above his bed. An area on the right side of his groin was shaved, the sheath still in place from the angioplasty in case the doc-tors needed access to the artery again. He was barely recognizable.

"Adam?" Grace walked over to the side of his bed and lay her hand lightly over his, careful not to disturb the tubes.

He turned his head halfway and opened his eyes.

"Goddamn Foley is killing me," he said.

"It won't be for long, Adam," Grace said.

"What are you doing here? Don't you teach?"

"They called me at the school. I came right away," she said, ignor-ing the sarcasm in his tone.

"Good thing this happened here, right, Grace? Not on some fucking island. I'd be a dead man."

She hesitated for a moment, realizing his anger was misdirected at her. Still, his words stung her. "Adam, if you don't want me here, I can leave. I'd like to stay, though. But I don't think we should talk about the island right now, do you?"

He turned his head away from her gaze and didn't answer.

"Adam? Do you want me to stay or leave?" she asked, her face stony. "Answer me."

He turned his head back toward her. His eyes were damp in the corners. "Don't leave me, Grace. Stay," he whispered hoarsely. "I need you."

"I won't leave you," she said, her voice choking as she looked at the monitor above his bed that graphed every singular beat of his heart. She took an unfinished breath. "I'll stay right here."

Chapter Twenty-five

Grace left Adam's bedside that afternoon only to pick up Kate. She hadn't called her at school. She wanted Kate to see her face and trust the look in her eyes when she told her what happened to her father. Grace stood outside the redbrick school building and watched the girls trail out in groups, laughing, their coats flung open, woolen scarves dangling loosely from their necks despite the cold January air and the flurries of falling snow.

"Mom! What are you doing here?" Kate called.

"I thought I'd surprise you," Grace said wanly.

"A bunch of us are going to go to the drugstore. We're buying makeup," Kate giggled. "Big dance Saturday night."

"Well, talk to me a second," Grace said. "Come, let's stand inside for a moment. It's cold out here."

"What's going on, Mom?" Kate asked as they walked into the school.

They sat on a bench outside the school nurse's office. "Everything is going to be fine, Kate, but your father had a heart attack this morning—"

Before Grace could finish the sentence, Kate wailed. "Oh, no. Oh, please don't tell me this." She buried her face in her hands.

Grace took her daughter's hands and pulled them from her face. "Look at me. He's going to be fine. He's in the coronary care unit but he's very lucky. They got to him early. I'm going to take you there right now."

"How do I know you're telling me the truth?" Kate asked, tears streaming down her cheeks.

"Because I would never lie to you and you're about to see for yourself. Now, come on." Grace was fishing in her purse. "Wipe your face," she said, handing Kate a limp tissue. "We'll grab a cab."

Patient visiting hours were over for the afternoon, but Grace knew the rules did not apply to doctors' wives. She and Kate walked past the security guard, who waved at them and nodded sympathetically. Word travels fast, Grace thought.

Kate held Grace's arm as they walked into the CCU. "Now, listen to me, Kate," Grace said, pausing outside Adam's room. "He still doesn't look so great. There are IVs in his arms and some bruising where they put the lines in. He's hooked up to tubes and a catheter for his urine and a heart monitor. And he's a little pale and can use a shower." Grace took a deep breath and smiled at Kate. "But he's starting to boss everyone around, so I know he's on the mend."

Adam's eyes were closed and his lips slightly parted when Grace and Kate walked into the room. *Oprah* was on a television tipped high on the wall, muted with white-on-black captions running across the screen. The room smelled like stale soup and rubbing alcohol. A stainless steel bedside table held a small gray box of tissues, water pitcher, and short stack of wax cups. There was a small plastic tray of untouched food pushed to the side, a crumpled napkin sitting on the top of what looked like baked fish, a small plastic fork wedged into a corner where a morsel had been removed. A small gold foil-wrapped packet of margarine had fallen to the floor. Grace noticed that someone had placed a blue surgical cap discreetly over the urine bag.

"What's wrong with him?" Kate gasped, clutching her mother's arm.

"He's sleeping," Grace whispered. "He's had a rough time."

"Why is he breathing like that?"

"He's not breathing like anything, Kate," Grace said.

"It's so slow."

"No, it's fine," Grace said, looking at the monitor. "He's fine."

"What should we do?" Kate asked.

"We can go to the cafeteria if you like. Are you hungry?"

"No, I want to wait right here," Kate said, lifting a small metal chair quietly, closer to the foot of Adam's bed. "I want to be here when he wakes up."

"I'll get another chair," Grace said, but Kate didn't answer her. She was staring, eyes fixed on her father, watching his chest move up and down.

Adam had awakened by the time Grace returned with another chair. Kate was leaning tentatively over the bed so that her face was cupped in Adam's right hand that he'd managed to raise despite the tubing.

"Don't you worry," he said. "It's going to take a lot more than this to take out your old man."

"You're not an old man," Kate sniffled.

But for the first time in his life, Adam felt like an old man. He turned to Grace as she set down the chair. "What the hell did they do with my boots? And my watch? Who's got my watch?"

"Your boots and clothes are in a locker, Adam. Your watch is in my purse. It's all safe and sound."

"What about my cell phone? Goddamn phone in here doesn't take incoming calls."

"It's in my purse. There's no one you need to call, is there, Adam? Certainly no one needs to call you right now. Besides, you know you can't use cell phones in the hospital," Grace said patiently. "You didn't eat your lunch."

"It's vile. Apple juice, for Christ's sake. And swordfish. I hate swordfish and this was bone dry."

"You need nutrition," Grace said.

"You two should go have dinner at Pasquale's," Adam said. "Bring me back a veal dish. What the hell? Get me the one swimming in that morel cream sauce."

"Adam," Grace said wearily. "You need to cooperate. Lew says you can get out of here by Saturday. Besides, you never have cream sauce."

"Well, maybe I should start," Adam said sarcastically.

"It's way too early for dinner, Daddy," Kate said. "It's not even four-thirty."

"Well, then go shopping or something. No point hanging around here."

"We don't mind," Grace said. "Unless you prefer to be alone."

"No, it's not that. I'm so damn tired. I just need to sleep," Adam said, looking away from his wife's face.

"Daddy, we could bring you something later," Kate said.

"A cognac would be good," he said. "And a Cohiba."

"Don't tease her, Adam," Grace said, leaning over and kissing his forehead. "We're going to go and let you rest. I'll be back in the morning."

"No work?"

"I'm taking the week off."

"You really don't have to do that, Grace."

"I know. But I'd like to."

"Take care of your mother, Kate," Adam said, pressing Grace's arm as she stood up from her kiss.

Grace caught his eye as he touched her arm. An image of Luke swept over her. She remembered Luke lying beside her, his arm enveloping her close to him. She looked at her husband's drawn, pale face and heard the steady beep of the monitor above his head and heaved an audible sigh. Her thoughts were broken by Kate's voice.

"I love you, Daddy," she said.

"I'll be racing you down the slopes again next winter, kiddo," Adam said. Uncharacteristically, he added. "I love you, too, Kate."

Grace felt guilty for her thoughts.

"See you tomorrow, Adam," she said.

Grace and Kate went home and changed their clothes. It was too much to go to Pasquale's. Grace had enough questions for one day. Going to Pasquale's without Adam required more explanation than she was prepared to give. Instead, the two wore blue jeans and went to a pub on Seventh Avenue. They ordered hamburgers and French fries.

"Your father would disapprove," Grace laughed.

"Yeah, but all those years of not eating this kind of stuff and look where it got him," Kate said bitterly. "Even he said so."

"He's going to be fine, Kate. You need to stop worrying. If he sees that you're upset, it's not going to help him."

"Why don't you ever tell him that you love him?" Kate asked suddenly.

Grace flushed. "Kate! I do. Of course I do."

"Well, I never hear you. I can't remember the last time I heard you tell him. Maybe you should once in awhile. I mean, especially now that he's sick, you know? Maybe it would help him to, I don't know, to recover."

"I tell him," Grace said defensively, wanting to ask Kate if she noticed that Adam never told her.

"Well, maybe not enough. You didn't tell him at the hospital."

"There are things between husbands and wives that have nothing to do with their children," Grace said uncomfortably. "I don't think you and I should necessarily have this conversation."

"Why not?" Kate asked defiantly.

"Why are you so angry?" Grace asked.

"I'm not angry."

"Yes, you are. Is there something that you have to say to me? Do you think this happened because your father and I had a fight last night?"

"I don't know," Kate said, her head down. "Maybe."

"Well, it didn't. That's not the reason."

"I thought these things come from stress."

"If they came solely from stress, then we'd all be having heart attacks and strokes. You know better than that, Kate. Sometimes bad things happen and the reasons are beyond our control," Grace said.

"Well, maybe for just a while we should make sure not to talk about things that might get him riled up. Like the island. Don't talk about the island anymore, okay?"

Grace nodded. "I won't talk about the island anymore. But, Kate, certainly you can't blame your father's heart attack on me."

"I'm not blaming you. I just think that maybe in the last few weeks since your parents died, things have been a little crazy."

"Yes," Grace said stiffly. "Things have been very unsettling."

"Well, Daddy's older than you are and maybe he's not as, I don't know, not as resilient."

"He's hardly an old man," Grace said. "Seems to me he gave you quite a run on skis a few weeks ago. He's very strong."

"Well, anyway, I don't think you should talk about the island anymore, at least not to Daddy. And don't talk about your parents, either. You can talk to Aunt Mel if you need to talk about things. And to me, I guess."

"Do you want dessert?" Grace asked, trying not to appear annoyed with Kate.

"No, I just want to go home. Do I have to go to school tomorrow?"

"Absolutely. We're going to have life as normal as possible until your father gets better."

"And then, once he's better, we go back to abnormal, right?"

"That was nasty, Kate. And unnecessary."

"I'm sorry."

"I know you're upset, but I think you can be upset without being unkind. Certain things happen that are no one's fault," Grace said. And as Grace spoke, she marveled at her own words.

Grace waited until Kate was sleeping before she dialed Luke's number. It was nearly midnight. The phone rang four times before he answered.

"Hello?"

"Luke?"

"Grace! Where are you?"

"I'm home. I woke you. I'm sorry. I should have waited until morning."

"No, no, it's okay." Luke pulled himself up in bed and reached for his cigarettes. "I've been thinking about you all day. God, it's good to hear your voice."

"But I woke you. You probably have to get up in a few hours."

"Forget that. I'm so glad you called. I couldn't call you, you know that, right, Grace? I wanted to. How was the drive yesterday?"

Was it only yesterday? Grace thought. It seemed like so long ago. "It was fine. I found the puzzle bark on the seat. I put them in my drawer."

"A souvenir so you wouldn't forget me," Luke said softly. "Everything okay?"

"I miss you," she said. "That's all."

"I miss you, too."

"Luke, Adam had a heart attack this morning."

"Oh, Jesus. Is he all right? See, I knew something was wrong. You didn't sound right to me."

"He's okay. He had it while he was operating so I guess if you're going to have a heart attack, no better place than in a hospital, right?" Grace said. "But he's sick, Luke. I mean, he's in the coronary care unit and he's hooked up to all this machinery and, well, I guess I'm not accustomed to seeing him look so weak."

"What do the doctors say?" Luke asked.

"That he's lucky. That they got to him in time. Adam and I had a huge fight last night. He wants me to sell the island. I can't remember the last time we had such angry words. Kate is upset with me now. I think she blames me for the heart attack."

"She heard the fight?"

"She was right there."

"She doesn't really blame you, Grace. She just doesn't know who to blame right now. I went through the same thing with Chris. He was so angry that Meg was sick and I became his whipping post. You'll just have to tough it out with her. She'll come around. She just needs to lash out at someone and you're it."

"Rationally, I know all that. But it's hard to take," Grace said, her fingers twirling the phone wire. "Last night, Adam said I should put the past behind me and that the island and the house are nothing more than liabilities. I don't know. He thinks I should get some professional help."

"Professional help? Like a real estate agent?"

"No," Grace laughed. "Like a psychiatrist. I tried to explain to him that I just need to digest so many things."

"There are grief counselors, you know. Maybe it would do you good to talk to someone."

"Maybe. But it's not just that I'm grieving for my parents, Luke. My husband is sick and I'm thinking about you. I feel like a terrible person." She lowered her voice. "I sat with him all day today, Luke. Mostly, I watched him sleep. And now, I'm home and I just want to be with you."

"You're not terrible, Grace, but he needs you right now."

"I know."

There was too long a silence on the other end of the phone.

"Luke?"

"I'm here."

"Do you understand what I'm saying, because I'm not sure that I do. Not that I've said much of anything. But when I left you yesterday— God, I can't believe it was just yesterday—well, I had all these dreams about going back there. I kept picturing the island in the spring and now . . . Now I just can't. Not anymore. I want to, but I can't. I can't even allow myself to go there in my mind. "

"You know, I never really thought you'd come back here to me. I dreamed about it all day today but I never really believed it, Grace."

"But why? Why didn't you believe it? I believed it until this morning."

"I'm not sure. Sometimes I think I almost have a sixth sense about things. It's as though you were a gift to me this past week. And I cherish that gift. But all this now with your husband . . . I just don't want to dream anymore right now, Grace. Maybe I've just awakened from my dreams one too many times."

"So have I. But until recently so many of them were nightmares. This seemed like such a good one this time."

"I don't know what to say," Luke said. "You know where to find me if you need me."

"I know," she whispered. "Same here." She caught her breath. "I'm doing the right thing, Luke. I have to do what's right, don't I?"

"Yes, you do," he said.

"Will you call?"

"No," he said. "You call."

"I'll try," she said, her voice breaking. "Take care of yourself, Luke." She hung up the phone and leaned her head back against the pillows, her eyes wide open as saucers to catch her tears.

Luke turned on the lamp by his bedside. He took the pillow where she laid her head beside him. It never occurred to him in the last several days that she wouldn't come back to him. He had said what he said to ease her pain. He could still smell her scent on the pillow. The pine shampoo she used in her hair. That perfume she wore, Anaïs. He loved the name. He saw a faint pink smudge of lipstick on the pillow slip. He lit another cigarette and mashed it out after two puffs, tossed the pillow on the bed, and went to the kitchen. He poured a Black Velvet from the bottle that sat on the counter, glanced at the sink, and realized he still hadn't washed their wineglasses from the weekend. He pulled a chair out from under the kitchen table and it shrieked across the floor. He took a slow sip of whiskey and slammed his fist on the table. How could he have believed his mother when she said the kingdom of God was in him and all around him? At that moment, he had never felt so alone.

Chapter Twenty-six

For the first few days, Adam mostly slept. There were mornings Grace sat in the stiff metal chair by his bed for hours and watched him, turning the pages of a magazine quietly so she wouldn't wake him, reading the captions on the television instead of turning up the volume. She would hear him stir on the precipice of wakening and fill the small stainless steel basin with warm clean water. She dampened a washcloth that she scented with Sea Breeze, gathered his toothbrush and paste, set a paper cup of cool water on the bedside stand. Both were silent as Grace bathed Adam's face with the cloth, wiped his hands that were still captive by the intravenous lines. He managed to raise them enough to brush his teeth while she held the basin below his chin, handing him the paper cup of water to rinse when he was finished. She combed his hair and dabbed some aftershave behind his ears even though he couldn't shave yet. She joked that he was beginning to strongly resemble Howard Hughes; when he didn't laugh, she apologized for saying the wrong thing. She felt foolish: He was always so pulled together and here he was, wearing a hospital-issue gown, unshaved, unkempt, unshowered. His humiliation was transparent. His dependency was staggering.

On the fourth morning, Thursday, Adam was transferred to the progressive coronary care unit, a step down from the confines of CCU. The electrodes that imprisoned him in the bed were replaced by a portable transmitter that clipped to his hospital gown. He was able to walk around the halls now, shave at the bathroom mirror while the transmitter relayed his heart sounds to a monitor at the nursing station. Although he could have showered, he preferred to sponge-bathe. He was too weak, he confessed to Grace in an even weaker moment, to feel confident standing in a steamy, slippery shower. She offered to help, but he refused.

Adam was loath to walk the corridors when the hospital was in full swing. He would only walk when visitors had gone home and the house staff wasn't milling about. As he began to heal and regain his strength, he insisted that Grace not sit by his bedside all day. "It's claustrophobic," he said. "You need to get out in the air. And I need some time alone. I feel enough like an invalid, Grace. Can't you understand that?"

She did understand. On Friday afternoon, the day before Adam was supposed to come home, Grace took a dance class on Broadway and stopped at the school to pick up her mail. She met Melanie and Jemma for lunch at a restaurant near Grand Central Station. Before Jemma arrived, she and Melanie ordered a glass of wine.

"Who's got the kids?" Grace asked, unfolding a napkin on her lap.

"They're in nursery school until two. Then Mrs. Hadley's going to pick them up," Melanie said. "Grace, have you spoken to him?"

"Adam?" Grace answered, confused.

"No, silly. Luke. Have you spoken to Luke?"

"I spoke to him the night after Adam's heart attack," Grace said softly.

"And? That was nearly a week ago."

"And nothing, Mel," Grace sighed.

"How can you say nothing?"

"Because there's nothing to say."

"What did he say? Did you tell him about Adam?"

"Of course I told him."

"And?"

"What can he say? Come on, Mel. This isn't high school."

"Exactly."

"What's that supposed to mean?"

"You had a love affair, Grace. Now you've got a sick husband. How do you feel, for God's sake? How do you think Luke feels?"

"I feel horrible. I feel angry and dutiful and lonely."

"Angry and dutiful and lonely. Gee, how come that rings a bell?"

"You should have been an analyst."

"No, this doesn't take analysis. Not when something is hitting you right over the head. You can't spend the rest of your life playing nurse. Until Adam's heart attack, you had a foot out the door. If you ask me, so did Adam."

"Everything's changed now."

"*Now* could be the operative word here," Melanie said. "What about the island?"

"Well, I guess it's still there, isn't it?" Grace said in a clipped voice.

"Grace, don't talk to me that way. I'm sorry. I don't want to fight with you. I'm just worried about you. You always do what you think is the right thing and I'm not so sure it's always right for you."

"Adam wants me to sell the island."

"No, I asked what *you're* going to do with it."

"I don't want to talk about this."

"Listen to me," Melanie said, leaning forward. "Once Adam is back on his feet, he's going to be back to his old self again, Grace. And God knows, that man will recover. Look, I am very sorry this happened to him and I would never wish him ill, but I don't want to see you in some guilt-ridden trap." If Melanie could have raised her voice any louder in the restaurant, she would have been yelling.

"I have a sick husband, " Grace said. "I need to do whatever I can so he heals. I don't want to agitate him."

"Just promise me one thing," Melanie said, lowering her voice, shutting her eyes for a moment. "Promise me you'll wait until he's better and then make your decision about the island. Don't just go along with him and sell it to humor him. You'll regret it. I swear, you'll regret it."

"Why are you so adamant?"

"Because I saw you on that island," Melanie said, her voice in a whisper. "And I saw the way Luke looked at you and the way you looked at him and I know you have a lot to deal with right now but things are going to change again. Just trust me, Grace."

"I'm going to tell you everything. Everything. I promise. You have to trust me. Please," Luke said. *"Give me your hand."*

"Okay," Grace said softly. "I'll listen to you."

"Promise?"

"Promise."

"I hope you mean it, Grace," Mel said, opening the menu.

"I miss him, Mel," Grace whispered on the verge of tears. "I miss Luke so much. I'm so confused right now."

Melanie reached across the table and patted her sister's hand. "I know, Grace. I know you miss him. That's why I just want you to wait before you make any decisions. Just wait." Melanie glanced toward the door. "Jemma's here. Quiet, now."

At ten o'clock on Saturday morning, Lew Erickson discharged Adam.

"You'll have to lay low for a while, though, buddy," Lew said. "I don't want to find you hanging around the hospital for at least three weeks. No surgery. No office hours. No teaching rounds. Not even paperwork. And don't be a wise ass, either, Barnett or I'll slap you back in here on some false pretense just to keep you still."

Adam was lying in bed, his breakfast tray pushed to the side, the food untouched, when Grace tapped on the half open door to his room.

"Good morning, prisoner!" she said brightly. "We've come to spring you."

"Are you excited, Dad?" Kate asked. "You're coming home!"

"I never want to see Jell-O again," he said. "Or egg whites. Unsalted egg whites, can you imagine?"

"You should eat, though. When we get you home, we'll make you something special," Grace said. "You look tired. Did you sleep last night?"

"I'm sick to my stomach."

"Is that a figure of speech or do you really feel ill?" Grace asked nervously.

"No, I really don't feel very well. Must be the rubber chicken I ate last night," he said. "I'm going to wash up so we can get the hell out of here." At that moment, he stood up from the bed. "Hand me my robe, will you, Kate? It's on the back of the door."

Kate held the robe behind him as he slipped his arms into the sleeves. Grace looked at him standing in the hospital gown. It was short on him, well above his knees. He looked painfully thin to her. He'd rejected the hospital food all week. Grace brought him some protein shakes, but he drank only half of them, saying they tasted like chalk. His arms still bore faint bruises from the intravenous lines. His beard was white and scruffy. He was pale; cadaverous.

"Maybe you should sit for a moment, Adam. You look a little peaked to me," Grace said tentatively.

"I'm fine," he said angrily. "I just need to shave. Haven't shaved in days."

He was rinsing his razor under the water when it happened. Grace and Kate were laying the clothes they had brought him from home across the bed when they heard the thud. Grace ran to the bathroom and saw Adam lying unconscious on the floor. He had struck the side of his head on the sink and a gush of blood poured over his right eye. Kate, behind her mother, screamed.

Grace could hear the cries from the monitoring station in the hall. She heard the nurse call out "V-T Room Ten." She heard her shout that it was Dr. Barnett's room and then the quick soft pads of rubber-soled feet as people flew down the corridor and into Adam's room. Before Grace and Kate knew what was happening, a nurse guided them swiftly but gently into the hall. Two doctors and two nurses lifted Adam's lifeless body back onto the bed. The intern on the unit, Sharon Parker, ran into the room.

"He's in V-Tach," Dr. Parker called out. "We have to shock him. Get me the paddles."

Dr. Parker grabbed the paddles that hung above Adam's bed and placed them over his chest. She glanced at the monitor. "Everybody clear," she said as the group around the bed took a step back. Adam's body lifted spastically as she depressed the paddles. She glanced at the monitor again. "Okay. We've got normal sinus rhythm," she said, inhaling. "Someone get a twelve-lead EKG on him."

An intern was attaching the electrodes to Adam's chest while a nurse took his pulse. Another nurse applied pressure to his head wound with a gauze pad.

"Can you hear me, Dr. Barnett?" Dr. Parker asked. "How do you feel now? Any chest pain?"

"It's the same goddamn thing," Adam croaked. "Artery shut down again. Get me to the lab. Get me to the fucking cath lab."

The cardiology fellow had come into the room and was looking at the electrocardiogram strip. "He's having another heart attack," he said. "He must have closed the artery. Call the cath lab. Get Dr. Stevens. Tell him we're on our way up."

"Dr. Barnett already made the diagnosis," Dr. Parker said somewhat coldly. "He knows exactly what's happening."

Grace and Kate were standing at the nurse's station during the commotion. Kate was sobbing as Grace held her, idly rubbing her back and murmuring "Sshh, all right, all right. All the doctors are in there now." Over and over, "All right. It's going to be okay." But Grace was frozen. The color had drained from her face.

"Mrs. Barnett? I'm Dr. Parker," a voice said. "I'm afraid Dr. Barnett's had another heart attack." And as Dr. Parker spoke, Adam was wheeled past them on a gurney, his chest bulging with electrodes under his hospital gown, someone trotting by his side steadying the portable intravenous pole that was hooked once again into his veins.

"Adam!" Grace jumped up from her seat and ran to the gurney.

Dr. Parker held her arm. "You can't go there right now, Mrs. Barnett. He's conscious. He knows just what's going on. Our guess is that the angioplasty closed down. We're taking him right back to the cath lab. You and your daughter can wait in his room. I promise to keep you posted."

"What about his head?" Kate cried. "He was bleeding so much."

"He's taking blood thinners so the wound bled more than usual, but it's not a deep one. We might give him a couple of stitches anyway, but his head is fine. Looks a lot worse than it is. That's the least of it right now."

"Why did this happen?" Grace asked. "Why?"

"It happens. Sometimes it just happens," Dr. Parker said patiently. "As I said, I'll keep you posted. It's going to be another thirty minutes, possibly an hour, until I get back to you. Please, try not to worry."

That night, Adam was back in the coronary care unit. The artery had shut down. The angioplasty was done again. Grace and Kate sat side by side on the same two metal chairs they had sat on earlier in the week and watched while Adam slept. Kate could barely take her eyes off the monitor above her father's bed. Grace could barely take her eyes off her daughter.

"We're going to let you rest, Adam," Grace said, standing at his bedside. It was just after seven o'clock. "We'll be at home, though. We're not going anywhere. I left the home number with the nurse's station. We'll see you in the morning."

"Daddy, by tomorrow you'll be feeling better," Kate said gently.

"Right," Adam murmured. "Typical, isn't it? The doctors always get screwed up."

"You didn't get screwed up," Grace said. "You're going to be fine, now." But she didn't know what was worse: the lines coming from his veins, the urine-filled bag hanging at the side of his bed, or the ugly contusion over his right eye. When Kate and Grace stepped off the elevator into the lobby of the hospital, Kate broke down.

"I have an awful feeling," she sobbed. "I'm so afraid he's going to die."

"He's not going to die, Kate," Grace said convincingly. "He's going to pull through. These things happen sometimes."

"What if you're wrong?" Kate demanded.

"Let's just go home, Kate," Grace said quietly.

"You didn't answer me, Mom," Kate said.

"It was just a complication. Everything's going to be okay," Grace said weakly.

But this time Grace was painfully aware that no one had reassured her that Adam's chances were good.

The hospital didn't call Grace when Adam developed a bleeding problem. They had drawn his blood several times during the night and the count continued to drop steadily. The entry spot in his groin where Dr. Stevens had reinserted the angioplasty tube had grown to the size of a small orange by 4 A.M. By nine in the morning, it had swelled as large as a grapefruit. At nine-thirty, Adam was transfused. When Grace and Kate arrived on Sunday morning, there was a sign on his door. ABSOLUTELY NO VISITORS. Panicked, Grace went to the nurse's station.

"What's going on?" Grace demanded. "Why is that sign on my husband's door?"

"He had a transfusion last night, Mrs. Barnett," the nurse said. "There was some bleeding. He needs to rest. Dr. Erickson told me to page him when you got here."

Minutes later Lew strode into the coronary care unit. "I'm on a tether for you," he said.

"Lew, this is our daughter, Kate," Grace said.

"Don't look so grim, Kate. We're going to pull him through this," Lew said. "He's going to have to stay here for another week or so. This time, we're just going to keep him right here in CCU. But you need to be a little upbeat. Keep his spirits up."

"Why did he need a transfusion?" Grace asked.

"Well, he's taking blood thinners and, as luck would have it, or not have it, he bled out during the night and became profoundly anemic."

"Why didn't anyone call me?" Grace demanded.

"Because Adam specifically asked us not to. You know, Grace. He's depressed. He's terribly depressed. He's a pretty macho guy, your husband. This isn't the state he wants to be in right now. I think that you and Kate should leave the medical end to me and you two just get him back on his feet emotionally. The worst thing for him right now is feeling like a burden," Lew said.

"Do you think he should see a psychiatrist? What about Dr. Muller? Adam seems to think well of him," Grace asked, remembering that was the name Adam suggested she counsel.

"I asked him if he thought it might help him to talk to a psychiatrist, but he wasn't very receptive. Sign of weakness for a guy like Adam, I think," Lew said. "As for Muller, I really don't think Adam would want to consult with a colleague. He's got a high profile here. I don't think he feels like airing his dirty laundry, if you know what I mean."

"Maybe his spirits will improve once he's home," Grace said.

"Oh, for sure. But, Grace, he won't be walking for a couple of weeks," Lew said. "He's got a substantial swelling in the groin. He's going to be immobile until that thing goes down. You'll probably have him home by the end of the week, but you better be prepared. . . . He's going to be out of commission for at least six weeks. You might want to get a private nurse."

"He'd never tolerate that," Grace said.

"Well, think about it. This isn't going to be easy. You'll have to shower him, help him dress, give him his meds. He's going to be weak. And he's going to be edgy. He's no day at the beach to begin with. You're setting yourself up for a tough one, Grace."

"I'll just have to take a leave from the school, that's all," Grace said.

"In sickness and health, right, Grace?" Lew sighed.

"Can't we see him, Dr. Erickson?" Kate asked. "Just for a moment?"

"Just for a moment," Lew said. "Come with me."

Lew walked ahead of them and tapped on Adam's door. "Only me, Adam," he said, poking his head in the door. "We're violating your sign. Two lovely ladies here would like to see you." He turned to Grace. "Call me any time at all, Grace. I've got to run back to the ER right now. But any time. Any time at all."

Kate entered Adam's room first. Just as he had been after the first heart attack, his face was turned to the window.

"Daddy? Daddy?" Kate said.

Kate gasped when her father turned to look at her. His complexion was a pasty gray. The bandage over his head wound was slightly crusted with blood.

"See why I put the sign on the door?" Adam said gruffly as she gasped. "I didn't want you to see me this way."

"I'd rather see you this way than not at all," Kate said, her eyes misting.

"Where's your mother?"

"Right here, Adam," Grace said from behind Kate. "I just spoke to Lew. He's quite confident about you, Adam."

"Yeah? Well, we'll see," Adam said, turning his face away again. "We'll just see."

Chapter Twenty-seven

Lew Erickson didn't discharge Adam until ten days after the second angioplasty. It was nearly the end of January. *Precautionary* was the word he used as an explanation when they opted to keep Adam for an extra three days. The swelling was still large; he was still anemic. Simply, Adam's recovery was not as swift as they hoped it would be.

When Grace and Adam got out of the taxi that pulled up to their apartment, Adam walked into the building with steps so painstaking, so unlike the broad strides that his long legs usually took across the lobby, that the doorman pretended to busy himself with a list of chores as Adam made his way to the elevator.

Grace had turned the guest room into a makeshift hospital room. She bought extra pillows for the beds, plain white sheets, a hand-painted bed tray, and had an intercom system installed between the guest room, master bath, bedroom, and kitchen. Each morning after Kate left for school, Grace tiptoed into the guest room and drew open the heavy, lined draperies. Glints of winter sunlight played on Adam's sallow face; his silver-streaked hair was noticeably thinner. Grace told herself that his demeanor was from lying down so much, perspiring in the middle of the nights as the doctors warned he might, not eating the way he should, but the masklike strain that crept over Adam's face even as he slept was distressing.

The school gave Grace eight weeks off until Adam's recuperation was complete. Both Dr. Stevens and Lew had promised her that he could slowly, steadily, return to work come the beginning of March.

But no surgical cases, they said. He couldn't be on his feet for too long. By March, they promised he could round with the medical students, consult on pre-ops and post-ops, and get back to his desk and medical journals. Nothing strenuous. It wasn't until the middle of February that Grace allowed Adam's office manager to bring him the mail, and then Grace insisted that only get well cards come for a while. No bills, no notices of conferences he was unable to attend. No controversy, Grace said. Nothing that might depress him and make his recovery seem more eternal than it was.

Grace made dinners of poached fish and boiled vegetables, lunches with fresh fruits and whole grain breads, pots of vegetable and chicken soups. She helped Adam when he showered. She bought a small shower chair at the medical supply outlet so Adam could sit while she washed his back and hair as he faced the wall. "Your turn," she would say discreetly as she turned away from him, listening to his breathing as he finished the shower alone, calling to her when he was done so he could lean on her arm as he stepped out over the tub, lifting the leg slowly and painfully that still suffered the hideous swelling in his groin. His body was still bruised and beaten. His skin was waxy; the sinewy definition of his lean muscles was gone.

"I never thought I'd come to this," he said bitterly one day as she combed his hair and fluffed the back of his neck with talc.

"It's not forever, Adam," she said.

"No, it's not, is it?" he asked. And she wondered exactly what he meant by that nearly cryptic phrase but was too afraid to ask.

As they approached the end of February, they walked around the block that circled their apartment building, her arm linked through his. He was bundled in a blue cashmere coat and gray muffler and she couldn't help but think she wished he'd worn something red to brighten his gaunt cheeks that seemed to fade into the pale hue of his scarf.

Perhaps the worst part of Adam's recovery was the sentiment that seemed to envelop him when it came to her. If he called to her from the guest room and she didn't answer immediately, his voice became raised and agitated, causing her to come flying in, almost panic-stricken. There were hours where Grace sat beside him as he clicked the remote control past channel after channel, complaining there was nothing worthwhile to watch. Grace suggested they play cards or Scrabble, or maybe he should just relax and read a book, something he normally had little time for. But Adam preferred the distraction of the television, opting for the shopping channel, so long as he wasn't by himself.

"Melanie is coming to the city today," Grace said early one morning as she fluffed the pillows around his head. "She has a dentist appointment so we're going down to the coffee shop for a bite to eat before she can't chew for hours. I'll just be an hour or so. Rosa is here if you need anything."

"Take the cell phone with you," he said.

"It's in my purse. You have an appointment with Dr. Stevens tomorrow, by the way."

"I know how these things go, Grace. I've done thousands of operations. More complicated than angioplasty."

"Then you should know and feel confident. You should feel this was rather routine."

"Do you know how many people I've lied to?" he asked. "It's a tough climb recovering from this. I'm just not sure I'll ever be the same. I'm not sure anyone is."

"You'll be better than before," she said. "Besides, you know that's not true. You have patients that were athletes and they're playing sports again. Snap out of it, now. You're going to be good as new." But he turned his face toward the window and she could see that the eyes that still seemed vacant to her had welled with tears. She kissed the top of his head. "I won't be gone long, Adam. I promise."

At first he didn't answer her. "Don't you see, Grace? You don't get it, do you? This time it's happening to me."

*   *   *

"How's the patient?" Melanie asked, pouring cream into her coffee.

"He won't let me out of his sight," Grace sighed. "He's afraid he's going to have another episode and he'll be alone."

"Why didn't you get a nurse to come in?"

"His pride. He's humiliated enough with me caring for him. He would never tolerate a stranger."

"I just hope he remembers how devoted you've been when he's back on his feet again."

"Oh, I think he will."

"Well, I hope you're right. Not everyone looks at these things like a religious experience, you know."

"I have to give it a chance," Grace said. "He's my husband. Don't you think you're being a bit harsh?"

"I'm sorry, Grace. I just don't believe for a second that he's having some sort of epiphany, you know? I don't want to see you get hurt."

"He's suffering," Grace said.

"He'd be suffering a lot more without you there," Melanie said. "Have you heard from Luke?"

"No," Grace said, pretending to look at the menu.

"Have you called him?"

"What for?"

"To see how he is. Just to talk. Grace, how would you feel if the shoe were on the other foot and he didn't call you? You have more of a bond than the time you spent together. You have Alex, too, you know."

"Don't you think Luke could have called *me*?"

"He would never call you. You know that, Grace. Especially now when he knows you have a sick husband at home."

"Why? He's a friend."

"Oh, for God's sake, Grace. He's more than a friend. He's your lover."

"Was."

"Really?"

"I think about him all the time," Grace said softly. "And it makes me feel so awful. There I am taking care of my husband like I have a halo and I'm thinking about Luke. What kind of person am I? I'm showering Adam and I'm feeling unfaithful to Luke. How messed up is that?"

"You haven't had a chance to come up for air since you got back from Sabbath Landing. I don't even know how you can think clearly."

Grace nodded her head ever so slightly and looked at her sister. "I'm suffocating, Mel. This time I'm really drowning."

"I know, Grace," Melanie said sympathetically. "I know. I just want to make sure no one holds your head under water."

Adam was sitting at his desk in the library when Grace came up-stairs. He wore a robe and slippers.

"Well, you've made progress," Grace said. "From the bed to the couch to the desk all without me. Pretty good."

"I've been going through the bills. Lots of past dues."

"We've been a little preoccupied," Grace said.

"I need you to help me shower," he said. "I'm still on the blood thinners. You remember what happened to John Glenn."

"Well, you're not an astronaut." Grace smiled. "You've got to give yourself some time."

"People are going to think I'm Kate's grandfather pretty soon."

Grace laughed. "Hardly. Maybe a rich uncle. Come on, Adam. Let's get you showered and into some decent clothes so you don't look like you're going to sleep again. And then let's take a longer walk. It's actually mild outside. The air will do you good."

They walked from the apartment to the Central Park Zoo and sat on a bench near the clock at the entrance.

"When I was a girl, I came here on a few Saturdays with this boy. God, what was his name? We'd take the train into the city and walk from Grand Central to the zoo. See that clock? On the hour, the animals turn around it like a carousel and music plays. I thought it was so romantic," she laughed. "Oh, Jake. That was his name."

"Jake? Isn't that the name of your brother's friend in Sabbath Landing?"

"No, that's Luke," she said, her face reddening.

"Yeah, that's it. Luke. Saw the phone bill this morning. Is that who you called in Sabbath Landing the night I had my MI?"

"What?"

"There was a call to Sabbath Landing."

"So?"

"Well, is that who you called? It was a pretty long call."

"Yes, I called him," Grace said, certain to look Adam in the eye. "Why?"

"Shouldn't I be the one asking why? You called him at midnight. Isn't that kind of late to call someone you barely know?"

"It was after you had the heart attack," she fumbled. "I was upset and didn't notice the time."

"Why would you call *him* after I had a heart attack?"

"I don't remember," Grace said evenly. "It was a long time ago."

"What were you calling him about that couldn't wait until morning?"

"I don't remember. I told you, I was upset."

"Seems to me that we call lovers and such at midnight."

"I wouldn't know," Grace said, cocking her head to the side. "Do you?"

"I hope you're telling me the truth, Grace," Adam said. "It would be a shame otherwise, don't you think?"

"Why do I feel threatened right now?" Grace asked.

"I don't know why."

"I don't want to start something, Adam. It was nothing. It was just a phone call."

"Is he married?" Adam asked.

"Widowed. He has a grown son."

"Does he have a lady friend?" Adam asked provocatively.

"I don't know," Grace answered, trying not to give her emotions away. The thought of Luke and another woman pained her. "Maybe. I never asked him."

"Well, did he have a lady when you were there?"

"I don't know," she said, her head down. "I told you. I never asked him."

"Do you love me, Grace?" Adam asked.

"Do you love *me*?" she asked, uncomfortable with his question.

"I asked you first," Adam said.

"Yes, Adam, I do," Grace answered, her face flushed. "And you? What about you? It's your turn to answer now."

"Let's go home now," he said. "I'm getting tired."

There was one last blast of snow in early April, shortly before Easter. It had blown in from the Great Lakes, blanketing the northeast corridor from Maine to Washington, D.C. Schools were closed. Traffic had come to a standstill. Airports were shut down. Even the mail didn't arrive until almost evening. Kate went ice-skating at the Wollman Rink. Rosa was unable to make it in to work from Brooklyn, and Grace and Adam were stranded together in the apartment. Grace pictured Sabbath Landing under a siege of snow, hoping the island house was withstanding the blizzard, picturing Luke sitting by himself as she was in front of a fire in the wood-burning stove, maybe brewing a pot of coffee on the stove. Maybe he managed to take the truck down the mountain and go to The Birch. Surely Trout and Bill would be there. After all, they lived within walking distance. Since Adam questioned her, she entertained the thought that perhaps there was someone else in Luke's life now. The notion of Luke with another woman made her feel empty and chilled. She wanted to pick up the phone and dial his number, if only just to hear his voice, to tell him she hadn't stopped thinking about him for a moment since she'd come home. Tell him how different the day would feel if she were snowed in with him.

Adam didn't start operating again until May first. He had put on the right amount of weight, his legs had become more muscular again from the walks and an exercise bike that Grace bought him as a going-back-to-work present. The color had come back to his cheeks and the wound on his forehead had healed with the faintest of scars. That morning, after he left for the hospital, Grace changed the sheets in the guest room, placed Adam's eyeglasses and medical journals on his nightstand in the master bedroom, hung his pajamas and robe in the master bathroom.

"You moved me back in?" Adam asked when he came home late that afternoon.

"I thought it was time," Grace said. "I thought you might be more comfortable in your own room. How was the hospital today?"

"I was comfortable where I was," he said, ignoring her question.

"Don't you think we should share the bedroom again?" Grace asked. "I think it would make Kate feel better. She asked me the other day when you would move back in. It was an odd choice of words."

"The day went fine," Adam said. "We'll see how the night goes."

He didn't reach for her that night when they went to bed. He flipped through the remote control as he had on the nights he lay by himself. She read a book and pretended she could concentrate with the television surfing through the channels. They turned out their lights at the same time. Grace said good night after the room was darkened, but Adam had already fallen asleep—or pretended to.

Grace had been sleeping for several hours when she awakened with the dream. It hadn't come to her in so many months. She had been certain it would never come again. She was awakened by her own cry, sitting bolt upright in bed, her back dripping with perspiration.

"What the hell is going on, Grace?" Adam asked.

"I'm sorry, " she said, breathless, her heart pounding. "I had the dream again. Remember I told you how I always had that dream about being in the lake? How Melanie and I were there and we were drowning? I haven't had it in so long. Months. It terrifies me." She reached over to him, placing her hand on his arm.

"Get a grip on yourself, Grace. Waking up like that in the middle of the night, for God's sake. I'm telling you right now," he said, shaking off her arm, leaning over to take a sip of water from the glass beside his bed. "You'd better sell that godforsaken island, get yourself to see Alan

Muller, and get rid of all your bloody demons because I can't take it anymore."

"Lew said he wanted *you* to see Muller after the heart attack," Grace said. "You refused to go. Why should I?"

Adam turned on the lamp on his nightstand. "That was different. I had an acute depression. Remember what happened the night before I had the heart attack, Grace. My blood pressure must have skyrocketed with your nonsense about islands and recurring dreams and all that mumbo jumbo about closure. I won't forget that, Grace. You may have done a swell job playing Florence Nightingale these last few months, but I'm telling you right now, I don't want to hear any more bullshit about your goddamn dreams. You either get yourself to a shrink or you keep it to yourself because I can't take it, do you hear me? Your histrionics are going to do me in. They almost did once."

"You blame me?" Grace asked slowly, as though she were talking to a child who couldn't comprehend. "You blame me for your heart attack? How dare you? All I did was reach out to you just now because I was frightened. You were frightened when you were sick, weren't you, Adam? You know what's it's like now, don't you? But you still can't find kindness in that damaged heart of yours, can you? At least not when it comes to me."

He went to grab his pillows. "I'm going to sleep in the guest room," he said. "I don't need this crap."

"No, please don't," she said haltingly so she wouldn't cry. Her face felt paralyzed; her jaws were clenched. "I'll go. And I'm turning off the intercom, Adam. If you need anything, call 911. But I'm certain you'll be just fine now. I think your heart is back to its old self again."

Chapter Twenty-eight

"I heard yelling in the middle of the night," Kate said the next morning as she and Grace ate breakfast.

"I had a bad dream," Grace said.

"No, Mom. I heard yelling. I heard the two of you shouting," Kate said.

"It was just the dream," Grace said. "That was all."

"I have to leave early today," Kate said, gulping her orange juice. "We're starting graduation rehearsals. I'm not a child anymore, you know. I don't believe you this time."

"I don't know what to tell you," Grace said.

"Who slept in the guest room last night?" Kate asked.

"I did."

"I'll see you later, Mom," Kate said. It was the first time she'd left the house without kissing her mother good-bye.

Grace heard the door slam and knew Kate had left. She resisted the urge to call Luke. It had been too long. Perhaps the romance they shared had paled in his memory. Maybe he had erased her, even erased Alex, once and for all. She was too embarrassed to call Melanie. Melanie, who had said months ago that she didn't trust that anything would change once Adam healed. And Jemma: Jemma would tell her that her place was with her husband no matter what.

But she had to speak to someone. Alan Muller? Not in a million years, she thought. No, it had to be someone else. She was amazed she was able to pull the name from the recesses of her mind. She made the call impulsively from the teacher's lounge at school that morning.

Sabbath Landing, New York, she said to the recording. The Reverend Albert Wood.

"Sabbath Landing Community Church," a lilting female voice answered.

"Can you tell me what denomination you are?" Grace asked tentatively, curious that there was no specific affiliation.

"We are nondenominational," the woman said.

"I don't understand."

"We've stood in this spot since 1876. Since 1948, we've been an independent community church. Basically, we try to just meld all the folks together. We're usable for everyone. Now, how can I help you?"

"I'd like to speak to Reverend Wood. Is he still there?"

"Oh, he most certainly is. Could you tell me what this is in reference to? Give me your name?"

"It's a personal matter," Grace said.

"Certainly. One moment please," the woman said, her voice a bit chilly.

It wasn't a moment before he picked up the receiver. "Reverend Wood."

"Reverend Wood? I don't know if you remember me. You presided at the funeral of my brother. I got your name from the newspaper. An old newspaper. My brother was Alex Hammond. It was a long time ago. 1959."

"Grace?" asked the reverend, leaning back in his chair. "Is it you?"

"Oh, my God," she said, embarrassed at her expression. "How did you know?"

"Lucas Keegan comes to see me quite often. Why, he was just here the day before yesterday. You must be on the same wavelength."

The Reverend Wood was a young man in 1959. Just thirty years old and new to Sabbath Landing, he had only been with the community church as their pastor for a year. During that time, he had performed two weddings, baptized three babies, and been courted at a dinner party given by the mayor. Alex Hammond was his first funeral.

"I am seventy-one years old and come the seventh of every November, well, I'll never forget that day," he paused remembering. "What can I do for you, Grace? Just tell me. Anything at all."

"Do you remember my parents, Reverend?"

"Jane and Alexander. I knew your family for only a few months before the tragedy. Long enough to know they were special people. Your family came to church every Sunday. Your mother always wore the most unusual hats," he reminisced. "I was often convinced the parish increased because the women in town wanted to see what she'd have on next. They say that Jackie started the pillbox hat trend—well, I'd say it was Jane Hammond, at least here in Sabbath Landing. As a matter of fact, I sat next to your mother at the mayor's dinner."

"What was she like?"

"Your mother? Oh, she was a delight. A charming dinner companion, although a bit nervous as I recall. The night of the party, you and Alex were staying at the Keegans' house with Edith and Bart Lambert's niece, Patricia. Your mother kept checking her watch, wondering if you'd gotten into bed on time. She hoped that Patricia would sit up with you if you couldn't fall asleep," he said. "She worried that Luke and Alex were behaving themselves."

"And my father?" Grace asked.

"Ham. Everyone called him Ham. I'll never forget Ham and his cigars. He and Will Keegan took me outside the city hall and we smoked a few Cubans after the mayor's dinner. After the funeral, I never saw either of your parents again. Your mother didn't come to the funeral. You know that she was hospitalized after the accident. She was under psychiatric observation," he said. "But they were your parents, Grace. Why are you asking me?"

"Because I'm beginning to realize I never really knew them. My mother was always distant. Removed."

"That wasn't the Jane that I remember," Reverend Wood said sadly.

"You have to understand, Reverend. She wouldn't play music.

Couldn't stand noise. She spent most of the time alone in her room. And my father, he tried, I suppose. It was like he could never find the words. Like they were stuck somewhere inside him."

"I see," he said.

"I didn't know anything about the accident until Luke told me last January. I never even knew that Alex existed. I don't remember him. And all my life I've been afraid of the water, Reverend. And all my life I've had these recurring dreams where Melanie and I are stranded in icy water and no one will help us. Now I've come to realize I was dreaming about Alex and me, not Melanie and me. I'm babbling, aren't I? I'm sorry."

"That's all right, Grace. Perfectly understandable. Who is Melanie?"

"My younger sister."

"Ah, yes. Luke mentioned her," Reverend Wood said. "You know, we called your father Ham because of his last name but also because he was always hamming it up, so to speak. He was so quick-witted, your dad was. And your mother was so warm, Grace. I would guess that she became distant because she simply couldn't deal with her world after the accident," he said gently.

"Luke says the same thing. Reverend, I listen to you and I can't believe my father was the way you and Luke describe him. He practically struggled when he spoke to us."

"Perhaps because what happened that day was unspeakable. You know that now, Grace. You hardly need me to tell you. They were grief-stricken. Their hearts were broken. We might have helped them but they closed themselves off."

"They committed suicide just before Christmas. Together."

"Luke told me. I was saddened to hear that. Deeply saddened. Such a desperate act. So tragic. Luke told me your father was suffering from what might have been Alzheimer's disease. I would guess that your mother felt she was losing him, losing someone she loved once again."

"They were so damaged, " Grace said, her voice breaking. "I'm in mourning, Reverend. Not just for the way they died or because they died, but for the way they lived. My husband doesn't seem to understand the notion of grief. As for the dreams, they're less frequent now."

"What does your husband do for a living?"

"He's a doctor. A heart surgeon."

"Healing the spirit is far less tangible. Perhaps he's simply more familiar with wounds that he can see and touch. Things that are more defined. Of course, after the spirit heals, we're often left with scars that are constant reminders."

"Like my parents?"

"No, from what you and Luke tell me, I believe your parents never even scarred. To scar, there has to be healing. I believe their wounds remained open."

"I need to make peace with all this," Grace said softly.

"You will."

"I don't know how."

"Oh, I think you do. Self-discovery can be tumultuous. Discovering or, in your case, uncovering a truth that you didn't even know existed can invite chaos. But once we accept the truth about ourselves and those around us, we will naturally find peace. You have to find a place for everything."

"Reverend, why do you suppose I can't remember Alex? Why can't I remember what happened that day?"

"I am sure there are theories about cognitive memory and selective memory that are quite scientific. As a layman, I can tell you that many of us don't remember back to when we were three. In your case, perhaps it's a blessing. Perhaps you chose to forget something too dreadful to remember. It's a form of protection."

"And my parents? How do you explain my parents? They closed their eyes as well."

"Oh, no. It's entirely different. They never forgot. I don't think they tried to forget as much as they couldn't bear the memory. Perhaps they thought if they never spoke of Alex, they could bury their pain along with him. Of course, they were unsuccessful."

"They were intelligent, though."

"Emotion is ruled by the heart, not the brain."

"They denied Melanie and me so much. I mean, look how they were before the accident. Look what they had inside them to give and kept from us."

"I don't think they denied you, Grace. The accident changed them. I understand your anger and frustration, but you need to forgive them."

"What if Alex's accident was my fault? I wasn't supposed to go near the lake. Maybe Alex was just trying to help me."

"Why are you so intent on blame? Listen to the word. Accident. By definition, there is no blame, no bad intention."

"But I need a reason. Why did this have to happen? And, you'll forgive me, Reverend, for what I am about to say. People chalk up things like this to the notion of God working in strange ways, but I can't. For the life of me, I can't understand what good could come of something like this. What on earth would the Divine reason be?"

"I have no answer for you, Grace," the reverend said quietly. "Sometimes there are no answers."

"How is Luke?" Grace asked, taking a deep breath. "I haven't spoken to him in months."

"He's fine," Reverend Wood said gently. "Lucas has always been strong and resilient, although he has always thought with his heart. He calls me often, Grace."

"He does?"

"Oh, yes. The last several months have been difficult and confusing for him. He's bouncing back, as they say."

"Because of me?"

"I just think there were a lot of old wounds reopened."

"Did he . . . did he tell you everything?"

"He told me a great deal," Reverend Wood said. "He's an old-fashioned sort, Lucas is. I had to keep reminding him that I don't take confession."

"Are you betraying his confidence now?"

"He said if you called, I could tell you anything I saw fit to tell. He knows me well enough to know I would never betray anyone's confidence."

"Why did he think I would call?"

"Oh, Grace, I'm not sure. Intuition, I suppose."

"You know I'm married, Reverend. You probably take a dim view of my relationship with Luke."

There was a long silence on the other end of the line. "Perhaps if I didn't know Lucas, I would say that I disapprove. I never like to see a child suffer because the parents part ways. I never like to see a home broken. But I also never like to see a heart broken," he said quietly.

She was embarrassed. "Could I ask you one more thing?"

"Anything at all."

"Would you tell me about Alex? Tell me what he was like."

"I only knew him as the child of parishioners. He was a sweet boy. Tousled red hair and hazel eyes. He had a way about him that was mischievous and he was most disarming. He squirmed a great deal during the service." He laughed. "I think that he and Luke preferred fishing to my sermons."

"Luke took me to the cemetery, you know. I have a picture of Luke and Alex that I took from the island house. I just wish I could remember Alex more than anything."

"Somewhere, deep down inside, you do."

Grace sighed, "I wish I could believe that."

"Perhaps he'll come to you in better dreams now."

"I hope you're right. I could use some better dreams," Grace said with a sigh. "I can't thank you enough, Reverend. You can't imagine how much you've helped me."

"Tell me, what are your plans for the house? I hear it's yours now."

"I'm not sure. I'm trying to figure all this out."

"And you will, I'm sure. Call anytime you need anything, Grace. And God bless."

Grace was tucking the reverend's phone number into her wallet when she saw her father's note. She had forgotten it was there. She unfolded it, saw her father's letterhead. It was scrawled and unreadable except for the capital letter A written a number of times, each time with a line through it.

A for Alex, she thought. Maybe my father was trying to tell me.

Chapter Twenty-nine

Adam moved back to the guest room. He placed his clothes in the empty bureau, hung his shirts and suits in the closet, moved his toiletries to the guest bathroom.

"Tell me what's happening," Kate demanded after Adam had left for work the next morning.

"It's just more convenient, Kate. That's all," Grace said. "He needs his sleep. I toss and turn. I'm so restless."

"Tell me the truth," Kate said.

"There's nothing to tell."

"I'm not blind, Mom," Kate sighed. "What's going to happen?"

"I'm not sure."

"Can't you do something?" Kate asked, her eyes welling up with tears. "What do you mean by 'you're not sure'?"

"Let's just wait and see," Grace said.

"You always say 'wait and see' when something isn't going to work out," Kate said.

"No, sometimes you really do just have to wait and see," Grace said. "Besides, Kate, it's not entirely up to me, is it? Be fair."

"I'm trying to be fair," Kate said. "I just feel that all this is so unfair to me."

In fact, the harsh words couldn't be forgiven. Grace and Adam were cordial around Kate, but inherent in the civility was a pronounced undercurrent of dispassion. There were no more arguments, let alone discussions. They had dinners out with Kate, attended her school play, planned her summer in Spain with Alison. All without intimacy.

On May 10, Adam turned sixty. He chose to spend the days preceding the event at an ashram of sorts in southern California. The evening of his birthday, he flew home. Kate and Grace took him to dinner at The Water Club where he ordered San Pellegrino instead of champagne, touted the benefits of green tea and gingko, and spoke of ridding the body and mind of toxins through therapeutic massage and meditation. Grace thought of Luke, his crushed pack of Camels and his short glass of Black Velvet. There were times she held herself still and closed her eyes, picturing his face, inhaling his scent, sensing his touch. Until the night she awakened from the dream, Adam was someone she thought she could live with. It frightened her that the more she thought of Luke, the more she felt he was someone she couldn't live without.

Kate's high school graduation fell on a Wednesday afternoon in early June. Folding chairs were set in the auditorium at the school, a high-ceilinged, cavernous space that once had been a factory. There were floating silver and white balloons, banners stretching the length of the room on either side congratulating the Class of 2001; tinfoil stars descending from invisible string dangled from the steel rafters. Grace and Adam sat in the fourth row: Grace on the aisle and Adam next to her. Melanie and Mike and Jemma sat behind them. "Pomp and Circumstance" began to play, the seniors began their parade to the stage, and Grace began to cry at the first chord.

Kate was one of the first in line. Her long blond hair flowed down the back of her navy gown, her mortarboard was slightly askew. She squeezed her mother's hand as she walked past. It was, to Grace, a gesture more than mere sentiment. Grace had a sense of absolution as she felt her daughter's smooth hand on her own. The lightness of Kate's touch was fleeting but so powerful that Grace felt an overwhelming sense of relief.

Still, there was no getting away from the fact that the day was not the way Grace had once pictured it would be. Once she had thought she would sit beside her husband, her arm linked through his, his hand perhaps covering hers, comforting her as she wept, wiping away a tear of his own. She once thought he might whisper something about a rite of passage, gently reminding her that this was the first threshold they would cross with their child. Perhaps he would dry her tears by telling her there would be college graduation, Kate's wedding, the birth of their first grandchild. More passages together. Just weeks ago, despite Melanie's cautions, she thought that Adam's heart attack in some way might have made them reborn. She talked herself into believing that her week with Luke was little more than a fantasy, one without the real history that makes up a marriage. But Adam ignored his wife's tears. He sat with one leg crossed over the other, the crease of his pant leg hanging perfectly, his arms crossed over his chest. He looked straight ahead, barely blinking.

Katherine Hammond Barnett, Grace heard the principal say. Honor Roll. Boston College will welcome Katherine in the fall.

"Where are you all going now?" Kate asked Grace as the reception thinned out. "The limos are leaving for our party. I've got to hurry."

"I don't know," Grace said, smoothing Kate's hair. "Adam, what do you think?"

"Oh, I'm tired after all these festivities," Adam said stiffly. "I think I'll head home."

"Well, I say we do some more celebrating," Melanie said. "We've got Mrs. Hadley booked through ten-thirty."

"You all go without me," Adam said. "I think I've had it."

Grace forced a smile for her daughter's sake, placed her hand on Adam's back, and asked if he wanted company. Fortunately, he took her cue.

"You go ahead, Grace. I'll be just fine." He gave his wife a perfunctory kiss on the cheek, gave the same kiss to Melanie and Jemma, shook Mike's hand.

"I'm proud of you, Kate," he said, embracing her, and he was off.

"Mom? Shouldn't you go with him?" Kate asked, her eyes following her father as he walked out the door.

Grace shook her head. "No, he's just tired," she said. "I won't stay out long. Leave it alone for now, Kate. Just have a good time." Kate was wearing a black sheath that had been hidden by the navy robe. She had glitter on her shoulders, a single pearl dangling from a chain around her neck. "This is your night, Kate, and you look beautiful. Now, go. Before I start to cry again." Grace smiled.

Adam was awake when Grace tiptoed in the house that night. It was just after ten. She heard the television in his study. He was wearing his robe, sitting on the sofa, his bare feet on the coffee table. He hung up the phone as she walked into the room.

"Have a good time?" he asked, turning his eyes to the television.

"We went for coffee and cake in Little Italy," she said. "Who were you talking to?"

"Answering service."

"But you're not on call."

"It was a mistake," he said.

"Adam, we need to talk."

"I guess we do, don't we?" he said, clicking off the television with the remote.

"Should I start?"

"You always do."

"That's not nice, Adam."

"You're right," he said. "Go ahead."

"This isn't much of a marriage anymore," she said bluntly.

"No, it's not," he said. "It's been a long time coming, though, hasn't it?"

"I suppose," she said quietly.

He stood up and walked over to the bar in his study. He poured a brandy. "Want one?" he asked, holding up a bottle of Rémy Martin.

She nodded. "I thought you were only drinking mineral water."

"I think this conversation needs something more potent than Pellegrino."

"At one point, I thought that maybe your heart attack was a silver lining. You know, that it might bring us together again. I thought you needed me."

"I did need you."

"Until you stopped," Grace said, and paused. "Until I needed you."

"That's not true."

"But it is true. When I needed you that night I had the dream, you just retreated again."

"I can't take the intensity, Grace. I'm sixty years old. I'm burning out professionally." He sat in his leather chair, spinning the brandy glass between his hands. "I've been operating for thirty-five years. I'm tired of the night calls. Fed up with answering inane questions from patients' families, explaining what I do to people who barely understand. I'm thinking about letting it all go."

"That's not all you want to let go, though, is it, Adam?" she asked softly.

"I should be content at this point in my life. I'm not," he said, facing her, his eyes almost fixed. "I'll tell you what that heart attack did. It made me realize how mortal I am."

"You didn't answer me. I asked what else you want to let go. Our marriage?"

"Don't pin it all on me. Don't make me the bad guy. You can't sit there and tell me you would choose to live with the way things are."

"I don't think there are too many choices left. But, no, this is no way to live."

"I want to be in Aspen this summer. I figure I can shuttle back and forth. A week there, a week here. I can't just leave the practice abruptly," he said, avoiding her eyes.

"You still haven't answered my question."

"I can't give you what you need, Grace," he said. "I can't deal with the nuances of your psyche, so to speak. I'm not comfortable with the abstract. You're too damn complicated for me, Grace. At this point in my life, I want simplicity."

"I see," she said quietly. "I'm not going to change any more than you are, Adam. I can't even try anymore."

"Nor can I," he said. "Honestly? It takes too much out of me."

"I suppose that's why you're a good surgeon," Grace said.

"What does that mean?"

"You don't have to get emotionally involved. You see your patients, you operate, they go home. That's it. Marriage is a more ongoing relationship, you know."

"Interesting analysis," Adam said coldly. "What do you want to do? I told you, I want to be in Aspen this summer."

"I'd like to spend time on the island."

"It's surrounded by water, I hear."

"Don't be that way, Adam. I'm trying to not be afraid. I don't think I'm afraid of water as much as I've been afraid about what happened on the water and can't remember."

"Kate and Alison leave for Spain on Saturday," he said.

"I know that," Grace said impatiently. "Why don't you address what I just said?"

"Because I can't. Don't you see, Grace? I can't deal with the amorphous. I need the stuff that's more concrete," Adam said, looking at her intently. "I can't deal with the vagaries of your memories and emotions. Let's talk about Kate."

"I don't think we have to tell her anything specifically right now, do you? I mean, she'll be so far away. Why spoil her summer? As far as she's concerned, can't we just be here and there? She'll be in Spain, anyway. Besides, a part of her already knows."

"Here and there," he mused. "Maybe that's at the bottom of all this, isn't it? We're just not together in the same place anymore."

"Did you hear what I said? A part of Kate already knows."

"I heard you."

"Answer me."

"What makes you think that she knows?"

"Because she lives here, for God's sake, Adam. She's a young woman. How could she not know?" Grace asked, starting to cry. "I'm sorry. I don't know why I'm crying. Despite it all, I suppose a part of me can't believe this is happening."

Adam ran his hands through his hair. "I suppose I do have a rather surgical approach to things. For me, you open, do what you've been trained to do, and then you close."

"Are we through, Adam? Are we closed?"

He took a deep breath, a sip of his brandy. "I guess the operation wasn't a success," he said uncomfortably. "Pretty trite, huh?"

"I'll never understand how you're able to tell the families when there's bad news," she said. "Don't misunderstand me. I'm sure this is like those cases when you feel it's all for the best and that sort of thing. But still . . ."

"You have to be detached," he said.

"Being detached isn't always the answer. It certainly isn't the answer in a marriage. You see, you can't make incisions in the soul and expect to just stitch them up again."

Grace and Adam drove Kate to the airport on Saturday morning. They kissed her and made her promise to call, waving good-bye as she walked down the gateway in the same way that all the other parents waved to their children as they left for the summer. They stood, side by side, their shoulders deliberately not touching as her plane taxied down the runway. Grace had an urge to slip her arm through Adam's, to feel the press of flesh on flesh somehow to ease the pain of watching her daughter leave, although she knew her marriage was all but over. Instinctively, she moved closer to her husband.

"I have a seven o'clock flight tonight for Aspen," Adam said, not looking at Grace while he spoke, ignoring the faint touch of her next to him. "You?"

"I'm meeting Jemma and Melanie at my parents' house this eve-

ning. The house goes on the market next Sunday. The tag sale's tomorrow. I'm bringing dinner from Pasquale's."

"Last supper, huh?" he said.

"Without the betrayal," she said.

"Great line, Grace. And then?"

"Then tomorrow morning, I'm taking a train to Fort Hope. I'm going to stay at The Alpine for a few days, then go to the island."

"You could drive," he said. "Just take the car."

"You don't need a car on an island," she said. The plane was gone
from view now. She slung her purse over her shoulder and walked away.

When Grace arrived at the house that night, her heart stopped
when she saw the small sign stuck in the front yard of her parents'
home announcing the tag sale. She walked the darkened path to
the front door, flicked on the outside lights for Melanie and Jemma,
hoping they'd be there any minute. She placed a bouquet of pink
sweetheart roses on the dining table, uncovered the tins from Pasquale's, set down a bottle of Chianti. Melanie and Jemma came in with
Jemma's key.

"Well, look at all this," Jemma said. "A feast."

"I'm so glad you're both here," Grace said with relief.

"Were you here long?" Melanie asked.

"Ten minutes maybe, but it seemed longer." Grace turned to Jemma.
"I want to see it before we have dinner."

"It's in her drawer. Between her slips," Jemma said.

"See what?" Melanie asked.

"Come," Grace said, walking up the stairs. "You'll see."

"I found it the other day when I was cleaning up the house for the
tag sale ladies," Jemma said, sliding the drawer open, extracting the
book, and handing it to Grace.

"Where's the letter?" Grace asked.

"Inside the book," Jemma said. "Where she left it."

"What letter?" Melanie asked. "What's going on?"

"*The Canterbury Tales,*" Grace said, showing the book to Melanie. The pages were tattered, the gilded edges chipped. The lace bookmark, its fringe draping over the cover, was yellowed with age. She opened the book where a pale pink envelope was stuck between the pages, her name scripted in her mother's handwriting. Grace's hands shook slightly as she opened the envelope, careful not to tear away more than she had to.

"Can you read it out loud?" Melanie asked.

"First, to myself," Grace said quietly, sitting on her mother's divan, the book on her lap.

Dearest Grace,

I know that at some point you and Melanie and Jemma will have the dreadful task of cleaning out this house. I am sorry for this. This is why we stipulated in our wills that the contents simply be sold. It will save you the effort, the time, and what I know would be the agony. Besides, anything and everything that is truly meaningful is in Sabbath Landing, save the few mementos and pieces of jewelry that I bequeathed to Melanie.

I suppose I could have left this letter for you in a more visible place and more immediately, but I feel that placing the letter within the pages of this book has a greater significance. This book is the only remnant of my past that I took with me from the island. You see, this is not a suicide note. This is an explanation. A letter I should have written to you many years ago. Or perhaps, more, it is something I should have told you with courage and love.

By now, I know that you have been to Sabbath Landing. You see, I asked Thompson (there was a letter to him within our wills) to place this letter in the book after you had made your journey to the island and leave it where you would find it. I knew that you would find it, Grace. Although you probably think I don't know you at all, I knew that you wouldn't waste any time going up there to see the mysterious gift we left for you.

It is with the deepest of regrets and apologies that the story of the

island didn't come to you from your father and me over the years. It
should have been a story you grew up with and acknowledged from
the time you were a baby. It should have been part of the fabric of
your life instead of threads you had to piece together for yourself. Of
course, I will never know who told you the story once you got to Sabbath Landing. My guess is that it might have been Bart Lambert since
he and his son, Kevin, have watched the house for us over the years.
Bart (we called him Trout since he was such a great fisherman) was
there on that dreadful day. But no one really knows our part of the
story. They can only guess. In essence, your father and I took you
and ran away. Ran away from every dream we ever dreamed, every
memory that haunted us, every friend we knew in the world. But
please understand that we ran away because what happened that day
was too unbearable to remember. The problem is, we never could forget. How foolish we were to think that we could. It is only at this
point in our lives, as your father is haunted by memories that he cannot fathom or unravel in his now damaged mind, that I realize how
alone I am with this truth. The memory of that day never became any
more bearable as time went on and, now, I can no longer tolerate the
pain alone. Perhaps if I had shared this tale with you earlier in your
life I would not feel the way I do now. Now, I fear it is too late. Or,
perhaps, I am simply too weary.

Why did we behave the way we did? Some people might say it was
cowardice. Others might call us delusional. The truth is, we knew no
other way to find peace. Peace, however, did not come with isolation.
Thank God, your father and I always found comfort in one another.

You were just a baby, Grace, when Alex died. Alex died. How
strange to see those words in front of me. Words I could never say.
You were three years old. And to this day we will never know whether
you wandered or Alex took you in that raft. It doesn't matter, though.
Alex was old enough to know better if he took you, and you were not
old enough to know better if you wandered. None of that ever mattered. It was just a terrible, horrible accident. Your father blamed

himself for not washing the deck so it wasn't slippery, for not remov-
ing that rock he always meant to remove. I blamed myself for being
distracted and not keeping track of you that day. Perhaps I relied upon
Alex too much, forgetting that as capable as he was, he was also still a
child. And you were like a little butterfly that was impossible to pin
down. The two of you, you and Alex, were constantly in motion.
Oh, how you both loved that island. How we all loved that island and
how we loved the both of you.

Before the tragedy, the four of us spent our happiest days there.
Our sweet Melanie was conceived there. It was a house that was
filled with love and books and music and laughter and then one day all
the joy was stilled.

You may wonder why we kept the island. We kept it because deep
down inside it was such a great part of us. To let it go would have
been letting go of Alex. Although he died there, he lived there as well.
Cherish that island, Grace. Make our dreams the way they were in-
tended to be.

Talk to Trout. He was there that day. Over the years, we have re-
ceived letters from our friends in Sabbath Landing through the bank.
Again, to my deep regret, we never replied. I know that our dear
friends the Keegans and Edith Lambert have passed away. I know
the Keegans' son, Luke, is still there, although he is widowed now.
Please call him. He was Alex's best friend and like a second son to us.
If he is as fine a man as he was a boy, then you should find a friend in
him, as well.

Take care, my darling Grace. Take care of Melanie. Your father
and I are so grateful that you and Melanie have each other. Tell
Jemma how we could never have done without her. And make sure
that you and Melanie teach your children the importance of facing the
truth, no matter how painful the truth might be. If and when you find
Luke Keegan, ask him to show you the puzzle bark tree on the island.
He and Alex loved that tree. It was so unusual and beautiful. They
would sit under its branches and chip off the bark and make their own
jigsaw. In some ways, the tree has a story not unlike yours, Grace.

Despite the odds, the dearth of water, the arid soil, the harsh winters,
it grew with an irrepressible strength and distinct beauty.
　　Your father and I love you.

　　　　　　　　　　　　　　　　　　　　　　　Mother

Grace sat still. Her face was motionless and stiff. "Oh God," she said. She began to turn the pages in the book, opening it to the book-marked page. "She marked 'The Prioress's Tale.' Look at this," she said, her voice quivering. "Mother underlined the inscription on the prioress's brooch. *Amor vincit omnia.*"

"What does that mean?" Jemma asked. "What language is that?"

"It's Latin. *Amor vincit omnia,*" she repeated, tears flowing down her cheeks. "Love conquers all."

The three women took their tea in the living room. Jemma brewed it in the old copper kettle. "One last time. Before it goes to the tag sale," Jemma said, placing the kettle on the stove.

"No, you keep it, Jemma," Grace said. "Mother wanted the tag sale to spare us the bother. But you just take it."

"Maybe we should cancel the sale," Melanie said. "I mean, it's no bother."

"I don't know," Grace said, hesitating. "I think we should respect their wishes. But, also, if you cancel the sale, I won't be able to help you." She took a deep breath. "I'm going to Sabbath Landing tomorrow morning."

"You are?" Melanie asked in disbelief. "When did you decide this? Why didn't you tell me?"

"I really wasn't sure until yesterday. Really, until this morning when Kate left. You see, Adam is going to Aspen," Grace sighed. "He's on his way as we speak. We're separating for a while. I'm giving notice at the school. It's a good time to do this with Kate in Spain."

"Oh, Grace," Jemma said, shaking her head.

"Please don't, Jemma," Grace said. "Don't preach to me about marriage. I don't have the kind of marriage I should have. For that matter, neither does Adam. I know how you feel about these things, but I've tried, Jemma. I really have. This is for the best."

"What will you do in Sabbath Landing by yourself?" Jemma asked.

"Well, I'm going to stay at The Alpine for a few days and then when I get my nerve, I'm going to the island."

"For how long?" Melanie asked.

"I have no plans," Grace said. "It will depend."

"On?"

"I don't know. How I take to the island, for one thing."

"Are you going to live there? Stay there for the summer?" Melanie asked.

"I don't know, Mel," Grace said. "I honestly don't know right now."

"You shouldn't be on that island by yourself," Jemma said. "I don't think that's safe."

Melanie smiled knowingly. "I have a feeling she won't be alone."

"Do you really, Mel?" Grace asked. "I could be setting myself up for a big disappointment."

"I don't think I want to hear this conversation," Jemma said, clearing the teacups. "This just makes me nervous."

"It's not what you think, Jemma," Grace said defensively, feeling like a child again.

"I don't know what I think anymore," Jemma said with a deep sigh, carrying the tray of cups to the kitchen.

Melanie and Grace heard Jemma run the tap at the sink. "Has he called?" Melanie whispered.

"No."

"Have you called him? Does he know you're coming?"

"No."

"Why?"

"I just haven't had the nerve to call him. Maybe he's met someone. I don't know, Mel. I figure I'll just see what happens when I get there."

"What is it about that place that makes you so impulsive?" Melanie asked with a smile. "First, you take off on New Year's Eve and now this—"

"Well, New Year's worked out," Grace said. "Listen, Mel, even Mother's letter said I'd find a friend in Luke Keegan. At the very worst, he'll be my friend."

"Call me. Promise me, you'll call."

"Of course I'll call you," Grace said, leaning over and hugging her sister. "You know, Mother wrote the letter to me and I felt sort of bad—for you."

"Don't," Melanie said. "That letter wasn't meant for me. It couldn't have been written to me as well. But, you know what, Grace? She loved me as best she could. You know, she was our mother but she was also Alex's mother. And can you imagine—?"

"I think in her own way, she had more courage than I'll ever have," Grace said. "She went on. I don't know that I would have been able to go on."

"You have more courage than you think, Grace," Melanie said.

"We'll see," Grace said, shaking her head. "Maybe I just have an impulse disorder."

Melanie laughed. "I don't think so. How are you getting there?"

"Train to Fort Hope," Grace said.

"He's going to be there," Melanie said. "You'll see."

"Oh, I'm sure he'll be there," Grace said. She looked at her sister. "I'm just afraid he might not be there for me."

Jemma came into the room, the empty teakettle in her hand. She looked at Melanie and Grace and then up to the ceiling and all around. "We should go," she said. "It's getting late." She walked over to Grace and placed her hand on Grace's shoulder. "You'd better get a good night's sleep, baby. You have a big day tomorrow." Jemma smiled. "And maybe the tomorrow after that and after that. Who knows?"

They took their coats from the rack by the door. Melanie took her parents' coats from their hooks and slung them over her arm. "I'm taking these," she said quietly. "I want them."

Jemma had gone to wait in Melanie's car. Grace flicked off the light switch in the vestibule and closed the door. "Good-bye house," she whispered, holding *The Canterbury Tales* tightly, the pink envelope jutting from the pages. Melanie waited for Grace in the front yard.

"Ready?" Melanie asked.

They walked away, their arms wrapped around each other's shoulders. They didn't have to say a word.

Chapter Thirty

Grace was aware of the difference in the air as she stood outside the apartment building waiting for a taxi the next morning. She thought of the first time she left for Sabbath Landing, how the air was so cold and bracing that January night, how she was filled with the anticipation of a journey. How little she knew about where the journey might take her. A pilgrimage, she thought to herself and smiled. She had placed the letter, *The Canterbury Tales*, the deed, the photograph of Alex and Luke, the pieces of puzzle bark, and Kate's graduation picture in her knapsack. She had almost everything she needed.

The city was quiet, as it always was on early Sunday mornings. The stale smell of diesel and coffee hung in the warm air of Penn Station. Her train was posted on the digital board. Was it her imagination, or did the lighted display flicker a bit? FORT HOPE. ON TIME. She walked to the ticket booth, bought a one-way fare, continued to the track, stopping to buy some bottled water and magazines at a kiosk. She hefted her smaller suitcase on the overhead rack, sat by a window, propped her feet on her larger suitcase in front of her.

She watched the urban landscape evolve from worn brick tenements to white clapboard homes with above-ground pools. Chain-link basketball courts and suburban depots were eventually replaced by cornfields and mountains. She watched the other passengers carefully. Everyone has a story, she thought. The old woman with a small leather bag got off in Poughkeepsie. She was greeted by a middle-aged woman who was, most likely, her daughter. They had the same sharp chin and sloped shoulders. What, Grace wondered, did she have just like her own mother? Her eyes, for sure. Her mother's hazel eyes that had witnessed more than any mother could bear.

The family with children carrying a large wicker picnic basket got off in Schenectady, greeted by an older couple. Grandparents, Grace thought. People I never knew. People my daughter never knew. Three young men with backwards baseball caps rode with her to Fort Hope. Three young girls in hip huggers and halter tops met them at the station in an old blue Dodge.

Grace stepped onto the jitney alone. She slipped the wedding band off her finger and put it in the pocket of her jeans. She had no idea what to expect now as the season had so drastically changed. Before she'd left the apartment, she started to dial Luke's number, but hung up before the final digit. How would she tell a man she thought she was in love with that she was sorry she hadn't called in nearly half a year? What if he had a whole new life, a new love, by now? But she remembered her mother's words about Luke: *If he is as fine a man as he was a boy, then you should find a friend in him, as well.*

It was hard to believe that Fort Hope was the same town Grace had driven through in winter. The streets, once deserted stretches of icy concrete, were crowded with tourists. Motels, shut down and boarded up last January, were open. NO VACANCY signs heralded the season, terraces streamed with baskets of alyssum in deep rose and purples. Curbside swimming pools were filled with children, their screams piercing the air as they splashed and dove into the water. Sunbathers, covered with oil, lay on cushioned chaise longues. Shops hung souvenir T-shirts and placed circular racks of postcards outside their doors. Lakeside restaurants brimmed with people drinking beer from plastic cups, waiting for tables under colorful awnings. Fairytale Town was open. The giant pirate was mechanized now, his eye winking, his mechanical hand beckoning tourists into the park. Fort Hope smelled as Grace had imagined it would, or perhaps it was that somewhere she remembered, of hot dogs and fried clams, fudge and saltwater taffy.

The jitney wove its way along Diamond Drive. Past the stables, flower marts, fruit stands, and delicatessens that were now open for business. There was The Birch on the right as they made the now-familiar turn into Sabbath Landing, its windowsills planted with bright lipstick-colored geraniums, a sign on the door advertising happy hour, tables and Cinzano umbrellas set on the deck overlooking Diamond Lake. The antique store, where she and Melanie shopped for junk jewelry and Mike's old Leica, was bustling. Patty Play Pal had shed her ski clothes for a broad-brimmed straw hat and overalls, a bouquet of flowers crooked in her hand. Children sat on the library's steps, its porch decorated with hibiscus bushes. And the lake. Diamond Lake was sapphire blue underneath a matching sky, the water sliced with shimmering frothy streaks as skiers and boaters flew over its span.

The Alpine, too, had changed. Several clerks stood behind the long front desk busily handling reservations. Tourists stood in line with matching luggage, waiting impatiently to check in. The lobby bar was filled with vacationers in shorts and sandals drinking pastel-colored drinks from martini glasses.

Grace's room, not a suite this time, again overlooked the lake. She parted the curtains and looked out the window. The path (she could see it was cobblestone, now that it wasn't covered with snow) was bordered with white Adirondack chairs and stone pots overflowing with flowers. The dock and the beach were dotted with bright blue-and-white-striped umbrellas. Hester's Peak was a lush forest green against the blue sky.

You won't recognize the place in summer, Luke had said.

Grace placed a call to Kevin Lambert. A woman answered the phone. A baby was crying in the background.

"This is Grace Barnett," Grace said. "I just wanted to leave Kevin a message to call me at The Alpine."

"Will he know what this is in reference to?" the woman asked, an edge to her voice.

"Oh, yes, I believe he's expecting me. I spoke to him last week. He said he could open my parents' house for me. The Hammond house? The one on Canterbury Island? I'm staying at The Alpine."

"Oh, yes," the woman said, relieved. "I hadn't made the connection. Your last name didn't ring a bell. I'll have him call you."

She took a shower. The pine shampoo she'd used in winter had been replaced with one that smelled like lavender. She put on a beige sundress embossed with small ecru flowers, placed a cardigan over her shoulders, fluffed her hair, traced on a pale pink lipstick.

She walked the cobblestone path and sat in an Adirondack chair with a clear view of the water. The sun was setting over Hester's Peak, painting the sky with fiery brush strokes of violet and burnt orange. The lake was sleepier. An occasional boat motored past. A few people rowed by in kayaks.

"Can I get you anything?" a waiter asked, a small round tray in his hand.

She pointed to a pink drink in a martini glass on the table next to hers. "What is that?" she asked.

"Cosmopolitan. Vodka, triple sec, Rose's lime, and cranberry juice."

"One of those, please," she said.

Luke is probably ending his day soon, she thought as she watched the fishing charters pull into the dock.

"Are there any good food shops in town?" she asked when the waiter returned with her drink. "Some place where I can get take-out?"

"There's Clyde's, right next to the liquor store. Right on the corner," he said. "You can walk it from here or take the jitney. One runs every ten minutes."

"And what about taxis? I need to get a car to take me to"—she fumbled in her purse for a slip of paper—"Twelve Ridge Drive. Off Route 47."

"I'm not sure where that is, ma'am," he said.

"About ten miles from here. Halfway between here and Minerva's Shelf."

"It might get expensive."

"How much?"

"Twenty-five dollars or thereabouts," he said. "I could call the concierge for you."

"Would you?" She looked at her watch. "Around eight. I need about an hour. I'll wait for him out front."

"Your name, ma'am?"

"Hammond," she said without skipping a beat.

She finished her drink and signed the check in the leather folder the waiter left on the arm of her Adirondack chair. She walked up the hill to the lobby entrance just as The Alpine jitney pulled under the canopy.

"I'm going to Clyde's," she said to the driver.

"Stops right in front of there," the driver said.

Clyde's was getting ready to close. The glass front counters were clearly picked over. She bought a half pound of cold shrimp, a jar of cocktail sauce, a half pound of smoked salmon. She laughed at herself thinking that Luke had been out fishing all day and here she was buying fish for dinner. She ordered a half chicken, some potato salad, a cucumber salad, a long loaf of crusty French bread, and a box of biscotti.

"Having a picnic?" the man at the register asked as he loaded the groceries into a white shopping bag.

Grace nodded and smiled, but she was thinking how dangerous it was to show up after five months, hoping you weren't forgotten, hoping that things might still feel the same. Yet, at this point, there was nothing to lose. Not anymore.

"Looks like no one's home," the taxi driver said as they pulled in front of Luke's house. "Are they expecting you?"

"Not really," Grace said vaguely. "You know what? I think maybe we should just head back to the hotel."

"I can wait while you have a look around," the driver said. "Maybe you'd like to leave them a note or something. Those groceries for them?"

She walked around the house and peered in the windows. It looked the same. The logs were still piled by the woodstove, newspapers were scattered on the living room floor. She saw the coffeepot sitting on the stove, a mug on the kitchen table next to a grouping of lures and open jars of paint.

It was then she heard the sound of water slapping against the dock behind the house. She walked slowly around back. Luke was leaning over the side of the boat, tying the lines to a post on the dock, his head down.

"So, who's to navigate and who's to steer?" she called to him.

He lifted his head slowly. "Grace," he said breathlessly.

She walked toward him. He put one foot on the railing. Started to step onto the dock.

"Wait," she said, taking a deep breath, gazing out at the lake and then back into his eyes. "I'm getting on. I'll come to you."

He reached out his hand, pulled her on deck, and gathered her in his arms.

Chapter Thirty-one

Nearly everyone in Sabbath Landing said they'd never seen a summer quite so busy. There wasn't a cloud in the sky, not a drop of rain; the temperature hovered around seventy-five. Luke took out his charter boat every morning at seven. Grace always walked him halfway down the island path, her arm linked through his. And every morning, as she sat and drank her tea, she read her mother's letter. It was hard for her to believe she was on the island with Luke, living in what seemed an almost perfect world.

They had finished what Luke called the "summerizing" of the island house on the Fourth of July. He said the only thing missing now was fireworks. Luke cleaned out the barbecue pit that his father and Grace's father had built one summer more than forty years ago. He refinished the old redwood picnic table and chairs, secured a double wicker swing that hung from a beech tree, pulled up the storm windows. Grace bought new sheets and blankets, new spreads for the beds. She scrubbed years of grease from the stove and polished furniture and washed every dish and pot and pan until they sparkled. Filled the bowl on the coffee table with new pinecones. She beat the braided rugs over the balcony outside her parents' bedroom, watching the dust fly in the sunlight. She filled the planters with flowers that Luke brought over from Buckley's nursery one Sunday afternoon. And as Grace pulled the plants from the flats and dug into the soil, Luke watched her, thinking how strongly she resembled her mother. Her auburn hair falling from under her sun hat, her pale muscular arms glistening in the sun.

Let's unload this boat, Mr. Hammond called.

But Dad, Luke and me are fishing, Alex protested.

Luke and I, Mr. Hammond laughed. Those fish aren't going anywhere, fellas. Let's go.

And he and Alex trudged up the path carrying cardboard boxes of flats.

What good boys you are, Mrs. Hammond said, waiting on the balcony, wearing an elaborate sun hat, taking the boxes from their muddy hands.

Race you to the dock. Alex punched Luke lightly in the arm. Last one there's a rotten egg.

"Hey, where are you right now?" Grace asked, wiping her face with the back of her hand, smudging dirt on her cheek. "Penny for your thoughts."

"They're worth more than that." Luke smiled. "You have dirt on your face. Here." He rubbed the spot with his thumb and kissed her. "I was thinking how much you remind me of your mother. The way she looked when she planted out here."

They thought they might invite people to celebrate, not just the Fourth of July but the opening of the island. They talked about buying flags and hanging Japanese lanterns but then, midconversation, they looked at one another.

"I'd rather be alone with you," they'd said in unison. Luke tossed his trademark steaks on the grill. They drank a bottle of red wine in the moonlight and made love under a blue velvet sky while fireworks from The Alpine shot over Diamond Lake.

They were sitting in the great room one evening in late July when Grace came to a decision.

"If I leave this house the way it is, the way it always has been, it becomes a shrine, not a home," she said, looking up from the book she was reading. "Do you think?"

Luke was fashioning lures. The coffee table was strewn with newspapers and brushes and jars of metallic paint. He set the lure he'd been painting on its side and moved next to her.

"I *do* think," he laughed, putting his arm over her shoulder. "As a matter of fact, I've *been* thinking. Listen, I can build a shed. If you had an attic here or a basement, you'd put everything there, right? But I can build a shed and that can be the place for all these keepsakes. Make this yours now, Grace. You can keep the past but, at the same time, you have to let it go. And so do I. Read your mother's letter again. This is what they would have wanted."

"I read that letter every morning." She smiled. "It's the way I start each day."

It wasn't a week later that Luke hammered the last nail into the shed, working into the night after he came home. Grace had bought several large wooden boxes and two old steamer trunks at the antique shop in town. She lined them with velvet and gingham. They placed children's books, old magazines, toys, and board games, things from long ago, into the shed. But they left the balsa airplanes dangling from the ceiling in Alex's room and the mounted bass on the wall. They moved the chess set to the great room and set Grace's ballerina music box next to Alex's old lures on a shelf in their bedroom.

"What about those old record albums?" Grace asked.

Luke grinned. "Hey, that's a turntable in there."

"You *are* a dinosaur," she laughed.

"Let's leave them here," Luke said.

"But put the Perry Como one in the shed," Grace said. "Please. I don't think I could bear that one, okay?"

Luke called Grace every day from the boat, sometimes stopping at the island in between morning and afternoon runs.

"You're ruining my career," he said one day after they made love at noon.

"Mine's already ruined," she laughed. "I haven't danced in weeks."

"You don't call dancing with me at The Birch dancing?" he asked with mock hurt.

"Oh, I do, Mr. Keegan. Forgive me," she said. "I miss the other kind of dancing, though."

"I know that," Luke said. "Why don't you call the dance school in Fort Hope?"

"I will. One of these days," Grace said. "I'm trying to take everything one step at a time."

"Pun intended?" Luke asked with a grin.

"You are too corny," Grace said, shaking her head.

"I love when I make you smile, Grace," he said.

"I love *you*, Luke," she said.

One night in early August, Helen and George invited them to Minerva's Shelf for dinner. It was their forty-first wedding anniversary. Trout would be there, they said. Kevin and his wife. Helen said life with George was getting too settled. "After all these years, we need a little distraction," she laughed.

Grace called to Luke from the bedroom as they were leaving for the party. "I'll meet you by the truck," she said. "I'm just getting my sweater."

"Get a warm jacket," Luke said. "We're taking the boat. It's easier by lake than by car."

"But it's dark," Grace said.

"Look at the moon," Luke said. "It won't be dark once we're out there. It's a beautiful night."

True, the moon lit the lake and stars dotted the sky, but a brisk wind was blowing. The waters were particularly choppy as the boat bounced over the wake.

"How much longer?" Grace asked, standing beside Luke as he steered, her arm linked through his, her head leaning on his shoulder.

"Ten, maybe fifteen minutes," he said. "We're okay."

"The lake still scares me sometimes," she confessed, gripping his arm tighter.

"I know," he said. "That's okay, Grace. More than likely, it always will. Some things you just learn to live with."

"Jemma once told me to look my fears square in the eye and stare them down." Grace smiled. "I'm trying so hard."

"You're doing just fine, Grace," he said, kissing the side of her head. "I'd never let anything happen to you."

"I know," she said. "That's why I'm here. Choppy waters and all."

"We need to talk about living together on the island," Luke said. "The summer's nearly over."

Grace felt her stomach sink. "I'm not sure what you mean," she said cautiously. "What are you saying?"

"Why do you look like that? All I'm saying is we can't stay there past September, Grace. It's not a good idea. Too many storms in the fall. And come October, it's too cold. The place has to be shut down for the season." He put his arm around her. "What did you think I was going to say?"

"I'm a little skittish, I guess," she said.

"Oh, Grace." He sighed. "What am I going to do with you?"

"I don't know. What *are* you going to do with me?" she laughed.

"Well, here's what I think, okay? We should live at my place off-season. We'll fix it up, Grace. I swear, I'll paint it. I'll sand the floors. Damn, I'll even clean out the garage. I know the place is a wreck. But I swear, it's got potential," he said. He had stopped the boat, letting it idle in the middle of the lake, rocking on the wake.

"I would live anywhere with you," she said.

"I don't want you to go home," he said, kissing her.

"I am home," she said.

It stormed one morning at the end of August. The first rain they'd had all summer. Thunder and lightning awakened Grace long before dawn. She got out of their bed, tiptoed to the kitchen, brewed a pot of coffee, and sat at the table.

"Well, you're an early bird," Luke said. He wore a bright orange parka over his shirt.

"The storm woke me. I wish you didn't have to go out on the lake today," she said, her eyes wide. "This storm . . ."

"This? This'll blow over by midmorning," Luke said. "The boat's as solid as a rock. This storm's nothing but a lot of noise. Best kind of fishing today, too. Those bass'll be jumping."

"But I have this funny feeling."

"In those bones?" he said, kneeling beside her, holding her to him. "I'll call you all day long, I promise. Weather report every hour on the hour, okay?" A pained look came over his face. "You stay inside, though. No walking around outside."

"I thought you said this storm wasn't so bad," she said. "It was this kind of day, wasn't it, Luke? Maybe something inside me remembers."

He nodded. "I'll call you," he said, kissing her neck. "Don't worry."

Grace was sitting on the floor in the great room when there was a knock on the door. Photographs and marking pens were spread out around her. She'd been putting together a photo album from a box of pictures she'd found in her mother's closet. She looked at the clock. It was just after three. She jumped up when she saw a figure in an orange parka through the window.

"Well, you're back early," she said as she flung open the door.

It wasn't Luke's face she saw.

"Grace."

"My God, Adam. How did you get here?"

He had driven up the night before, he said. Stayed at The Alpine. A charter brought him to the island.

"Everyone in town knows you," Adam said. "When I said Canterbury Island, the guy at the marina said, 'Oh, Grace Hammond's place.' Hammond? Well, that didn't take long."

"What are you doing here, Adam? Why didn't you call first?"

"Truth? I couldn't remember your cell number. I suppose I could have called Kate and asked, but I thought that would look awfully bad."

"Yes, it would have. I just spoke to her yesterday. She'll be home in ten days, you know."

"That's why I'm here. We need to talk."

"Well, come in," she said. "Give me your coat. You're soaked."

He stood in the middle of the great room and looked at the ceiling as she hung his coat on a hook near the kitchen door.

"Interesting place," he said. "A little isolated though, don't you think?"

"Not really. You get used to it. Isolation is more a state of mind."

"Where did you tell Kate you've been?"

"Back and forth, as you and I agreed. Although lately, I've eased her into things a bit. She knows I've spent more time here than Manhattan. That you've been in Aspen. She hasn't asked for details."

"How did she take all that?" he asked.

"She's no fool. She's having a wonderful time, which helps steer the conversation away from reality. But you've spoken to her, haven't you?"

"Not in great depth," he said. "I guess there's not a better way to say what I have to say." Adam sat on the sofa. "I want a divorce, Grace."

She nodded. "So do I."

"That's it? So do I?" He was stunned.

"Oh, Adam. This doesn't really come as shock to you, does it? What do you want me to do? Would you like me to cry and carry on? I have cried. Cried more than I ever care to cry again," she said. "I want us both to be happy, that's all."

"I'm moving to Aspen in November. I sold my practice. I want to sell the apartment. Fifty-fifty, Grace. Everything."

"I think Kate needs a place to come home to in the city. All her friends are there."

"I want the Aspen house, though. I'll buy you out."

"I don't care about Aspen."

"Then maybe I'll get a small place in the city. We can share it. Meet her there on school breaks."

"I just don't want her more displaced than she has to be."

"I agree."

"Well, there's one thing that we agree on," Grace said.

"You'll have to get a lawyer. I've already retained one," he said. "Not to worry, though. I'll absorb your fees."

She nodded. "Thank you," she said. "You're very efficient, Adam. You do realize I'll be in the city in a couple of weeks when Kate's home. I have to get her packed. And I think we should both take her to Boston."

"I'm aware of that. That's fine. We'll have to tell her about the divorce before she leaves. It's not going to be easy."

"I'm sure she won't be surprised," Grace said with a sigh. "But it's a lousy thing to do right before she goes off to school."

"I'll handle it," he said.

"I'll handle it, too, if you don't mind. Our tacks are different, Adam."

"I'm painfully aware of that."

"Would you like a tour of the house?" she asked, preferring not to engage him any longer. "Something to drink?"

She set the kettle on for tea. He watched her as she moved deftly about the kitchen, reaching for the cups from a high glass-enclosed cabinet, her delicate arms stretching like a dancer's.

"You look good, Grace," he said softly. "You're happy here, aren't you, Grace?"

She turned quickly, looked at him and smiled for what she thought was the first time in years. "I *am* happy. It feels right."

"What about the lake? The water?"

"I'm making my peace with it. I'm making my peace with a lot of things."

She took him room by room, chatting as they walked, telling him what had been in places where it no longer was, how she had changed things, kept certain things the same. The last room they came to was the bedroom. Luke's work boots sat by the armchair.

"I take it those weren't your father's," Adam said, pointing his chin in their direction.

"No," she answered, her face reddening. "They weren't."

"It doesn't matter, Grace, really. Who is he, though? I'm curious."

"Luke Keegan."

"Ah, your fisherman friend. Your midnight call."

"Alex's friend," she said self-consciously. "My friend, too."

Adam sat down in the chair, picked up one of the boots, turned it over, and set it back down. "Clearly, he's more than a friend. I haven't been alone either. I met someone in Aspen."

"Who?"

"She's a decorator."

"Shelby."

"How on earth did you know?" Adam asked, rather shocked.

"Kate mentioned her last January. She said you spent a lot of time together choosing carpet and tiles," Grace said, a smile playing on her lips. "It's okay, Adam. Really. No hard feelings. Come, let's go have our tea."

"It just happened," he said, sitting at the kitchen table.

"Did Shelby go to the ashram?" Grace asked, then shook her head from side to side. "Never mind. That wasn't fair of me. It really doesn't matter. Does Kate know?"

"Not yet. Kids are pretty resilient, though. She'll get used to it."

"You don't have to tell me how resilient kids are," she said. "She's not going to like this though, Adam. "

"She'll get over it."

"It might take her a long time. You're going to have to be very patient with her."

"And what about your fisherman? You think she's going to like that?"

"Don't call him that. His name is Luke," Grace said. "I'm sure she won't like it at first. But she'll grow to like Luke. You can't help but like him."

"Still have those bad dreams, Grace?"

"Not for months, Adam. I only have good ones now."

"Well," Adam said, setting down his cup. "Thanks for the tea and sympathy."

"I'll see you in a couple of weeks, Adam," she said coolly. "We'll get everything settled. I want you to be happy, Adam. Truly."

"See you," he said.

"Adam?" She was going to tell him about the letter from her mother.

"Yes?"

"Never mind. It wouldn't matter anyway," she said.

Grace stood on the balcony and watched Adam walk the dirt path to the dock where his charter waited. It was a long way from the morning he stood outside her studio and pretended to be interested in Toby Abbott. A long time ago that he proposed to her in a room filled with strangers. She watched him disappear as the path curved around and then saw him again, his back to the house as he stood on the deck of the boat as it backed out from the slip. It was just as Adam pulled away that Luke's boat came in. A glance passed between the two men in their orange parkas. She saw Luke look up at the house. She waved but he couldn't see her through the trees. She called his name but she knew he didn't hear. She ran from the balcony and down the path. She wasn't a quarter of the way down when Luke came running up.

"Where are you going?" he said, stopping her, both hands on her shoulders.

"To meet you," she said, bewildered. "I called to you. You didn't hear me."

"That was him, wasn't it?" he asked, out of breath. "That was Adam."

"Yes," she said. "What's wrong with you? Why are you running?"

"I knew it was him," he said, sitting down on the wet ground, placing his head into his hands, trying to catch his breath. "What was he doing here? He wants you back, doesn't he?"

"He came to tell me he'd hired a lawyer. And I should get one, too. I'm afraid you're stuck with me, Keegan," she said, sitting down beside him. "Not that you weren't before he showed up here, mind you. Hey, look where we are."

Their backs leaned against the puzzle bark tree. Grace stood up and chipped off two pieces with the nail of her thumb.

"Open your hand," she said. She took the pieces and locked them together, pressed them into his palm, and closed her hand over his. "This is us. Locked together. The fitting pieces of the jigsaw. For always, okay?"

"Forever," he said, closing his eyes, kissing her hand over his own. "Forever."

Chapter Thirty-two

Luke drove Grace to the Fort Hope depot on the Sunday before Labor Day. Kate's plane was arriving that evening from Barcelona.

"I'll be back on Thursday or Friday. I'll let you know for sure," Grace said, putting her train tickets in the pocket of her jacket. "Don't look so worried."

"I *am* worried," Luke said. "Is he staying at the apartment tonight?"

"He is. He'll be there all week. Of course, he'll stay in the guest room. And Kate will be there."

"That's not what's worrying me," Luke said. "I don't want him to upset you."

"He doesn't anymore, Luke," Grace said. "I'm upset about Kate, though. We're going to tell her tomorrow morning. She'll be tired tonight so I thought we should wait. Maybe we'll take her to breakfast or something."

"She's going to know the moment she sees your face," Luke said, running his hand down Grace's arm. "You wear your heart on your sleeve, you know."

"I know," Grace said. "But we'll be so busy this week, too. We've got to get her things together for school. Clothes, sheets, towels. I'll have my work cut out for me."

"It may not be quite enough to distract her," Luke said gently. "Or you."

"I know." Grace nodded. "This is the hard part of telling the truth."

* * *

Adam was at the apartment when Grace arrived. He had a clipboard and pen in his hand.

"What's that?" she asked, setting down her small suitcase, dispensing with hello.

"I'm making a list of things to go to Aspen and others for Sabbath Crossing."

"*Landing*. For God's sake, Adam. Sabbath *Landing*," Grace said, irritated.

"Are there specific things you'd like to have?" Adam asked, overlooking her correction.

"The photo albums and videos of Kate. Things that my parents gave us. Things from Melanie and Kate and Jemma. That's all."

"Well, write them down and I'll have everything labeled and shipped," he said. "The movers come next Saturday. Oh, I didn't tell you, did I? The real estate agent called last week. They sold the apartment."

"No, you didn't tell me," Grace said coldly. "Look, I was planning to go home either Thursday night or Friday morning but I can stay for the movers, if you like."

"Not necessary," he said, reddening a bit.

"Well, you might need some help."

"Shelby's flying in Friday night."

"I see," Grace said. "Don't you think you could have checked with me first?"

"I didn't think it mattered," Adam said.

"I'll pack and label my own boxes. Just make sure they get shipped, would you? There won't be that much."

"Look, we should head out to the airport," Adam said, checking his watch. "It's nearly four. Kate's plane gets in at six."

"That's not for two hours. We have more than enough time."

"It's Labor Day weekend. Traffic is murder."

"Adam, I don't think we need to mention either Shelby or Luke to Kate at this point. One thing at a time, do you agree?" Grace asked.

"Agreed," Adam said. "By the way, what about the crystal? Do you want anything? Need anything?"

"I have everything I need," Grace said. "Let's just go."

The news of Adam and Grace's divorce never waited until morning.

"Just a few things tonight. We can do the rest tomorrow," Grace said, unpacking Kate's suitcase. "Get me a glass of ice water, would you, Kate? I'm just going to sort out these sweaters so we can get them to the dry cleaner first thing. Then we can all go to dinner."

"The red one's clean," Kate called as she walked to the kitchen.

Kate returned with the glass of water and the clipboard. Adam had left it on the kitchen table. "What is *this*?" she asked, waving it in front of her mother.

"It's Dad's."

"What's it for?"

"It's a list."

"A list for what?"

"I think your father should be here, too," Grace said uncomfortably.

"No, you talk to me first. I'm not stupid, Mom," Kate said hotly. "This is a moving list. You and Daddy were never together this summer, were you? Just because I was in Spain, don't think I wasn't aware."

"No, we weren't."

"What's going on, Mom?" Kate asked, her eyes blinking.

"Your father and I are getting divorced, Kate," Grace said softly.

"When were you planning on telling me?"

"In the morning," Grace said. "We didn't want to tell you on your first night home."

Kate's eyes welled up with tears. She took a balled up pair of socks that were on the bed and threw them at her dresser. "I knew it," she said. "So, what's with the list?"

"We sold the apartment."

"You sold the apartment? Without asking me? Oh, my God, how can you do something like that?" Kate cried.

"It just wasn't a question, Kate. Dad is retiring his practice. He's going to Aspen. I'm going to Sabbath Landing."

"You're going to live on that island?" Kate asked, her eyes wide.

"Not the whole time," Grace said. "I have a place on the mainland."

"No! That's not what I mean. You're leaving the city? I don't believe you! Aspen and Sabbath Landing are so far away! My *friends* are here!" Kate shouted.

"Kate. I'm sorry," Grace said helplessly. "I don't know what to say. Dad did say that he was thinking of getting a small place here in the city. He said we could share it. Meet you here on breaks."

"But what about Thanksgiving and Christmas? What about my birthday?"

"You'll be at school on your birthday this year, Kate."

Kate was crying. "What about the holidays, though?"

"We'll have to share you," Grace said. "We've always shared you."

"I don't understand any of this," Kate sobbed. "How can you do this?"

"But you do, Kate," Grace said. "Deep down inside, you do understand."

"You loved each other once. You must have."

"It was there once, Kate," Grace said. "It really was."

"So, what happened?" Kate asked.

"People change. If you're lucky, you grow together. We grew apart."

"But everyone says that people *don't* change," Kate said.

"Well, not fundamentally, I suppose. But you change in terms of each other."

"You don't love each other anymore," Kate said, sitting on the bed, her head bowed.

"No, not in the way that we should." Grace shook her head. She sat down on the bed beside her daughter. "We tried, Kate. We need to move on now. We'll be better friends this way. You'll see."

"But you've always been in the same place. Now he'll be one place and you'll be another and I don't know where that leaves me. I don't know where it leaves me in the summer. On weekends. Everything."

"You can stay with your city friends sometimes. Your friends can come to us sometimes. We'll work everything out, Kate. I promise. You'll see. It will all work itself out. The human spirit is amazingly resilient."

"How can you do this to me?" Kate repeated.

"I know it feels like we're doing this to you, but we're not. At least not intentionally, Kate. There's no good way to do something like this."

"But why can't you at least stay in the city?"

"If you think about it, Sabbath Landing is the same distance from Boston as New York."

Kate stood up and walked over to her dresser. She wound the key on the music box. "Like where will this be?" she asked, holding the music box. "I mean, I'll take it to school but then where will it be in the summer? How will I know what to keep where?"

"It's hard, Kate. I know it's hard. I hope you'll share your summer between your father and me, although I'd be a liar if I said I didn't wish I could have you with me the whole time. The three of us will have to figure it all out as we go along. The only thing I know is that I love you. Your father loves you."

"What difference does it make if you don't love each other?" Kate asked bitterly.

"It makes a tremendous difference," Grace said. "Your father and I will always hold a special place in each other's hearts because of you."

"That's so contrived, Mom," Kate said. "It's so irrelevant."

"No, it's not irrelevant. You have to try to understand: You're our child but we have a marriage. You're always going to be a part of us and a part of our lives. It's the marriage that has to end, not our relationship with you as parents." Grace looked at Kate to see if she was hearing her. "Even you had a sense that your father and I were pretending the last few years. You can't tell me that you prefer a make-believe marriage to this."

"Not great choices," Kate said.

"No, they're not," Grace said. "But this is the only choice right now. This is the reality that works. The reality that's fair to your father and me."

Adam knocked on the open door. "I've been standing out here for a few minutes," he said. "I've been listening. Please, try to understand, Kate."

"I think part of her understands very well," Grace said softly. "Don't you, Kate?"

"Does Aunt Mel know?" Kate asked.

Grace nodded.

"Jemma?"

"They both know," Grace said.

"What did they say?"

"They've been supportive as always," Grace said. "There's not too much they *can* say."

"We have a table at Pasquale's tonight," Adam said. "Kate? Can we all go?"

"If we can have a meal together where there's no tension, no bickering," Kate demanded. "Then I'll go. This is one of my last nights before I go to college. This wasn't what I was counting on."

"We know," Grace and Adam said in unison.

"Well, at least you agree on something," Kate said. "I just need to wash my face. I'll meet you at the elevator."

Early Thursday morning, Adam picked up a rental van and by late afternoon, Kate was in her dorm at Boston College.

"We thought you might like to get some lunch before we leave," Grace said as she put sheets on Kate's narrow dorm bed. "Sort of a late lunch, early supper. Interested?"

"Where's Dad?" Kate asked.

"He's down at the van, checking that we emptied everything out," Grace said. "Your roommate seems like a nice girl. Cory? Is that what she said her name was?"

"Cory Gilbert. Her parents left early. She does seem nice, doesn't she? She's from Arkansas, you know."

"Why don't you ask her to come with us to lunch?" Grace asked brightly. "I saw a cute pub on the corner before we pulled into campus."

"I think I'd like to just go alone with her. You know, get to know each other. I mean, we *are* going to live together."

Grace smiled. "I understand. Columbus Day is sooner than you think, Kate. There's no school that Monday and Sabbath Landing is only four hours from here. What do you say we make a date for that weekend?"

"It's a date." Kate nodded with a half-smile.

"It's going to be okay, Kate," Grace said, tears pooling in her eyes. "I promise."

"I sort of know that," Kate said. "We do always manage to figure things out, I guess."

"Now, that's the best thing I've heard in months," Grace said, drawing Kate close to her.

Epilogue

Luke and Grace closed the island house in mid-September for the winter. Luke painted his house on the mainland a periwinkle blue. He rehung the porch swing, cleaned out the garage, got rid of the old couch. They bought a love seat and two overstuffed chairs for the living room, and a dresser for Grace, a daybed for the room where Kate would sleep. Grace put her touches here and there. She hung two of her mother's watercolors, filled vases with fresh flowers, and tossed embroidered pillows and woven throws over the love seat. *The Canterbury Tales* was placed on a book stand in the living room alongside family photographs. Luke placed the photograph of Meg in a trunk in the basement.

"You didn't have to do that," Grace said.

"Life has to go on," Luke said.

"But she's Chris's mother," Grace said. "Put it back."

In October, over Columbus Day weekend, Grace and Luke drove to Boston College.

"I was planning not to like him," Kate said as she and Grace sat in a coffeehouse while Luke took a deliberate walk around the Charles River. "But he's awfully nice, Mom. You really can't help but like him, can you?"

Grace smiled. "No, you can't."

"How's the new job, Mom?"

"Still a little too new," Grace laughed.

"Did your old school take it well?"

"Oh, very well. They couldn't have been nicer."

"What's the name of this new one again?"

"Fort Hope Dance Arts," Grace said. "I'm even teaching an adult tap class. I haven't taught adult classes in twenty years." Grace reached her hand across the table. "I am so happy to see you, Kate. To be here with you."

"Me, too," Kate said. "Me, too."

Grace and Adam's divorce was final in November. The documents arrived the day before Thanksgiving, addressed to Grace, in care of Luke Keegan. Luke didn't say a word as he handed Grace the envelope. She sat at the kitchen table and looked at the papers. It was strange to see her name and Adam's at the top of a legal form. Plaintiff and defendant. Barnett against Barnett. A division in no uncertain terms. Adjudged that the marriage of Grace Hammond Barnett and Adam Winthrop Barnett is dissolved by reason of irreconcilable differences. It was all so final and true. It would be false to say she didn't feel a twinge to see proof that the marriage had ended, even though it had ended so long ago. The silence was broken when she heard Luke open the damper of the wood-burning stove, the spark and pop of the embers as the dry logs hit the flame. She put the papers in a kitchen drawer, walked into the living room, and put her arms around Luke as he knelt in front of the fire.

"You okay?" he asked.

"Never better," she said, and kissed the side of his neck.

"You sure?" he asked, turning around.

"Positive," she said.

Kate had flown to Aspen for Thanksgiving. It was the first Thanksgiving Grace hadn't shared with her since the day she was born. Kate called after supper.

"Mom? It's me," Kate whispered. "So, listen to this. Shelby made a tofu turkey."

"No drumsticks?" Grace laughed.

"It was absolutely absurd. I mean, there were no drumsticks, not to mention that soy gravy just isn't the same," she laughed, and then asked solemnly, "What did you do?"

"Oh, it's quiet here. We just stayed home," Grace said. "Chris went to his girlfriend's house this year. I miss you, Kate."

"Me, too. But I'll be home for Christmas. Home in Sabbath Landing, okay?"

"Music to my ears," Grace said.

Jemma had driven up several days before Christmas with Melanie, Mike, and the twins. They were staying at The Alpine. Kate arrived in Fort Hope, by train, on Christmas Eve morning.

"Chris will be in later this afternoon," Grace said as they wove their way up Diamond Drive in Luke's truck. "He's bringing his girlfriend. I think it's quite serious."

"What's he like?" Kate asked. "Wow, Mom, you can really drive this truck."

"A little shy," Grace said. "But sweet. He's a lot like his father."

"What's his girlfriend's name?"

"Betsy."

"I have a boyfriend at school, Mom," Kate said. "Joshua. He's a music major. Plays the piano."

"Is he good to you?" Grace asked.

Kate nodded. "He's kind of old-fashioned, though. Opens doors for me and stuff like that."

"Don't let him get away," Grace said knowingly. "That's the best kind."

Grace and Luke had a Christmas tree in the living room decorated with angels, and mistletoe hung in every doorway, but Luke said it had become his tradition over the last several years to spend Christmas Eve at The Birch. The tourists were long gone from Sabbath Landing. The streets were quiet once again, strung with icicle lights. The air smelled like snow and smoking chimneys. Diamond Lake was nearly frozen, still and glistening under a crescent moon. The circle was beginning again, Grace thought as Luke drove the truck down Diamond Drive to The Birch with Kate, Chris, and Betsy chattering in the backseat.

Helen and George were dancing as usual, this time to Christmas carols. Trout sat in his place at the end of the bar. Kevin and his wife and baby were there as well. Bill, the bartender, wore a Santa Claus hat. Sam and Jeannie from the Sunoco were there along with Margaret Buckley, the librarian, and her husband, Gus. Gus said he sold his last Christmas tree that night at the nursery and wanted to sleep until the New Year. The Reverend Wood stopped by with his wife, Susan, between sermons.

"The whole town is here," Grace said as she danced with Luke.

"I'm getting our coats," he said.

"We're leaving?"

"No, I have something for you. It's in the truck," he said.

"I thought we agreed not to exchange gifts until later," Grace said. "Yours is at home."

"This is different," Luke said.

Luke took Grace out the back door of the tavern. "Hop in," he said, opening the driver's side for himself.

"I think this is the first time you didn't open the door for me," Grace said. He started to run around the truck. "Never mind, silly," she laughed. "Just get in. It's freezing out here."

He reached into the glove box and took out a split of champagne, two glass flutes wrapped in red napkins. He popped the cork and filled the glasses, put the Dan Fogelberg tape in the cassette player, and blasted the heat.

"Champagne? What are you doing?" Grace asked.

He reached into the pocket of his leather jacket and took out a small red felt bag tied with a gold drawstring. "I was planning to get down on my knees," he said. "But there's snow on the ground and it's too cold outside. You know me, I am an old-fashioned guy, Grace. I can't say it any better than this. I love you with every ounce of my being. I never want to be without you. Marry me, Grace."

"Oh, Luke," she said. "I love you. I will marry you, Luke."

"I swear, I'll catch the stars for you, Grace. I'll take away all your bad dreams."

"You already did," she said, crying.

"So, why are you crying?" he asked, his arms around her.

"Because I'm so happy," she said through her tears.

"Here," he said, handing her the velvet bag. "Open it."

There was a pair of dangling earrings, a shimmery moon and three silver stars. When Grace held them, they clinked together like wind chimes.

"I got them at the antique shop," Luke said.

"They're beautiful," Grace said, putting them on.

"They're not real, though, you know," Luke said. "The moon is only crystal."

"They are real. The most real."

"See? I gave you the moon, too." He smiled. "I didn't get you a ring, Grace. I saw these and somehow they just seemed right."

"They're perfect," she said. "Everything is perfect."

The room was silent as they walked into the tavern. Everyone was standing in a half circle on the dance floor.

"So?" Jemma asked, walking over to Grace, taking her hands and shaking them in hers. "Did you say yes?"

"You knew?" Grace cried. "How did you know?"

"There was something in Luke's eyes," Jemma said.

"I told you she's a witch," Melanie laughed, putting an arm around Jemma.

"A witch? Well, I'm not sure I like that, Melanie," Jemma sniffed.

"A good witch," Melanie said.

"Jemma kind of made an announcement," Mike said, smiling at

Luke. "Got everyone to come to attention and wait for you two to come back inside. It's been a vigil since you've been gone."

"Well, hold on," Melanie said. "So, what's the verdict here?"

Luke grinned. "She said yes."

"Well, well, well," Melanie smiled. "What a surprise."

"Merry Christmas, Luke," Kate said, kissing his cheek. She turned to Grace and hugged her. "Merry Christmas, Mom. I love you."

"Did he give you a ring?" Melanie whispered in Grace's ear as she hugged her.

"No. Better," Grace said, moving her hair behind her ear to show off the earrings.

"Oh, Grace, they're beautiful. They're you. He knows you, doesn't he?" Melanie threw back her head and laughed. "Oh, I love that man. Now, aren't you glad you listen to me sometimes?"

Trout came up behind Grace and took her hand. "I need to borrow the bride and groom for a moment," he said. "Come, there's a room upstairs. I have something to say to you."

The three trudged up a small, dark staircase. Trout flicked on a switch that lit a bare bulb over an old pool table. There were chairs folded and propped against the wall. Trout took three, dusted them off, and motioned to Luke and Grace to sit.

"Maybe I have no right doing what I'm about to do, but I feel some, well, some obligation. I've known you two since you were little kids. Now, I know you're both all grown up and all, but seeing that your folks are gone and I'm the last one of that generation . . . Well, I've been through a lot with both of you," he said, faltering for words. "I'm not sure how to put this. . . ."

"I hope you're about to give us your blessing, Trout," Luke said. "Because it'll save me having to ask."

"Well, that's just what I was trying to do." Trout smiled, wiping away a tear. "This couldn't be a more blessed union. Lucas and Grace, I swear, if anything was ever meant to be . . ."

"I only wish they knew about us, Trout," Grace said. "I wish they were all here to see us."

"I swear to you, Grace, they're all watching you right now," Trout said. "They see us. You can bet they do."

"I can feel them," Luke said, taking Grace's hand and pressing it to his lips.

"So can I," Grace whispered. "Finally, so can I."

About the Author

Stephanie Gertler is the author of the acclaimed novel *Jimmy's Girl*. She writes a monthly lifestyles column called "These Days" for two Connecticut newspapers, *The Advocate* and *Greenwich Time*. She lives in New York with her husband, three children, and four dogs.

Visit Stephanie's Web site at www.stephaniegertler.com